Isobel's Wedding

Sheila O'Flanagan

First published in Great Britain in 2002
by HEADLINE BOOK PUBLISHING

First published in paperback in 2002
by HEADLINE BOOK PUBLISHING

This edition published in paperback in 2006
by HEADLINE REVIEW
An imprint of HEADLINE BOOK PUBLISHING

15

ISBN 0 7472 6566 6 (A format)
ISBN 0 7553 2998 8 (B format)

Typeset in Galliard by Palimpsest Book Production Limited,
Polmont, Stirlingshire
Printed and bound in Great Britain by
Clays Ltd, St Ives plc

Headline's policy is to use papers that are natural, renewable and recyclable products and made from wood grown in sustainable forests. The logging and manufacturing processes are expected to conform to the environmental regulations of the country of origin.

HEADLINE BOOK PUBLISHING
A division of Hodder Headline
338 Euston Road
London NW1 3BH

www.reviewbooks.co.uk
www.hodderheadline.com

Terms and Conditions

This voucher entitles the bearer to £1 off *How Will I Know?* by Sheila O'Flanagan in paperback. Voucher may only be redeemed against one purchase and must be handed in instore upon redemption. One voucher per transaction. Voucher valid between 15th June 2006 and 16th July 2006, in any Woolworths store excluding Ireland and Northern Ireland stores. This voucher cannot be redeemed in conjunction with any other offer. Offer not available in Ireland or Northern Ireland. Cash value of voucher is 0.001p. No cash alternative. Not to be redeemed online. Subject to availability.

Promoter – Woolworths plc, Woolworth House, 242/246 Marylebone Road, London NW1 6JL

Thanks to:

My agent and friend Carole Blake who introduced me to a great group of people at Headline and changed my life for ever.

My extended family, the best PR people I know.

Colm, who'd rather be in Spain.

And, of course, to those of you who buy my books – I hope you enjoy reading them as much as I enjoy writing them.

Chapter 1

The Wedding (Francisco Goya, 1791)

I was trying on the wedding dress when Tim phoned. Actually I was twirling around in front of the full-length wall mirror, admiring the way the skirt billowed around me in a carefree puff of white chiffon, when I heard the phone ring. It had taken me longer to make this wedding dress than any other I'd ever done, but this was *my* dress. This was the dress I'd wear when I married Tim in two weeks' time and it had deserved all of my time and all of my attention. I smoothed the skirt and fingered the tiny white pearls neatly hand-sewn onto the bodice. There were four hundred and twenty of them. I'd never sew a pearl onto a dress again.

'Isobel! It's for you!' Alison stood at the bottom of the stairs and yelled at me. 'It's your fiancé.' She broke into a guffaw at the word 'fiancé'. She always did. Alison, who was twenty-one, thought I was out of my mind to be getting married. Alison didn't approve of marriage; she believed that husbands only tied you down, limited your potential, trapped you for the rest of your life. She thought I was too young to tie myself down to one person. But I wasn't. I was exactly the right age. Twenty-seven. Long enough on my own to have had some fun and make a few elementary mistakes. But mature enough, now, to know exactly what I was doing. To be ready to become Isobel Malone instead of Isobel Kavanagh.

I stared at my twenty-seven-year-old reflection. Brown eyes, red-rimmed from spending too much time at my sewing machine, a pale face that was looking forward to our honeymoon in Rhodes, and soft brown hair which was halfway between lengths because I wanted to be able to put it up for the wedding. It was a pity I wasn't taller because the dress would have looked truly gorgeous if I'd been a tall, willowy, Stella Tennant sort of person. But I'd stopped growing around the five-foot-one mark and remained the short one in our family. At least I was slim, although that was probably because I'd almost stopped eating in the last two weeks. There simply hadn't been time.

Alison (unlike me in almost every respect – taller, tousle-haired and bigger-boned) thumped her way up the stairs and pushed open the bedroom door. 'Are you deaf?' she demanded. 'It's Tim—' She broke off and stared at me. She hadn't seen the finished dress before. 'Oh, Isobel.' Suddenly her face was softer, gentler. 'It's beautiful!'

I grinned at her. 'Thank you.'

'I mean it,' she said. 'It's lovely. *You* look lovely.'

'I'll look more lovely when my hair is done properly and I'm wearing all the right bits and pieces.'

'You're like Cinderella going to the ball,' she breathed as she fingered the gossamer-light material. 'I never thought it would look like this.'

'Oh, for heaven's sake!' I laughed at her. 'Come down to earth, Ali. You're the one who thinks I'm off my head to be getting married in the first place.'

She shrugged. 'I just don't think that women can be

themselves if they're chained to some man,' she said. 'As soon as a girl gets married she puts her husband's needs ahead of her own. It's this nurturing thing. We can't help ourselves. That's why you shouldn't get married in the first place.'

'And what if you're truly in love?' I asked her as I slipped out of the dress and placed it carefully on the padded hanger. 'What then?'

She shook her head. 'Love is delusion,' she said. 'People only think they're in love.'

'Wait until you've fallen for someone yourself before making that judgement,' I told her briskly. 'I'll remind you of this conversation when you're mooning about over some bloke who doesn't take a blind bit of notice of you.'

I pulled my dressing-gown over my white slip and hurried downstairs, leaving her still gazing at the dress.

I picked up the receiver. 'Hi there.'

'What on earth were you doing?' asked Tim. 'I've been hanging on for ages.'

'Discussing the meaning of love with Alison,' I told him. 'She doesn't believe in it.'

Tim broke into a fit of coughing.

'I hope you're not getting a cold,' I said. 'It'd be terrible if you were too sick to say "I do".'

'I wanted to meet you,' said Tim.

'We're going out tomorrow,' I told him. 'And I was going to finish off the bridesmaids' dresses tonight.'

'I need to see you tonight,' said Tim. 'Really I do, Isobel.'

I sighed. 'It's not that I don't want to see you. It's just that I've so much to do!'

'Please, Isobel.'

'But there's only two weeks and—'

'Isobel, please.'

'Oh, OK.' I ran my fingers through my hair. 'I suppose I can practise with the headdress another evening.'

'Meet you in Kiely's?' he said.

'Tim!' Kiely's, in Donnybrook, was close to Tim's red-bricked, bay-windowed townhouse. I lived in Sutton, at least a twenty-minute drive over the toll-bridge.

'I left the car in for a service today,' he said apologetically. 'I thought I'd have it back this evening but it wasn't ready. So I'm without wheels.'

'Oh, OK,' I said again. I always gave in to Tim, I couldn't help it. Maybe that was what Alison was talking about.

'Half an hour?' he said.

'An hour,' I told him. 'I need to get dressed. I was trying on my wedding dress when you called.' I laughed suddenly. 'I hope it's not bad luck to be trying on the dress when your fiancé phones – like him seeing you in it!'

Tim laughed too but he didn't sound convincing. It was all getting a bit much for him, I thought. Endless discussion about who to invite and what sort of menu to have, and which band to choose. All sorts of things that seemed so important at the time but probably weren't important at all really. In the end, the only important thing was that Tim loved me and that I loved him. The rest was incidental. But the incidental things took up most of our time these days.

I reversed my white Peugeot 205 out of the driveway and turned onto the coast road.

It was a grey, depressing evening. A thin layer of cloud blocked out any trace of blue sky and a cool easterly breeze whipped across the bay taking the struggling warmth out of the sun. I hoped it would be fine for my wedding day. I dreamed of blue skies with cotton-wool wisps of cloud and still, warm air. I could be lucky, I thought, as I sped along the road. It would be May by then and the weather might have turned.

It took me half an hour to get to Kiely's. Cars littered the surrounding streets and I abandoned mine on a double yellow line. I hoped I wouldn't get a ticket but, if I did, I'd make Tim pay for it. Friday night was a bad night to arrive late to a pub.

I pushed open the door. A haze of blue-grey smoke wafted towards me and my eyes began to water. I looked around the heaving throng of people for Tim. Why on earth did he insist on meeting in crowded places?

Finally I saw him, leaning against the wall, pint of Guinness in his hand. He was incredibly handsome, I thought smugly. His hair was jet-black and fell in an endearing fringe over his navy-blue eyes. His face was tanned and healthy, with high cheekbones, the sort I'd die for myself. He wore an oversized maroon Aran jumper and ragged Levis.

My heart skipped a beat when I saw him – sometimes I found it hard to believe that he was mine.

I wormed my way through the crowd and tapped him on the shoulder.

'Oh, hello.' He looked startled. 'I didn't see you come in.'

'You can't see anyone in here,' I said. 'It's just one pulsating blob of people. Why didn't you pick somewhere quieter?'

'It was quieter when I came in,' he told me. 'It seems to have filled up in the last half-hour.'

'Do you want to stay here?' I asked. 'Would you like to go somewhere else?'

'No, here is OK. Do you want a drink?'

'Orange juice is fine,' I said.

He nodded, handed me his pint, and made his way to the bar. He wasn't in a good mood, I thought, as I watched him. There was something wrong. I hoped it wasn't his mother again. She'd kicked up blue murder because we'd limited the family invitations to twenty-five from each side and Tim had refused to allow her to add on some distant cousin he couldn't even remember.

'It's all right for Isobel,' Denise Malone had told him. 'She has a small family. There probably aren't twenty-five people on her side anyway.'

'Of course there's twenty-five on my side,' I'd retorted angrily when he told me. 'I'm not squeezing my family out just so that she can invite a crowd of freeloaders!'

It had all been very silly, got very heated, for no real reason. In the end, Denise's sister rang from the States to say that she'd love to come but that she really couldn't afford the trip over in May, since she'd already booked her holidays for July. So there was space for Cousin Maddy or Dotty or Biddy after all and no need to rearrange anything.

'Here you are.' Tim handed me the glass of orange juice and retrieved his pint.

'Cheers.' I raised my glass but he was already taking a deep mouthful of Guinness.

'I needed to talk to you,' he said. He wiped the thin cream line from his upper lip. 'I'm sorry I dragged you out tonight.'

'I don't mind.' I put my head on his chest. 'I know I said I was busy, but I'm never too busy to see you. Darling,' I added teasingly.

'It was important to talk to you,' he said.

I looked up at him. Something was wrong, and from the tone of his voice it was a bit more serious than trouble on the Dotty, Maddy and Biddy front. 'What's the matter?' I asked.

He wiped at the condensation on the outside of his glass.

'What's the matter?' I asked again.

He looked up at me. 'I can't go through with it,' he said abruptly.

I heard the words but they didn't mean anything to me. 'What?'

'I can't go through with it,' he said again, a touch of desperation in his voice. 'I can't, Isobel. I need some time. I want to postpone it.'

'The wedding?' I stared at him. 'You want to postpone the wedding?' I clutched at my glass of orange juice.

'Yes.' He nodded and took another mouthful of Guinness.

I could still hear the buzz of the people around us, but their voices were muted, distant. I felt as though I was wrapped in a cocoon, separated from the world outside. My voice was paralysed. I opened my mouth and closed it again. I blinked a couple of times. 'You're joking,' I croaked finally.

'I'm not joking, Isobel.' His look was anguished. 'I need more time.'

'More time for what?' I demanded, the words tumbling out now. 'What could you possibly need time for? We've known each other for nearly two years. We've been engaged for six months! If you had a problem with it, why didn't you say so before now?'

'I didn't feel this way before now.'

'Feel what way?' I asked.

'Trapped,' he said.

I rummaged in my bag and found my asthma inhaler. I shook the canister a couple of times and then squirted the fine spray into my tightening lungs. Tim watched me.

'Are you all right?' he asked.

My breath was coming more easily again. 'No,' I said. I clutched the inhaler in my hand.

'Put it back in your bag,' he said. 'You don't really need it.'

'It's smoky in here,' I told him. 'You know I wheeze when it's smoky.'

'I thought it was me,' said Tim. 'I didn't mean to upset you.'

'And what did you think telling me you wanted to postpone the wedding would do?' I demanded. 'Make me dance around the pub with delight? I can't believe this, Tim. I really can't. Tell me you're joking. Tell me you don't really mean it. Why do you feel trapped? Is it just nerves? Is it—' I broke off. I couldn't talk any more. The tears were streaming down my face.

He watched me uncomfortably. He pulled a cotton hanky from his jeans pocket and handed it to me. I was crying far too much for it to be of any use. I knew that people were looking at me, but I didn't care. I could cry if I felt like it. I could have an asthma attack if I felt like it. I could die if I felt like it. I gulped and started to cough. I couldn't breathe properly. I thought, frantically, that maybe I *would* die.

'Isobel!' Tim's voice was harsh. 'Stop crying like that. You'll make yourself sick.'

'*You're* making me sick,' I said, gulping the smoke laden air through my sobs. 'You're the one that's doing this to me.' I shook the inhaler again and took another dose.

'Isobel!' Tim grabbed me by the arm. 'Stop it. Stop it now.'

He steered me out of the pub and into the darkening street. I rubbed my eyes with his hanky.

'How could you do this to me?' I asked. 'Why? Why

now? If you don't love me, why have you let it go this far?'

'I'm not saying I don't love you.' Tim pushed a lock of hair out of his eyes. 'I *do* love you, Isobel. I just don't feel that I can marry you. Not yet.'

I stared at him as I twisted the hanky around and around in my hands. I really couldn't believe I was hearing this. Part of me expected him to tell me it was all a joke, but I knew it wasn't. He looked too uncomfortable, too miserable, too serious for it to be a joke.

'We've been practically living together since we got engaged,' I said, trying to breathe calmly and evenly. 'Surely that must have helped you to think we could live together for ever.'

He sighed. 'That's just it, Isobel. Right now, everything is perfect. You stay with me most weekends, you go home during the week. You stay with me if we go out somewhere. But you're not there all the time. I know sometimes I'd like you to be there all the time – that's why I thought we should get married – but now I'm afraid. I like being on my own too. I'm not comfortable with the idea of having someone wanting to know where I am every minute of the day.'

'But I don't want to know where you are every minute of the day,' I said despairingly. 'I only want to know that you'll be with me every night.' I blew my nose and shoved the hanky into the pocket of my jeans.

Tim leaned against the wall and stared ahead of him. I remembered the day we'd met, at a twenty-first birthday party in the St Lawrence Hotel, in Howth. It had been a noisy, crowded party and I'd gone outside for a breath of fresh air. Tim was outside too, busily typing something into a personal organiser.

'What on earth are you doing?' I asked. I'd had a few

drinks – normally I wouldn't have butted into someone's private business.

'Making a memo of something I have to do tomorrow,' he said.

'You don't look like the business type.' I hiccoughed gently.

He laughed. 'I'm the computer type,' he said. 'I design computer software. I've been stuck on something for days and it suddenly came to me. So I thought I'd better get it down because sure as hell I'll never remember it in the morning!'

I grinned at him. 'Sounds reasonable.'

'Are you at the party?' he asked.

I nodded. 'But it was so hot and crowded I thought I'd come outside for a while. It's lovely out here, isn't it?'

'Want to go for a walk?' he asked.

'Why not?'

We walked along the pier together. The water lapped gently in against the wall and the wires from the boat-sails jingled against the masts. The moon sent a shaft of silver light across the harbour. We chatted as though we'd known each other for ages. Tim was unlike anybody else I'd ever met. I worked in a print and packaging company as the personal assistant to the managing director. I was used to people in suits, to graduate trainees wanting to get on, to the factory floor and the commercial work ethic. Tim was a creative sort of person. I'd always thought that computer people were boring and obsessed. I thought that they had to think in logical progression, like machines. I was way out of date. Tim said that he saw the results of his programmes before he'd ever written them; he thought in broad pictures as though he were making a film or writing a book.

'Wow,' I said. 'That's a sort of computer-nerd thing to say, isn't it? "Wow"?'

He laughed and put his arm around me. 'Wow,' he whispered as he drew me closer to him.

It was love at first sight. It was always like that for me, though; I fell fast and hard and then fell out of love as quickly. But it was different with Tim. With Tim, I knew that it would last for ever.

How could it all have gone wrong? I thought bleakly. We were so right together. Not opposites, exactly, but complementary. When he was working on a project, he was lost to me. When he'd finished, he was devoted. And I was always there, content to be with him, secure in the knowledge that no one else could love him as much as me, and that there was no one else in his life to usurp me.

He earned a lot of money as a software designer. The day I met him, he'd bought his townhouse in Donnybrook. He had a company car. He took two holidays a year: one to the sun any time between May and September, and a skiing holiday in February. I didn't weigh him up in monetary terms and decide that he was a good catch, but he was. I loved him and I thought he loved me.

I thought we worked as a couple. I thought that everything between us was perfect. I thought that I understood him. How could I have understood him when he was going through such agonies?

'I'm sorry.' I slipped my arm into his. 'I didn't realise it was getting to you so much.'

'I'm sorry too.' He hugged my arm to his side. 'I thought I was ready for this. Truly I did, Isobel. But I can't do it. I can't stand in the church with our friends and family and make such a big issue out of it all.'

I looked at him hopefully. 'Would you go through with a quick wedding in a register office?'

He disentangled my hold on him. 'Not yet. I can't do anything yet.'

We stood silently beside each other. Part of me felt sorry

for him. Part of me wanted to kill him. Part of me wanted to kill myself.

How could I walk into the office on Monday and tell them all that my wedding was off? The wedding that had been practically the sole topic of conversation in the company for the past month? How could I tell them that the Conrad was cancelled, that the gifts were being returned, that the honeymoon to the Greek islands wasn't going to happen? It would be awful. They'd be sorry for me. They'd put their arms around me and tell me that it wasn't the end of the world and then, when I wasn't there, they'd discuss it in breathless whispers and say that they knew it wouldn't have worked and that I'd made such a fool of myself over Tim Malone.

'I just need some time,' he said. 'That's all.'

I said nothing. There was nothing I could say. I stared across the road without seeing anything.

'I thought perhaps you might like to go on the honeymoon,' said Tim suddenly.

'What?'

'The honeymoon. It's paid for. I feel terrible about this, Isobel. I thought you might like to go on the holiday.'

'With you?' I stared at him incredulously.

'Of course not,' he said. 'With a friend.'

'Oh, Tim.' I burst into a fresh paroxysm of tears. '*You're* my best friend. I don't want to do anything without you.'

He held me to him and allowed me to sob all over his jumper. He patted me gently on the back and whispered that he still loved me.

'So why won't you go through with the wedding?' I cried. 'Why?'

'I've told you,' he said helplessly. 'I just can't. I still want to see you, Isobel. I don't want us to break up. I just want to postpone things for a while, that's all.'

'How can we go on seeing each other?' I sniffed. 'People will think we're insane.'

'When did we ever care what people thought?' he murmured into my ear. 'When?'

I leaned against his chest, the rough wool of the jumper coarse against my face. My eyes were closed. I still couldn't take it in. I couldn't believe that Tim felt the way he did. He hadn't shown it before now. I sighed deeply and he held me closer.

'How can you hug me like this?' I asked as I lifted my head to look at him. 'How can you hold me tight and not want to marry me?'

'It's not that I don't want to marry you, Isobel. I do. I just don't want to do it now. It would be a mistake to do it now. Really it would.'

'Is there someone else?' I hadn't wanted to ask, was afraid of his reply.

'Of course not,' he said sharply. 'How could there be? I haven't had eyes for anyone but you.' He kissed me on the forehead. 'It's such a big step, that's all.'

I leaned against his chest again. 'But I thought we were ready for it.'

'I'm so busy in work at the moment,' he continued. 'I'm working a twelve-hour day. I don't have time to be with you. I don't want to feel guilty that you're at home without me.'

I was silent.

'When I get myself sorted out,' he said. 'Later in the year.'

I moved away from him. 'What makes you think you'll be more likely to marry me later in the year? What if there's another project, something else to keep you working so hard? I know that you're busy. I understand that, Tim.'

'It's different now,' he told me. 'I know that if we were

married I'd be rushing a job just to get home. And I know that you'd be pissed off with me for not being there when you wanted. It's the wrong time, Isobel. That's all.'

'And you still love me?' I looked at him doubtfully.

'More than anything,' he assured me, and drew me towards him again.

~

There was a ticket on my car. I ripped it from behind the wiper, crumpled it into a tiny ball and flung it into the oily puddle in front of the Peugeot. Tim had half-heartedly asked me to go back to the house with him, so that we could talk things over. But I didn't want to talk things over with Tim. I needed to be on my own for a while. I needed to get my thoughts together, to make sense of what he had told me.

I still couldn't understand why. It was easy for him to say that he needed time, or that he felt pressurised, or that he was too busy at work. But it was hard for me to believe that they were insurmountable obstacles to true love. And I'd thought that what Tim felt for me and what I felt for him was true love. I'd never been this close to another person before. I'd never shared their dreams or desires or the trivial details of anyone's life the way I had with Tim. I knew the kind of toothpaste he preferred. I knew that biological washing-powders brought him out in a rash. I knew that he liked jazz music, mountain walking and Chinese food. I knew that he was cranky in the mornings, at his best late at night. I knew that when he was taken over by a problem he couldn't leave it alone until he'd worked it out. I knew so much about him, I thought, as I unlocked the car door, but suddenly it wasn't enough. I hadn't known that the thought of marrying me had been so truly terrible to him.

~

My parents were watching TV when I arrived home. Alison had gone out with some girlfriends, but – unusually – Ian, my loose-limbed, nineteen-year-old brother, was sprawled across the sofa, his legs dangling over the armrest.

'Susan Purcell rang a few minutes ago,' said Mum as I walked into the living room. 'She's dropping around tomorrow night with your wedding present. She told me that she's bought a Paul Costello suit for the wedding!'

'She should have saved her money.' I'd taken another puff of my inhaler before coming into the house but my breathing was still uneven.

'Oh, Isobel, a suit like that will last her for years,' said Mum. 'It's the kind of thing you can wear over and over again.'

'I meant, she should have saved her money on the wedding present,' I said. It was an effort not to cry again. 'I won't be needing her sheets or toaster or waffle-maker or whatever she's bought.'

Mum pointed the remote control at the TV and silenced Pat Kenny. 'What happened?' she asked.

'The wedding's off.' I flopped onto the sofa beside Ian, who sat upright and stared at me in amazement.

'Off!' Mum, Dad and Ian echoed my words together.

'Off,' I repeated.

They exchanged glances. 'Why is it off?' asked Dad finally.

'We've postponed it,' I said.

They were silent for a moment.

'Why?' asked Ian.

I twirled my glittering diamond engagement ring around on my finger. It had never occurred to me to give it back to Tim – to make some kind of gesture by flinging it at him in temper.

'Tim feels that he's not quite ready for the commitment.'

'The bastard!' Ian stood up, his six-foot-one frame towering over me. 'I'll tear him apart. Who does he think he is? Not ready! Hasn't he been sleeping with you for the past year and a half!'

'Ian!' I looked at him in horror. It wasn't that my parents didn't know that Tim and I had slept together – given that I spent so many nights in Donnybrook it would have been pretty strange not to – but we never spoke about it, as though by ignoring it they could pretend that I was still an innocent virgin.

'He's got a bloody nerve.' Dad was angry. The tip of his nose was red, which was a sure sign.

'Oh, Isobel.' Mum put her arms around me. 'I'm so sorry.'

I felt the lump in my throat and swallowed hard, blinking furiously to get rid of the tears that threatened to spill down my cheeks. I was tired of crying. I didn't want to cry in front of my family.

'It's for the best,' I said shakily. 'It'd be terrible to get married and then decide it had all been a mistake. Anyway,' I cleared my throat, 'we haven't broken off our engagement. We've just postponed things until later in the year.'

'But you won't be able to book the Conrad for later in the year,' said Mum. 'It was a struggle getting it for Saturday week! Don't you remember? You won't get any decent hotel at such short notice. How much is it going to cost to cancel it now?' She put her hand over her mouth in dismay. 'Not that the money is important, of course, darling. Your happiness is. But all the same—'

'I don't want to talk about it now,' I said. 'I'm tired. I'm going to bed.'

'I'll bring you up some hot milk,' said Mum. 'Help you sleep.'

'I don't need hot milk,' I told her. 'I'm perfectly well able to sleep, thanks. I'm exhausted.'

I opened the door of the front room. The presents were there, neatly piled to one side. The Egyptian cotton bed-linen. The set of Newbridge cutlery. The Waterford glass decanter. I wanted to pick up the Waterford glass decanter and hurl it across the room. But I didn't. There wouldn't have been any point. Besides, it wasn't my decanter to throw anywhere. Half of it belonged to Tim.

I couldn't sleep, of course. I lay in the bed and stared at the ceiling, wondering how my life could crumble around me like this. My wedding dress hung on the outside of the wardrobe, mocking me. I hadn't the heart to put it away. I couldn't bring myself to touch it.

I heard Alison come in around one o'clock and the muted tones of her conversation with Ian. I pulled the covers around me and tried to make myself fall asleep. I didn't want to talk to Alison.

She pushed open my bedroom door and tiptoed to the bed.

'Are you awake?' she whispered.

I kept my eyes tightly closed and tried to breathe deeply and evenly.

'You can't possibly be asleep.' Her voice was louder.

I didn't move.

'OK,' she said. 'Don't talk to me now. I understand. But you're well rid of him, Issy, and you know it. He's a shit. He always was a shit. I never liked him.'

You liar, I thought, as I kept my eyes closed. I've seen you looking at him. You know as well as I do that he's an attractive, sensitive bloke and you probably fancy him yourself.

'I'll talk to you tomorrow,' she said finally. 'It's probably for the best.'

I supposed everyone would tell me that. It's for the best. People always say it when something rotten happens, as though rotten things can actually make your life any better. I couldn't see how calling off the wedding I'd dreamed about since I was a child was for the best. I wanted to believe that it was simply postponed for a few months, but there was a band of ice around my heart that told me it could be postponed for ever.

I don't know when I eventually fell asleep. When I did, I dreamed of my wedding. It was taking place as though nothing had happened. Tim stood at the altar and smiled at me as he took my hands in his and promised to love me. I promised to love him too. It was only when we posed outside the church for the photographs that I realised I wasn't wearing my beautiful wedding dress but some old net curtains which had been in the hot-press for years.

'It isn't a valid wedding,' Father O'Brien told me mournfully. 'You have to wear a dress to make it a valid wedding. I'm very sorry, Isobel, but it's all been a dreadful mistake.'

Chapter 2

The Lovers' Complaint (Joan Miró, 1953)

Mum was waiting for me when I got up on Saturday morning. I stumbled downstairs and took some Hedex from the box in the cupboard while she hovered around me, teapot in hand, an anxious expression on her face.

'Do you have a headache?' she asked.

'No,' I snapped. 'I'm overdosing on paracetamol.'

She looked hurt. 'I only asked.'

'Thanks,' I said. 'But I'm fine. It's just from tiredness.'

'I couldn't sleep either.' She poured a cup of tea and handed it to me. 'I kept thinking of what I'd like to do to him. How dare he treat my daughter like that!'

'Oh, Mum, please.' I sat down at the table and listlessly buttered a slice of overdone toast.

'But, honestly, Isobel! How can he just change his mind like that? Didn't he talk to you about it? Hasn't he said something before now?'

I shook my head. I didn't want this conversation.

'But if he felt that strongly it can't have taken him until now to decide. You've been engaged for six months.'

'I know,' I said.

'What does his mother think?'

'I don't know. I haven't spoken to her.'

'I hope she's proud of him.' Mum refilled the kettle. Water splashed angrily from the tap.

'It's not her fault,' I said.

'It's her fault the way she's brought up her son,' said Mum. 'And that's what I'll tell her.'

I stared at her in horror. 'Tell her?'

'You don't think I'm going to sit around while her precious son throws my daughter over, do you? I'm going to tell her exactly what I think of him!'

'Mum!' The thought was terrifying. 'Please don't. It'll only make things worse. Besides, we haven't called off our engagement. We've just postponed the wedding.'

'Huh!' Mum snorted.

She went on and on at me. I stopped listening and played with my toast. I wasn't hungry. A great way to diet, I thought bleakly. I wasn't even thirsty.

In the afternoon I borrowed Ian's mountain bike and went for a cycle along the seafront. It was still windy and I was buffeted from side to side as I tried to keep the bike upright. I hadn't cycled since my schooldays. I was out of practice. But at least it kept me out of the house and away from Mum. I didn't know which was harder to bear, her rage or her comfort.

She was on the phone when I got home.

'Of course I see your point of view,' she was saying. 'But I can't believe that he's just dumped her like this.'

Thanks, Mum, I thought. Dumped her. A very sensitive way of putting it.

'Well, my daughter is worth ten of your son!'

Oh, God. My worst nightmare. She was on the phone to Denise Malone. For some reason, despite their similar backgrounds, Mum and Mrs Malone had never hit it off. Neither of them thought that their offspring's choice of partner was the one they'd have chosen themselves. Mum didn't like Tim's studied scruffiness. Mrs Malone wouldn't have liked any girl Tim brought home.

'Get off the phone,' I hissed as I took off my sweatshirt. I was sweating from the exertion of cycling against the wind.

Mum made faces at me and continued the conversation.

'I think it's ridiculous. Two weeks! Of course it's better now than later – but even still. No, I don't think he's being fair.' I could see her cheeks redden and her grip on the receiver tighten. 'You might think so.' Silence. A sigh. Gritted teeth. 'Yes. No. Goodbye.' She turned to me. 'Stupid woman,' she said and put her arms around me.

I half-thought that Tim might ring me even though I'd asked him not to. Every time the phone rang my heart jumped and, even when I found out that the call wasn't for me, my whole body trembled for ages afterwards. I wondered what he was doing. Working, I supposed, that great panacea for all men. 'I'm too busy, I'm working.' Tim had used it a lot as an excuse in the past, but I always thought it was genuine. Now, for the first time, I was unsure. I felt insecure and frightened. The family didn't help – they went on and on at me.

Alison was the only one who was pleased.

'It's not that I want you to be miserable, or anything,' she said. 'But you don't need Tim Malone to make you happy.'

'Oh, sod off,' I replied and banged the bedroom door shut.

Mum wanted to know about cancelling things. 'Because you'll have to inform the hotel, you know, Isobel. God knows how they'll react. And there's the band, and the photographer. I don't know what you should do about the cake. I'm sure it's baked already, but maybe it's not iced. That way we'll be able to use it as a Christmas cake—'

'Oh, for God's sake!' I stared at her in exasperation and walked out of the kitchen and into the back garden.

The tulips splashed vibrant red in the flowerbeds, surrounded by yellow, purple and white pansies. The lawn was emerald green, with neat stripes. Dad loved the garden and spent hours working in it. Usually I felt it was an oasis of peace and serenity, but today its structured elegance made me want to pull up the flowers and trample on them.

'D'you want me to go around and talk to him?' Ian was sitting on the garden bench. I hadn't noticed him at first.

'And say what?' I asked.

'Dunno.' Ian motioned to me to sit beside him. 'Tell him that he's a fool and that he's missing out on a really great woman.'

My brother never normally spoke to me like this. I laughed sourly. 'We've just postponed it,' I said. 'There's no need to tell him anything.'

'You look far too upset for someone who's happy about postponing things,' said Ian. 'You're too pale and you look sick.'

'Thank you for the vote of confidence,' I said. 'You can rush around and tell him I'm wasting away.'

'I'm only trying to help,' said Ian glumly.

'I know.' I leaned my head on his shoulder. 'I'm sorry.'

Thankfully, Dad didn't try to talk to me. He just squeezed my arm every time I walked by him, and allowed me to read the newspapers before him.

It was a long weekend. I couldn't get Tim out of my mind. Everything I did, I imagined doing as Tim's wife. My soon-to-be-married state had become so much a part of me, I couldn't adjust to it not happening. I still couldn't understand why Tim felt trapped. I'd never pressurised him. I didn't force him into asking me to marry him. It didn't make sense. None of it made sense. I wished I could stop thinking about it for even a couple of minutes but I couldn't. I didn't sleep on Sunday night either.

I toyed with the idea of staying out of work on Monday, but that would have only made things more difficult. I went in early instead. I wanted to be at my desk, outside Barry Cleary's office, before any of the other staff arrived. I didn't want to walk the length of the open-plan floor while someone called out '*Only two weeks to go!*' and made me burst into tears again. I'd tell them, of course, but in my own time.

I switched on my computer and called up the memo files. The folder marked 'personal' contained the list of people we'd invited to the wedding and the presents that they'd given us. I'd need that list to return the presents. Or should I return the presents, I wondered, if Tim and I decided to get married in the autumn? What were the chances? I asked myself savagely. Did he really mean 'postpone' or did he mean 'call off'? How could I know? I'd been too shocked to talk to him properly on Friday night. I should have gone back to his house as he'd suggested and made him tell me exactly what the problem was and exactly when he intended to go through with things. I should have phoned him yesterday, despite telling myself I didn't want to. Now I was in limbo. I leaned my head on the monitor and sighed deeply.

'Are you all right, Isobel?' Lesley Morrissey stopped at my desk. 'Have you got a headache or something? I've got Panadol in my bag if you want.'

I looked up at her. 'No thanks, I'm fine.'

'You don't look fine,' she said, putting a green folder bulging with invoices on the edge of my desk. 'You're white as a sheet and you've got black circles under your eyes. All this wedding stuff is getting you down.'

I took a deep breath. Might as well start with Lesley, I thought. Let her be the one to break the news to the rest of the people in the office. 'There isn't going to be a wedding,' I told her. 'Not in two weeks anyway.'

'Isobel!' She looked at me in shock. 'Why?'

I wanted to say that I'd got cold feet, that I was the one to call it off, but I was afraid that she'd find out the truth. I didn't want her to feel sorry for me. I didn't want sympathetic looks following me around the office.

'We've been talking about it,' I said. 'We decided it was getting out of hand. The preparations, the fuss. There were arguments about the guests.' I shrugged. 'It didn't seem like an enjoyable thing any more. So we've decided to postpone it.'

'Until when?' Her grey eyes were wide in surprise.

'I'm not sure. October maybe. Or November. Or next year.'

'But, Isobel—' Her expression was a mixture of sympathy and amazement. 'I thought you were really happy about getting married. I thought that you couldn't wait to be with Tim.'

'There's a difference between being married and the wedding itself,' I said, although I was saying the first words that came into my head and I hadn't a clue if they made sense. 'I'm not sure we were ready for the wedding, even if we did want to be with each other.'

'Why don't you call off the big do, and get married quietly instead?' she asked. 'If it means that much to you.'

'Maybe we'll do that,' I said. 'But not on Saturday week.'

Then Barry Cleary, the managing director, walked into his office and Lesley scurried back to her desk. I could see her telling the other girls, Niamh and Anna, who tried hard not to look in my direction, but who shot surreptitious glances at me when they thought I didn't notice. I didn't care. I wasn't sure whether or not Lesley would give my version of the events, or whether she'd end the conversation with 'she's putting a brave face on it, but he's obviously dumped her'. What were they to think, after all? People don't call off their weddings just because the fuss is getting a bit much. I wondered, suddenly, if they'd already had a collection for me. A brown-paper envelope passed surreptitiously around the office with much giggling. For Isobel's wedding present. I felt sick.

I brought Barry his cup of coffee. He was reading the *Irish Times* business page. 'Interest rates down again,' he commented as I put the cup in front of him. 'Good news for mortgage holders.' He stirred the coffee. 'I suppose that's the sort of thing that'll occupy you now, Isobel. Things like the cost of your mortgage and carpets and furniture.'

'Possibly,' I said. 'But not in the immediate future.'

'You'll have to take responsibility for your own financial affairs.' He took off his gold-rimmed glasses and placed them on the desk. 'Don't be kept in the dark by that husband of yours.'

Why were they all talking about him today? Barry had hardly mentioned the wedding since the day I'd got engaged.

'Actually, Barry, I'm not getting married as soon as I thought after all.' I tried to sound nonchalant, but the words came out as a croak.

'Pardon?' He looked at me quizzically.

'The wedding,' I said succinctly. 'It's off.'

'Isobel!'

Couldn't anyone come up with a different reaction? Couldn't somebody, for once, just look surprised? Couldn't they say 'that's a shame' without saying 'Isobel!' and looking at me as though I'd contracted a fatal disease?

'We've changed our minds,' I said. 'We've postponed it.'

He stared at me. 'Sharon will be disappointed,' he said finally. 'She was looking forward to it.'

'Maybe later in the year,' I said.

'Really?'

'I'm not sure.'

I couldn't stay in his office. The shreds of my self-control were beginning to disappear. I picked up my notebook and fled to the ladies'.

I didn't want to stay in there too long. If I did, someone would be dispatched to find out if I was OK. There seemed to be a kind of antenna around the office, something that let the other girls know if one of us was upset. They knew the difference between going to the loo to answer the call of nature and going to the ladies' to cry your eyes out.

So I wouldn't cry my eyes out. I would get myself under control and I'd go back to my desk to get on with my work. I looked at myself in the mirror. Lesley was right. My face was ashen and my eyes were smudged with black shadows. I pinched my cheeks to bring the colour back. It didn't really work. I should have come into the office layered with make-up so that I didn't look so awful. But I hadn't the heart to put it on before I left the house. Now I wished I had.

'Would you like to come to the pub for lunch today?' asked Niamh as I passed by her desk.

'Thanks, but I'm actually busy,' I lied.

'Feeling OK?' she asked.

'Fine.'

My phone was ringing when I reached my desk.

'What's this I hear?' Marion, the receptionist, was at the other end.

'Hi, Marion. Can you call me back? I'm kind of busy at the moment.'

'Don't play games with me,' said Marion. She was the oldest of us, in her late thirties, married with three children. 'Is it true?'

'If you're asking about the wedding, yes, it's true.'

'But why?'

'Marion, please.' I clutched the receiver. 'I'll talk to you about it later, not now.'

'All right,' she conceded. 'You don't sound great, Isobel. Take care of yourself.'

'Thanks,' I said.

I got through the day. I kept myself to myself and ignored the glances of the other girls. The men knew something was up but they weren't as clued in as the girls. None of them made any comments to me.

By half-past five I was exhausted. I saved my work, switched off the computer and locked my desk. Lesley, Niamh and Anna had all left around five. I called to Barry that I was going home, and then I hurried out of the building and into my car.

I felt as though people were looking at me, although I knew that they couldn't be. I thought that they were noticing my engagement ring and nudging each other to share the knowledge that it was all a sham. Tim Malone had never intended to marry Isobel Kavanagh. How dare I strut around the streets flashing that diamond as though it was a symbol of something? It was only jewellery. Jewellery I wasn't entitled to wear.

I ripped the ring from my finger and threw it into the glove compartment. My hand felt naked without it.

The traffic was heavy and it took over an hour to get home. The family were sitting in front of the TV when I got in. My mother told me that there was some bolognese in the pot and she'd re-heat it for me if I wanted. She'd put on some spaghetti, too, if I liked. I was getting tired of her fussing around me all the time. I knew that she was trying to be supportive but she was killing me with kindness. I wanted her to stay watching *999* and shout to me that I was late and I'd have to make my own dinner.

'I'm not hungry,' I said as I curled up in an armchair with a well-thumbed copy of *Rebecca*.

'You've got to eat,' she said. 'You can't sit around pining.'

'I'm not pining,' I told her. 'I had lunch with the girls in the office. I'm fine.'

'Where's your engagement ring?' asked Alison suspiciously. 'Have you sent it back to him?'

'Shit!' I exclaimed, jumping up from the armchair. 'It's in the car.'

'What's it doing there?' asked Dad.

I didn't reply.

I retrieved the ring and slid it onto my finger again. It sparkled in the evening sunlight. I felt the ice around my heart again and took a puff of my inhaler.

'So is Shitface going to call you?' Alison looked up at me as I came in.

'Don't talk about him like that,' I snapped. 'I'm still engaged to him, we're still going to be married.'

'Leave your sister alone,' said my mother to Alison.

'Why don't you all leave me alone?' I snarled and went upstairs to my room.

I wished I'd moved out of the family home before now. I'd thought about it a couple of times, but I liked living with my family and I had expensive tastes when it came to property. Nothing I liked was ever remotely within my reach. In an apartment, I wanted somewhere bright and airy, with views over the city. In a house, I wanted a period home with a huge sunlit garden. Even Tim's townhouse wasn't really my cup of tea. But I'd have happily lived there if I was married to him.

I looked at my watch and wondered whether my friend Julie was back from her weekend away in Kerry with the girls from her tennis club. I needed to talk to Julie. She'd understand how I felt.

'I've just got in,' she said breathlessly, when I phoned. 'We had a wonderful time and I'm glad I took today off so that we could stay a little longer. It's amazing how refreshed you feel after a couple of days away.'

'Would you like to go for a drink?' I asked.

'Oh, Isobel, I'd love to, but I'm exhausted. I drove home and it's such a long drive from Killarney. The back of my neck aches.'

'I'd like to talk to you,' I said.

'I could meet you for lunch tomorrow,' she suggested.

'I'd really like it if you could meet me tonight.'

'Is there something wrong?' she asked. 'You sound funny.'

'Meet me,' I said.

'OK.' She knew that there was something wrong now. 'The usual?'

'Fine.'

'See you in half an hour?'

'Perfect.'

I changed into jeans and a sweatshirt and brushed some bronze onto my pale face. 'I'm going out,' I called to my parents. 'See you later.'

The pub was half-empty, quiet enough on a Monday night for us to be able to talk. Julie arrived a couple of minutes after me and strode over to the corner table where I sat.

I'd known Julie Donegan since we'd done a business course together eight years before. She was tall and slim with flawless skin and grey-green eyes. Her hair was naturally brown but she changed its colour every few weeks; today it was shining copper and fell around her shoulders in ordered disarray. She wore black jeans pulled tight at the waist, teamed with a crisp white blouse. I wished that I could look as graceful and elegant as Julie, but I was born too much of a tomboy for that. My hair was a mess, my sweatshirt had an old chocolate stain on the cuff and my jeans were the ones I'd worn doing the garden the previous week, so that there were grass stains on the knees.

'You look great,' I said as she sat beside me.

'You look like shit,' she told me. 'What's the matter?'

I fiddled with my engagement ring. 'The wedding's off,' I told her.

'Isobel!'

Even Julie, I thought wryly. Even my best friend could only exclaim my name and look at me in horror.

'Postponed indefinitely,' I added.

She waved at a lounge-girl. 'A couple of Southern Comforts, please.' She looked at me. 'Why?'

It was easier to tell Julie. I didn't feel that I had to pretend with her. 'He felt trapped.'

'Bullshit,' she said. 'He got cold feet.'

'I don't know what he got,' I said unhappily. 'But he got enough of it to decide that he couldn't marry me.'

'But, Isobel.' She grabbed me by the hand. 'It doesn't make any sense. Why didn't he get cold feet before now?'

'I don't know.' I took back my hand so that I could rummage in my bag for a tissue. I knew that the tears were going to fall again.

'Here.' She handed me one.

I blew my nose.

'So you're still engaged?' She looked doubtful.

'I think so.' I knew I looked doubtful too. 'He says he still loves me. He just feels that everything has got out of control.'

Julie paid for the drinks. 'What do you think?'

'Right now, I don't think anything. I feel terrible. My family keep looking at me as though I've got only weeks to live. Ian wants to beat the crap out of Tim. Alison keeps telling me that it's definitely the best thing that could have happened. Mum doesn't know what to say to all the people we've invited, and Dad sits there saying nothing but looking mournful.'

Julie laughed, and the sound of her laughter made me feel a little better.

'I told them in work,' I said. 'You know the way they are in my office – the wedding was the only topic of conversation. They kept looking at me when they thought I was preoccupied. Half-sympathetic, half-ghoulish looks. I'm sure they'd just bought me a present too. All last week Lesley kept asking me about the colour of things in the kitchen.'

'I bought you a present,' said Julie blankly. 'A set of crockery.'

'Oh, Julie!'

'Never mind.' She laughed again. 'Mum'll be pleased to have more dishes. Since she got the dishwasher she doesn't care how many odd cups of coffee or snacks we have.'

I swirled the golden drink around in my glass. 'I thought I had it all,' I said. 'I thought I was so lucky. I thought I was marrying someone who loved me. Even better that he was successful and happy in his own right. I felt part of him, Julie. I don't understand.'

'Men are impossible to understand,' she said briskly.

'Not Tim,' I said. 'Tim was always straightforward.'

She raised an eyebrow enquiringly at me.

'Until now,' I said.

'D'you think there's someone else?'

I picked up a beermat and broke it in half. 'No.'

'Are you sure?'

'I can't be certain.' I broke the two halves into halves again and dropped the pieces into an ashtray. 'But I truly don't think so. Why would he want to stay engaged if he had another girlfriend? It would be easier just to tell me and get it over with.'

She shook her head. 'You never know what people will say or do if they think they're making life easier for themselves. Even Tim.'

I drained my glass. 'I want to kill him.'

'I'm glad,' she said.

'Glad?'

'At least you're angry. It's better than being miserable.'

'I'm miserable too,' I said. 'I still love him.'

We had another couple of drinks. The pub filled up some more. I looked around at all the couples sitting close to each other, sharing secrets, whispering into each other's ears, occasionally kissing each other. It wasn't fair, I thought. I'd been part of all that and now he'd changed everything.

'Come on,' said Julie. 'Let's have one for the road and then go home.'

We had one for the road, then another for the road, then one for the bumps on the road and finally one for the holes in the road. My head was spinning by the time we left the pub and I almost fell as I stepped off the pavement.

'Be careful,' giggled Julie. 'Don't break a leg or anything.'

'I am careful,' I said as I clutched at her for support. 'I'm very careful. Very careful, very drunk.'

'You probably haven't been drunk in ages.' She put her arm around me. '*I* haven't been drunk in ages.'

'It's not a solution,' I said sanctimoniously.

'Nobody said it was.' She burped gently and looked surprised. 'But it can be a comfort.'

'You're my best friend,' I told her. 'And I love you.'

'And I love you.' Her words were slurred. 'You're my best friend too, Isobel. And you're more important to me than any – man.' She spat the last word.

'But you have Declan,' I protested, surprised at myself for remembering the name of her latest boyfriend. Julie wasn't exactly a one-man kind of woman. 'He's nice.'

'He's OK. But I don't love him.'

'I love Tim,' I moaned. 'I can't stop loving him, Julie. He's part of my life.'

'He's a bastard,' she said.

'He said that we might get married at the end of the year.' I almost walked into a lamp-post. 'He just needs some time.'

'He just needs a boot in the arse,' said Julie.

I laughed. 'A boot in the arse. Good idea.' I kicked out at an imaginary Tim. 'Gotcha!'

We reached the turning for Julie's house.

'I'm going to have a hangover in the morning,' I said.

'Me too.' She tried to focus her eyes. 'But it was worth it. Don't let him get to you, Isobel. Keep your chin up.'

'Sure,' I said. 'Absolutely.'

But it was hard not to let him get to me. It was hard when I felt that my whole life had been ripped apart.

DeltaPrint, the company I worked for, had its main offices in Stillorgan and two factories, one in Leopardstown and the other in Tallaght. I sat in the morning traffic, my hangover headache nailed behind my right eye, and wished that I worked somewhere nearer to home. The cars crawled towards the booths on the toll-bridge. One of the things I'd looked forward to when I'd married Tim was not having to cross the river every day. The journey would have been against the traffic every morning. I'd have had to put up with this nightmare for only another fortnight. I leaned my head against the side window. I felt rotten.

Alison had left a note for me on the kitchen table. '*Shitface rang*' was all it said. I wondered when Tim had called. If, perhaps, he'd changed his mind, realised that he was suffering from nerves. I laughed bitterly. Changing his mind again would cause even more chaos. I'd cancelled the hotel, the band and the photographer yesterday, trying to ignore the compassion in their voices as I told them that we were delaying the wedding.

I wondered if I should sell my dress. My wonderful Cinderella dress would end up as a small ad that said '*Wedding dress, size 12, never worn*'. People would look at it and cluck with sympathy, but they wouldn't want to buy it because it might be unlucky. I couldn't bear to think of that beautiful dress never being worn.

Dressmaking was my hobby. I'd thought, once, that I might make clothes for a living, but I didn't want to go to college and study design. I preferred doing my own thing, once-offs for friends and family. People around home knew that I made clothes. I'd done heaps of wedding dresses before I'd done my own. I thought of all the other girls wearing Isobel Kavanagh originals as they floated happily down the aisle, and I ached to be one of them.

Barry was in the office before me. I popped in to see if there was anything he wanted.

'Are you taking your holidays?' he asked bluntly. 'You're down for two weeks in May and you've arranged for someone from the agency to temp for you. Do you want to cancel that?'

I liked the way Barry was being matter-of-fact about it. There was no sympathy in his voice, only practicality.

'No,' I said. I needed the time off. I was drained from the preparations anyway, even if they hadn't come to anything.

'That's fine,' said my boss. 'Can you run me a report on the orders from DeltaPac?'

'Sure,' I said, and went back to my desk.

I'd worked with Delta for five years. I liked the company, I got on with Barry and I received regular salary increases and a bonus every Christmas. I'd have happily stayed with Delta after my marriage, although I'd told Tim that I wanted to have a baby before I was thirty and maybe give up work then. I'd always thought he was happy about the idea but perhaps that was what had spooked him. From being a carefree single man to someone whose wife wanted to be surrounded by nappies in a couple of years. Maybe I'd seemed too clinical about it. I clenched my fists under the desk. I wished I knew what I'd done. That was the worst part. I felt as though it must be my fault, but I didn't know how.

The phone rang, my private direct line.

'Good morning,' said Tim.

'Hi.' I felt my face flush.

'How are you feeling?'

'OK.'

'I'm glad. I feel terrible.'

'Really?'

'Of course. You don't think I'm pleased with myself,

do you? I've handled everything so badly. I didn't mean to do it the way I did. I upset you and I never wanted to upset you. I need to talk to you. Can we meet for lunch?'

I needed to see him. 'I suppose so.'

'Thanks. I'll pick you up around twelve-thirty.'

'I'll be outside,' I said.

I stood outside the yellow-bricked office building and watched the cars whiz by, scanning them for sight of Tim's sporty red Alfa. He was five minutes late. I tapped my foot impatiently on the pavement and tried not to think about the girls in the office who'd walked by me on their way to the village for lunch.

Eventually the car pulled up beside me.

'Sorry I'm late,' he said as I climbed in. 'Some idiot had blocked me into the car park. D'you want to go to Gleeson's?'

'OK,' I said.

Tim executed a horrendous U-turn and headed back towards Booterstown.

'How are you feeling?' he asked.

'You asked me that on the phone,' I said. 'I'm fine.'

'Good.' He changed down a gear and screamed past a builder's truck.

'Could you drive a bit slower?' I asked.

He glanced at me. I never asked him to drive slower.

He pulled into the car park of the pub and switched off the engine. 'I'm starving,' he said. 'I could eat a horse.'

He ordered steak and chips with mushrooms and potatoes. I ordered an omelette.

'You should eat a bit more than that,' he protested.

'It's all I want.' I fiddled with the silver chain on my wrist. 'I'm just not hungry, that's all.'

He was silent. He picked up a sachet of sugar and shook it, then replaced it in the little chrome dish.

'I didn't mean to be so abrupt on Friday,' he said eventually. 'I know that I should have talked to you properly. Told you how I felt, but I couldn't. Everything seemed to be so out of control. I didn't know what to do. Whenever I wanted to talk about it, you'd tell me something about the bridesmaids' dresses or the menu or the cars or a million other things. There never seemed to be the right moment to say I was getting overwhelmed by the whole thing.'

'I thought you wanted to get married,' I said. 'If you wanted to get married then all the stuff about the wedding day shouldn't matter. It's only one day in your whole life.'

'I know.' He picked up the sachet of sugar again. 'I don't know why I got cold feet.'

'Have you changed your mind again?' I looked at him, half-hopeful, half-horrified.

'No.' His response was definite and my heart sank. 'I can't do it yet, Isobel.'

'Do you think you ever can?' I asked.

'I don't know.'

'So we're not really talking about postponement here, are we? We're talking about it being over.'

He looked anguished. 'I don't want it to be over.'

'Well, it has to be, doesn't it?' I was impatient now. 'If you don't want to marry me, then it's going nowhere.'

'Why do we have to get married?' he asked. 'Why don't you come and live with me for a while?'

I was silent. Was this what he really wanted? Me without the marriage? I'd thought about living with him, we'd discussed it before, but then we'd decided that we wanted to show our commitment to each other by getting married.

'It would work,' he said. 'And we could both get used to being with each other all the time.'

The waitress put our food in front of us. Tim rubbed his hands and sprinkled salt onto his steak. The steam rose from my omelette and the smell of eggs made me feel sick.

'It's not that I don't want to be with you,' he went on through a mouthful of chips. 'It's just that marriage is such a big step.'

'So why did you want to get married in the first place?' I demanded. 'You were the one that asked me, Tim. I never made you do it.'

'Well—' He made a face. 'You were always talking about friends who were engaged. We seemed to spend a lot of time with married people. It got to me, I suppose.'

'Did I force you into it?' I was perplexed. I honestly hadn't thought that I was making him feel like that.

'Not forced,' he said. 'I don't know, Isobel. I just felt I had to ask you, and then it seemed to have a life of its own.'

I knew what he meant. There was so much paraphernalia attached to getting married that you tended to lose sight of what it was all about.

'I'm sorry you felt like that.' I poked dispiritedly at my chips.

'There's so much about you that I love,' he said. 'It's the marriage thing I'm uncomfortable with.' He grinned. 'So, if you want to move in with me for a while, help me get my head together—' He looked like a little boy when he put his head to one side like that and peered through his fringe. It was hard to resist him. But I was supposed to marry him, not just live with him. Maybe a year ago, if he'd suggested it then, I would have happily moved in. But he hadn't asked; he'd asked me to marry him and I knew that now I couldn't settle for less, stupid and all though it seemed.

'It wouldn't work,' I said.

'Oh, come on, Isobel, you haven't even thought about it properly.'

'But it's not what I expected.'

'Sometimes people have to settle for what they didn't expect.'

I moved the chips around on my plate. This wasn't what I wanted. But was he right? Did I want too much?

'I don't know,' I said finally.

His mobile phone rang. I almost jumped out of my skin.

'I'll be there soon,' he told the caller. 'I'm entitled to a break. I need some time. Of course it'll be done by four. Give me a rest, Greg! No. Yes. Talk to you later.' He shrugged. 'Never a dull moment. Told you I was busy. I can hardly get out of the office these days.'

'Poor you,' I said.

'Look.' He wiped his mouth with the paper napkin. 'I know that this has been a shock to you, Isobel, and I know that I've been a shit about it. But I also know that I love you. Why don't you do as I suggested on Friday, go on the honeymoon with one of your friends, and we'll talk about it again when you come back. It'll give us both time to think things over, and at least you'll have a break.'

A break would be nice, I thought wistfully. And I needed to get away from the solicitous glances, the well-meaning sympathy.

'OK,' I said.

'Great,' said Tim. He kissed me on the cheek. 'I'm glad you understand.'

Chapter 3

Women Running on a Beach (Pablo Picasso, 1922)

It had seemed ideal when Tim and I first discovered that the flight to Rhodes departed at one o'clock in the morning. Our plan was to go straight from the reception to the airport and hop on the flight to our honeymoon destination. No messing about with an overnight stay in Dublin where Tim's friends could have arranged practical jokes on us – just a night-time flight to the sparkling Aegean and two weeks of sun-soaked bliss.

Sitting in the departure lounge with Julie, waiting for the delayed flight to be called, didn't have quite the same appeal. She kept looking anxiously at me as though I'd suddenly disintegrate into a sobbing wretch, and kept up an inane conversation which I supposed was meant to distract me from the fact that, by now, I should have been a married woman.

I closed my eyes and leaned back in the seat. It had been a truly awful day.

I'd woken up at seven, to the birds singing joyfully in the apple-tree outside my bedroom window and the sun streaming through the light cotton curtains. It was a beautiful morning. I gazed out into the flower-filled back garden, where I'd intended to have some pre-wedding photos taken, and tears of misery and disappointment flooded down my cheeks. I tried to tell myself that it was very insecure to feel like this, that no girl in this day and age needed a husband to feel complete, that I shouldn't be crying for something that might never have worked in the first place. I tried to reason that, if Tim felt so unsure about things, it was better to wait until he was more certain. But it didn't stop me from crying. I did my best to sob silently because the thought of my mother rushing into my bedroom to comfort me was too much to bear.

Each time I looked at my watch I thought of where I should have been – at the hairdresser's, getting my make-up done, arriving at the church, walking down the aisle, saying 'I do' to Tim. I wondered what he was doing, half-expected him to call. But he didn't.

I went into town. It was the easiest way of avoiding Mum's stricken face and Alison's triumphant one. Dad and Ian had gone to a football match and had left the house without saying anything. I think Dad wanted to pretend it was just another Saturday.

Grafton Street was hot, crowded and dirty. I spent a fortune on clothes that I didn't need. I bought two linen suits in Monsoon, a beautiful silk jacket in AirWave, two pairs of Bally shoes, half-a-dozen T-shirts, a wraparound skirt and three one-piece swimsuits in M&S.

I arrived home with dozens of carrier bags and a hole in my bank balance and I didn't care.

'My God,' said Alison when she came into my bedroom. 'Did you go completely mad?'

'Why not?' I asked. 'I don't need the money for anything else.'

'Are you bringing that lot on holiday with you?'

'The T-shirts, I suppose.' I folded them neatly and put them into the suitcase. 'And the swimsuits.'

'You'll have a great time in the sun,' she promised. 'It'll be lovely to get away and you'll feel miles better when you come back.'

'Yes.' I tried to sound enthusiastic but it was very hard.

'What time's Julie calling around?'

'About eleven,' I said. At eleven, Tim and I should have been dancing together in the ballroom. At eleven, I should have been married for nearly eight hours. I snapped the suitcase closed.

'I'll be thinking about you tomorrow, lying on the beach having a great time,' said Alison.

'Shut up, will you,' I said, and went downstairs.

~

Julie slept all through the flight but I couldn't. So I was relieved when we finally touched down in Rhodes. It took over an hour to retrieve our luggage and nearly another hour before the bus trundled into the town of Rhodes. I'd been tired and cranky until then but I gasped with sudden delight when we turned onto the quayside and saw the hundreds of boats and ferries bobbing up and down in the water. The sunlight was dazzling off the white flagstones, the walled city made me feel as though we'd stepped back in time and the fishermen selling sponges, even at this early hour, looked like they'd been there for ever.

'Isobel!' gasped Julie. 'It's wonderful.'

'Gorgeous,' I breathed.

When I'd thought of Rhodes, I'd pictured tourists and restaurants, sunbathing and late-night bars. I hadn't imagined anything quite so timeless.

The Hotel Kos was a five-minute walk from the beach. It was very modern – smoked-glass, pink marble and very cool. I was glad to be out of the scorching sun for a while

– I wondered what on earth it would be like at midday if it was this hot already.

We were on the second floor. We threw our suitcases on the bed, pulled open the heavy curtains and stepped out onto the balcony.

There were people lying around the pool already, smearing themselves with lotions as they settled down for the morning. The pool was big – kidney-shaped with a small bridge running across the narrow part. Children jumped from the bridge into the deep end despite the notice that told them not to. I wished I had the nerve to jump into the water like that but swimming was never one of my strong points. Maybe it was because of my asthma, but whenever I swallowed water I was never able to cough it out properly and always ended up gasping for breath and clinging helplessly to the side of the pool while people clustered anxiously around me.

There was a small bar at the far end where a few people had gathered for poolside drinks.

'Tell me you're glad you came.' Julie wriggled her shoulders with pleasure at the warmth of the sun.

'Of course I'm glad I came,' I said. I was glad I had come, but I wished it wasn't Julie beside me. I should have been here with Tim. I tried not to think about him, tried to push him to the furthest recesses of my mind, but it was impossible. I felt the easy tears welling up again and I turned into the room so that Julie wouldn't see them.

'D'you want to unpack now, or go out straight away?' she asked.

I shrugged. It didn't matter. Nothing mattered.

We unpacked. When we'd put everything away, we wandered around the hotel and out to the pool. We draped our towels over a couple of sunbeds and turned them so that they faced into the sun.

'This is the life,' sighed Julie happily. 'I think I'll

lie on my stomach. Will you rub some cream onto my back?'

'Sure.'

She yelped as the cold cream hit her shoulders and I laughed as I rubbed it in.

'Are you OK, or do you want me to rub some on you?' she asked.

'I'm fine,' I said. 'I'll sit up and read for a while.'

I covered myself with Factor 10, perched my sunglasses on my nose and opened my book. But after five minutes the words jumbled in front of my eyes and I felt myself getting sleepy. I lay down on the sunbed and stared up at the cloudless blue sky. It wasn't fair, I thought miserably, it truly wasn't fair.

My eyelids fluttered closed. I fell asleep. I woke up when somebody jumped into the pool and sent a tidal wave of water over my feet. I turned to the sunbed beside me to see if Julie was awake too. It was empty. I looked around for her and finally spotted her at the far end of the swimming-pool. She was treading water and talking to two men. Quick work, even for Julie. I stood up and stretched.

'Isobel!' She waved at me. 'Come in! It's lovely.'

Julie would have walked to the side of the pool and dived in beautifully, but I lowered myself gingerly into the cold water. I gasped as I launched myself into my inelegant breast-stroke and lumbered down the pool to Julie.

'So you finally woke up,' she giggled as she held on to the rail. 'I thought you were going to sleep for ever.'

'I was exhausted,' I said.

'I was going to wake you up just to turn you over.' She disappeared underwater for a moment, then emerged again. 'I thought you might burn to a crisp.'

I glanced down at my chest. It was turning red.

'I'm OK,' I said.

'I want you to meet my two friends.' She gestured at the men she'd been talking to, who'd swum across the pool and back while I swam to her. 'This is Ari and Andreas – Andy for short.'

'Hi,' they said in unison.

'Ari and Andreas?' I looked at them quizzically. 'Are you Greek?'

They laughed. 'No,' said one. 'We're American.'

'American!' I said. 'I always thought when Americans did Europe, they just did capital cities.'

'We're Greek-American,' the nearest of the two explained. 'Ari and Andy Jordan in the States, but Ari and Andreas Iordanopoulos in Greece. We were at a family wedding in Piraeus, now we're here for a holiday.'

'They've been here a couple of days already,' explained Julie. 'They've offered to take us to dinner tonight.'

I looked from them to her.

'We're full board in the hotel,' I said blankly.

'That doesn't matter,' she said. 'Nobody says we have to eat here every night.'

'I suppose not.'

'Hey, if you don't want to eat with us it's no problem.' The Greek-American didn't look at all put out. 'We thought it'd be kinda nice to go out with you guys, but don't feel obligated.'

I felt dreadful. They were so polite and I was so rude. 'I'm sorry,' I said. 'I didn't mean that I didn't want to eat with you. I'm a bit sleepy still – my brain isn't functioning all that well.'

He laughed. 'Don't worry. We're going to the beach this afternoon. We'll see you back here – maybe around eight?'

'Sounds great,' said Julie.

'Fine,' I said.

I climbed out of the pool and went back to my sunbed. The paving stones were scorching underfoot.

'You didn't have to sound so enthusiastic!' said Julie sourly as she joined me.

'I'm sorry,' I said. 'I didn't mean—'

'It doesn't matter.' She wriggled her toes. 'But I want to have fun, Isobel, and I want you to have fun too.'

I smiled at her. I'd do my best.

~

My nose was burned. It glowed in the evening sunlight and sent Julie into a fit of giggles every time she saw it.

'Leave me alone,' I said good-naturedly. 'A different bit of you could be glowing – we just can't see it.'

'Too right,' she laughed. 'Here, put some powder on your nose, bring it down a little.'

I dabbed at my nose with *Lancôme*. 'What d'you think?'

'Better.' She nodded. 'What are you going to wear?'

'Denim skirt, white T-shirt.'

'Oh, Isobel, that's too boring. Why don't you wear that lovely printed sun-dress?'

I stared at her. 'I'm not dressing up,' I said. 'Just wearing something comfortable.'

'But you should make an effort,' she said.

'I'm on holiday. I don't need to make an effort.'

Julie ignored me as she did her face, draped herself with jewellery and slipped on a bright yellow Lycra dress.

'Are you planning on seducing one of those blokes?' I asked her. 'Because if you are, the other one will be very disappointed if he doesn't get me.'

'Fancy your chances, do you?'

'Don't be stupid. But I don't want them to think that there are two of us on offer.'

'I'm not on offer, as you so delicately put it.' She sprayed herself liberally with *Trésor*. 'I'm just dressing for dinner.'

I sighed and put on some lipstick.

Ari and Andreas were waiting for us in reception. They were both tall and dark and, I guessed, in their mid-twenties. They both wore faded Levis and cotton shirts.

'I'd better re-introduce us, since we're wearing clothes,' said the taller of the two. 'I'm Ari Jordan and this is my brother, Andy.'

'Pleased to meet you,' I said. 'I'm Isobel Kavanagh.'

'Don't tell me you don't remember my name?' Julie pouted.

'You're Julie,' said Andreas, linking his arm with hers. 'Do you want to go tourist or local?'

'I know that it's naff to want to be touristy,' said Julie. 'But could we leave the tiny little ethnic doesn't-look-much-but-the-food-is-wonderful until another night? I'd like to go to somewhere brash and bright where I can see what's going on.'

Andy laughed. 'Let's go into the old town.'

The restaurant they brought us to was perched high in the walls of the old town. From it, we had a wonderful view of the renovated market square with its fountain, its brightly lit cafés and restaurants and hundreds of small shops. The pedestrian streets were thronged with carefree people strolling around in the balmy warmth of the evening.

Julie, Andy and Ari talked about holidays. I heard the conversation but couldn't bring myself to take part. I ached with loneliness inside. I wanted to go home.

I listened as the talk covered a range of topics. Andy worked as an analyst in a petro-chemical company while Ari was a chiropractor. They lived in Florida. They came to Greece every year. I liked them but I still wanted to go home.

After the meal they walked back to the hotel with us.

'Fancy a nightcap?' asked Julie.

'I'm practically asleep on my feet as it is,' I told her. 'You go ahead if you like.'

She looked at the Jordans enquiringly.

'Why not?' said Andy.

I said goodnight and went up to the room, leaving it unlocked so that Julie wouldn't disturb me when she came up later. I pushed open the balcony doors and sat on the wrought-iron chair. Sounds of music and laughter floated up from the bar. I leaned my head against the whitewashed wall and tried not to think that, if Tim had been with me, we would have been in the bar together, laughing and joking, listening to the music. And then we'd have come back to this room and made love. I definitely didn't want to think about that. I wrapped my arms around myself and rocked back and forward in the chair. It was all wrong being here without him. It had been a mistake to come with Julie.

I sat on the balcony for about half an hour and then decided to go to bed. I'd no idea when Julie might come up and I'd no intention of sitting waiting for her as though I were her guardian.

But as soon as I'd slid under the single sheet I was wide awake again. The demon thoughts chased around and around in my head. Thoughts of Tim. What was he doing now? Was he missing me as much as I was missing him? Did he regret what had happened? Was he pacing up and down in the Donnybrook house, wishing that he'd kept his mouth shut because he'd made a dreadful mistake?

Probably not, I thought bitterly, as I twisted and turned, unable to get comfortable. He's probably out with his mates, having a few pints, perfectly happy. I groaned and punched the pillow a few times. I wanted to be asleep. I didn't want to think about Tim.

It was about an hour or so later when Julie came up. She tiptoed around the room, then clattered into the edge of my bed. She gave a muffled curse but I lay still and I heard her sigh with relief that she hadn't woken me.

She got into bed and was asleep almost instantly, snoring very gently.

I tossed and turned some more, before finally falling into a fitful sleep. But I woke early the next morning, early enough to be sitting on the balcony again when the sun rose to spill pink-gold light across the sky and begin another scorching day.

We slipped into a lazy routine of sunbathing, swimming and meeting the Jordans in the evening. I didn't mind going out in a foursome, but I felt uncomfortable when Julie sidled up to Andy and he put his arms around her while Ari and I sat beside each other like brother and sister.

There was a reason for that, and it wasn't all because I had no interest in meeting another man. Ari Jordan had no interest in meeting a woman either. I'd prepared my speech the second day, to tell him that I liked him, he was a decent bloke, and I didn't want to appear pushy or anything, but I was trying to get a relationship into perspective and I didn't think it would be a good idea to get involved with anyone else. It was a pretty good speech and I rehearsed it a couple of times to get the tone right. But Ari pre-empted me.

'I don't want you to get the wrong idea about me and my brother,' he said as we sat beside each other while

Julie and Andy smooched on the dance floor. 'He's obviously very keen on your friend. It's just that I—' he looked at me anxiously. 'I'm not actually interested in girls.'

I didn't catch on straight away. 'I'm not interested in men at the moment either.'

'No.' Ari shook his head. 'You don't understand. I am not interested in girls. At all.'

I stared at him. 'At all?'

'At all,' he said firmly.

I looked at his tanned face, amber-flecked eyes and sun-bleached hair. He was very attractive. 'But you're interested in – um, men?'

He grinned nervously. 'Well, yes.'

'Oh.' I didn't know what to say. I'd never met a guy who'd said he was gay before. I knew *of* gay people, I'd met a few blokes who were *supposed* to be gay, but I'd never sat face to face with a guy who told me that he was interested in other men.

'Does your brother know?' I asked curiously. I couldn't understand why Andy Jordan would try to double date with a couple of women when his brother would prefer to be somewhere else.

Ari sighed. 'He knows. He's OK about it. But I don't think he entirely believes it.'

'You don't look gay,' I said.

'And what does that mean?' asked Ari. 'That I haven't got a tattoo across my face saying *Gay Pride*?'

'No.' I blushed. 'I'm sorry. Of course not. I just meant that, well, you know, some gay men look very pretty and you're not pretty, you're good-looking.'

Fortunately Ari laughed. 'I'll take that as a sort of compliment.'

'Thanks.' I smiled at him. 'And your brother is interested in girls?'

'He seems very interested in your friend,' said Ari. 'Although sometimes I think Andy goes out with hundreds of girls to prove himself. You know, his older brother is gay but he wants everyone to know that he's one hundred per cent hetero. So he lines up as many women as he can.'

I nodded in understanding. 'But I hope he doesn't break Julie's heart. Although her heart is pretty OK. She usually does the breaking, I think. Not like me.'

'Tell me about your boyfriend,' said Ari. 'What's he like?'

'Want his phone number?' I asked glumly.

'No,' said Ari.

'I'm sorry.' I sighed. 'We'd been going out for a couple of years. We decided to get married. Then he decided that he'd been pressurised into it and he called it off. Julie and I are on my honeymoon at the moment.'

'The shit!' Ari smiled sympathetically. 'The least you can do is have a fun time while you're here.'

'That's what I keep telling myself,' I muttered. 'But I don't know whether I can or not.'

'You've got to,' said Ari. 'No guy is worth it. Take it from me.'

He grinned and squeezed my shoulder. I squeezed him back.

'Why don't you loosen up a bit,' said Julie as we got ready to go out the next night. 'Ari's a nice guy.'

'I know,' I said. 'He's very nice. He just happens to be gay.'

'Isobel!' She stared at me in shock. 'He can't be.'

'He is.'

'But—' She looked bemused. 'He doesn't *look* gay.'

'How did you expect him to look?' I demanded. 'Have *Gay Pride* tattooed across his forehead?'

She looked as abashed as I had done. 'I suppose not.' Then she glanced anxiously at me. 'But Andy isn't gay.'

'No,' I said. 'As I'm sure you've already verified.'

'Not yet,' she said. 'But maybe he's one of those blokes who's unsure about his sexuality.'

I grinned. 'He seems pretty sure about it to me.'

'Well, me too,' she conceded. 'But who knows?'

'Ari does,' I said. 'And he says that Andy is one hundred per cent.'

'I hope so. I wouldn't have believed it about Ari.'

'Neither did I until he told me,' I admitted.

'Bit of a waste,' said Julie pensively.

'For womankind generally, I suppose.' I fastened my Majorcan pearls around my neck. 'But not as far as I'm concerned. He's a nice guy and he's good company. That's all. Besides, even if he was interested in women, I'm still engaged to Tim.'

'You can't sit around and mope,' she said briskly. 'Is Tim sitting around moping?' She dabbed perfume behind her ears.

'He might be,' I said.

'Grow up, Isobel.' Julie looked at herself in the mirror and adjusted her earrings. 'Men don't sit at home and mope.'

'Even if he's out having the time of his life, it doesn't mean that I want to.'

'You can't spend all your life waiting for him,' she said.

'I'm not going to.'

She flicked a brush through her hair and turned to me. 'And what are you doing now?' she asked. 'You're on holiday. You should be having a good time. But you're miserable because he's let you down and he didn't even have the guts to tell you that it's for good.'

I stared at her. 'We've only postponed the wedding.'

'Oh, Isobel.' She sighed deeply. 'You haven't rescheduled it, have you? When exactly is it meant to take place?'

'I don't know. We haven't decided yet.'

'You mean *he* hasn't decided,' she retorted. 'Hasn't decided whether he wants to keep you hanging on a string or whether he does need someone to wash his socks and cook for him every night.'

'That's not fair.' I got up and went into the bathroom. 'He's just unsure of himself, that's all.' I stared at my reflection in the mirror. My face was tanned and healthy, but I still had shadows under my eyes.

'Isobel, maybe he really was overwhelmed by everything.' Julie stood in the doorway. 'But was it really fair of him to decide that, a couple of weeks before you got married? And he hasn't given you any decent commitment for the future.' She bit her lip. 'I don't want to preach at you, honestly I don't. But I can't see how you can trust him. What happens when you get near the next date? Does he get cold feet all over again?'

'I don't know.' I washed my hands. I hadn't needed to wash my hands, but I wanted something to do. The water cascaded over my engagement ring. I didn't wear it during the day so that there was no fine white line on my finger. But I needed to wear it at night.

'I'm sorry,' she said. 'I shouldn't have said any of those things.'

'It doesn't matter.' I patted my hands dry. 'You're probably right. I don't know any more, Julie. I don't know whether I love him or I hate him.'

'I'd hate him, personally.' She hugged me. 'But I won't preach any more – no matter what you decide to do.'

'Do you think I should break it off with him completely?' I asked.

She leaned her head against the door frame. 'Yes.'

'Why?'

'Like I said – you'll never be sure of him.'

'But maybe I can be.'

'Maybe.' She stretched her arms over her head. 'It's just that I wouldn't feel comfortable with someone who did what Tim did.'

'You've never loved someone like I love Tim,' I said.

'No.' She bit her lip. 'I don't want you to be hurt. Not by someone who isn't worth your tears.'

I smiled lopsidedly at her. 'Thanks.'

'Come on,' she said. 'We'll be late for dinner.'

~

The Jordans brought us to a restaurant near the port. I watched a huge cruise ship, decked from bow to stern in coloured lights, gently glide into the deep-water dock. That would have been a nice honeymoon, I thought. Drifting through the Mediterranean, stopping at different ports. I wondered whether I ever would go on honeymoon with Tim. Whether Julie was right. Whether I would ever truly trust him again.

~

It was as though we'd known the Jordans all our lives. Later in the week we went back to Andy and Ari's villa after the meal. It was a small, two-bedroomed house, with tiled floors and whitewashed walls. Andy went to get some beer from the fridge, while Ari disappeared somewhere.

'Would you mind if I stayed here tonight?' whispered Julie.

I'd expected this to happen. I shook my head.

'He might not ask me,' she murmured. 'But I'd like to if he does.'

'Whatever you want,' I said. 'Be careful, that's all.'

'Don't worry.' She grinned at me. 'Be prepared, that's my motto.' She patted her bag and winked.

I drank a beer and then told them I was going back to the hotel. 'But you stay a little longer if you like,' I told Julie. 'I'll fall asleep straight away. Don't worry about what time you come in.'

'I'll walk with you.' Ari got up before I could stop him.

It was a sixty-second walk from the villa to the hotel. 'Not much of a walk,' I said.

'Do you want a nightcap?' he asked.

'I'm tired,' I told him. 'I want to go to bed.'

'I'm sure that's where my brother and your friend are right now,' he laughed. 'That's why I suggested the nightcap.'

We sat together in the bar. To anybody watching us, we probably appeared to be a perfectly happy couple. They'd think that we were a perfectly happy engaged couple, I thought, as I glanced involuntarily at my ring. How wrong they'd be. I laughed suddenly.

'Nice to hear that.' Ari smiled.

'Just thinking.'

'About?'

'Us.' I grinned at him. 'People think that we're going out together. That we're a normal couple.'

'What's normal?' he asked.

I flushed. 'I meant—'

'I know what you meant.' He looked tired. 'It's OK.'

'Is it difficult for you?' I asked.

'Yes,' he answered. 'Some guys cope very well. Some don't cope at all. I'm somewhere between the two.'

'Do you have a boyfriend?' I hadn't wanted to ask before now, felt the question was too personal.

'I had,' said Ari. 'We were together for a year. He left me.'

'For another man?' I asked.

'At least it wasn't for a woman,' said Ari wryly.

'So you're miserable too,' I said. 'And every night you sit and listen to me wallowing in self-pity.'

He shrugged. 'I like you, Isobel. And you need to talk about it.'

'That's very American,' I told him. 'Talking about everything. I need to think about it. That's all.'

'Have another drink,' he said. 'We could get bombed tonight.'

I shook my head. 'Better not. We'll feel awful in the morning.'

'Have one more anyway.' Ari glanced at his watch. 'Give your friend and my brother time to—'

'Oh, God, yes.' I ran my fingers through my hair. 'I'd forgotten about them.'

He got the drinks and we sat in companionable silence for a while.

'What are you going to do about your boyfriend when you go home?' Ari asked.

'I don't know.' I swirled the drink around in my glass. 'I couldn't believe he'd do what he did to me.' My voice shook. 'He humiliated me.'

And that was the whole thing. Leaving aside the shock, the hurt and the betrayal, it was the feeling of humiliation that had bitten so deep. Knowing that people would look at me and say, 'There's Isobel Kavanagh – she was practically left at the altar.'

'You'll get over it,' said Ari.

'How do you know? I might be deeply scarred for life.'

'You might be, but I doubt it.' Ari smiled gently at me. 'You're a tough person.'

'No, I'm not.'

'You are,' he said. 'You're here, holidaying with your friend. Going out with Andy and me.'

'I feel safe with you,' I said dryly. 'I know that's very unfair.'

'No.' Ari shook his head. 'I'm glad you feel that way.'

'I don't like dumping my life in your lap. Especially when you've got your own problems.'

'Don't mind me,' said Ari. 'Your fiancé is a shit. When you go home you should fling that ring in his face.'

'I couldn't do that.'

'Well, keep the ring, but break it off with him anyway.'

'Did Julie put you up to this?' I asked curiously. 'Because I had a very similar conversation with her earlier tonight.'

He shook his head. 'But the two of us have independently come to the same conclusion. Don't waste your life on him, Isobel.'

'Thanks for the advice.' I finished my drink and stood up. 'If you don't mind, Ari, I'm going to bed now. Julie and Andy can take their chances.'

'Goodnight.' He took me by the hand and squeezed it gently. His touch was warm and dry.

I held his hand for a moment. 'Goodnight,' I said, and went upstairs.

Chapter 4

Woman Lying Down (Salvador Dalí, 1926)

I was nervous about going home. I didn't know what to expect from Tim and I didn't know exactly how to behave with him. Julie continued to tell me that I should make a clean break, start all over again. Ari Jordan thought the same. But that didn't make them right, I told myself. They didn't know Tim. If the same thing had happened to somebody I knew, then probably I would have offered similar advice – he's not worth it, forget him. But you can't just forget people and you can't just throw away two years of a wonderful relationship.

Alison told me that I looked great. 'Healthier,' she said critically, 'although you still have a pained look about you.'

'That's because the flight is so long,' I told her. 'And I dozed off at a funny angle. I've got a crick in my neck.'

'He didn't ring while you were away,' she said.

'Who?'

'Shitface.'

'Why should he?' I asked. 'He knew I wasn't here.'

'Ha!' she exclaimed triumphantly. 'You knew who I meant.'

'Of course I knew who you meant.'

'Have you decided to give him the order of the boot?' she asked. 'Have you come to your senses at last?'

'Give me a break, Ali,' I sighed. 'I'm not making any major decisions at the moment.'

~

The girls in work told me I looked great too.

'And your hair is lovely like that,' said Niamh.

I smiled. My hair had grown enough to be tamed into a single plait. I liked it that way too, although I knew I'd probably get it cut again. I wasn't really a long-haired person.

I sat at my desk and took out my diary. Barry was at a meeting in Naas all day which suited me. It meant time to catch up on some paperwork. It also meant that I'd be able to phone Tim.

I'd called the previous night but his answerphone cut in with its jokey '*Tough, you've missed me*' message. I didn't want to leave a message on the machine, I needed to talk to him myself. I still didn't know what to do about him.

I phoned his office at noon which was usually a good time to catch him. 'He's not here this week,' said Shauna, the receptionist. 'I think he's gone to the States.'

He did that from time to time. The software company was owned by an American parent, which in turn was owned by some company in the Far East. Tim had been to California a few times, and to Tokyo twice. I often wondered if anyone knew exactly who owned what in the corporate world. Whether there was one single company that owned everything, only nobody quite realised it yet.

'Do you know when he's due back?' I asked.

'At the weekend, I think,' replied Shauna. 'If you hold on a moment, I'll check.'

Classical music played while I waited. I preferred silence.

'He'll be back on Friday night,' she said. 'Isobel?'

Shauna clicked back into the line.

'Yes.'

'We're all really sorry about what happened.'

'Thanks,' I said.

'But if both of you were unsure then it was a wise decision.'

Was that what he'd told them? Better, I supposed, than saying it was his idea.

'Thanks,' I said again.

'I hope you *do* get married. I always thought you were perfect together.'

'We'll see,' I said, although I hoped so too.

I couldn't give up on Tim although I was disappointed that he hadn't left a message for me to say that he'd be away. But he was a laid-back person, the sort who doesn't think about leaving messages, or washing last night's dishes or filling the car with petrol before going on a long journey. I put it down to his brilliance at computers. Maybe even genius. You don't expect a genius to be the same as a normal person.

I went to the townhouse while he was away. I'd left a pair of shoes there which I needed, and some lipstick which I didn't really need but wanted to retrieve anyway.

His car was in the driveway. I parked behind it and slid the key into the hall door. The alarm beeped at me and I tapped in the code numbers to silence it.

The house was still and quiet. I pushed open the door to the living room. A foil tin sat on the coffee-table, the remnants of a curry congealed inside it. I wrinkled my nose at the smell. A number of computer magazines were strewn across the floor and one of Tim's workpads lay open, the writing and squiggles on it proof of his industry over the past few weeks.

I picked up the remains of the curry and deposited them in the bin. I tidied up the magazines and left the workpad, still open, on the table. I put away the dishes that were on the draining-board and wiped breadcrumbs from the kitchen table. I filled the vase of flowers with fresh water. Not like Tim to have flowers, I thought. They were gladioli, my favourites. I wondered if he'd bought them because of me.

His bed was unmade, the duvet piled into a heap in the centre. The bedroom smelled, unmistakably, of Tim. A combination of *Badedas* shower-gel and *Ralph Lauren* aftershave. I sat on the bed and buried my face in the duvet. I missed him so much it really, truly hurt.

My shoes were in the wardrobe. I put them into a plastic bag along with the lipstick which had been on the chest of drawers. I straightened the duvet and plumped up the pillows. I should have been doing this anyway, I thought, suddenly. If things had gone according to plan I would be Isobel Malone and I would be plumping up the pillows and making the bed because Tim would expect me to. And because I'd be happy to do it. I would be living in this house instead of simply visiting it.

'How could you do this to me?' I said the words out loud. 'How could you!' I threw the plastic bag containing my shoes and my lipstick across the bedroom. 'Why did you do this to me?' Then I collapsed, sobbing, onto the bed.

The phone rang and startled me. I heard the answering machine whir into life and Tim's voice echoed around the house.

'It's me.' The caller was female. 'I thought I might catch you before you left. I wanted your first set of notes on the Saracen project. It doesn't matter. Catch you later on.' I heaved a sigh of relief. It was work. For one horrible, heart-stopping moment, I thought that the strange female voice might have had something to do with Tim calling off our wedding. But that was silly. I was creating monsters for myself.

I gathered up my shoes and lipstick and let myself out of the house.

I rang him again on Friday night, but the answering machine was still on. This time, though, I left a message for him to call me when he got home.

He phoned on Sunday afternoon.

'How did you enjoy your holiday?' he asked.

'It was lovely,' I answered steadily. 'The hotel was nice, the weather was gorgeous and I had a wonderful rest.'

'That's good,' he said. 'Isobel, were you in the house while I was away?'

He sounded aggrieved.

'Well, yes,' I replied. 'I wanted to get a pair of shoes that were there. I phoned your office and they said you'd be away until this weekend and I needed the shoes before then.'

'So you're responsible for tidying everything up.'

'I didn't throw anything away,' I said. I knew that sometimes the most awful rubbish was very important to Tim. 'I just threw out your disgusting curry left-overs.'

'Thanks,' he said. 'But you really shouldn't have cleaned up after me. I can do it myself.'

'I couldn't help it,' I told him. 'It was so horrible and I couldn't imagine what it might be like by now.'

'It was very good of you,' he said.

'That's me.'

'D'you want to meet for a drink?'

'Tonight?'

'I suppose so.'

'OK,' I said. 'I'd like a drink.'

We met in Clontarf Castle. Alison made a face at me when I said I was meeting him, Mum looked worried and Dad rustled his newspaper.

'I need to talk to him,' I told nobody in particular as I grabbed my keys from the mantelpiece.

The castle was bathed in evening sunshine and it seemed a shame to go inside. But I found a couple of seats beside the window, ordered myself a beer and waited for Tim. I was early. I was annoyed at myself for being early – I should have been late and left him waiting for me. That's the least that Julie would have advised. But the traffic-lights had been green all along the coast and I'd got here much quicker than I'd intended. I took my diary out of my bag and made a show of studying it so that people wouldn't think I was waiting for someone.

I'd almost finished my beer when he arrived. I sensed his presence before I saw him. He hadn't seen me yet. I waved in his direction and he nodded at me.

'Sorry I'm late,' he said as he sat down. 'There was an accident on Morehampton Road. Delayed me a bit.'

'That's OK.' I signalled to a lounge-boy and ordered drinks.

'You look wonderful,' he said. 'The holiday seems to have done you the world of good.'

'I feel a lot better,' I admitted. 'I was pretty shattered, you know.'

He took my hand. His touch was soft and familiar. I felt myself dissolve inside.

'I'm really sorry, Isobel.' He squeezed my hand even

tighter. 'I wouldn't have hurt you for anything. You know that.'

I nodded.

'Afterwards I thought that I was an idiot. That I should have gone through with it anyway. That we would have worked it out. But I couldn't be certain.' He pushed his fringe out of his eyes but it flopped back again almost immediately. 'You're very special to me, Isobel.'

'I should hope so,' I said. 'Allegedly, we're still engaged.'

'Of course we are,' said Tim.

I sighed with relief. 'And do you have an idea of when we should get married?'

'Not yet.' He tapped the edge of the table. 'I'm sorry, Isobel, I really am. I need a bit more time to think.'

Alison and Julie's warnings flashed through my head.

'I need to know,' I told him. 'I need to be sure about things.'

'I'm sure that I want to marry you,' said Tim. 'I'm just not sure when.'

I bit my lip. This wasn't really what I wanted to hear.

'I'd still like it if you lived with me,' he added. 'I was put out when you came and collected your shoes. It seemed like you were trying to move away from me.'

'It wasn't that,' I told him. 'They were my flat shoes. I needed them to wear with jeans.'

'When I see you sitting in front of me, I know that I was mad,' said Tim. He shook his head. 'Everybody told me that I was mad.'

'It was a horrible thing to do.' All at once my anger returned. 'You made a fool out of me, Tim. Everyone looks at me and thinks "There's that poor girl who was dumped at the altar". I had to go and face everyone in work. I had to cancel the hotel and the band and the photographer and everything. Mum and Dad are devastated. Ian wants to kill you. Only Alison thinks I've had a merciful release.'

He smiled. 'She would.'

'She might be right,' I said tartly. 'It was cruel, Tim. Really cruel.'

'I know.' He took my hands again and enveloped them in his. 'I hated myself for doing it. But it seemed right to me at the time. Maybe it was all wrong, I don't know. But it would have been awful to get married when there was a nagging doubt there. You do see that, don't you?'

'Oh, I see it all right,' I said. 'Julie thinks I'm far too understanding.'

'We've had a good relationship,' said Tim. 'It can withstand this, can't it?'

He looked so vulnerable sitting in front of me. My anger melted away. 'Of course it can,' I said.

~

The family was gathered around the TV. I sat down in my favourite armchair and picked up the paper.

'Well?' said Mum.

'Well what?' I turned over a page.

'Well what has he got to say for himself?'

'Nothing new,' I told her. 'He's sorry, of course.'

'Huh!' She snorted. 'I don't want you wasting your time with him, Isobel. There's other fish in the sea.'

'Mum,' I sighed. 'I'm sure there are plenty of other fish in the sea. You've told me that often enough. Remember when I split up with Alan Davenport? That's exactly what you said then. And the Niall Dillon episode? There's no need to trot out all the old lines.'

'I'm only trying to help,' she said.

'I know,' I said. 'But this is something I can work out for myself.'

'I wish I could believe that,' she said moodily, and turned back to the feature film.

~

Tim asked me to go to the launch of one of the company's new software packages the following Friday. There was to be a corporate presentation in the afternoon and a dinner that evening. I wasn't going to the corporate presentation, but I was looking forward to the dinner. I rushed home from work to get ready and locked myself in the bathroom, much to the annoyance of Ian who was going out too.

'It'll only take you a couple of minutes to shower!' I yelled through the locked door.

'I need to shave as well,' he protested. 'Hurry up, Issy, you're not the only member of this family who goes out, you know.'

I was wearing a midnight-blue dress with a low-cut back to show off my tan. I pulled my hair into the plait again and tied it with some dark blue velvet ribbon. I was pleased with the effect. I made sure that my make-up looked very natural and doused myself in *Allure*, which was Tim's favourite perfume.

'You look fantastic,' said Alison as I came downstairs. 'Far too good for Shitface.'

'Stop calling him that.' I tightened the butterflies at the back of the diamond and sapphire earrings Tim had given me for my last birthday.

'I'm just concerned about you,' she said.

'Give it a rest.' I looked out of the window. Tim was picking me up but he'd balked at coming into the house. I wasn't too keen on him running the gauntlet of my family either, so I said that I'd watch out for him if he just parked outside. I heard the distinctive roar of his car coming down the road, picked up my bag and hurried out.

'God, you look beautiful,' he said as I got into the car.

I knew I did. I'd spent a lot of time working on looking beautiful.

'Thanks.'

'I won't be able to keep my hands off you, looking like that.'

'You'd better,' I told him. 'Unless you want to scandalise the board of Softsys.'

'It'd take a lot to scandalise them,' Tim laughed as he sped down the coast road.

'Well, don't try anyway,' I said.

The dinner was in Jurys. I'd expected Tim to moan about picking me up, because he could have walked to the hotel, but he didn't seem to mind. Guilt was working wonders on him.

We walked into the hotel together and I knew that we looked good as a couple. Tim, as I often told him, cleaned up well. When he was prised out of his T-shirt and jeans and forced into a suit, he looked handsome and desirable.

Tonight's dinner was black-tie – not very usual with the software crowd – but Tim said that they all liked to dress up occasionally. He looked fantastic in his tux and he wore it with a confidence he said he didn't feel.

'It's great on you.' I adjusted his bow-tie for him. 'You look like a grown-up.'

'I don't want to be grown-up,' he said. 'I want to be young for ever.'

'Come on, my little Peter Pan,' I said. 'Let's join the throng.'

I knew most of the Softsys people. Shauna, the receptionist, was standing just inside the door, a glass of wine in her hand.

'Isobel!' she cried when she saw me. 'It's great to see you!'

'Thanks.'

'You look wonderful. Have you been away?'

'I went to Rhodes,' I said and the penny dropped.

Shauna blushed furiously.

'I'm sorry,' she said. 'I've put my foot in it.'

'It's OK.' I grabbed a glass of wine from a passing waiter. 'There's a lot of people here tonight.'

'This is one of our biggest products this year,' she told me. 'Some of the US guys are over.'

'Great,' I said. I watched Tim as he walked over to a tall, fair-haired man and shook his hand.

'Tim's been very quiet these last few weeks,' said Shauna. 'Of course he had his US trip, but I think he really missed you, Isobel.'

'It's his own fault,' I told her.

'Isobel!' Dave Brennan, one of the other designers put his arm around me. 'How are you?'

'Great, Dave, thanks.'

'You're very good to come along,' he said. 'We weren't sure you would.'

'Why shouldn't I?' I asked.

'Oh, well.' He looked embarrassed. 'We thought you mightn't like to.'

'Don't worry about me, Dave,' I said. 'I'm fine.'

People began to take their seats at the tables. Tim and I were near the top table. 'High in the pecking order,' he told me. 'Not that I really want to worry about that sort of thing.'

Maurice Fitzgerald, the company MD, made a speech about the new product, telling us how it would make other, similar systems, obsolete. Industry standard, he said a few times. I didn't listen to Maurice but glanced through the menu. The different courses had been given computer-speak names – '*Melon bytes*' for starters, followed by '*Megabytes of beef with a lyonnaise potato interface*'. Maurice finished his speech and the food was brought around.

I sipped my wine then spluttered as I felt Tim's hand on the top of my leg. The midnight-blue dress had a slit along the side which Tim had noted approvingly in the car. Now I could feel his fingers moving gently across my thigh. I looked at him, but he was turned away from me, talking to the man on the other side of him. I squeezed my legs tightly together and Tim slapped me softly with his fingers. I opened my legs slightly and, when he moved his hand between them, squeezed them closed again and trapped him. I could feel him flex his hand between my legs but he couldn't move it. I continued to eat the starter and began to talk to Dave who was sitting on the other side of me.

Finally, Tim leaned towards me and whispered into my ear, 'Let go.'

'Why?' I whispered back.

'Because I want to butter my bread-roll.'

'You should have thought of that earlier.'

'I know.'

'Keep your hands to yourself until later.'

'Spoilsport,' he said as I loosened my grip.

Tim didn't like dancing. I adored it. But there was no chance of getting him to dance with me.

So I danced with Dave and Maurice, with two other software developers, Keith and Greg, and with the bloke from the Californian office, Duane. It was fun dancing with Duane because he was well over six feet tall and was the thinnest man I'd ever met. He was, he told me, African-American. I told him that I'd recently met Greek-Americans. I wondered were there any people who were simply Americans.

'Native Americans,' he said politically correctly and very seriously and I dissolved into a fit of giggles which he didn't understand.

It was nearly one-thirty when Tim finally decided to suffer the obligatory dance with me. The band was playing smoochy love songs and he held me close to him while the music washed over us.

'I've had too much to drink,' he murmured sleepily. 'I didn't mean to.'

'It's OK,' I said.

'Not really. I wanted to be awake.'

'You'll wake up when you go outside,' I told him. 'The fresh air will do it for you.'

'Come home with me tonight,' he said as he pressed closer to me. 'Stay with me tonight.'

I wanted to stay with him more than anything. I'd thought about it before I'd even left my house earlier that night. I'd wondered would he ask.

'But will you still love me tomorrow?' I breathed the words of the song into his ear.

'I love you right now,' he said.

The night air was cool. I shivered as the breeze hit my bare back.

'Here.' Tim took off his black jacket and hung it around my shoulders.

'I don't need your jacket,' I protested.

'I've a long-sleeved shirt on,' he said. 'You'll freeze to death. Much good you'd be to me if you froze, Isobel, don't you think?'

'But imagine the fun you'd have warming me up.'

He took me by the hand and we walked up Pembroke Road. The leaves of the trees rustled in the breeze. The road, normally so crowded with traffic, was quiet, the tall houses in darkness.

Tim whistled softly as we walked and I cuddled up to him. They would be so annoyed with me, I thought as I smiled slightly to myself, Alison and Julie, Mum and Dad, Ian – and Ari Jordan. All those people who thought I shouldn't give Tim a second chance. All those people who were ready for me never to forgive him. And they were all so wrong.

We turned into his narrow driveway. The yellow porch light glowed dimly. Tim fumbled for his keys and dropped them. I picked them up and handed them to him. He opened the door. I switched off the alarm.

We stood facing each other in the hallway. I let Tim's jacket fall from my shoulders. He loosened the straps of the midnight-blue dress. It slid from me into a circle of blue velvet. I was wearing a navy body underneath, no stockings. Tim looked at me wordlessly. I looked back at him.

He picked me up and carried me up the stairs. He put me onto the bed. He stood at the end of the bed while he fumbled at his bow-tie, took off his shirt. I liked Tim's chest. Not a hugely muscled chest, but firm with a springy covering of curly black hair. Sometimes I would run my fingers through the curls and he would gasp in pain and in pleasure.

I lay immobile on the bed. He positioned himself over me and undid the silk body. His expression was serious as he made love to me. Sometimes he moved very slowly, so that he was hardly moving at all. Then he would pick up his rhythm until he seemed to be possessed, before suddenly slowing down again. He was wonderful to me that night. He touched me in all the places I liked most to be touched. He left gentle kisses all over my body. And when I told him that I could stand no more, he entered me again, more fiercely, with more determination and I shuddered and cried with pleasure.

We crawled under the duvet together. He fell asleep straight away, his eyelashes forming straight black lines on his cheeks. I looked at him in the shadow of the darkness and I wanted to cry with love for him.

I knew that he was the only man I would ever love. I knew that one day I would marry him. And be happy.

Chapter 5

La Vie (Pablo Picasso, 1903)

It was warm, but the rain hissed against the window and formed tiny pools of water in the cracks between the paving slabs of the patio. I pressed my nose against the glass and looked up at the sky. The grey clouds were skimming the top of the trees and it seemed impossible that somewhere up there was a blue sky and a fiercely burning sun.

I searched the utility room for my rain jacket but I couldn't find it. It was probably in Tim's house.

The front door slammed as Ian went out. A few moments later, Alison was gone. I wondered how my parents felt about their children growing up. Would they be sorry or relieved when we all finally left home?

The jacket might be bundled onto the top shelf of my wardrobe, I thought suddenly. That was where I usually threw clothes that weren't in daily use. I ran upstairs to check, but it wasn't there. I was on my way downstairs again when the phone rang.

'I'll get it,' I called as I picked up the receiver.

'Isobel! Glad I caught you.'

'Hi, Tim.' I glanced at my reflection in the hall mirror, smoothed my eyeshadow a little with my middle finger.

'Isobel, I'm really sorry but I can't see you tonight.'

'Why not?' I hadn't seen Tim in almost a fortnight – he was working very hard on the new software application.

'Because I'm up to my tonsils in work,' he said. 'I'm ringing from the office – haven't had time to get home yet.'

'How long will you be there?' I asked.

'I'm not sure. It depends on how this thing looks after I fiddle about with it a bit. Could be an hour, could be twelve hours.'

'Oh, Tim. I was looking forward to seeing you.'

'I was looking forward to a night out too,' he said. 'I need to come up for air! But I absolutely can't leave this at the moment.'

'Why don't I come over to your house and cook you dinner?' I suggested. 'I could have it ready for you when you come in, and you could flop in front of the TV.'

'Nice thought.' I could almost see Tim smile. 'But I really don't know how long I'll be, and I'd hate you to go to all that trouble.'

'It wouldn't be any trouble,' I said.

'All the same.' Tim was firm. 'It wouldn't be fair. Why don't you go out and have a good time and I'll give you a buzz tomorrow?'

'Oh, OK then.' I knew I sounded mulish but I couldn't help it.

'I'll be finished by tomorrow,' promised Tim.

'I said it's OK.'

'All right. I'd better go. Sooner I start again, sooner I finish.'

'OK. Take care.' I replaced the receiver and sighed.

Not for the first time I wished that Tim's job didn't seem to mean so much to him, that he didn't commit himself so completely to every project he was involved in.

I wandered back into the living room and sat down.

Mum looked up from the TV. 'I thought you were going out.'

'I was. Tim's working late. That was him on the phone.'

She made an indeterminate clucking sound.

'Don't,' I said.

'Don't what?'

'Make that noise.'

'What noise?' She looked the picture of innocence.

'You know quite well,' I said as I picked up the *Evening Herald*.

Saturday night, I thought glumly, and I'm stuck here watching boring TV with my parents. What a frumpish thing to do. I flicked through the newspaper without reading it and came to the cinema pages. Maybe I'd go to the pictures, I thought. There was a new James Bond movie showing. Tim hated James Bond. I wouldn't care if I was on my own. Maybe Julie was home. She liked Pierce Brosnan. I threw the paper to one side and phoned her.

'I'd love to go,' she said.

'Great. I'll phone and book seats on my credit card. D'you want me to pick you up?'

'Fine,' she said. 'What time's the film?'

'Eight forty-five,' I told her. 'I'll call around for you in fifteen minutes.'

Mum clucked again when I said I was going out with Julie. Dad was immersed in the newspaper.

The rain was heavier now. It hammered against the pavement and beat against the windscreen of the car. I turned the wipers on fast, so that they flapped over and back in their own demented dance.

'What a foul night,' gasped Julie as she climbed into the car. 'Maybe I should have stayed in and watched TV after all!'

'Nonsense,' I told her. 'You know you wanted nothing more than to come out with me.'

'I thought you'd be out with Tim tonight,' she said, brushing rain from her jumper.

'I should have been,' I admitted. 'But he's working.'

Julie didn't mind being second choice. 'I suppose if I was in love with someone I'd want to be with him rather than a girlfriend,' she said jauntily. 'Even if the man is Tim Malone.'

'Oh, shut up.' I turned onto the main road.

We ran from the car to the cinema but we still got soaked. I'd thought I had an umbrella in the car but it had unaccountably disappeared.

'It doesn't matter.' Julie looked around the heaving throng in the foyer. 'Let's get some popcorn and ice cream.'

We loaded up with supplies and made our way into the darkness.

Afterwards, Julie suggested we go for something to eat.

'After popcorn and ice cream!' I exclaimed.

'I didn't have any dinner,' she told me. 'And popcorn doesn't exactly fill you up.'

So I drove to a small restaurant in Malahide, where the food was inexpensive but very good. It was full of couples gazing into each other's eyes over the flickering candles on the wooden tables.

'God,' murmured Julie. 'I feel like a complete gooseberry.'

I laughed. 'Who cares?'

We ordered blackened chicken and garlic potatoes. When the food came, I realised that I was hungry.

'Have you heard from Andreas the Greek lately?' I asked Julie casually as I blew on a portion of chicken.

Even in the candlelight, I could see her blush.

'Oh?' I grinned at her.

'He phoned tonight,' she said. 'Just before you, in fact.'

'Well, well, well.' I bit into a piece of chicken and the spices nearly blew my head off. I gulped at my glass of water.

'Serves you right,' laughed Julie as I dabbed at my watering eyes. He'd rung her a couple of days after we'd got home from Rhodes but she hadn't mentioned him since.

'He's phoned a few times,' she said.

'Julie!'

'I really like him,' she said defensively.

'He must really like you,' I said, 'if he's the one doing all the phoning!'

'He might,' she said non-committally.

'Julie Donegan! Are you conducting a long-distance affair with this bloke?'

'I'd like to,' she said. 'But it's very difficult when you're at the other end of the phone and you know the person you're talking to is hundreds of miles away.'

'I guess so.' I ate another piece of chicken, more cautiously this time.

'There was something about him,' she said dreamily. 'I haven't felt this way about anyone before.'

'Really?'

'Really. And I know you'll say it's because we were on holidays and everything was idyllic, but it isn't like that, Isobel.'

I scratched my cheek. 'I'm delighted.'

'It's all very well being delighted,' she told me waspishly, 'but he's in Florida and I'm in Dublin. It's not exactly an easy relationship.'

'I can see that.' I filled our glasses with more water. 'Are you going to go and see him or anything?'

'He's asked me to,' she said. 'In September.'

I whistled under my breath.

'Don't look so surprised,' she said. 'I might go.'

'*Do* go,' I said, surprised at my own insistence. 'Go and decide whether you love him or not.'

'Goodness, Isobel.' She laughed at me. 'That sounds very intense.'

'I know.' I smiled ruefully. 'I just want you to be happy, Julie.'

'And what about you?' she asked. 'Are you happy?'

I sipped my water. 'Of course.'

'Resolved your differences with Tim?'

'Yes.'

'When are you getting married?'

I sipped my water again. 'I'm not sure.'

'Haven't you set a date yet?'

'No,' I said. 'But that doesn't mean anything, Julie. We're still going to do it. It's just that he's really busy at the moment, finishing some project. When it's wrapped up, then we'll discuss the wedding.'

'I'm glad you're happy,' she said seriously. 'But don't let him hurt you again.'

'I won't,' I said, and applied myself to the serious business of eating.

Alison was making toast when I came downstairs the following morning. The rain of the previous day had disappeared and the sun was brilliant in the washed blue sky. I poured some cereal into a bowl and sat in the cane chair near the kitchen door.

Alison leaned against the wall and yawned widely. Her hair fell into her eyes and she pushed it back lethargically.

'Where were you last night?' I asked. 'You look wrecked.'

'I feel wrecked,' she admitted, yawning again. 'Suzy had her going-away drinks last night. I didn't get in until half-four this morning, but I couldn't sleep.'

'When does she leave?' Suzy, an old friend of Alison's, was going to Australia for six months.

'Tonight,' said Alison. 'If she wakes up.'

'Will she enjoy it?'

'Australia?' Alison poured some milk into a glass and drank it in a single gulp. She wiped the white moustache from her lip. 'I'd say so. She says she'll do a lot of travelling. She has an aunt or cousin or something in Perth so she'll go there for a while, then get around.'

'It'd be nice to work abroad,' I mused.

Alison nodded, then winced. 'Bloody head,' she muttered.

'Your toast is burning,' I said.

'Shit!' She fiddled with the toaster and held the two blackened pieces of bread between her fingers. 'I hate burnt toast.'

'Put on some more,' I said.

She sighed and threw the toast into the garden. 'Doesn't matter. The smell of it burning has put me off.'

She filled the kettle and plugged it in. I watched her while she leaned against the wall again. Most people never thought of Alison and me as sisters because we were so unalike. But despite the fact that we disagreed on hundreds of little things we managed to get on well together.

The kettle boiled and she made coffee for both of us.

'I begin to feel more human,' she said as she sipped hers. 'I can feel my red corpuscles getting up and wandering around in my bloodstream again.'

I laughed. 'Mine are marching around already. I feel

very energetic today. Maybe I can persuade Tim to play tennis with me.'

'Oh!' Alison put her cup on the table and stared at me. Then she blushed. The colour started at her neck and very slowly flooded her face. She put her hands to her cheeks as though to hide it.

'What's wrong?' I asked in surprise.

'Nothing.' She picked up the cup and sipped her coffee again.

'Alison!'

She looked uncomfortable.

'Come on,' I said. 'Whatever it is, you might as well tell me.'

A wasp came in through the open kitchen door and buzzed around the kitchen. Alison flapped a towel ineffectually at it as she tried to persuade it out of the door again. It careered into the window and buzzed frantically. Alison threw the towel at it and scored a direct hit. The wasp fell onto the draining-board and spun around.

'I think I've killed it,' she wailed.

'Maybe not,' I said. 'Put it outside, it might recover.'

She scooped it onto some kitchen paper and threw it out onto the grass. 'That way I won't know whether it dies or not,' she said as she emptied the remains of her coffee down the sink and rinsed her cup. 'I'd better go and get dressed.'

'Not until you tell me what you were so put out about,' I told her.

'It was nothing.'

'Don't give me that crap,' I said with sisterly feeling. 'Tell me.'

I could always make her tell me things.

'It's just – I thought you were going out with Tim last night,' she said.

I looked at her in surprise. 'I was. But he couldn't

meet me so I went out with Julie instead. There's nothing wrong with that, is there?'

'No,' she said.

'So, what's the problem?'

'I met Tim last night.'

'Oh?'

'Well, not met, exactly. I saw him. And I thought he was meant to be with you.'

'Where did you see him?' I asked.

'In Donnybrook,' said Alison.

'Probably went out for a drink after he finished his work,' I told her. 'I know that if I ever work late all I want to do is flop in front of the telly, but Tim likes going for a drink to unwind. He says that some of his best ideas come to him in a haze of alcohol, only he can never remember them afterwards.'

Alison still looked uncomfortable.

'So did you talk to him?' I asked. I could imagine what their conversation would be like. Alison held a grudge. That was another difference between us. I can never stay angry with someone, but Alison can store up rage to use months later on her unsuspecting victim.

'No,' she said. 'I was going to, but I didn't.'

'I still don't see what the fuss is about.' I drained my cup. 'Just because you don't like him any more.'

'I don't want to cause you any hassle,' she said defensively. 'Really I don't. And I don't want you to get mad at me.'

'What have you done?' I asked, suddenly alarmed. 'Don't tell me you did something awful?'

'Of course I didn't.' She sounded indignant. 'What d'you take me for.' She sighed deeply. 'It's only – well – there was someone with him.'

'What do you mean?'

'I didn't meet him in a pub,' she said. 'We went for

something to eat. And he was there, in the restaurant. I thought you were with him because the girl who was there looked very like you. Only her hair was longer. And I think she had blue eyes. Maybe it was just blue eyeshadow. I can't remember properly. We'd had a few drinks by then. And I was going to go up to him and say hello – maybe say that he was a shit or something – I don't know—' she looked at me unhappily. 'But this girl was with him.'

'So what?' I tried to ignore the painful pounding of my heart in my ribcage. 'He was probably working late and decided to go and have something to eat.'

'I know,' she said miserably.

'So why are you getting so upset?'

'I don't know.' She rubbed at her eyes. 'I suppose – I saw him with this girl – I don't know what I thought.'

'The worst obviously,' I said angrily. 'Just because you didn't want me to get married in the first place! And he let me down! And you think he's going to let me down over and over again! Well, that's not going to happen, Alison Kavanagh. OK, so things went wrong a couple of months ago. That doesn't mean that Tim and I haven't sorted out our differences and made decisions about our lives. And I'm not going to get upset because he has dinner on Saturday night with a work colleague.'

'I know. I'm sorry,' she said.

'Fine,' I told her.

I pulled my dressing-gown tighter around me and went upstairs. I locked myself into the bathroom and turned on the shower. The room filled up with steam. I hung my dressing-gown on the bathroom door, and slipped out of my pale pink pyjamas.

I wished Alison hadn't told me. It wasn't that I didn't believe that Tim had been working. I was sure he had. I knew how involved he became in every project and

I knew, too, that he often had someone working with him. But I was unhappy that he'd gone to dinner with this unknown girl instead of phoning me and asking me if I'd like to see him.

Silly, I told myself, as I stepped under the spray. Why should he ring? Would I, if it had been the other way around? If I'd been in the office and wanted something to eat, would I have tried to call Tim or would I have suggested to one of the girls that we'd go out together? I wasn't sure. It had never happened.

He might have phoned, of course. He could have called and found out that I was at the cinema with Julie and so decided to go and eat with this girl. Sensible thing to do, really.

I turned off the shower and wrapped a towel around me. I'd phone him myself and sort things out. That was the best thing to do.

Condensation dripped from the wall mirror. I drew a heart on the steamy surface and wrote Tim's name in the middle. It was a stupid thing we used to do in school. Write some guy's name in the steam and he'd fall for you. I shook my head and rubbed the mirror with some toilet roll. I was engaged to Tim, for God's sake! I shouldn't feel the need to write his name on the mirror.

'Isobel?' Alison rapped at the door.

'I'll be out in a minute.'

'Isobel, I'm sorry.'

'For what?' I asked as I towelled myself briskly.

'For telling you. I shouldn't have said anything.'

'Don't be daft.' I ran a wide comb through my hair and winced every time I reached a tangle.

'But it was silly of me. I mean, you're right, she was probably just from work and everything.'

'It's OK,' I told her.

'All the same—'

'Forget it, will you!' I shouted. 'It doesn't bloody matter.'

But of course it mattered, I thought, as I sat on my bed and blowdried my hair. No matter how innocent it was, I hated to think of him sitting in a restaurant on a Saturday night with another woman. Especially as he'd broken off a date with me – just minutes before I'd set out to meet him! There couldn't be anything in it, could there?

'You'll never be able to trust him again,' Julie had said, and although I'd dismissed her dire warnings, her words came back to echo around my mind. Now the seeds of doubt were growing into a wilderness of mistrust, much as I tried to stop them. I flung my brush on the bed. I wished that Alison had kept her mouth shut. Then I wouldn't know about Tim. It wouldn't make any difference.

I sat on my bed and curled my knees up under my chin. But why should it make any difference? It wasn't as though he was having a relationship with this woman. Was it?

The chill band of insecurity wrapped itself around me. Maybe he was. Maybe she was the reason he'd called off the wedding. Perhaps he was in love with her.

But if he was in love with her, my distracted mind tried to reason, why would he say that he wanted to stay engaged? Why didn't he just break off the engagement, tell me it was a dreadful mistake and that he was crazy about someone else? Why would he have sent me on holiday with Julie and then made love to me so wonderfully when I came home? It didn't make any sense.

I would ring him now, I decided, and find out. There was no point in sitting here allowing my fevered imagination to get the better of me.

Alison was in the kitchen again when I went downstairs.

'Don't worry,' I told her. 'Everything's fine. I'm going to phone him.'

She looked anxiously at me.

'Why don't you go out?' I said. 'Stop hanging around looking like a sad spaniel.'

'Maybe I will,' she said. 'Clear my head.'

'It'll do you good,' I told her.

I waited until she'd gone before I rang Tim's number. The answerphone responded. I hung up.

Maybe he was still in bed. He did that sometimes, stayed in bed really late on Sundays. Often, when I met him on Sunday afternoons, he was only just up and we'd go into town and have brunch. He always left the answerphone on when he was in bed.

I tried again half an hour later. The answerphone clicked in again.

He couldn't be in bed with her, could he? I hadn't wanted to formulate the thought, had firmly resisted the picture of him lying beside a lovelier model of me. He wouldn't be in bed with her. It was disloyal of me even to think it.

Alison came back from her walk. Mum and Dad came back from theirs. Ian was out with friends.

I rang again. Still the answerphone.

I couldn't take it any more. I had to go and see him. If he was in bed and asleep, I would tell him I was sorry and then get into bed beside him. Of course, he might be working. He left the machine on when he worked too. And I hadn't left any messages, had been too nervous to leave any messages.

I was acting like a teenager. He was my fiancé, after all. He loved me. He'd said so.

But he hadn't proved it, said the demon in my head. When it came to the crunch, he couldn't prove it.

I took my car keys from the hall table and went to see Tim.

Chapter 6

Dismal Sport (Salvador Dalí, 1929)

A wall of warm air hit me when I opened the car door. The smell of hot vinyl was overpowering. I wound down both driver and passenger windows and wished I had a sunroof. The steering wheel was almost too hot to touch. It was amazing that today was so hot, given the almost torrential rain of yesterday.

The sun dazzled me as I drove. It reflected off the sea in brilliant sparkles of light. I felt around in the glove compartment for my sunglasses – I hadn't needed them since I'd come back from Rhodes. I shoved my Tina Turner tape into the cassette and turned the volume up.

I couldn't make up my mind whether to drive quickly or slowly. Part of me wanted to be beside Tim now, this very second; another part of me was scared that my worst fears – the ones I didn't even allow to come into my head – would be realised. I hated him for putting me through this.

The Alfa was in its place. He was at home, although I wasn't sure whether that made things better or worse. I sat outside the house for a moment, the engine idling, afraid to confront him.

This is silly, I told myself finally, and switched off the engine. I left the windows open and the door unlocked.

It was ages before Tim answered the doorbell. He was wearing a blue T-shirt and grey shorts and his feet were bare. He looked at me in surprise.

'I didn't think you were coming over this afternoon.'

I stared at him. 'You were supposed to ring me.'

'Not until tonight.'

'Can I come in?' I felt like a stranger standing on his doorstep.

'Of course.' He opened the door wider and I stepped inside. 'I'm sorry,' he said. 'I was busy. And I didn't think you'd come all the way over here.'

The back door was open. Tim walked through the house and into his small patio garden. 'We were working,' he said as I followed him outside.

The girl was sitting on Tim's swing chair, her feet curled underneath her. She wore a long, shocking pink T-shirt that almost covered her figure-hugging Lycra shorts. Her hair was pulled back from her face but I knew immediately what Alison had meant. She was very like me.

'This is Laura,' said Tim. 'She's my partner on the Saracen project.'

Laura took off her huge, wrap-around sunglasses. Her eyes were brilliant blue. 'Hi,' she said lazily. 'You must be Isobel.'

I nodded, not trusting myself to speak.

'Tim was right,' she giggled. 'We could almost be sisters.'

'You've the wrong colour eyes,' I said, looking directly into them.

'Otherwise she's just like you, isn't she?' said Tim. 'I thought I was seeing things when she walked into the office.'

She got up from the seat. She was also much, much

taller than me. A better height for him, I thought. Her head would nestle comfortably on his shoulder, not somewhere halfway between his stomach and his armpit like mine.

'Maybe I'd better go,' she said. 'We've got most of the work done anyway.'

'But we still have to figure out that program-freezing problem,' protested Tim.

'I've got a theory about that.' Laura launched into some explanation which made no sense to me whatsoever. I sat on an upturned terracotta pot and listened to my fiancé and his colleague argue about it while I pulled at the leaves of his escallonia bush.

He couldn't really be having an affair (can you call it an affair when you're not actually married?) with this girl. Surely if he wanted someone else, he wouldn't have picked a clone of me – even a taller, more intelligent, blue-eyed version? Tim's fantasy girls were always blondes with gravity-defying busts, tiny waists and voracious sexual appetites. I wished she'd go away. I wanted to talk to him.

Eventually they finished their discussion. She would work on the freezing problem. He'd put the final package together. It would only be a week behind schedule.

She waved at me as she left. I smiled at her, although I don't think I'd have liked it very much if someone had given me that kind of smile. It didn't reach my eyes. It hardly reached my mouth.

They spent ages at the front door but they were still only talking. I could see them from where I sat.

Tim came back into the garden carrying a couple of cans of Carlsberg. He opened one and handed it to me. He always opened cans of beer for me because I could never seem to manage it without breaking a nail.

'Thanks,' I said.

'Lucky you didn't arrive earlier.' He took a deep draught of beer.

'Why?'

'We were really busy.'

'Is that why you didn't answer the phone?'

'Did you phone?' He looked surprised. 'I didn't hear it. The machine is on anyhow.'

'I know. I didn't bother leaving a message.'

'You should have. I've been in and out. I would have seen the light blinking.'

'I didn't know what to say.'

'You could have done what you're supposed to do.' He laughed. 'Left your name and number and the time of your call and I'd have called you back!'

'Yeah, right.'

'Oh, for God's sake, Isobel. What's the matter with you?'

Now that the time had come to confront him, I was afraid. I'd rehearsed it in the car on the way over, as the music had soothed me, and I thought that I could sound reasonable and fair. But now, with Tim sitting opposite me, I knew that I'd sound shrewish and whining. The sort of girlfriend I detested. Clinging. Suspicious. Untrusting. But it was his fault that I was untrusting, I thought miserably. He shouldn't have treated me the way he did.

'Ali saw you last night,' I said casually. 'In Furama.'

'Did she?' He looked surprised, but not guilty. 'I didn't see her.'

'You were with someone. Laura, I suppose.'

'Is that what this is about?' he demanded, his voice suddenly harsh. 'An inquisition into my movements last night?'

'It's not an inquisition,' I protested. 'I just wanted to know, that's all. You were supposed to be going out with me. Ali saw you. She thought it was me with you and then she realised it wasn't.'

'So she rushed home to tell tales.'

'That's not fair,' I said. 'She told me this morning, but only after I'd wormed it out of her.'

'I'll bet that was hard,' he muttered. 'Your sister never liked me.'

'Your mother never liked *me*,' I said with false brightness.

He swallowed the rest of his beer and kicked the can to the end of the garden. It echoed noisily off the flagstones.

'Laura and I were working late. I took her to dinner when we'd finished. That's not a crime and I don't like you acting as though it was.'

'I'm not,' I said.

'Yes, you are.'

We stared at each other for a moment and I thought there was more than anger in his eyes. I didn't like it.

'I'm sorry,' I said.

'We were working here this afternoon, too. We'd almost finished. Would have finished if we hadn't been interrupted.'

'I didn't mean to interrupt you.'

'I said I'd ring you tonight, and I would have.'

'It's just that I haven't seen you in ages,' I said.

'You don't own me,' said Tim.

A bird flew into the garden and hopped around. Its body was brown with a greenish tinge. Its beak was yellow. I didn't want to speak because I might disturb it. I couldn't speak anyway because I knew that if I did, I would cry.

There was too much resentment in Tim's voice. Too much hostility. At that moment I knew that Tim didn't love me any more.

I shivered in the warmth and bit my lip. I stood up. The bird flew out of the garden with a noisy flutter of its wings.

I cleared my throat. 'It isn't going to work, is it?'

'What?' Tim looked up from the weeds he'd been pulling.

'Us.'

'Don't be stupid, Isobel.'

'I'm not being stupid,' I said. 'I'm being realistic. I should have been realistic before. I was stupid before. How could you possibly decide not to marry me in May but still want to go out with me? Why did I think that it was a reasonable idea? What pathetic sort of creature did you think I was?'

'I never thought you were pathetic,' said Tim.

'But you don't want to marry me.'

'It's not that.' Tim looked uncomfortable. 'I'm just not ready to get married. I explained all that to you, Isobel.'

'I know you explained it to me,' I said. 'But I didn't listen to you. I didn't want to listen to you. I wanted to pretend that everything was all right. But it isn't all right – it can't be all right.'

'I needed some time.'

'You did. I didn't. But I was going to give you time because I thought I should.' I shook my head. 'No wonder everyone kept looking at me so anxiously. They thought I was cracked. You did the closest thing to ruining my life and I still ran after you like a lovesick teenager!'

'Stop being dramatic.' Tim looked angry. 'I didn't ruin your life or anything like it. I would have ruined it a lot more if I'd married you and then decided that I should have waited. I did you a favour, Isobel.'

'Oh, right.' I laughed bitterly. 'It was a great favour

letting me cancel everything. Knowing that I had to face everyone and tell them that you didn't want to get married. It's a great favour to be humiliated like that, Tim.'

'I thought you understood.'

'I understood that my heart was broken,' I said. 'I understood that all right.'

'But you seemed to be OK.'

'I'm good at that,' I told him. 'I'm a PA. I'm good in a crisis. I could work my way out of the crisis. Rearrange things. Cancel things. I could do all that without bursting into tears but I cried every single night of my so-called holiday in Rhodes.'

He looked uncomfortable. 'I'm sorry,' he said again.

I didn't want it to be like this, but I didn't have any choice. I'd been living in some kind of dream world myself lately. Trying to pretend that the wedding wasn't due to happen until next year. Trying to pretend that it could be exactly as it was before.

I eased the engagement ring from my finger and handed it to him.

'I should have done this before,' I said. 'I was a fool.'

He turned it over and over in his hand. For a second, I thought he might give it back to me, but he clenched his fist around it.

'I'll keep it.' He looked up at me. 'Maybe we'll use it again.'

I shook my head, bit my lip and walked out of the house.

~

I drove as far as the canal, then pulled over to the side of the road. I fumbled in my bag for my inhaler and squirted a dose of the fine mist deep into my lungs. I held my breath for ten seconds, then released it slowly. The rattle in my chest had subsided. I felt a little calmer.

They had been right and I was wrong. Even if Tim's relationship with Laura was purely professional – and it could easily be, I'd seen no real signs to prove otherwise – I couldn't accept his word. It was no way to plan a marriage and no way to live my life. I would have to forget Tim and find someone else. Or not. I shivered in the warmth of the sun. There was no need to find someone else. I was perfectly capable of living life on my own. I could get an apartment after all. Perhaps I could afford something near work. I'd be getting away from home then, and from the places I knew since childhood. There was, after all, something ridiculous about the idea of a twenty-seven-year-old woman living in the parental home.

I shuddered at the thought of arriving home without my ring. I didn't want to go through it all again.

I drove past our house and around the corner to Julie's. She was sitting in the back garden, topping up her tan. Her parents had gone for a walk, she told me, and would probably be out for ages. I sat on the neatly mown grass and extended my hand to her.

'What happened?' she asked calmly.

I'd thought I'd be able to tell Julie without bursting into tears, use her as practice before I went home, but the tears flowed anyway. She said nothing while I scrubbed at my eyes with a crumpled tissue. She went into the house and came back with a box of Kleenex man-size.

'So?' She handed the box to me and I took another tissue.

I blew my nose. 'I've broken it off with him.'

'I thought you'd sorted everything out?'

'I wanted to think that we had.'

'But what went wrong?'

I pulled at a blade of grass and tore it into tiny pieces.

'Was it last night?' she asked. 'When you didn't go out?'

Only last night, I thought. It seemed like years ago.

'Ali saw him,' I told her. 'He was with another girl.'

'The shit!' Julie's eyes blazed with fury. 'The absolute shit! How dare he? After all he's said. I'd like to strangle him.'

'It wasn't like that,' I protested, wondering why I was defending him. 'She was from work. They were doing a project together.'

'Oh, really.' Julie's voice was full of disbelief.

'I believe him,' I said. 'He told me that they worked late and went for something to eat. It's not exactly a crime, Julie.'

'Huh,' she said.

'But I couldn't help wondering.' I pulled another blade of grass. 'And I thought about what you said – that I'd never be able to trust him again. And I knew that I was suspicious of him and that I didn't trust him.'

'I'm sorry if I made you feel—'

I shook my head vigorously. 'It's not your fault. I kept wondering, that's all. He said he'd ring today but I rang him instead. There was no answer. So I just thought the worst and hurtled over to see him.'

Julie's eyes opened wide. 'And?'

'She was there,' I said. 'But there wasn't anything going on, really there wasn't. They were working in the garden. They had books and papers with them and I believe him when he said that was all they were doing.'

'So, why have you broken it off?'

'Because I'll never be certain,' I wailed. 'I'll never feel

one hundred per cent convinced that he married me because he loved me and that he really wanted to. He got really pissed off because I wanted to know about her and I don't blame him. We were never like that before, Julie. You know that. He went out with his friends, I went out with mine. We never questioned each other.'

'Maybe you should have,' she said darkly.

'I don't think so.' I leaned my head on my knees and closed my eyes. My finger felt strange without the ring, knowing that I'd never wear it again. I couldn't quite believe that I was the one who'd actually done it, who'd decided that we wouldn't be getting married in the future. I still felt that it was Tim's decision, not mine.

'So what are you going to do now?' asked Julie.

I sighed. 'I don't know. I thought maybe about getting a flat, something near work.'

'Buying one?'

I shrugged. 'I could probably afford it. I was thinking about it on the way home. I don't want to live at home any more, Julie. It's too constricting. And they'll be following me around, oozing sympathy. Mum'll be trying to get me out and about meeting other men – you know her, it's a husband or nothing as far as she's concerned.' I wiped my eyes with the back of my hand. 'Maybe that's why I felt so strongly about marrying Tim. She was always going on at me about getting married before I was thirty. The last time we talked about it she said that I was leaving it a bit late to have a family! I told her that I was young enough but she handed me an article about infertility in women over thirty and how having a career and putting off babies until you're older can be a drastic mistake. I tried to tell her that I haven't actually got a career, I just have a job, but it didn't cut any ice with her.'

Julie laughed. 'Your mum was always the homebird type.'

'You'd think that she'd want us to go out and have a good time,' I said. 'After all, she was married when she was twenty and I was born a year later. You'd imagine she'd like me to have fun.'

Julie sighed. 'You know parents. They always want the opposite of what you'd expect. Remember when I was going out with Will? My mother did everything she could to split us up, even though she'd been nagging at me for ages to find myself a boyfriend.'

I laughed unconvincingly. 'Well, yes, Julie – but *Will*?'

'OK.' She grinned at me. 'So he looked like a Hell's Angel, but he was a decent bloke all the same.'

'Julie, he used to scare the living daylights out of me,' I told her. 'I was always terrified I'd meet him with a gang of his mates and they'd do unspeakable things to me.'

'Isobel!' She looked offended. 'He wasn't like that.'

'I know that,' I said. 'It was the way he made me feel.'

'He didn't last long anyway,' she sighed. 'He was just my rebellious phase.' She waved her hand at the freshly painted house, the immaculately tended garden and frowned. 'I needed to have something different to this.'

I nodded. Julie's house was similar to mine. Both four-bedroomed, semi-detached, built in the nineteen-fifties. Big rooms, big gardens and all rewired, double-glazed and owned by people of my parents' age. People who'd gone through the lean, early, married years, had accumulated a little money, who'd spent it on a yearly holiday and fitted kitchens, new bathrooms and sunny conservatories.

I hadn't gone through a rebellious phase. I wanted to be one of those people. Only Tim and I wouldn't have had lean times, we would have been a successful, happy, married couple.

Oh God, I thought despairingly, I'd had it all planned

so neatly. And it had nearly happened. Why hadn't I seen that Tim was getting cold feet? Why hadn't I anticipated his doubts? Why hadn't I stayed the sort of girl he wanted to marry? Why me, I cried silently. Why me?

Julie was silent beside me. She stared into the distance and allowed me to regain my composure.

'It feels awful now,' she said after a few minutes. 'But you *will* get over it.'

I gave a wry smile. 'I know I'll get over it. People get over things. But I'll never feel the same about anyone again.'

'You'll find someone else someday and you'll feel even better,' she told me.

'Let me wallow in my misery,' I said wanly. 'I'll tell you when it gets better.'

'OK.' She hugged me. 'D'you want to come inside and see the new suit I bought?'

I nodded and we went inside to talk about things that really matter.

~

Strangely, it was Ian who noticed that my engagement ring was missing.

They were having dinner when I arrived home. I could smell the roast beef as soon as I walked into the house and I wondered why Mum would want to cook a Sunday roast in weather like this.

'It was wet and cold yesterday,' she pointed out when I told her that she shouldn't have bothered cooking.

'Besides—' Ian helped himself to more potatoes, 'I'm a growing lad. I need my food. You girls might want to wander around like half-fed waifs, but I need to build muscle.'

'Muscle!' I jeered, pinching his waistline.

He caught me by the wrist and held up my hand. 'Where's your ring?'

There was silence at the table. Dad put his knife and fork in the centre of his plate and looked at me expectantly.

'I gave it back,' I said. 'I changed my mind.'

'Oh, shit,' said Alison.

'Alison Kavanagh!' Dad looked angrily at her. 'You know I don't like that sort of language.'

'Sorry,' she muttered as she looked at me from beneath her long lashes. 'Is it definitely off, Isobel?'

I nodded.

'But I thought you'd sorted it out,' cried my mother. 'I thought you said that you'd get married in the autumn. I thought you were going to go through with it.'

'I thought you'd be pleased,' I said shortly.

There was silence again.

'I'm pleased,' said Dad.

'Me too,' said Alison.

'Whatever you want,' said Ian.

'Well, of course I'm pleased.' Mum sounded unconvinced. 'I told you he wasn't worth it, after all! But you don't seem to know your own mind, Isobel. I just don't want you to do something you'll absolutely regret. I don't want you breaking it off out of pique.'

'I didn't break it off out of pique.'

'Why did you?' asked Alison quietly.

I clenched my fists under the table. 'Because I didn't think I could be sure about him. Because I felt that it would take him a long time to be sure about me. Because I didn't want to take the chance.'

I'd ruined dinner for them. Possibly Ian would keep eating, but I could see from everybody else's expression that my news was almost as great a blow as the postponement of the wedding.

'I'm going up to my room,' I said. 'Don't all come charging up to make sure I haven't slit my wrists or anything. I'm fine.'

I lay on the bed and stared at the ceiling. I wanted to make plans for the rest of my life. There was no point in thinking about Tim Malone any more. He had to be consigned to the past, with the other boyfriends whom I'd once thought I loved. I remembered Alan Davenport, the first guy I'd ever been truly crazy about. Our romance had only lasted a few months – it had been based more on physical attraction than anything else – but I was shattered when we split up. It was the same sort of feeling now, I told myself. As though part of you has been suddenly ripped away. But you get used to it after a while. Then one day you wake up and it doesn't hurt any more. You try to remember what he was like and you can't. You forget what your favourite song was, or his favourite colour. You stop wearing the perfume that made you sneeze but that he liked. You go back to wearing cotton knickers and bras instead of wispy bits of voile. You turn into a normal person again.

But while you're waiting for the pain to go away, for time to kick in with its healing powers, it's hell. And for me, right then, it was the worst hell I'd ever been in.

Alison knocked at the door a few hours later. I hastily scooped the photographs of Tim and me into a shoebox and shoved them back underneath the bed. I opened the biography of Jackie Kennedy Onassis that was on my bedside locker.

'Are you OK?' she asked as she came into the room.

'Of course.'

'What happened?'

'Nothing.'

'Oh, come on, Isobel. Something must have. Why did you decide to break it off?'

'I didn't exactly decide to break it off,' I said. 'He was the one that started it.'

'I know. But you said – I thought—' She looked miserable.

'It's nothing to do with you,' I told her. 'I mean, nothing to do with what you told me.'

'But, Isobel—'

'Really it isn't. I went over to him and we talked. While we were talking I realised that I can't wait for ever for him. And he wasn't certain about anything. So I thought that it was better to make a clean break of it there and then. Get it over with.'

'Oh, Isobel!' She put her arms around me and hugged me. 'I'm so sorry!'

'What have you got to be sorry about?' I asked as I disentangled her arms. 'You've probably done me a favour.'

'I may be stupid, but I'm not that stupid.'

'Really, Alison. It could have been a dreadful mistake to marry him.'

'But you seemed to have worked it out. If it wasn't for me—'

'—it would have been something else,' I finished for her. 'Don't feel guilty.'

'I feel guilty because I'm glad you broke it off with him,' she admitted. 'I just didn't think you should get married to him. He was always such a super-confident person. I thought he didn't give you enough credit.'

'I thought you just didn't believe in marriage.' I smiled at her.

'That too,' said Alison. 'But – he was so sure that he had a great job and you were just a secretary.'

'I'm not just a secretary,' I told her. 'I'm a PA. It's much more than typing and making coffee!'

'I know.' She hung her head. 'I'm sorry. I'm saying all the wrong things.'

'It doesn't matter.' I kissed the top of her head. 'Leave me alone now, Alison. I'll be fine.'

Easy to say, I thought, when she'd closed the door behind her. Easy to say, easy to pretend. I'll be fine. I was still telling myself that when I finally fell asleep.

Chapter 7

Inverted Personages (Joan Miró, 1949)

But, of course, I wasn't fine. I went into the office every day, came home again every evening, even went out occasionally with Julie – but I wasn't fine. I tried to behave as though everything was OK. I didn't sob over my computer terminal. I answered the phone briskly and efficiently. I did the shopping for Mum at the weekends. I tried not to talk about Tim when I was with Julie. But nothing could take away the empty feeling inside and nothing could make me believe that I would ever be happy again.

I told myself that time was all I needed. A great healer. I reminded myself of all those clichés over and over again as I peered at folders full of invoices through eyes that were blurred with unshed tears.

'Isobel.' Barry stood at the door to his office. I blinked a couple of times to clear my eyes. 'Can you come in for a moment?' he asked.

I followed him into the office and sat in the chair in front of his desk. He took a pen from the black leather container on the desk and rolled it around in his hands a couple of times. I watched him silently.

He cleared his throat. 'How are you feeling?' he asked abruptly.

I was surprised at the question. I looked at him in astonishment. 'How am I feeling?'

'Yes,' he said. 'Generally.'

I swallowed. Whenever people asked me how I felt, the urge to cry washed over me and it was all I could do not to burst into tears again. 'I'm fine.'

'Are you?'

I nodded. 'Absolutely.'

He said nothing.

'Well, almost absolutely.' I shrugged. 'Sometimes I feel a bit down, to be perfectly honest, but most of the time I'm OK.'

'You've got over the thing with Tim?'

'It's hard to be sure you're completely over something,' I told him. 'But, yes, I am.'

'I'm glad to hear it.' He smiled slightly. 'But I'm not sure that I'm as confident as you are about that.'

'Why not?'

He took a file from his desk. 'These invoices. You sent DeltaPac ones to DeltaCon and vice versa.' He took out another file. 'Staff payroll. You left it in the top drawer of your desk last night. You didn't lock it away as you're supposed to.'

My lips were dry. 'I'm sorry, Barry. It was an oversight.'

'Finally—' He opened his diary. 'Can you tell me why you booked me on a flight to Manchester for tomorrow when I'm supposed to be going to London?'

Oh God, I thought. How could I have done all these things wrong?

'I'm sorry,' I said again. 'I don't know what happened. I wasn't concentrating properly. I'll sort it out.'

He looked at me thoughtfully. 'You've been with me a long time, Isobel. We work well together, I think.

You've made a positive contribution to the company. Up until now.'

I felt a stab of fear. Was he going to fire me? He could, because of the payroll. I couldn't believe I'd left the payroll in an unlocked desk drawer.

'I've never had to talk to you like this before,' he continued, 'and I don't much like doing it. But it can't go on like this.'

'I know that these are bad mistakes,' I said. 'I do. Really. And I'm truly sorry. I didn't realise how much I'd let my concentration slip.'

'It's not only major things like this,' said Barry. 'It's not passing on messages. Being abrupt with callers. Not being part of the team.'

I bit my lip. So much for thinking that I answered the phone in an efficient manner. I was going to lose my job. Not content with losing a fiancé, now I was about to become unemployed. Careless, as Oscar Wilde might have put it.

Barry got up from behind the desk and sat on the edge of it. 'I'm sorry about your wedding,' he said, his tone marginally warmer. 'I know it must have been a terrible blow to you. But life goes on, Isobel, and you can't spend your whole life pining away.'

'I'm not pining,' I told him.

'You're not working either,' he said.

I fiddled with the belt of my skirt. I couldn't meet his eyes.

'This is a warning, Isobel.' He sounded tired. 'I don't want to lose you. As I said, you're a good worker. Usually. But you have to get back into gear. Stop wearing dreary clothes to the office. Perk up a bit. It's not as though you've been bereaved.'

But, for me, it was. I couldn't see how anyone who'd lost a partner could be less gutted than I was.

'Thanks, Barry.' I glanced at him. 'I appreciate what you've said.'

'That's OK,' he told me. 'I'm sorry I had to say it, but—' He grimaced. 'Everyone has something happen to them at some time in their lives that is as heart-rending and miserable as what happened to you. It takes different forms for different people. But there's always something. That's the way life is.'

I wondered what heart-rending and miserable thing could have happened to Barry Cleary. I couldn't think of anything offhand.

But Barry was right. I had allowed myself to be consumed by my own unhappiness. I had to snap out of it. Let myself live again. Take control of my own destiny.

I stood up. 'I promise you won't have to talk to me about it again,' I said.

'Good.' He smiled at me. 'It's important that we all pull together.'

I went back to my desk and tried to clear my thoughts. A trickle of sweat slid down my back. My job had been on the line. I knew that Barry liked me, but it wouldn't have stopped him firing me if he believed that I couldn't work as I had before. I bent my head over the invoices and checked them more thoroughly than ever.

I bought a new suit in red wool and wore it into the office the following week. Red suited me and I knew that it brought the colour back to my cheeks. I wore more make-up, some nice jewellery and made an effort. I went to lunch with Niamh and Anna. I was bright and cheery every time I went into Barry's office and I cultivated an air of super-efficiency that surprised even me.

I was sitting at my desk, correcting a draft of a speech that Barry intended to give at a management conference in Killarney. It was the first time he'd been asked to speak at something like this and he wanted it to be perfect. It nearly was, I thought, as I read through it. It hit the right note. Not too boring, not too light-hearted. Competent, I decided.

'Isobel?' John Ferguson, from the marketing department, stood in front of me.

'Hi.' I put the text of Barry's speech to one side and looked up at him.

He smiled nervously. 'How are you?'

'Fine,' I replied. 'You?'

I didn't know John very well. He'd joined DeltaPrint the previous year and, although I'd worked with him a couple of times, he kept himself very much to himself. I didn't think he particularly liked me – thought, perhaps, that I was too fun-loving, too flighty.

'I was wondering,' he said, 'if you were doing anything on Friday night?'

I stared at him. 'Friday night?'

'Yes.' He made a face. 'I've got tickets, you see. For the Mary Black concert. I thought you might like to come.'

'Oh.' I didn't know what to say. I'd no idea he'd intended to ask me out. Ask me out! A date! Was this time, I wondered sardonically, trying to help the healing process along?

'Of course if you're busy—' he said hastily.

'No,' I told him. 'I'm not busy.' I was silent for a moment. 'It's very nice of you to ask me, John. Truly it is.'

'But?' he said.

I smiled crookedly. 'But I can't go out with you. Not yet.'

'Why not?' he asked.

'I'm not quite ready to go out with someone yet,' I told him. 'I'm sorry.'

'Don't worry about it.' His tone was even. 'It doesn't matter.'

'Maybe some other time,' I said.

'Sure.' He forced a grin. 'Let me know.'

'Yes,' I said. 'I will.'

He walked back through the office and I pinched my nose between my fingers. I should have said yes. It wouldn't have hurt to go out with him. He'd obviously gone to the trouble of getting the tickets. Now I'd hurt his feelings and I didn't want to hurt anyone's feelings. I was too much of an expert on hurt feelings myself.

Damn, I said, drawing a black line through a repeated word in Barry's speech. Damn, damn, damn.

The speech was a great success. *Business & Finance* did a report on the company which caused a flurry of activity in the office. We landed an important contract, I worked late three nights a week and Barry didn't have to talk to me again about efficiency and commitment. But time, even as it marched inexorably onwards, still wasn't doing much healing for me. One day in early September I went to Mum's wardrobe to look for a jacket and I saw my wedding dress. It was still swathed in tissue paper and covered in plastic. It hung there, white, immobile, haunting.

There was no one else in the house. I took out the wedding dress and laid it carefully on the bed. It was beautiful. Really beautiful. I slipped it from the hanger and held it in front of me. I was darker now than I'd been in April and my tanned skin accentuated the white of the dress. The four hundred and twenty tiny pearls glistened in the afternoon sunshine.

I took off my jeans and top and slid the dress over my head. My heart was thumping in my chest as though I were committing a criminal act. I pulled up the zip, ran my fingers through my hair and stood in front of the mirror.

I'd lost weight. The dress had been a perfect fit, now it was slightly looser around my waist. I turned around slowly. The material rustled. I stared at myself. Face, paler than usual under the dusting of my tan, eyes dark and miserable, hair long and lank. Had I looked like this before? I didn't know. I felt as though the person in the mirror was a stranger. A woman in her wedding dress. I watched my eyes fill up with tears and refused to blink to stop them from falling.

I took off the wedding dress and brought it into my own room. I laid it out on the bed. It was like a ghostly shroud. I took my dressmaking scissors from the cupboard and sliced it neatly up the centre. My tears fell as I cut it again and again, lengthways, sideways, across the bodice, through the skirt, until it was reduced to a rubble of white ribbon and pearls. Then I bundled it into a plastic bag and shoved it under the bed.

Julie and I went for a walk around Howth Head the following day. It was hot when we started, but one of those days when grey clouds can appear out of nowhere and send a torrent of rain onto the unwary. For most of our walk, though, the sun glittered on the deep blue water of the open sea and the gorse lit up the hill in a blaze of yellow.

'I'm going to Florida next week,' said Julie while we sat on a boulder and gazed at the horizon.

'Really?' I turned to look at her. 'To stay with Andy?'

'Of course to stay with Andy.' She laughed. 'There's no other reason to go to Florida!'

'I know.' I picked at the corner of my nail. 'I hope you have a great time.'

'I hope so, too,' said Julie. 'I was wondering if you'd mind giving me a lift to the airport?'

'Of course not.' I stretched my legs in front of me. 'You lucky thing.'

'Well, even if Andy and I decide we hate each other, I'll still have a good time,' said Julie. 'And another holiday would be nice.' She looked critically at me. 'You could do with one yourself, Isobel. You look wretched.'

'Gee, thanks.' I punched her gently on the shoulder. 'You make me feel so good.'

'These last few days,' said my friend, 'you're paler and listless and – oh, not yourself.'

'I don't know what's myself any more.' I sighed and rested my head in my hands.

Julie was silent. A gull screeched overhead.

'I thought everything was going well for you,' she said eventually. 'You were busy in work and you seemed OK.'

'I know.' I didn't look up and my voice was muffled. 'But sometimes I feel as if I want to forget everything, Julie. Just sit down somewhere and fall asleep and not bother waking up.'

'Isobel!' She sounded horrified. 'You don't mean that.'

'I don't know what I mean,' I said miserably. 'I don't care any more.'

'Oh, Isobel.' She put her arm around me. 'Don't feel

like that! Of course you care about things. You just need something to keep you interested.'

'Like what?' I looked at her. 'Like what? My whole life is pretty useless. What have I ever done, ever achieved? I've got a crummy job in a boring paper factory; despite all my talk I haven't managed to move out of the family home; I've lost my fiancé and I can't get over it. I'm hopeless.'

'No, you're not,' said Julie firmly. 'You're depressed and feeling sorry for yourself, but you're not hopeless. And you'll get over Tim, you know you will.'

'But I don't want to get over him,' I cried. 'I want to love him!'

Julie sighed. 'There's no point in wanting that.'

'I can't switch it off,' I said. 'I thought I could. But he's in my mind, in my heart, in my dreams. All the time. I can't see anything or do anything without thinking of what it would be like with him. I thought it would get easier with time, Julie, but it's not. It's worse.'

'Oh, God,' said Julie as she put her arm around me again. 'I wish I could help. Truly I do.'

There was no one who could help me. I thought that maybe I was really ill. A girl I'd gone to school with, Eilish Murphy, had been off for an entire term with depression. We'd laughed about it in the cloakrooms, wondering what on earth someone who had porcelain skin and sapphire-blue eyes had to be depressed about. Someone said it was because she'd split up with her boyfriend but I was convinced that there had to be more to it than that. Now, I wasn't so sure. And I hated the me that had mocked Eilish behind her back. I was sure people were mocking me.

One evening, when I was alone in the house, I took out the phone book and looked up Tim's name. It felt strange to see it there, in black and white, confirming that he still existed. I touched the print, feeling incredibly silly. *Malone, T. J., 8 Berkeley Mews, Donnybrook.* And his phone number. The phone number I knew off by heart.

I needed to talk to him, to hear his voice. Not to be with him, exactly, but to know that he was there. To share a couple of stories with him, perhaps. I picked up the phone and dialled, remembering to withold my number. It'd probably be the answering machine and I wouldn't leave a message. Didn't want him to think that I was a nutter.

'Hello.' His voice, well-remembered.

I opened my mouth but no sounds came out.

'Hello,' he said again.

I held the receiver away from me and looked at it.

'Hello.' Impatient this time.

I put the receiver back to my ear.

'Is there anyone there?' Angry now.

I said nothing, could say nothing.

He replaced the receiver at his end. I listened to the buzz of the line.

I hung up. My hands were trembling, my knees shaking. I swallowed a few times, then dialled again.

'Hello?'

I still couldn't speak.

'Look, is this the same person as before? I can't hear you.'

Of course you can't, I thought. I'm not speaking. But you should know it's me, Tim. You should sense it.

'If it's a real phone call, try later. If you're some crack-head, then piss off!'

I smiled bitterly. 'Piss off,' I mouthed silently.

He hung up.

I dialled again.

'Yes.'

I love you, Tim. I sent the message to him by thought. Surely he'd understand. Surely he knew it was me. Who else could ring him?

'If you don't stop this, I'm calling the police.'

But not for me, Tim. You can't call the police for me.

He hung up again. I dialled his number once more. But he'd left the phone off the hook. I supposed I would have done the same.

I wondered if I was going a little bit crazy. I didn't think so but I couldn't be sure. The last week or two had seemed so unreal. It was as though I was alive but not living. Watching everything rather than being part of it.

I'd ring him again later. I needed to hear his voice.

I brought Julie to the airport. She bubbled with excitement at the prospect of seeing Andreas the Greek.

'I know it'll probably be completely different,' she told me as we sat in the coffee shop together. 'But I have to know.'

'He was really nice,' I assured her. 'He probably won't want to let you come home.'

'I'll have to come home.' She grinned and broke a piece off her pastry. 'I don't have any more holidays left.'

'You're a lucky bitch going to the States like this,' I said.

'Andy was hoping that you and Ari—' Julie made a face.

'He's *gay*, Julie, for heaven's sake!' I shook my head. 'I certainly wouldn't try pursuing a gay man. Do irreparable damage to both our psyches! Besides, even if he wasn't gay, he wasn't my type.'

'Nobody's your type right now,' she told me.

'I know.' I spooned the froth from the top of my cappuccino. 'I'm beginning to think that Alison's right. I shouldn't get married.'

'I bet you anything she's hitched before she's twenty-five.' Julie grinned at me. 'And she'll have you hard at work making some fairy-tale wedding dress for her.'

I said nothing.

'You haven't done any dressmaking in ages,' Julie continued.

'Haven't felt like it,' I said shortly. How could I? When nearly everything I did was a wedding dress or a bridesmaid's dress? Where could I summon up the enthusiasm for that?

Julie looked at her watch. 'I suppose I'd better get going.'

I walked to the departure area with her.

'Have a good time,' I said. 'Don't do anything I wouldn't!'

'Gives me great scope,' she giggled. She hugged me. 'Thanks for the lift. See you in a week.'

'See you,' I said as she walked away.

The following Friday I went out with the girls from work. We went to the Orchard for a few drinks, then into town for something to eat.

I wasn't hungry. My head ached from the drink which was stupid because I should have been able to drink more than two beers without feeling weird. But I still felt detached from reality, still felt that there was someone else living my life.

Marion was in good humour. 'I don't get out enough by myself,' she said as she ordered Pavlova for dessert.

'The trouble about being married and having kids is that you always put them first.'

'Not always, surely,' said Niamh. 'After all, you have a life too.'

'I know,' Marion said. 'But my life is so tied up in their lives. You have kids, you want everything for them.' She shrugged. 'I like what I have but I like to get out.'

'I like getting out, too.' Niamh was the youngest in the office, she was twenty. 'I can't imagine what it'd be like to have children.'

'My sister is always tired,' said Lesley. 'She had her second during the summer. He's a lovely baby but he just cries and cries. Poor Simone is exhausted. Even though Stephen wants to help, Noel won't go to anyone but his mother. And Phoebe is so jealous! Simone is afraid that she'll try to poke Noel's eyes out or something.'

'That's terrible,' said Anna.

'They usually get over it.' Marion's eyes lit up as the Pavlova was put in front of her. 'Joyce hated Len when he was born, but it only lasted a few months. And she adored Betsy. Still does.'

I listened to the conversation but didn't participate. I'd no interest in talking about babies and children.

Everyone wanted to go to a nightclub but I was too tired. They didn't try too hard to persuade me – I knew that I'd been a drag all evening. I'd wanted to be bright and witty and cheerful, but I couldn't.

So I walked down Grafton Street, swarming with people at midnight, and stayed miserable.

Tim was standing outside River Island. He wore black jeans, a white shirt and a multi-coloured waistcoat. He needed a haircut. There were three other people with him. All male, I noted with some relief. They were talking animatedly.

I didn't know whether to go over to them or not. I

stood indecisively outside McDonald's among a chattering throng of teenagers and wondered where Tim and his friends were headed. Suddenly Tim nodded to them and began to walk towards College Green. I hurried after him. Tim always walked quickly. I was getting breathless as I tried to catch up with him.

He stopped at the pedestrian lights and I stood beside him.

'Hi,' I said casually.

He turned around in surprise. 'Isobel.'

'That's me.' I smiled at him. My smile was safe, friendly.

'How are you?' he asked.

'Great. You?'

'Not bad,' he said. 'I was out with some friends.'

'Me too.'

The lights changed and we both crossed the road.

'Where are you off to now?' I asked.

'Home.'

'You should have gone the other way to try for a taxi,' I said, nodding at the long queue. 'It takes for ever.'

'I have my car,' said Tim. 'I parked it in a sidestreet.'

'You'll have been clamped,' I told him. 'Or towed away.'

'Probably.' He grinned at me. 'But that's life.'

I wished he hadn't smiled. His face lit up when he smiled.

'Are you going home?' he asked.

I nodded.

'Do you want a lift?'

'It's the wrong way,' I said.

'I don't mind,' said Tim. 'I don't like to think of you hanging around here on your own.'

'If you're sure—?'

'Of course I'm sure. I wouldn't have said it otherwise.'

'Thanks.' I followed him through the streets until we came to his car. Still there, no ticket, not clamped.

'You see,' said Tim. 'You gotta take a chance.'

I fastened the seat belt as Tim started the car.

'So, how's everyone?' he asked.

'Fine.'

'Alison?'

'She's great.'

'Got a job yet?'

Alison had a degree in town planning, but she was working in a shoe shop at the moment.

'No,' I said. Alison didn't regard the shoe shop as a job.

'She'll get something eventually.' Tim went through amber lights on O'Connell Bridge and I winced.

'She hopes so.' I shifted in the seat. 'How is the Saracen project coming along?'

'Completed, thanks,' he said. 'It was one of those nightmare things. Seemed so simple but we kept running into stupid problems all the time.'

'How's Laura?' I asked casually.

'She's in California at the moment,' he replied. 'Lucky cow.'

'Very,' I said. 'Julie's in Florida.'

'Is she? Holidaying again?'

'Remember I told you that she'd met a bloke in Rhodes? A Greek American?'

He furrowed his brow.

'I did tell you,' I said. 'Anyway, she's gone to see him.'

Tim whistled. 'A holiday romance!'

'Maybe,' I said. 'I can't see it coming to much myself, but you never know.'

I clasped my hands together. I was suddenly conscious of my ringless engagement finger. I rubbed it gently and wondered what Tim had done with my ring.

He turned on the radio. They were playing sixties songs. Tim liked the sounds of the sixties. I always told him that he was just being pretentious.

We drew up outside my house. The windows were in darkness.

'Thanks for the lift,' I said. 'It was very good of you.'

'No problem,' said Tim.

'Drive safely home.'

He laughed. 'Isobel!'

'Sorry,' I said. 'I know, I sound like your mother.'

'Not quite,' he said. 'But almost.'

There was real amusement in his voice. I turned to him and smiled. 'And wear your vest when it's cold.'

He laughed again. 'Goodnight, Isobel.'

'Goodnight, Tim.'

I hadn't meant to kiss him and I hadn't meant to let him kiss me. But it was one of those things that just happened. One minute we were sitting in the car as polite friends, the next we were kissing as though we were lovers who hadn't seen each other in years. Which we almost were, I told myself as I kissed him. His kisses were long and searching. I let him hold me, revelling in the warmth of his body and the strength of his arms.

'Isobel,' he murmured as he came up for air.

'Oh, Tim,' I gasped. 'I've missed you so much.'

He broke away from me and regarded me with his huge, thoughtful eyes.

'I'm sorry,' he said. 'That was a mistake.'

I stared at him. 'A mistake?'

'I shouldn't have kissed you. It wasn't fair.'

'On who?'

'On you. On me.'

'Why wasn't it fair?' I tried to calm my racing heart.

'You know why,' said Tim. 'I'm sorry.'

I touched him on the cheek. He recoiled as though I'd slapped him.

'I'm not trying to hurt you,' I said.

'But I'll hurt you,' said Tim. 'I don't want to hurt you any more than I already have.'

I counted to ten. I had to be calm. 'It's OK. We're friends.'

'Are you sure?' Tim looked curiously at me.

'Of course. A kiss between friends.' I laughed lightly.

'I haven't been a very good friend to you.'

'You have tonight,' I said. 'You drove me all the way out here.'

'I'd have done that for anyone,' said Tim.

'But you did it for me.'

'I'd better go,' he said.

'Are you sure? Do you want to come in and have coffee?'

He shook his head. 'Really. I have to go.'

'OK.'

'Take care, Isobel,' he said as I got out of the car.

'Give me a call sometime.' I waved at him as he drove away.

I hugged his kiss to me as I got into bed. Of course he'd been shocked when he kissed me. Surprised, I guessed, at the depth of the passion that was still there. He still loved me, I thought. Must still love me. To drive out of his way like that. To kiss me in the way he did. He might not be ready to live with me but he hadn't got over me yet.

I fell asleep cuddling my pillow and dreamed of him again.

~

I wasn't going to ring him but I did. Saturday afternoon, when Ian and Dad were watching *Grandstand* on TV,

Mum had gone shopping and Alison was working. I dithered around beside the phone for a while, then dialled Tim's number.

Sometimes I thought that the person who invented the answering-machine should be shot. Tim could be at home, working, but I wouldn't know because I hated leaving messages for him. Besides, there wasn't a message I could leave. I hadn't any real reason to ring him, I just wanted to talk. I listened to him telling me to leave my name and number after the tone and hung up without saying anything.

I wished Julie was here. I didn't want to be on my own. I wanted to talk to someone about Tim and, even though Julie would simply tell me that I was off my head to still care for him, I needed to talk about him.

In the light of day, and without a couple of drinks inside me, I knew that I was silly to think he might still care. So he drove me home. So what? He didn't take me up on my offer of coffee (couldn't I have thought of something more original?) and he didn't try to raise false hopes by saying anything remotely loving to me. But he'd kissed me and it had been the sort of kiss that you dream about. So maybe he did still love me. I shook my head. Why is life so complex? Why aren't things more cut and dried? Tim dumped me – it was over. That's how things should have been. I should hate him. Yet I couldn't do that and, no matter how much I tried, I couldn't prise him out of my heart.

I rang later that evening, too, but this time the machine was switched off and nobody answered the phone. I wondered where he'd gone, who he was with, what he was doing. When I woke up at four o'clock in the morning I had to fight the impulse to ring him then, to talk to him while he lay in bed, hair tousled, eyes dulled by sleep.

Grow up, I told myself as I thumped my pillow. You're twenty-seven, not seventeen.

~

Barry wasn't in on Monday. He phoned the office to say that he was going to Cork to meet someone and that he'd be out for the day. I had things to do but I wasn't wildly busy. At eleven o'clock I rang Tim's office.

'He's away,' Shauna told me. 'He's in California.'

'California,' I repeated dully.

'Yes,' she said. 'There was a presentation on the Saracen project. Tim, Jack Benson and Laura Hart have gone.'

'Oh,' I said.

'He'll be back next week.' I could hear the curiosity in Shauna's voice. 'Was there anything urgent, Isobel?'

'No,' I said. 'Nothing at all.'

I stared blankly in front of me. He was in California. He was in California with Laura. Laura who looked like Isobel, only more beautiful. Laura who knew what he was talking about when he said things like 'Token Ring' and 'Ethernet' and 'Extension Folders', all of which used to send me into a fit of giggles. Tim was in California with Laura and I was a fool.

'We're going bowling after work.' Lesley stood in front of me. I hadn't even noticed her. 'D'you want to come?'

I blinked at her and shook my head. 'Things to do.'

'Like what?' demanded Lesley.

'Bits and pieces,' I said.

'Oh, come on, Isobel. You can't sit around doing nothing your whole life.'

'I'm not,' I told her. 'I'm making a dress for a friend. She's coming around for a fitting tonight.'

'Oh.' Lesley looked abashed and I thought how easy it was to lie to people. 'OK.'

'Have a good time, though,' I said as I rummaged around in my desk drawer for something to do.

'Sure,' said Lesley. 'Next time, maybe.'

'Next time,' I said.

My fingers closed around a set of keys. I'd forgotten that they were there. Keys to Tim's house. The spare set. I'd given him back my keys but I'd forgotten about the spare set. I supposed he'd forgotten too.

I stared at them in my hand. I should post them through his letterbox. There was no need to leave a note or anything, he'd know they were from me.

I left work early and drove to his house. His car wasn't there. I stood at the front door and opened the letterbox while I clutched the keys in my hand. It seemed such a final thing to do. I debated with myself for a moment, then unlocked the door.

As the alarm beeped at me I hoped that Tim hadn't changed the code. I couldn't quite see how I could explain myself to the guards if they arrived. He was my fiancé, officer, and I was returning a set of keys. It sounded lame.

But the numbers were still the same. The silence of the empty house wrapped itself around me and I felt light-headed from simply being there. The last time I'd done this, there had been a reason and Tim and I were still engaged – however tenuously. This time I had no right to be there whatsoever. I was probably committing some sort of crime although it couldn't really be breaking and entering when I hadn't actually broken anything. I closed the hall door gently behind me.

It was unnaturally tidy. Cups and saucers were washed and stacked neatly on the drainer. There were no foil containers half-filled with curry, no magazines and workpads strewn across the living-room floor. Even the desk where his computer sat, silent and dark, was tidy. Well, that was going too far, tidier than usual anyway. It didn't look like Tim's house any more. I didn't feel part of it any more.

I tiptoed upstairs. My heart was pounding. I kept telling myself that I'd no right to be here and that I should go home straight away but I couldn't stop myself. God, I thought suddenly, what if he's still here after all? What if he only pretended to go to California and he's here, in bed, with the lovely Laura? I nearly vomited onto the stairs at the thought.

The bedroom was empty, but the bed was neatly made. I stood in the doorway and looked around. A gleam of light caught my eye and I walked over to the dresser.

My engagement ring lay there and it was the diamonds that had sparkled. I picked it up and slipped it back onto my finger again, but it seemed to burn against my flesh and I knew that I shouldn't have done it. I replaced it carefully on the dresser and looked at the other jewellery that was there – a signet ring that I'd given Tim when we got engaged and a pair of earrings that didn't belong to me. The stones shone blood-red in the gold setting.

I stood there for a moment feeling dizzy. Then I took the earrings and flushed them down the toilet.

I don't know how long I stood in the bathroom. Time didn't have any meaning for me and my legs were frozen. I couldn't move, couldn't think.

The sound of a car pulling up outside finally galvanised me into action. I ran back into the bedroom and peeped out through the net curtains. Tim's next-door neighbours were arriving home. I heaved a sigh of relief and went downstairs again. I'd have to wait until they were safely indoors – I didn't want to meet them and risk them telling Tim that they'd seen me.

I stood beside the silent computer and couldn't resist the urge to switch it on. It whirred and gurgled into life as the icons popped onto the screen. I dragged the file entitled 'Saracen 2' into the trash. I knew that Tim, like all good programmers, would have backed up his files. And that he probably had files at work as well as at home. So I wouldn't be doing anything more than inconveniencing him by my actions. I slid the disk that he'd so carefully labelled into the zip drive and dragged its contents into the trash too. Then I selected the *Empty Trash* command.

'*The trash contains 4 items which use 30mb of disk space. Are you sure you want to permanently remove these items?*' asked the computer. I clicked on the OK icon and watched the files disappear.

Then I replaced the disk in its box and switched off the computer. I put the second set of keys to the back of Tim's desk drawer where he wouldn't find them for ages, set the alarm and drove home.

Chapter 8

Mother and Child (Pablo Picasso, 1971)

Tim didn't ring to find out whether it was me who'd erased the data on his machine. I didn't know whether he'd even noticed – whether, perhaps, he thought that he'd managed to erase it himself. He never rang looking for the second set of keys either, so I presumed that he'd forgotten about them or that he'd found them in the desk and imagined that he'd put them there himself.

I waited for him to call, of course. Each time the phone rang my heart started to thump in my chest and I was sure that everyone could hear it. But they continued to take their phone calls – Mum's friends at the bowling club, Ian's pals, Dad's workmates, Alison's eclectic gathering of friends. Julie was the only one who telephoned me. I hadn't realised that my circle of friends had dwindled so much over the past few years. But I'd lost touch with a lot of people when I'd started going out with Tim. The only other phone calls for me were from people asking me to do dresses, but I hadn't the heart to accept any orders. I didn't feel able to do a wedding dress again, and all of the calls were for wedding dresses.

I still lived each day in a world of my own. I knew that

I was going through the motions – that I was getting my work done, sitting around at home, occasionally going out – but all of those things seemed to be happening to someone else, not to me. Sometimes – despite my desperate efforts to be always efficient – Barry had to buzz the intercom on my desk a couple of times before I even realised that he'd called me; sometimes I read whole chapters of books before I noticed that I'd read them before; sometimes I sat through entire TV programmes without remembering a single thing that had happened on them.

I still thought about moving out of the house but I couldn't summon up the enthusiasm to go apartment-hunting. That was my trouble – I couldn't summon up the enthusiasm to do anything very much.

The days grew shorter, the weather more atrocious, the thought of dragging myself out of bed every morning more and more difficult.

Every now and then I sat at my desk and typed Tim's name onto my computer screen over and over again in one big word – *TimTimTimTim* – until someone approached and I deleted it with a single keystroke. Sometimes I still practised how my signature should have looked, writing Isobel Malone in my big, loopy handwriting before shredding the paper I'd written on into tiny pieces. Sometimes I told myself that I was better off without him; that, when I got over things properly, I'd be thanking God it was over between us.

And sometimes I disappeared into the loo and bawled my eyes out as quietly as I could.

Andy Jordan was visiting Ireland for Christmas. Julie had invited him when she was in Florida and he'd accepted straight away. Julie was crazy about Andy and I was pleased for her but envied her too.

'He makes me feel all fizzy inside,' she confided one

evening when we'd gone for a drink together. 'Even when he talks utter rubbish, I enjoy listening to him speak!'

I laughed. 'That's because he sounds different. Makes him more attractive.'

'He is attractive, isn't he?' She beamed at me. 'You've only seen him in casual clothes, Isobel, but we went out to dinner one night when I was over there and he wore this fabulous suit. Navy-blue silk jacket and trousers! God, you'd never get an Irish man into navy-blue silk.'

She was probably right.

'I hope he won't freeze to death here,' she continued anxiously. 'He's never been anywhere really cold in his life.'

'I thought you said he went skiing in Colorado?'

She made another face. 'That's different. That's crisp cold. Not the dark, miserable sort of damp wetness that we get here.'

'I hope you didn't tell him that it'd be dark, miserable and damp,' I said.

'I told him to pack lots of jumpers and a raincoat. He said he didn't have a raincoat.'

'I bet he does,' I told her. 'He's only having you on, Julie.'

'D'you think so?' She shook her head, since last week a cascading tumble of auburn curls.

'Probably,' I said.

'I can't wait for him to get here. I bought him an Aran jumper for Christmas. Although he'll probably never get to wear it when he goes home!'

'There's probably not a great call for them in Florida,' I agreed.

I could see Tim in the maroon Aran jumper the night he'd told me that the wedding was off. I could see the pull in one of the diamond patterns where he'd caught the jumper on a nail in his garden shed. It was crystal clear, as though he was standing in front of me.

'Isobel?' Julie looked at me curiously. 'Are you OK?'

'Sure.' I let the image of Tim dissolve. There were only strangers surrounding us and none of them wore maroon Aran jumpers.

'You looked miles away.'

'Just thinking,' I said. 'What colour is the Aran?'

She stared at me as though I'd gone off my head. 'Cream, of course. Are you sure you're OK?'

'Of course I am,' I said impatiently. 'D'you want another drink?'

She shook her head. 'I'd better get home. I promised Mum I'd ice the cake for her tonight. Honestly, Isobel, you'd think she'd just go out and buy a cake like most people do these days, but no, it has to be home-made.'

'Mine's the same,' I said as I pulled on my soft red coat. 'Puddings, cakes, mince-pies – she does the lot! I wouldn't mind but she says she hates it.'

'Why does she bother?'

'I don't know. It's probably some primeval nurturing thing. Of course Ali goes mad and tells her not to bother – but my darling sister doesn't say no when a plate of mince-pies and cream is put in front of her!'

Julie laughed. 'I hope Andy has a good appetite when he comes over. Mum'll be very disappointed if he doesn't.'

'I'm sure he'll have a ravenous appetite,' I told her, 'and I bet it won't be for food.'

She made another face but she didn't tell me I was wrong.

Mum's sister, Rachel, her husband Dennis and their

fourteen-month-old baby daughter, Sorcha, were spending Christmas with us. Rachel and Dennis had moved to London when they married five years ago, but they wanted to come home for Christmas. They were going to spend three days with us and three days with my grandmother before going home. Rachel and Dennis were the only family we had. Mum and Rachel were Granny Behan's only children and Dad was an only child himself. There was a twelve-year age gap between my mother and her younger sister and Rachel sometimes seemed more like an older sister to me. I'd certainly never called her Aunt Rachel and it would have sent her into a fit of giggles if I had.

Rachel worked in an insurance company. I wasn't sure exactly what she did but she had an office of her own with her name on a chrome plate on the door, a company car and she earned a good salary. Dennis was a recruitment consultant in the City. Between them, they earned a lot of money.

I was taking sausage rolls out of the oven when Dad arrived home with them.

'Hello, Issy!' Rachel swept into the kitchen and threw her arms around me.

'Hi, Rachel, don't touch any of those, they're hot.' I pecked her on the cheek.

'Hello, Rachel,' said Mum.

'Helen! You look great!' Rachel hugged my mother and kissed her on both cheeks.

'Steady up,' warned Mum. 'You're not in London now. Although I didn't think they went in for all this kissing business in England.'

'Not usually,' admitted Rachel as she unwound a knitted scarf from her neck. 'I always wanted to come home like a prodigal emigrant and cause a fuss in the family.'

I laughed and Dennis walked into the room. Dennis was one of life's wonderful people. He wasn't hugely attractive – not the sort of man who'd draw gasps of admiration for his looks – but he was always kind and attentive and easy to get on with. Mum said he suited her flighty sister down to the ground because Dennis was a stabilising influence on her. For once I think my mum was right.

Dad followed them, carrying Sorcha.

'Good God,' I exclaimed as he came into the room. 'She's grown!'

The last time I'd seen the baby had been at her christening, when she'd behaved very demurely and had slept through the entire ceremony, only opening her dark-blue eyes when the priest splashed water on her forehead but never uttering a sound.

'She weighs a ton,' moaned Dad as he set her down on the floor and she tottered unsteadily towards a chair.

'She's lovely.' Mum wore the particular besotted look that most women use when they're looking at babies. 'Isn't she a pet?'

'I hope you think so when she wakes up screaming in the middle of the night,' said Rachel darkly. 'She's teething at the moment. See how red her cheeks are? They're driving her mad.'

'Poor little thing.' Mum picked her up and cuddled her. 'Don't you worry, honey, we'll look after you.'

Sorcha beamed at Mum, nestled up to her, then bit her on the ear.

'Sorcha!' Rachel looked horrified but Mum pretended she wasn't hurt.

I chuckled to myself as I put the sausage rolls on a wire cooling tray.

'So, how's business, Dennis?' The men disappeared into the living room while we stood around the kitchen.

Mum was still rubbing her earlobe while Sorcha had buried her face in her mother's chest.

'She's tired,' said Rachel apologetically. 'She does things like that when she's tired.'

'Do you want to put her to bed?' asked Mum. 'Or would you like some tea or coffee first?'

'Tea would be great,' said Rachel. 'I'll give her some milk and a biscuit. The gnawing should help.'

It was after midnight when we finally got to bed but I didn't care that it was late because I didn't have to go to work on Christmas Eve and I knew I could lie in bed in the morning.

~

I didn't get much sleep on Christmas Eve morning, or on Christmas Day either. Sorcha was awake at six and insisted on going on a tour of the house both mornings.

By Christmas night, Rachel confessed that Sorcha's insatiable curiosity and boundless energy were sometimes exhausting.

'You were like that too,' said Mum.

'As a child, perhaps,' Rachel said. 'Not now.'

'You should have had her sooner,' Mum told her. 'Then you wouldn't be so tired. It's much harder when you're an older mother.'

There was a taut little silence and Rachel raised an eyebrow. 'I hope you don't mean that the way it sounded, Helen.'

Mum looked uncomfortable. 'Probably not. It's just so tiring looking after children. I was tired when Isobel was born. I can't imagine what it must be like for you, at work all the time, rushing around the place. And that little bit older.'

'I'm fourteen years older than you were when you had Isobel,' grinned Rachel. 'And I know that it's exhausting. But I'm in good shape, good health and I have a wonderful husband who looks after both of us.' She squeezed Dennis's arm affectionately.

'I don't think it's a good idea to work and have a child. Particularly late in life.' Mum persisted with the conversation and I could have shot her.

'Don't be so old-fashioned.' Rachel bounced Sorcha on her knee. 'I couldn't look after myself when I was in my twenties, let alone another person.' She smiled at Mum. 'Look at her, Helen! She's completely dependent on me. Can you imagine her being completely dependent on me when I was in my early twenties?'

Mum looked abashed. 'No.'

'You see?' Rachel tickled Sorcha under the chin and the baby squealed in delight. 'You see? My big sister is just a nag, Sorcha. Just – a – nag!' She held the baby over her head and both of them laughed uproariously.

Mum sighed and opened a box of Dairy Milk. We sat back and watched the movie.

~

I offered to baby-sit on St Stephen's Day while Mum, Dad, Rachel and Dennis went out together.

'You're sure you can manage?' Rachel looked unusually worried.

'Rachel! I have a younger brother and a younger sister. It comes back to you, you know.'

'She should be OK but she might fret because she's in a strange house.'

'We'll be fine,' I promised. 'Honestly.' It was strange to see Rachel looking so worried. I guessed that motherhood did that to even the most laid-back of people. 'Honestly,'

I repeated, 'once you've put her to bed there isn't exactly a lot to do.'

Eventually they went out, followed shortly by Ian (meeting his mates) and Alison, who refused to say where she was going.

'You're not my guardian,' she snapped when I asked.

'OK, OK.' I made a face at her. 'Do whatever you like. I don't care.'

It was odd to be in the house on my own with a baby. Rachel had set up the baby monitor so I curled up in the armchair with *Wuthering Heights.* My reading material was still bleak. I couldn't take sugary sentiment, especially at Christmas.

I peeked in on Sorcha an hour later. She lay stretched out in the cot that Mum had borrowed from a neighbour, one hand gently resting on her cheek. She was so pretty, so small, so vulnerable. I knew that I was looking at her in the exact same gooey way as Mum looked at her. But it was hard not to. God, I thought, wouldn't it be great to be a baby again. Nothing to worry you, just lie there and wait for people to pander to your every whim.

I leaned over and touched her. Her skin was soft and warm. It must be incredible to have a baby of your very own, I thought. Someone that was part of you. What must it be like to touch a person that you had created yourself? I resolutely put images of Tim out of my mind. I didn't want to think of the baby I could have created with Tim.

She woke up around midnight. I shot out of the chair as her thin wail came from the baby monitor and ran upstairs two at a time. She was sitting up in the cot, eyes laden with tears, cheeks wet.

'What's the matter?' I asked. 'What's wrong?'

She wailed again.

I picked her up and she stopped crying. I held her

close to me and breathed in her baby smell. 'Are you all right?'

Her cry was more half-hearted this time. I walked around the bedroom with her, rocking her gently in my arms. 'Who's a good baby?' I asked, then laughed at the absurdity of the question.

She stared at me, her eyes huge in her round face. 'You're so lovely,' I whispered and held her close to me.

I sat down in the high-backed wicker chair in the corner of the room. It was peaceful holding her like this. It was nice to feel that someone needed me. I felt more relaxed than I had in ages. Sorcha opened her eyes and looked straight at me. I leaned down to her and kissed her. Her eyes flickered, then closed.

I woke up when Rachel pushed the bedroom door open and tiptoed inside. Even when I woke I didn't move so that the sleeping baby was undisturbed. I was amazed that I'd slept holding her in my arms.

Rachel smiled at us. 'Was she a lot of trouble?'

I shook my head. 'She woke up and whimpered for a few minutes, then fell asleep again.' I shifted in the chair and pins and needles ran through my arm. I grimaced and Rachel laughed under her breath.

'She's heavy,' I said.

'I know.' Rachel gathered her from me and put her back in the cot. Sorcha sighed deeply but stayed sleeping. We stood and looked in at her.

'They're so innocent,' said Rachel wistfully.

'It's hard to imagine that either of us was once that small,' I said.

'Everybody says that they grow so fast, too.' Rachel rearranged the pink and yellow blanket over her daughter.

'Will you have any more?' I asked.

'I don't know,' replied Rachel. 'I'd like to, I think. It's hard work, though.'

'Give up your job,' I said blithely. 'Follow Mum's advice. Then you'll have plenty of time and you won't be so tired.'

'I think you get tired anyway.' Rachel smiled at me. 'And I wouldn't dream of giving up my job. I've worked too hard to get where I am.'

'I think I'd give up mine,' I said dreamily. 'It would be wonderful not to have to clock in every morning.'

Rachel was silent for a moment. 'So how are you doing?' she asked finally. 'Since you broke up with Tim?'

I'd wondered when she was going to ask me, how she'd work it into the conversation. I knew that eventually she'd have to ask. I'd want to ask if I were her.

'Fine,' I said.

'You sure?'

'Of course.' I was *not* going to cry, I told myself. There was no need to cry. It was eight months later, for God's sake!

'Must have been pretty horrible for you.'

'Mmm.'

'And I guess Helen wasn't a lot of help.'

'She was a bit cut up about it,' I admitted.

'Gone out with anyone else?' asked Rachel casually.

'You must be joking!' I laughed bitterly.

'Oh, come on. You'll want to go out with someone else,' Rachel said. 'You know you will. Have you got over him?'

'I don't know,' I said, and started to cry again.

Rachel said nothing but handed me a tissue from the box beside the cot. I wiped my eyes, blew my nose and took a puff of my inhaler.

'You haven't got over him?'

'I keep thinking I have,' I said. 'And then something happens and I start to cry like this all over again. It's not fair, Rachel. I've tried, really I have. But he won't go away. I imagine him all the time. Everywhere I go, everything I do, he's there in the background. When I go out with the girls – admittedly not very often – I think of how I should be a married woman. When I go out with my pal, Julie, she talks about her boyfriend and I feel a total failure. When I drive around town I see places we've been, pubs we've been in, cinemas, restaurants, everything! And I can't look anywhere without seeing him there!'

'Oh, Isobel.' She put her arms around me and hugged me to her. 'It'll get easier, truly it will.'

'Everybody says that,' I sniffled. 'But nobody knows. They're just assuming.'

She reached out for another tissue and I took it from her.

'Why don't you come to London for a while?' she asked. 'Get a job there, give yourself a bit of a break.'

'I don't think so,' I said. 'I've never wanted to work in London.'

'But it would break the cycle for you,' said Rachel. 'You wouldn't picture Tim everywhere you went. You'd be with a whole new set of people. It'd be good for you, Isobel.'

I sighed. 'Maybe.'

'Definitely,' she said. 'Why don't you give a few of the agencies a ring? They're crying out for good secretarial and admin staff. I bet you your first week's salary that you'll get a job straight away.'

I smiled weakly. 'I'll think about it.'

'Promise me,' said Rachel. 'Don't just say it.'

'I promise,' I said. 'I really promise.'

I went to a New Year's Eve Ball with Julie and Andy.

I didn't want to go because I thought that I'd be a wallflower and a gooseberry all at the same time, but both of them insisted. It was for a good cause, Julie told me, as she handed me the ticket and asked for a cheque. The more people that came along the better.

I took my midnight-blue cocktail dress from the wardrobe. I hadn't worn that since the night of Tim's software dinner. I was certain I could smell the lingering traces of *Ralph Lauren* but I'd had the dress cleaned since then so it wasn't possible.

'You look wonderful,' said Andy as I got into the taxi with them.

'Thank you.'

'Fabulous dress,' said Julie. 'Did you make it yourself?'

I nodded. 'Ages ago. It's nearly two years old.'

'It's ageless,' said Julie. She wore a black sheath dress with a tiny diamond brooch on the shoulder. With her auburn curls piled on top of her head she was about six feet tall and looked extremely elegant. She'd had her nails done, I noticed. Julie was an occasional nail-biter, but tonight they were long, even and polished a vibrant red. 'Sculptured,' she whispered when I nodded at them.

'Look great,' I whispered back.

'I'm getting left out of things,' Andy complained and Julie laughed and told him we were having a girly conversation and he should just butt out.

The hotel was crowded with people in party dress, crushing their way to the bar. A silver banner wished us all a Happy New Year and a band mangled some well-known melodies. I sighed. I wished I hadn't come. It was all very well to say that I'd done it because it was for a good cause, but if I wanted to support a good cause I should have just given Julie the money.

I hated New Year at the best of times. Everyone being nice to everyone else, singing stupid songs, making stupid resolutions, grimly determined to have a good time.

'Southern Comfort on the rocks.' Andy handed me a drink.

'Thanks.' He stood there with Julie's gin and tonic in his hand. 'She'll be back in a minute,' I told him.

He put the drink on a nearby table. 'So how are you doing?' he asked. 'Gotten over your ex-boyfriend yet?'

'Sort of,' I replied. I took a gulp of Southern Comfort and enjoyed the warm glow of the alcohol as it went down.

'You're far too nice to worry about a shit like that,' said Andy.

'He wasn't a shit,' I said.

'Of course he was.' Andy looked angry. 'You don't leave a lady at the altar.'

'He didn't quite leave me at the altar.' I laughed and was surprised that it came out as a genuine laugh and not somewhere between a laugh and a sob. 'There were two weeks to go, you know.'

'Even so.' Andy still looked angry. 'It wasn't a very nice thing to do.'

'No, it wasn't,' I agreed. 'But it was better than getting married and then deciding that it was all a horrible mistake.'

'Julie told me that you went out with him for a while afterwards,' he said. 'Why on earth would you want to?'

'Because I thought that we might get back together. I still cared about him.'

Andy shook his head. 'I don't understand women. I never will.'

'You're not meant to understand us,' I teased.

'Not meant to understand what?' asked Julie.

'Women,' I told her.

'Exactly,' she said. 'You just have to love us.'

'Oh, I sure do that.' Andy smiled at her. 'Do you want to dance with me?'

She looked at me enquiringly.

'I don't mind,' I said. 'Go ahead.'

They walked onto the dance floor and he put his arms around her. He really was very attractive, I realised. I wondered if Ari had been as attractive. They'd looked alike, I remembered, but I wasn't sure how alike they'd been. I couldn't recall Ari very much – I couldn't conjure up his face.

I finished my drink and went to the bar. I wondered if I'd get blind drunk tonight. Maybe I should. Maybe my New Year's resolution should be to spend the next year in a haze of alcohol which would numb me completely so I wouldn't think about Tim or feel devastated whenever I realised that he wasn't part of my life any more.

I knew that I wouldn't. I didn't get drunk very often because, if I did, I usually had a raging hangover the next day. Besides, I didn't really like being drunk. I didn't like the loss of control, the muzzy, floating feeling. I drank another Southern Comfort and reflected that I could always just get drunk tonight.

Julie and Andy didn't mean to leave me alone for huge chunks of the evening but they spent ages wrapped around each other, swaying to the music and oblivious to everybody else.

At midnight we formed a circle and counted down to the New Year, the band played Auld Lang Syne and everybody kissed and hugged each other. Julie told me that this year would be the best year ever for me and I smiled and said that I hoped so. Andy hugged me and told me that Ari had said hello and that his brother thought I was one of the nicest girls he'd ever met and if I wanted to come to the States later in the year he was sure that Ari would be delighted to see me. I put my arms around them both and said that they were wonderful friends.

Andy ordered champagne and popped the cork very expertly so that none of the drink was wasted. I decided that if I was going to have a hangover, a champagne hangover was more exclusive than any other sort and I might as well drink it.

I suppose I had a good time. I wasn't really sure. I wondered would the time come when I could feel properly again, when I would know that I was happy or when I knew that I was sad. I watched Julie and Andy share a private joke and I cried inside.

I had a really rotten hangover the next day.

Chapter 9

Spain (Salvador Dalí, 1938)

The apartment was dark. The heavy, lined curtains effectively blocked out the light and the gentle heat of the afternoon sun. I supposed that in the summer months I'd be grateful for that but right now I wanted light and I wanted warmth. I pulled the curtains apart and stepped out onto the balcony.

It wasn't much of a view. I stared across the city at the jumble of apartment buildings and office blocks so different from the Dublin skyline I was used to. There were no landmarks for me, each building was new and unfamiliar. I felt my breath catch in my throat as I suddenly realised how very alone I was.

I hadn't chosen Spain. It had never been a lifetime's ambition to come and work here, but when the opportunity arose I knew that I'd be mad not to take it. Coming to Spain meant getting away from Dublin and its incessant reminders of Tim and how bloody awful my life had been since we split up. For the second time, I reminded myself. And, after all, the second time I'd been the one to pull the plug.

But it still didn't feel like that. I might have been the person who said it wasn't working, but I still felt like the person who'd been let down. I knew plenty of women would think that I was a complete loser, some sort of pre-feminist sad case, but I couldn't help it. Despite trying to fool myself day after day, I knew that things weren't getting any better.

And landing the job in Spain avoided the possible unpleasantness of Barry deciding to sack me.

After he called me into his office to 'talk to me' I tried really hard to get back to my old self. But my old self was too bound up in what I used to be – Tim's fiancée. Sometimes I'd walk into the coffee room at DeltaPrint and the chatter would stop and I'd know without a shadow of a doubt that I was the topic of conversation. Of course I was – nothing this dramatic had happened in DeltaPrint before.

Occasionally, I'd take a half-hearted look through the papers to see if there was another job. I told myself that Rachel was right, I'd be better somewhere else, but I looked without enthusiasm and was never convinced that I'd find anything to suit me. Barry caught me reading the *Guardian* supplement one day. I tried to close it as he walked by the desk but I only succeeded in knocking a box of paper-clips onto the floor in front of him.

'Oh, God, Barry, I'm sorry!' I scrabbled under the desk to retrieve them.

'Come into my office, Isobel.' Not a request – a demand. Very unlike him.

I perched on the edge of the chair and looked nervously at him. I hadn't made any huge mistakes, I was certain of it. Jim Loughlin had gone to London earlier in the day and I knew that I'd booked the right flight for him. I'd made backups of all the previous months' accounts. I'd confirmed Barry's attendance at the print and packaging conference at the IMI. There wasn't anything left to do.

He went straight to the point. 'It isn't working, Isobel.'

I stared at him.

'What d'you mean?'

'You know exactly what I mean.'

'But I've tried, Barry, honestly I have. And I know my work's been OK.'

'OK, maybe,' he said. 'But efficient, no. And it's so difficult to work with you now, Isobel. I'm afraid of saying the wrong thing and upsetting you.'

'You've never upset me,' I told him.

'That's because I try so hard not to.'

I was hurt and I felt the familiar sting of tears behind my eyes, but I said nothing.

'You don't act on your own initiative any more,' said Barry. 'I have to tell you to do things. I have to be on your case all the time. I have to check things in case you make mistakes.'

'I don't make mistakes,' I said tonelessly.

He sighed. 'No, you don't. But there's no joy in you any more, Isobel. No fun. No laughter.'

'I'm at work,' I said. 'There's no fun here anyway.'

'You didn't always feel like that.'

I studied my nails.

'However,' Barry paused and I looked up again. 'This might be of interest to you.'

He handed me a newspaper and I frowned because it was in Spanish. It took a few minutes for my Spanish to kick in. 'The actress and singer Madonna visited Madrid today,' I translated into English.

'Not that,' Barry interrupted. 'The advertisement beside it.'

'*Administrative Assistant. Fluent English. Computer literate. Required for prestigious training company.*' I glanced up at him.

'That's it,' he said. 'What do you think?'

'What d'you mean – what do I think?'

'Doesn't it sound like you?'

I looked at the paper again. 'Well, I suppose so, but it could be anybody. My English is fluent because it's my mother tongue. What about my Spanish?'

'You put on your CV that you were fluent in French and Spanish,' said Barry.

'I was,' I said. 'But I haven't spoken either of them in years.'

'I thought you went to Spain the year before last,' he said. 'Malaga, you said.'

'Yes, but Malaga is a touristy sort of city,' I pointed out. 'I didn't exactly need to use a lot of Spanish.'

'It doesn't matter,' said Barry. 'You're still fluent.'

'So what's this about?' I asked.

'Sharon's friend put that ad in the paper,' he told me. 'And Sharon thinks you'd fit the bill.'

Sharon was Barry's wife.

'Why did she think of me?' I asked.

'Because we talk about you at home,' said Barry. 'I asked her for advice on how best to deal with you and she gave it.'

'Get rid of me was the advice?' I stared at him.

'Don't be ridiculous,' he said. 'She thinks you need a change of scenery. Get away from Dublin for a while. Get out and about and have a good time.'

I swallowed the lump in my throat. 'I don't feel like doing that.'

'Not here, maybe,' said Barry. 'But, Isobel, Madrid! Think about it. Warm and sunny and such a beautiful city.'

Yeah, I thought, and me out of your hair.

'And if I'm not interested?'

'Isobel.' He frowned. 'Why shouldn't you be interested? It's a new life for you. You should be having fun, not sitting around moping over someone who isn't worth it. You're still young.'

I sighed. 'It's a big change.'

'You need a big change,' said Barry, 'and, Isobel, to be perfectly honest, I need a change from you.'

~

I stepped back from the balcony into the apartment. It was small but perfectly adequate. There was a living area, a galley kitchen, a bedroom and a bathroom. My first apartment, I told myself. A place of my own. I said it out loud to make it seem more real.

Gabriela Suarez, Sharon's friend and the Managing Director of Advanta, had organised the rental of the apartment for me. The company was paying my first month's rent, which was helpful. I was very grateful to Sharon for saying good things about me to Gabriela, but at the back of my mind I couldn't help thinking that they were all doing this to get me out of Barry's way. He had wanted to fire me, I thought bleakly, but he was afraid that it would tip me over the edge.

~

My mother nearly had a fit when I told her. She couldn't understand why I would leave my family and my well-paid job.

'I need a break,' I said.

'But why Spain? Why not somewhere in Ireland? Or London? Somewhere you can get home easily?'

'It's only a two-hour flight to Madrid,' I told her impatiently. 'I can come home any time I like.'

'It'll be too expensive,' she said. 'You won't be able to afford it.'

'There are plenty of cheap flights.'

She sighed. 'I don't like it, Isobel.'

'Oh, for God's sake.' I stared at her. 'I should have done this a long time ago.' I ignored the hurt look in her eyes.

~

'I don't believe you.' Julie looked at me in astonishment. We'd gone to the Bloody Stream for a drink and were wedged into a corner of the crowded bar. 'Madrid!'

'Why not?'

'No reason,' she said. 'I think it's absolutely marvellous. I'd love to go abroad to work. I don't know why I didn't.'

'I'm not sure about it,' I confessed. 'I know that Barry basically got me the job and I'm sure he did it because he couldn't stand me in the office any more.'

'He wouldn't have recommended you if he didn't think you could do it.'

'Sharon, his wife, recommended me.' I sipped my drink. 'I think she decided that I was driving her husband around the twist and she had to do something about it.'

Julie laughed. 'So what! It's a great opportunity, Isobel.'

'I know. But I'm scared.'

'Scared?'

'That I won't like it. That I'll be useless. That this Gabriela woman will hate me when she meets me.'

'Oh, don't be stupid.' Julie looked at me without any sympathy. 'You spend too much time navel-gazing, Isobel. Of course you'll like it. You won't be useless. And there's no reason for Gabriela to hate you.'

'I know,' I said. 'I just—'

'That bastard Malone sapped all your confidence,' said

Julie angrily. 'You never used to worry about new things before.'

'It's not that,' I said.

'It bloody is,' said Julie.

'I think it's great,' said Alison as we sat in the living room the night before I went. 'It means I'll have somewhere to stay if I want to get a break.'

'I'm glad that's all I mean to you.' I grinned at her.

'Don't be silly,' she said. 'It means I can have your bedroom too. More space for my stuff!'

'I wish I was going.' It was the first time in years Ian had been up before midday on a Saturday. 'I bet you'll have a great time.'

'I hope so,' I said.

'Send me photographs of gorgeous Spanish women,' he said.

'Why?'

'So's I can see what I'm missing.'

'There are plenty of gorgeous women at home,' said Alison severely.

'Not the same as continental women,' said Ian seriously. 'They all look so classy. They dress so well.'

I looked down at my frayed jeans. Ian was right. Continental women always looked sophisticated, even in frayed jeans. Whereas I looked as if I'd grabbed these out of the bottom of my wardrobe. I'd lost the ability to be stylish. I hadn't made a dress since the wedding dress. I hadn't bought new clothes in ages. Maybe Madrid was a good idea after all.

I opened my suitcase and began to unpack. I couldn't quite believe that I was here and that I didn't know when I'd be going home. It wasn't a holiday. I said that over and over again on the plane as we flew over the Pyrenees and I looked down at the snow-capped mountains. 'I'm going to live in Spain.' But it didn't sink in, somehow, and it still hadn't sunk in.

The only sound in the apartment was the faint hum of the fridge. Otherwise it was uncomfortably quiet. I couldn't even hear sounds from the adjoining apartments, and I wondered if anyone lived in them or whether they were vacant. I felt the quiver of loneliness again and tried to ignore it.

I went into the living area and switched on the portable TV for company. TVE was showing a football match between Real Madrid and Juventus.

I listened to the commentary as I continued to unpack, letting my ear become accustomed to the words and the cadence of the language. I'd been worried in case my Spanish had declined more than I thought, but I'd conversed reasonably well with Gabriela and now I could follow the commentator's anguish at the referee's decision to allow Juventus a free kick on the edge of the penalty area. '*Gooooo-aaa-lll!!!!*' he cried a moment later and I understood him when he said that Real were behind due to a monumental travesty of footballing justice.

Finally, all of my clothes were put away. I walked back into the living area and surveyed my apartment with the eye of someone who felt, marginally, more proprietorial.

It was sparsely furnished, but that wasn't a bad thing considering its size. A heavy darkwood table with four high-backed Spanish-style chairs was pushed against the counter that separated the living and kitchen areas. There was also a two-seater sofa and a small armchair. The TV stood on a corner unit with space for a video, but there wasn't any video. Not that I cared. I was relieved it had TV. That was it as far as the living room was concerned.

There wasn't room for furniture in the galley kitchen. There was an assortment of plates, cups and glasses in one cupboard and some knives and forks in the floor unit beside the sink.

I thought of the complete set of Royal Doulton china that Tim's aunt had given us as a wedding present and wondered what he had done with it. I should have kept one of the token toasters, I thought, as I rummaged around a bit more. And the coffee-maker.

There was shopping to be done, but I wasn't in the mood to do it today. I had to get some food, but everything else could wait.

The apartment was on the fifth floor of the Edificio Gerona, on a side road near the Paseo de la Castellana, one of the city's main streets. I took the lift down to the ground floor and walked out into the bright afternoon sunshine, clutching my map and trying not to look too much like a tourist. Even this early in the year Madrid had its fair share of them.

I walked all the way down to the Plaza de Colon before I noticed how much my feet were hurting. I bought water, bread, milk and fruit in a small shop and a copy of the newspaper *El Pais.* Then, feeling almost part of the city at last, I ventured down into the metro and caught the Liñea I back to the apartment.

The lift shuddered its way to the fifth floor. There was still nobody around. I wondered was I the only person living in the Edificio Gerona. Maybe it was condemned or something and that was why Gabriela Suarez hadn't minded paying my first month's rent.

By eight o'clock I was sick of my own company and sick of TVE. Juventus, I discovered on the evening news, had beaten Real two goals to one. José Maria Olazabal had won a golf tournament in the USA. King Juan Carlos and Queen Sofia were visiting Italy. The Prime Minister had called for greater productivity in the increasingly competitive global market place. And tomorrow would be cloudy with a possibility of rain.

I switched off the TV and pulled on a sweatshirt. I braved the shuddering lift and went outside again. This time I turned the opposite way at the end of the road and, almost immediately, found a row of shops which included a brightly lit, crowded bar-café. I found a seat inside. The TV behind the bar was showing the highlights of the Real versus Juventus game and a cluster of men groaned aloud at the free kick decision and the subsequent goal. I leaned back in my seat and ordered a San Miguel.

I opened *El Pais.* A man squeezed into the seat beside me. I folded the paper so as to give him more room.

'*Gracias*,' he said.

'*De nada.*' It came quite naturally.

Juventus scored their second goal and the collective groan was louder. The man beside me clucked in disapproval and caught my eye. 'Real are playing like headless chickens,' he said.

'It was a poor decision earlier,' I murmured.

'You are English?' Obviously my accent wasn't as good as I thought.

'No,' I said. 'Irish.'

'*Irlandesa!*' He smiled at me and switched to English. 'I worked in Dublin for six months.'

'Really?' I said politely.

'Yes. In a restaurant in Temple Bar. It was called La Cocina.'

I nodded. 'I know it.'

'I never saw you there.'

'You wouldn't remember.'

'Of course I would,' he said gallantly. 'Nobody could forget such a beautiful face.'

I smiled. I knew it was a chat-up line but he did it so well.

'What is your name?' he asked.

'Isobel.'

'A lovely name,' he said. 'I am Ignacio.'

'Pleased to meet you.'

'For how long are you visiting Madrid?'

'Oh, I'm not sure,' I told him. 'I've just started to work here.'

'Really. Where?'

'A training company,' I told him. 'Advanta. We run computer courses as well as seminars to help business people become more efficient.'

He shrugged. 'I am sorry. I do not know it. I work for the Banco de Bilbao myself.'

'Perhaps I will open my bank account there,' I said.

'Please do,' said Ignacio. 'Here is my card. I will be delighted to look after you personally.'

I took the card and slid it into my bag. 'Thank you.'

'Can I buy you a drink?'

I shook my head.

'A coffee perhaps?'

'No, thank you, Ignacio.'

'Perhaps you would like to have dinner with me some night?' He smiled at me. 'It is difficult when you start work in a new city. I know. I would be delighted to show you around.'

'It's very good of you,' I said. 'But—'

'You do not have to decide now,' said Ignacio. 'But I often come to this bar. I would be glad to see you again.'

I smiled at him. 'Thank you very much.'

The Juventus Real match was over and the station had switched to British football and was showing Liverpool and Chelsea.

'They are a good team,' said Ignacio when Chelsea scored. 'But they will never be as good as Real.'

'No team will ever be as good as Real,' I said, although I hadn't a clue really.

'Spoken like a true Madrileña,' said Ignacio and gave me the full force of his Latin good looks in his smile.

'Not bad,' I could hear Julie and Alison say in unison. 'Your first day and someone has tried to pick you up.'

~

I arrived at Advanta's office early on Monday morning. So early that only the security guard was behind the receptionist's desk in the lobby. I sat down and waited while he phoned Gabriela Suarez to tell her that I was here.

I was nervous about meeting her. I'd imagined all sorts of people – from plump and homely to tall and elegant – but I couldn't pin a picture to the lilting voice I'd spoken to on the phone. She must be in her early forties to be a friend of Sharon's, but I couldn't guess at anything else.

The woman who emerged from the lift and stepped confidently across the foyer was close to my tall and elegant picture. She had short black hair, wore a dark brown Donna Karan suit and her watch, which I noticed when she extended her hand to shake mine, was a Rolex.

'Welcome to Madrid, and to Advanta,' she said. 'I hope you had a good journey and the apartment is all right.' Her English was flawless.

'Thank you, yes.'

'Come this way.'

I followed her into the lift and she pressed the button for the eighth floor.

'We have two floors in this building,' said Gabriela. 'The eighth is where we have the offices and the administration, and the seventh is where we have the conference and training rooms.'

I nodded.

'We have a full-time staff of twenty people and contract staff of thirty,' she continued. 'Some of the contract staff just do a couple of sessions a year – they are not full-time lecturers. But some are. We pride ourselves on the quality of our lecturers and the standard of our courses. It is our aim to be the best training company in Spain.'

The doors of the lift sighed open and we went through some wooden doors into Advanta's offices. They were bright and modern. The desks were light wood, the walls panelled in what looked like walnut. The carpet was silver-grey. Gabriela opened the door of her private office. It was a medium-sized corner office. Barry Cleary had once told me that all managers wanted corner offices because it was a sign of authority.

Gabriela sat behind her desk and looked at me. 'Sharon speaks very highly of you,' she said.

I was embarrassed. I didn't know Sharon Cleary all that well.

'I hope I'll work well for you,' I said.

'I hope so too.' She smiled slightly. 'You are the answer to a prayer really. I lost three of my best staff in one week. Careless, no?' I was silent. 'One girl got a better job offer, one decided that she wanted to go back to college and the third got married and moved to Barcelona.'

'A bit unfortunate,' I said.

'Well, I knew that Berenice was going to Barcelona,'

said Gabriela. 'That was why I advertised. But when the others handed in their notice too, I was in big trouble. I don't like taking temporary staff because I want people to be committed to the company, but it's hard to get the experience you need quickly.'

'I know nothing about training,' I told her. 'I did say that to you on the phone.'

'But you do have organisational experience,' she said. 'You are an administrator.'

'That's what I do best,' I said, trying to forget some of Barry's comments over the past year.

'Excellent,' said Gabriela. 'So I will take you to your desk, introduce you to some of your colleagues and leave you to it.'

She was very businesslike. I'd never worked for a woman before and I didn't know what to expect.

I soon learned that Gabriela Suarez was almost frightening in her efficiency. And, according to the other people in the office, she expected the same level of efficiency from her staff. People that were loyal to the company and who worked well were rewarded with good salaries and bonuses. Anyone who didn't work out left very quickly. I hoped that I'd work out. I'd been rejected by Tim and, I thought, by Barry. I couldn't stand it if I was rejected by Advanta too.

Chapter 10

Standing Nude (Joan Miró, 1918)

The days were easier than the nights. I was busy during the day, but when I got back to the apartment each evening I felt cut off from everyone. And at night, when I lay in the creaky double bed, I wondered what would happen if I was suddenly taken ill and nobody knew about it. The people in Advanta might just think I'd had enough and had hared back home. My family wouldn't know that I was lying unconscious in Madrid. Sometimes I couldn't sleep and I lay there wondering what was happening at home, what Julie was doing. What Tim was doing.

It never seemed so bad in the mornings, but the fears were very real at night.

On Friday nights the administration staff hit Leon's Tapas Bar for a drink and tapas before going home. It was, literally, one drink, but at least it was a way to get to know them better.

Sometimes Gabriela came along too, which she did that first Friday. She ordered drinks for everyone and handed me a glass of San Miguel.

'So how was your first week?' she asked.

'Busy.' That was true. I'd had a lot of familiarising to do, as well as the normal work.

'Do you think you can cope?'

'Of course.' I smiled at her. 'I think I'll enjoy it here.'

'That's good news.' She returned the smile. 'Magdalena tells me that you have changed the filing system for the assessments.'

'Not changed exactly.' I looked at her anxiously. 'It was on computer but I think you were using a less efficient application. I shifted it to Grail.'

'I know very little about the different programs,' said Gabriela. 'Once it is working and it doesn't cause extra administration, I don't mind what you do.'

'You should find this will be much quicker,' I said. 'And you'll be able to transfer files more easily.'

'Sounds good to me.' Gabriela looked pleased. 'What do you think, Magdalena?'

Magdalena Moyet was Gabriela's personal assistant. 'It's good,' she said. 'Isobel showed me a shortcut for moving the data around. It's very efficient.'

'My goodness.' Gabriela laughed. 'Perhaps I have done us a great service by offering you this job.'

'I'm glad you did,' I said. 'Thank you.'

'Luis!' Magdalena waved at one of the men who worked in the administration department. 'Come and talk to us.'

I hadn't spoken to Luis before although I'd seen him in the office a few times and knew that he had a reputation of being a real ladies' man. Went through Advanta like a dose of salts, Magdalena had told me on the first day. Nothing much to look at but absolutely fantastic in bed apparently.

He wasn't particularly good-looking. He was medium height with unkempt hair, blue eyes and absolutely no dress sense. Which was unusual in Madrid because, if the women were chic, the men were just as fashionable. But

Luis wore ancient suits and even older ties to work, and his shirts were a riot of clashing colours. All the same, he had a certain charm and when he smiled he seemed to smile especially for you. Not that he'd actually smiled for me yet.

'Hi.' He manoeuvred himself into a space beside us. 'A good week, Magdalena.'

'Not bad.' She grinned. 'Keep Gabriela in a few new suits.'

I glanced at the Managing Director, but Gabriela had turned to talk to someone else and hadn't heard her PA's comment. Her suits were all designer and her home was in a very fashionable area of the city. I hadn't realised that training was so profitable.

'So, Isobel, how did you enjoy this week?' asked Luis.

'It was good,' I said. 'I think I'll like it.'

'Excellent.' He looked at me appraisingly. 'And I like you already.'

'Luis!' said Magdalena warningly.

'I only meant that Isobel is a wonderful addition to our company.' He shrugged expressively. 'I have an unfair reputation, dearest Isobel, and one which Magdalena thinks I absolutely deserve.'

I watched them warily. Magdalena hadn't said anything about a relationship with Luis herself, although she'd winked when she told me that he was fantastic in bed.

'Don't be silly.' She punched him gently on the arm. 'Just because I never gave in to your advances.'

'There are only two women in the office that never succumbed,' said Luis. 'And Isobel is the other one.'

'What about Gabriela?' I asked, and the two of them exploded into laughter.

'She doesn't count,' spluttered Luis. 'She's the boss.'

'So?' I looked at him archly. 'If the man is the boss,

it doesn't stop him from chasing the women who work for him. Or it doesn't stop the women from chasing him. Why should this be different?'

They weren't sure whether I was joking or not.

'Gabriela wouldn't,' said Luis finally. 'And, to be honest, I wouldn't have the nerve!'

'So tell us about yourself, Isobel.' Magdalena pushed her long black hair out of her eyes. 'Why did you come to Spain?'

Nobody knew me here, I reminded myself. I could reinvent myself. I didn't have to bare my soul to them.

'Oh, I needed a change,' I told her. 'I was bored in my old job, I'd dumped my pathetic boyfriend and I didn't know what I wanted to do with my life. So I thought it would be nice to work abroad.'

'I wish I'd thought of that when I broke up with Francisco,' said Magdalena. 'I could have got a more interesting job somewhere else. That would have made him stop in his tracks.'

'Were you going out with your boyfriend a long time?' asked Luis.

'We'd got into a rut,' I explained. 'I'd fallen into the habit of going out with him.'

'I know exactly what you mean,' said Magdalena. 'And it's a habit that's hard to get out of.'

I nodded and drained my glass. 'Anybody want another?'

They shook their heads. 'Got to get home,' said Luis. 'But I'm meeting a group of friends at the Hard Rock Café later. Would you like to join us?'

'I don't think I can,' I said.

'Whatever you like,' said Luis. 'It's an informal group. We'll be there at ten.'

'Perhaps,' I said.

'Hope you can make it.' He smiled at me. 'Surely there's nothing else you have to do on a Friday night?'

'Not really,' I said. 'Perhaps some tidying of the apartment.'

'Isobel!' He looked at me as though I had two heads. 'On Friday!' And we all laughed.

I'd bought wine during the week and stashed it in the fridge along with some cans of lager, half a melon and some smelly cheese. I opened a bottle when I went home and debated whether or not I would turn up at the Hard Rock. In the end I didn't go. I wasn't ready to socialise yet, to try out the new Isobel. A drink on Friday was enough for now. And I didn't want to get to know them too well. I didn't want to get involved.

I poured wine into a wide tumbler. I hadn't bought any wine glasses, just the wine. Luis probably doesn't have the slightest interest in you, a little voice muttered in my ear. Still, it'd be nice to think he had. Good for the ego.

The phone rang and startled me so much I almost dropped my glass. This was my first phone call. I'd rung home, of course, but nobody had rung me.

'Isobel?'

'Julie! How are you?'

'Great,' she said. 'And you? I rang to see how you were getting on.'

'OK,' I said cautiously. 'The work isn't too bad, although there's a lot of it. I'm in charge of booking lecturers and keeping tabs on them, that sort of thing. The boss, Gabriela, is quite nice. She—'

'Isobel! Shut up about work. I was enquiring about your *social* life.'

'I haven't had much time to have a social life yet,' I said. 'It's still my first week.'

'But you must have done something in the evenings,'

she said. 'I mean, you don't just go home and sit in front of the TV, do you?'

'I went for a drink with the people after work tonight,' I told her. 'Although they don't seem to have the kind of sessions we have at home. But that was nice. And I've enrolled for advanced business language classes on Wednesday nights.'

'Anything else?' asked Julie. 'Any gorgeous Latin hunks inhabiting your apartment block?'

'Not that I've seen so far,' I said. 'But you never know. Actually, I haven't seen anyone else on this floor yet. There is someone in the apartment across the hall because I've heard their radio. And I've seen people in the lobby. But I haven't met any of the neighbours yet.'

'Bet there's somebody,' said Julie.

'I don't work as fast as you,' I told her. 'But – I did meet a guy in a bar around the corner last Saturday.'

'The day you arrived!' she cried. 'I knew it, Issy, I knew you could do it!'

'Hang on,' I said. 'I haven't done anything yet.'

'But you spoke to him, didn't you?'

'A few words.'

'You see!' She was triumphant. 'I knew once you'd left here you could get back on track. And the best thing of all, Isobel, is that none of them know you're recovering from a mauling by the shit Malone.'

'Julie!'

'Oh, come on, Isobel. He almost wrecked your life. Now you can have a little fun again. Get out there, girl. Live a little.'

I laughed. 'You know me, Julie. I'm not that sort of girl.'

'When I met you first, you were exactly that sort of girl,' she said seriously. 'Remember? You had loads of boyfriends. Your only trouble was choosing one at a time.'

'I was younger then.'

'So what? You think you're ready for a pension now?'

'No.'

'Then have a good time,' said Julie. 'Remember, if it all gets too horrible you can always come home.'

'You're dreadful, Julie Donegan, really dreadful.'

'But I give good advice,' she told me. 'Every time.'

~

It rained on Saturday. I couldn't believe it. I thought the rain in Spain should be falling somewhere else. I needed to go shopping, rain or no rain.

The nearest metro station was a five-minute walk away. I caught the metro to Sol, the lopsided square that didn't much look like its name as rain cascaded down the street. I hurried into the Corté Ingles, one of Spain's best-known department stores.

I wandered around the household department, stamping down the thought that if I'd married Tim I'd have been doing this in Arnotts or Roches instead. I bought towels and bed-linen, some really pretty cups and saucers, and a cutlery set with brightly coloured handles. Then I realised that even these few purchases would be a nightmare to get back to the apartment, so I called a halt and caught the metro home again.

It didn't quite feel like home. But it was beginning to look like somewhere with a piece of my personality in it. I arranged the cups and saucers on the hardwood table and nodded my approval.

I listened to the TV while I cleaned the apartment. If you can call scrubbing a sink and tiles and polishing woodwork fun, then I had fun. It wasn't bad actually. In a kind of way, I enjoyed myself.

At five o'clock I made myself some soup and cut wedges

from the crusty bread I'd bought earlier. Nothing to this living alone, I thought, and it's great not to have Ian or Alison barging in and changing channel just as I'm getting into the movie. I was watching a dubbed version of *Pretty Woman* – I'd seen the film about a dozen times before. More than that, probably, because it had been one of Tim's favourite films and he'd regularly hire it out from the video store no matter how many times I told him it was rubbish.

'But she's so lovely,' he'd say as he drooled over Julia Roberts.

'You should be so lucky to find a hooker like that,' I remembered telling him. 'It's a complete male fantasy movie.'

'So what?' And he rolled over and pulled me closer to him. 'I need my fantasies.'

And so do I, I thought as Julia Roberts insisted on the fairytale. So do I.

~

The movie was over by half-eight. I had to make the effort. Julie was right. There was no point in hanging around. I'd come here to have a good time and forget about Tim and that was what I was going to do.

I am Isobel Kavanagh, I told myself as I left the apartment. I am a confident woman. I can do whatever I like.

I went into the bar-café and sat in the corner again. I recognised some of the faces from last week, but not everyone. Then Ignacio pushed open the door and looked around. He smiled when he saw me.

'Isobel! It's nice to see you again.'

'You too,' I replied.

'You haven't called into the bank yet.'

I smiled. 'I haven't had enough money to call into the bank yet.'

'You don't need a lot.' He unzipped his soft leather jacket. 'Can I get you a drink?'

'That would be nice,' I said. 'I'd like a beer.'

'One beer.' He ordered a couple from the bar and sat down beside me. 'So, how have you enjoyed your time in Madrid so far?'

'Very well,' I told him. 'I like the company I work for and the people are very nice.'

I didn't know whether it was because I was speaking a different language or whether it was because I was out of practice chatting with men that my conversation sounded so stilted.

'Watched any good football matches lately?'

I grinned. 'Afraid not.'

'You should come to a game sometime. When Madrid play Barca. That's always a good contest.'

'You think so?'

'Oh, absolutely.'

Were the men in Madrid like the men in the tourist resorts? When I was twenty-two I'd gone to Magalluf in Majorca with a crowd of girls. We'd behaved very badly, got drunk every night and practically thrown ourselves at any man who came along. There had been plenty of English or Irish men in the resort but I preferred the Spaniards even though I knew that they were only interested in unencumbered sex. I'd slept with one of them, a skinny dark-haired guy whose name I couldn't remember. I came home feeling ashamed of myself. Sleeping with – Raul, I think – had been the only one-night stand of my life. Even though I'd had lots of boyfriends, I only slept with the ones who meant something to me, the ones I thought might be for ever.

'You are dreaming, Isobel.'

'Oh, sorry.' I looked at Ignacio. 'Did you say something?'

'I asked if you would like to eat with me later? There are some nice restaurants here.'

'Well, thank you, Ignacio but I'm sure you had other plans for this evening. Last week you were here with some friends. Surely you must be meeting them tonight too?'

'They are only my sporting friends,' he said. 'We play football together. I certainly don't want to spend the evening with them.'

'I'm not hungry,' I told him. 'Truly, I'm not. But another beer would be nice.'

'OK,' said Ignacio and called out to the barman.

The bar was packed with people but it had a different feel to it than a bar at home. There wasn't the intense seriousness about drinking that I always felt in a Dublin pub. Maybe it was because of the group of men in the corner playing dominoes as though they were in a tiny rural bar. Maybe it was because the women at the next table were drinking frothy cappuccinos and eating sugared almonds. Maybe it was simply that I didn't really know anyone.

'You are doing it again,' said Ignacio.

'What?'

'Dreaming.'

'No.' I smiled at him. 'I'm just taking in the atmosphere, that's all.'

I bought the next drink and he bought the one after that.

Isobel Kavanagh, independent woman. I lowered my fifth beer. I am free of the past. I have put it behind me. I can do what I want, when I want. I am not attached to Tim Malone any more. It's over. Completely.

It was quiet in his apartment.

'You are the most beautiful girl I've ever known,' he whispered softly.

'Don't be silly.'

'It is true. Your skin is so smooth. Your hair is so soft. Your eyes are like lakes.'

That was laying it on a bit thick, I thought.

He brushed the side of my cheek with his index finger. 'You are *muy frágile. Muy guapa*.'

Fragile and pretty. Not bad.

He drew his finger over my lips and down my throat. I was lightheaded from the drink, wished it had been Southern Comfort instead of beer. I didn't want to think that I might taste of beer.

He did. A mixture of San Miguel and Camel cigarettes. Very, very different to Tim. I couldn't help thinking of Tim, even as I allowed Ignacio to unbutton my red silk blouse. I was outside myself now. I could see him standing beside me and I could see my head on his shoulder. None of this was actually happening to me. It was like a scene from someone else's life.

'Oh, Isobel.' He slid the blouse from my shoulders. 'How beautiful.'

He unhooked my Wonderbra and it joined the blouse on the floor of his bedroom.

I didn't know how I felt. I didn't know why I'd come here, to Ignacio's small apartment on the other side of the city. When we'd left the bar I simply got into the taxi with him, he'd put his arm around me and suddenly I felt so protected that I wanted to stay there for ever. I knew so little about him but it didn't matter. Except for my one-night stand I always talked with my boyfriends before I slept with them. I knew their surnames for a start! And their parents' names and the names of their brothers and sisters, and what they liked doing and their favourite food and a whole heap of other things which I thought essential to a loving and committed relationship.

But maybe this was better. It was physical and exciting and it made me feel good.

He felt different to Tim. He moved more slowly, more deliberately. He asked me if I was happy, if it was pleasurable for me.

'Oh, *sí*,' I murmured, as I held him close to me. '*Sí, sí, sí.*'

I woke up at three o'clock with a thumping headache and wheezing chest. I struggled out from beneath the crumpled sheets and scrabbled under the bed for my handbag, my breathing worsening all the while. Eventually I found the inhaler and took a deep puff.

Ignacio grunted and rolled over in the bed, pulling the sheets with him. I sat immobile in case I'd wake him, then exhaled slowly. The air rattled out of my lungs. That's the thing with asthma. You can breathe in easily enough, it's pushing the air out that can be the problem.

But the inhaler had worked. I always wheezed when I had too much to drink, especially if it was beer or red wine. Red wine had the added disadvantage of making me sneeze.

It was cold in Ignacio's bedroom. I slipped quietly out of the bed and got dressed. I tiptoed into the bathroom and pulled a brush through my dishevelled hair. My eyes were faintly bloodshot and my mascara had smudged.

I'd come to Spain and I'd reinvented myself and I'd gone to bed with someone whose surname I didn't know. It was an appalling case of callous recklessness. Julie would have been proud of me.

I felt guilty about slipping out of Ignacio's apartment. But I didn't want to see him in the morning. I didn't want to see him again. He was a nice guy and I'm sure I would have got on well with him. But I didn't want to find out what his surname was, or what his parents' names were or anything about his brothers or sisters.

I wanted to be Isobel Kavanagh, free and single and happy to be that way. I wanted to be Isobel Kavanagh, heart-breaker. Isobel Kavanagh, the girl who had fun.

~

I woke up at eleven o'clock and I didn't know where I was. I looked around the room in confusion, expecting to see the Vincent van Gogh *Sunflowers* print that was on my bedroom wall at home. But the bare white wall seemed to rush at me and I closed my eyes because my head spun. Too much drink, I remembered now, and – Ignacio. The memory of Ignacio flooded my mind, blotting out everything else. I couldn't believe I'd gone to bed with him.

My cheeks burned. What had I been thinking about? Where had I left my senses? Somewhere over the Pyrenees? Isobel Kavanagh didn't go around jumping into bed with people. I remembered telling myself that last night, even as Ignacio had cupped my breasts in his hands and told me that I was the most beautiful girl in Madrid. I grew hotter at the memory. It was all very well to reinvent myself at night, I thought, but in the cool light of day the reinvention was a bit much to take. Julie had told me to have fun, but she couldn't have meant hop into bed with someone new a mere week after coming here.

I clambered out of bed, pulled my dressing-gown around me and went into the bathroom. My face looked the same. There was nothing in my eyes to tell the world that I'd slept with someone for the first time since Tim Malone. I smiled very slightly at my reflection. At least I'd done it, I thought. When I thought about sex I could think of someone other than Tim. He wasn't the last person I'd been with.

It gave me a feeling of comfort. Maybe it had been worth it after all.

Chapter 11

Vines and Olive Trees, Montroig (Joan Miró, 1919)

The phone on my desk rang and startled me out of a daydream in which I met Tim Malone while I was in a sports car driven by a handsome Madrileño. 'Oh it's you – um, Tim,' I was saying, looking at him as though trying to place his face. 'Nice to see you again.'

I picked up the phone. '*Hola!*'

'Isobel, it's Luis.'

'Luis.' I peered around the pillar so that I could see his desk even though his face was hidden by a tall potted plant. 'What can I do for you?'

'Do you have the file on the autumn courses? I can't find it anywhere.'

'No.' I knew I didn't have it, even without looking.

'Have you any idea where it might be?'

'Why should I, Luis? I've nothing to do with that right now.'

'I just wondered.' He sighed. 'I have mislaid it, and I cannot think of where to find it.'

'You probably left it in the boardroom after this morning's meeting,' I said, irritably. 'You're forever leaving things there.'

The red light on my phone flickered, a sign I had to take

another call. 'I'll talk to you later,' I said as I switched to the other line. '*Hola!*'

'I'd prefer if you answered the phone by using your name,' said Gabriela and I almost dropped the receiver. 'It's much better than just *hola*.'

'Of course,' I said. 'I'll remember that.'

'Please do.' She was calling from her mobile phone and static crackled along the line. 'Magdalena is out of the office today, I know. There are a number of people I was meant to meet this afternoon but I've been delayed here. Can you phone around and reschedule my appointments, Isobel? My diary is on my desk so it shouldn't be difficult.'

'No problem,' I said, pleased that she'd phoned me rather than anyone else. 'Is there anything else I can do?'

'No,' said Gabriela. 'But be nice to those people. I hate having to cancel engagements and I think it's rude to do it at such short notice. But I'm in negotiations at the moment and I simply cannot break them off.'

I'd no idea where she was or what she was negotiating about. All I knew about Gabriela was that she seemed to thrive on combining a highly successful business with raising two children. She seemed to really care that people were happy working with her and she took time to make everyone feel as though she knew them personally. But I still didn't want to get on the wrong side of her. Apparently she had an unbelievable temper if things went wrong. It didn't last long, Magdalena had told me, but it was truly awful at the time.

I rang around Gabriela's clients, told them that she'd been unavoidably detained and rearranged all the appointments with the minimum of fuss. It was the first time I'd felt efficient in ages.

At four o'clock Luis sat on the edge of my desk.

I looked up and knocked over my tray of pens and pencils.

'Don't sneak up on me like that,' I snapped.

'I didn't.' Luis made a face. 'You were engrossed in staring at your computer screen. What are you working on?'

'Nothing.' I bit my lip.

He leaned around to look at the screen, but it only displayed one of Grail's Screensavers.

'You're looking at that?' he asked curiously.

'No,' I said shortly. 'I was thinking.'

I'd been thinking about Tim. It had come to me suddenly, and in an overwhelming rush. I'd been typing in some figures on course attendances and I'd suddenly been transported back to Tim's house and an evening when I'd been lying on the sofa while he played around with the computer. And I'd walked up behind him and kissed him on the neck.

He'd been working on Grail then, on the very screen I'd been using. Seeing it now, working on it myself, had brought all the feelings and all the pain and all the humiliation back. And I'd almost cried, sitting in front of my personal computer, two thousand miles away, looking at something from my past.

'Are you all right?' asked Luis.

'I'm fine,' I said.

'I found the file,' he told me. 'You were right, it was in the boardroom.'

'Good,' I said.

'Can I ask you a question?' Luis gazed at me with his big, brown eyes.

'Sure.' I double-clicked on the spell-check icon. My Spanish spelling wasn't brilliant.

'Do you prefer women or men?'

I stared at him.

'It's a fair question, no?'

'It's a bloody cheeky question,' I snapped. 'And it's absolutely none of your business.'

'It is my business,' he protested. 'I need to know.'

'You don't need to know,' I said.

'Oh, *mia* Isobel.' He looked pained. 'It was an honest question. After all, you do not join us very often after work. You only talk about female friends out here. I thought, perhaps—' He shrugged.

'Luis,' I said dangerously. 'Piss off.'

~

He couldn't seriously have believed I was attracted to women. He'd heard me tell Magdalena that I'd broken it off with my boyfriend. He was just getting at me because I wasn't flirty and charming with him like everyone else in the office. Even if Luis had been my type I couldn't have had a relationship with him that would end in tears and me being unable to stay with Advanta. And any relationship with Luis *would* end in tears, I was pretty sure about that.

~

I went to my evening class that night and afterwards a crowd of us went to the bar in the nearby Lux Hotel and got blitzed. I was flirty and charming with Stefan from Norway and he told me, drunkenly, that I was the sexiest woman he'd ever known.

He was incredibly attractive. Unfortunately, he told me he was going back to Norway in two weeks. 'Otherwise I would try to know you better, Isobel.'

'How much better?' I could hardly speak. We'd been drinking vodka and I never drank vodka.

'I would want to know every centimetre of you,' he said. 'You are so lovely, so beautiful.'

I snuggled up closer to him. 'So, why can't you?'

'Because I will soon be back in Oslo.'

'But you're not there yet.'

He gazed into my eyes. I blinked a couple of times to get him into focus.

'My apartment is a ten-minute journey by taxi,' he said.

'What are we waiting for?' I asked.

~

I stood in front of the delegates to our conference on managing human resources. My hands shook and a trickle of sweat ran down my back even though the room was air-conditioned. This was the first conference I'd arranged by myself. The total responsibility had been mine – booking the room in the hotel, making sure we had the right speakers, arranging the buffet afterwards, checking that all the presentational equipment was ready. And then making sure that we had the right number of attendees and that they'd all signed in and received their information packs.

It was very interesting and exciting but it was scary. I'd never done anything on this scale in Delta.

Gabriela had been offhand when she mentioned it to me. 'I'll leave the organisation up to you, Isobel,' she said. 'Just let me know if there look like being any mishaps.'

But there weren't. Everything had run smoothly and now I was standing in front of an expectant audience ready to give my opening speech and introduce the speakers to them. I was terrified that I'd forget what to say and that my Spanish would desert me so that I'd be left standing like a goldfish opening and closing my mouth.

I moistened my lips, clenched my fists so that no one could see the tremble in my hands and launched into my introduction.

Nobody noticed that I'd left out one of the speakers. I remembered Cristina halfway through my presentation and managed to slot her name in as though I'd always meant to mention her out of turn. Then I was finished, Sofia took her place at the front of the room and I slipped out of the side door to grab a *café solo*. My legs were shaking so much I thought I'd collapse but I was elated. I'd got through it all and I hadn't made a mess of it and Sofia (known for her granite-like demeanour) had actually smiled at me as I made way for her. I exhaled slowly and leaned against the wall.

It was a good day so far.

It stayed like that. The seminar was a great success. Afterwards, as I sipped a glass of wine, I checked through the comment forms and was delighted to see that the delegates had rated the day highly. I floated back to the office.

Most of the staff had gone home but Gabriela was still in her office.

'Isobel!' she called as I walked by. 'How did it go?'

I couldn't keep the grin off my face. 'Great.'

She smiled at me. 'Good. I am pleased.'

'So were they, Gabriela.' I opened my briefcase and took out some forms. 'Look. This guy says that the organisation was excellent and the speakers couldn't have been better!'

'That must be my father,' she said, her face straight. 'I told him to write something nice.'

It took me a second to realise she was joking. 'They're all like that,' I said. 'Only one guy thought that Mario could have answered more questions. But everyone else was really pleased.'

'That's good.' She closed the file in front of her. 'I'm proud of you, Isobel. Sharon told me that I'd get a good worker in you and she was right.'

I blushed. 'Really?'

'Really. And I'm glad you're working with us.'

'So am I,' I said.

She switched off the desk light. 'Would you like to have a quick beer before going home?'

'Oh, I—'

'You don't have to.'

'Thank you, Gabriela. I'd like to.'

'OK, then,' said my boss. 'Let's go.'

Leon's, the tapas bar, was crowded but we managed to get stools near the door. Tapas bars are meant more for standing than sitting, but neither of us had the energy to mill around in the crowd.

'What would you like?' asked Gabriela.

'*Jamón serrano*, please.' *Jamón serrano* is a naturally cured ham and was one of the few tapas dishes that I really liked. Lots of bars are into shellfish, or squid or olives, none of which I'd managed to develop a taste for.

'Is that all?' asked Gabriela. 'You sure?'

I nodded.

'*Jamón serrano*,' she called to the waiter, '*y una ración de gambas y aceitunas por favor. Y dos cervezas*.'

Prawn and olives weren't too bad, I thought. It was when people ordered snails and octopus that I felt ill.

The beers were wonderfully cold.

'Congratulations,' said Gabriela. 'Your first seminar.'

'Thanks.'

'I meant what I said. You are an excellent worker, Isobel.'

'I'm glad you think so.'

She nibbled an olive. 'I was doubtful. I hadn't met you. But Sharon was so sure you would be good.'

God, I thought, she must have been absolutely desperate to get me away from Barry. I must have been making his life hell. What on earth would she have done if Gabriela had said no – or, even worse, if I turned out to be completely useless?

'And you like it here in Madrid?'

'Oh, yes,' I told her. 'It's wonderful.'

'You are not lonely?'

'Why should I be lonely?'

She shrugged in the expressive way that all continentals have. 'You are away from home. From your family and friends. It would be strange if you were not even a little lonely.'

'I suppose I am sometimes.' I wouldn't admit to Gabriela the terror of waking up on my own, gasping for breath and unable to find my inhaler, convinced I was going to die. It didn't happen often, but when it did it was utterly terrifying.

'I would be.' She smiled at me and her brown eyes were warm. 'But I have always been a very home-loving person.'

'I suppose I was too, in a way,' I said.

'But you still decided to leave.'

I looked straight at her. 'What did Sharon tell you about me?'

She ate another olive. 'That you were a capable, nice, hardworking woman. That you had had a misfortune in your life and you wanted to get away for a while. That I would do well to employ you.'

'Really.' I made a face.

'That is all she said. I do not know what your misfortune was. Nor do I care. As an employer.' She smiled at me. 'But as a friend, yes, I care.'

I blinked a couple of times. 'It's silly really.'

'Nothing is silly,' said Gabriela.

I was silent for a moment. I didn't know whether it was a good idea to tell her about me. I was trying to change my history, after all, and what was the point in trying to change if I told everyone my life story? And it wasn't really a very interesting life story. My God, other people really suffered. All I'd been was self-indulgent.

'I was engaged to be married,' I told her finally. 'We called it off. I was very upset.'

'But of course you would be upset!' she exclaimed. 'Who wouldn't be?'

'I was silly,' I said. 'He wanted to be friends. I thought we could make it go back to the way it was.' I sighed. 'But you can't, can you?'

'No. But you can go forward.'

I laughed. 'That's what people said to me. But, Gabriela, I didn't want to go forward. I didn't want things to change.'

'I can understand that.'

'Can you?' I asked in surprise. 'Most people thought I was stupid, I think. My friends kept telling me to go out and have a good time. But I didn't want to.'

'So you came to Madrid to – get away from it all?'

'I suppose so.'

'And have you had a good time here?'

'It's different. I'm enjoying the work. And the language classes.'

'And do you go out?'

I flushed as I remembered Ignacio. I still couldn't believe what had happened with Ignacio. And I thought about Stefan from Norway who'd passed out before we'd got anywhere, which was just as well. I'd caught a taxi home again, half-relieved but half-disappointed. I'd kind of fancied Stefan.

'Sometimes.'

'You have made some friends?'

'I've gone for a drink once or twice with some people from the language classes. There's a hotel opposite the college and sometimes a few of us go into the bar after class.'

'Irish people?'

I shook my head. 'English mostly. Some French and Dutch. And a Norwegian.'

'And have any of them become special friends?'

I laughed. 'I'm not in the market for special friends right now.'

'And how about the people from the office?' she asked casually. 'Have you gone out with them?'

I looked up from my beer. 'Not really. Only to this tapas bar once or twice. But I haven't been here very long, Gabriela.'

'Luis would like to go out with you.'

I smiled faintly. 'Luis likes to go out with everybody. So I've heard.'

She smiled too. 'Yes. He is not a faithful person, that one. But I like him.'

'I like him too,' I admitted. 'But I don't want to go out with someone from the office.'

'You are right,' said Gabriela. 'It makes life complicated and it is complicated enough already.'

I ate some *jamón serrano.*

'I was thirty years old when I met Alfredo,' said Gabriela suddenly. 'I hadn't been going out with anyone for a long time. Then I met him and I knew, instantly.'

'Really?'

She nodded. 'It was strange. We were at a dinner party. He knew the hostess, I knew the host. Alfredo sat opposite me. We both looked up at the same time and that was it. I knew.'

'Straight away?'

She nodded again. 'But, yes, Isobel. Immediately.

There was chemistry. I don't know what causes it. But, yes, straight away.'

I sighed. 'In that case I'm quite safe. I haven't met anyone who's made me feel that way here yet.'

'I had been very much in love with my previous boyfriend,' said Gabriela. 'I was surprised that I could fall in love with someone else.'

I made a face at her. 'Are you trying to be some sort of counsellor?'

'Of course not,' she said. 'But it's true, Isobel. I was crazy about Marco. We broke up. Well, actually, he dumped me for a Catalan girl who was working here. I couldn't believe it. I was absolutely broken-hearted.'

Somehow I couldn't imagine the controlled and capable Gabriela Suarez ever being broken-hearted. I said so.

'But, yes,' she said. 'I cried into my pillow every night!'

I laughed. 'You sound so dramatic.'

'To me it was,' she said. 'I thought I would never get over it. But I did.'

'How did you get over it?' I asked.

'I left my job and set up Advanta,' said Gabriela simply. 'It was the best thing I've ever done.'

So that was it, I thought. Simple. Instead of haring off to Madrid I should have stayed at home and started my own hugely successful business. Then I could be as rich as Gabriela, marry someone as successful as me – Gabriela's husband was a vet and hugely busy all the time – and when Tim Malone came looking for a job I could tell him that sorry, he wasn't up to it. Pleasant thought.

'So.' Gabriela drained her glass. 'I must get home. It was nice to have a drink with you, Isobel.'

'Thanks for asking me.'

'You will get over it,' she said. 'Have a good time in Madrid. But remember I want efficiency around the office. So please, I would like you to be in time every morning, and to be fit for work.'

I wondered if she was getting at me because the morning after I'd gone off with Stefan I'd been late for work. And so hungover I could hardly speak.

'Don't worry,' I assured her. 'I like this job and I want to get on here.'

She smiled. 'Glad to hear it. *Buenas noches*, Isobel.'

'*Buenas noches*, Gabriela.'

~

Tonight's movie was *Alien 2.* I was glad it wasn't some weepy romantic drama. Or a light romantic comedy. There was nothing funny about romance. I poured myself a glass of wine and cheered when Ripley said, '*Get away from her, you bitch!*' She was a good role model, I thought, as I sipped the wine. Vulnerable, but tough in a crisis. An excellent role model, in fact. I finished the bottle of wine and went to bed.

~

In Advanta, you were only as good as your last seminar. There were more courses to be organised, more lecturers to contact, more brochures to proof, more updating to be done on the computer. By now, I had completely reorganised the way we kept our records and it was much easier to cross-reference things. Magdalena muttered that the best thing ever to happen to the company was for that stupid cow, Camille, to have left. I bathed in the glow of her appreciation and was glad to go to lunch with her sometimes to hear of Camille's eccentricities or to share the latest office gossip.

'Luis has a new girlfriend,' she told me one afternoon.

'Really?'

She nodded. 'Her name is Maria. She works in the Corté Ingles.'

'In a shop!' I laughed. 'How could Luis meet anyone in a shop? I don't think he's ever voluntarily bought anything.'

Magdalena laughed too. 'No, it's odd. But even Luis goes into shops occasionally. And he met her and asked her out.'

'Is there anyone Luis doesn't ask out?'

'Probably not,' said Magdalena. 'But he doesn't mean any harm.'

'How long will his affair with Maria last?'

She shrugged. 'Who knows? With Luis it can be all charm and romance for a few weeks and then bang, it's over.'

'How long did you go out with him for?'

'Long enough for him to realise he wouldn't get me into bed,' she chuckled. 'It was fun, really.'

'But don't you find it wrong?'

'Wrong?'

'That he behaves like that.'

'Some men are made that way.' She accepted it quite easily. 'Luis is one of them. But you can't be angry with him because he always looks so helpless.'

She was right about that. The uncoordinated clothes, the ruffled hair, the air of having better things to do than worry about his appearance—

'And he is sweet,' she said. 'When my mother was ill he sent her flowers every day.'

'Was he still trying to sleep with you?' I asked, a little sourly.

'Not by then. He was just being nice.'

'Luis Cardoso isn't my type,' I said. 'So I won't be hopping into bed with him. I've better things to do.

Anyway, from what you say, Luis likes to sleep with his conquests more than once. That's not my style.'

'Isobel!' She stared at me. 'Have you slept with lots of men?'

'Not lots,' I said. 'But I hope to change all that.'

'Isobel!'

'Why not?' I demanded. 'Why should Luis sleep with as many people as he likes and I can't?'

'I don't know.' She looked confused. 'But it is different for a woman, don't you think?'

'I don't know,' I said briskly.

'Do you think about your Irish boyfriend a lot?'

'What?'

'The boyfriend you said that you had left. The one that caused you to come to Madrid.'

'He didn't cause me to come to Madrid,' I said tautly. 'I wanted to come anyway. And I think about him sometimes, but I'm having far too much fun here to think about him often. He's probably got another girlfriend by now anyway.'

'Are you sure you do not miss him?' asked Magdalena.

'Why should I miss him?' I made a face at her. 'I'm much too busy here to miss anyone.'

'You're so calm, Isobel,' said Magdalena. 'I wish I could be like you.'

I nearly choked on my coffee when she said that.

~

I walked down to the bar-café that evening. I didn't know whether I wanted Ignacio to be there or not. I ordered a glass of wine and sat in the corner watching Sky Sports. They were showing Manchester United and Spurs. Ian was a United fan. Went to a lot of their matches. Had posters of the team on his bedroom wall. Well, not now.

They'd been taken down on the last redecoration and eighteen-year-olds don't stick posters of football teams on their bedroom walls. But he probably would have liked to. I missed Ian.

I ordered another glass of wine. The bar was half-full but there was no sign of Ignacio.

It had been stupid to come and expect him to be here. Especially since I'd sneaked out of his apartment without saying goodbye. But I needed to be with someone tonight. Someone who would call me wonderful and beautiful and would touch me in all the places I wanted to be touched.

I went home and drank a bottle of wine. It was easier to be on my own when I'd had something to drink.

Chapter 12

The Invisible Man (Salvadore Dalí, 1929/33)

Sometimes I felt as though I was two different people. There was the Isobel who was really happy about being in Madrid. Who enjoyed her work, drank *café solos* with Magdalena after work and walked along the winding streets at the centre of the city absorbing its history. And there was the other Isobel, who hated being away from home, who was afraid to be on her own in the apartment, who drank too much and who despised herself.

It was on one of the bad days that Julie rang.

'Hi,' I said unenthusiastically. 'How's it going?'

'Goodness, Isobel, you sound dreadful. What's wrong?'

'Nothing,' I said as my eyes welled up with tears. 'Why should anything be wrong?'

'For God's sake, I know you. I know that miserable tone of voice.'

I sniffed. 'I'm fed up.'

'Of what?'

'Everything.'

'Why?'

'Oh, Julie, I don't know why I came here!' I rubbed my eyes. 'People are OK, I suppose, but I'm not truly friendly with any of them. I need someone to talk to.'

'You need to get out and about,' she said briskly. 'You're in a great city and you're sitting in watching TV.'

'How do you know what I'm doing?'

'Well, I kind of assumed that's what you were at,' she said. 'If you were living the hectic social life you should be living, you wouldn't have been there when I called.'

I sighed. 'My social life is useless.'

'Come on, Isobel. What about the bloke you told me about? The bloke you met the first night you were there and—'

'Julie.' I interrupted her. 'I haven't seen him since. I don't want to get involved.'

'Who says you have to be involved?'

'Oh, Julie, you know how it would be. He'd take me to dinner or the movies and he'd phone me in work and suddenly we'd be a couple. And I don't want to be a couple.'

'Nobody's asking you to have a long-term commitment to the guy. Surely you'd be better off out with him than sitting in moping.'

'I'm not moping.'

'Don't lie.'

'Oh, OK,' I sighed. 'I *was* moping. I'm just going through a bad patch, I suppose.'

'Isobel, your bad patch could cover half a lifetime! Now stop sitting around and get out there.'

'Why are you so keen to have me out there?' I demanded. 'When you're so obviously in yourself?'

'Yes, well,' she muttered, 'I'm waiting for Andy to call.'

'How is Andy?' I asked.

'How should I know?' She snorted. 'He said he'd ring on Monday but I haven't heard a word. And I'm damned if I'm going to call him!'

'Don't be silly,' I told her. 'Call him. Maybe he's busy.'

'Maybe he is,' she said. 'But I'll tell you something, Isobel, this long-distance relationship isn't much fun.'

'I guess not.'

She laughed suddenly. 'We're a hopeless pair. You sitting around in front of the TV pining for a lost boyfriend, and me pining for one that's thousands of miles away.'

'I'll invite you to my next wedding if you invite me to yours,' I said gloomily. 'The way things are going, it's a safe invitation.'

'Never mind,' said Julie. 'We're women. We're strong. We'll survive.'

Oh yeah, I thought, as I pulled the sheet around me that night. But just surviving isn't enough.

~

I did make other friends in Madrid. Two of them, Barbara and Bridget, who taught at the college where I studied Spanish – invited me to a party at their apartment.

The apartment was crammed full of people by the time I arrived. They sat on the floor, draped themselves over the sofas and squeezed onto the balcony. I didn't know many of the people there and I sat around for ages feeling totally out of things before I poured myself a treble measure of Southern Comfort and decided to get blitzed.

It wasn't a bad party, I thought, as I drained my glass. There was a buzz about it and all I had to do was get involved. I refilled my glass and squeezed myself past a group of girls dancing flamenco.

'Sorry,' I said as I bumped into a fair-haired guy who was leaning against the wall.

'It's OK.'

'You're Irish?' I opened my eyes a little wider.

'Sure am.'

'From Dublin?'

'Drumcondra,' he said.

'I'm from Sutton myself.'

'Another Northsider.'

'What are you doing here?'

'God knows.' He made a face. 'I came with a gang of people. But they've disappeared. And you?'

'I know the girls who live here.'

'Lucky you.'

He was good-looking, although not by my usual criteria. He had the lean look, all right, but the blond hair was against my rules, as was the silky-smooth skin and the pale blue eyes.

'Finished?' he asked.

'What?'

'Looking at me.'

I blushed. 'Sorry.'

'If I looked at you like that you'd call it leering.'

'I wasn't leering.'

'What do you call it then?'

'Gazing.'

'Let's gaze somewhere else,' he said as he slipped his arm around my waist and pulled me close to him.

He wanted to go to my apartment but I didn't want anyone in my home.

'I share with four other guys,' he told me. 'There won't be any privacy.'

'I'm sure you'll think of something.'

He thought of something. He had the keys to the building where he worked. It wasn't a big modern office block like Advanta's – just a small, converted building.

He wasn't as good as Ignacio but it was the first time I'd made love on an executive swivel-chair.

Afterwards I insisted on getting a taxi home alone.

Barbara had seen me disappear with him. 'Where did you go?' she demanded the following week when I met her and Bridget for coffee in the college's small café.

'Nowhere.'

'Isobel!'

'I can't remember.' I didn't want to talk about it. It had been a mistake.

'Can't remember?'

'I brought the Southern Comfort with me. We walked for a while. We drank.' I shrugged. 'I can't remember what else.'

'Isobel!' She grinned at me. 'When I met you first I thought you were such a strait-laced person. You didn't want to come to the party. I told you to lighten up. But I was completely wrong.'

'Not completely.'

'Come on. You disappear with probably the only decent-looking single male of the night and you can't remember where you went or what you did.'

'Actually,' I said, 'I just don't want to remember.'

'Remember what?' asked Bridget as she sat down at the table. 'Hi, Isobel. Guess you and John had a good time on Friday night.'

'John?'

'Christ, Isobel, don't tell me you can't even remember his name.' Barbara looked stunned.

'It's not that I don't remember.' I stirred my coffee. 'I never asked.'

'You are incredible.' Bridget looked at me with a mixture of awe and disbelief. 'How could you possibly spend the night with someone and not even bother to ask him his name.'

'I didn't spend the night with him,' I said.

'So you don't know whether you're seeing him again or not?'

I shuddered. 'I doubt very much I'll be seeing him again.'

'Why not?'

'I don't want to.'

'But—'

'Look, Barbara,' I said harshly. 'Any chance we could drop this subject? I'm bored with it.'

'Sure. No problem.' She exchanged glances with Bridget. 'Do you want to nip across to the hotel? See Tomás.' Tomás Medina was Bridget's boyfriend.

Bridget nodded. 'Just for an hour.'

'Coming, Isobel?'

I was very tired. We'd been extremely busy in work. I should go home and get an early night.

'OK,' I said.

The bar in the Hotel Lux was tiny. Tomás stood behind the horseshoe-shaped counter and polished glasses until they sparkled.

Bridget sat on one of the high stools at the bar and cooed at him while Barbara and I brought our drinks into the foyer. The Lux was a mid-priced hotel, probably used by businessmen who had a strict limit on their expenses and tourists who were on package weekends. There was a night-show too – Spanish Culture – which mainly featured flamenco dancers who weren't half as good as the girls who'd danced at Barbara's party.

Life was pretty much the same everywhere, I thought. Sitting in the Lux was no different to sitting in Jurys or the Burlington or the Conrad. The same crowd of people milling about. Standing impatiently in front of the lift. Looking around for a porter. Celebrating a birthday or an anniversary or a wedding. And then the business conventions in places called the Seville Suite or the Granada Rooms.

I drained my glass of Southern Comfort. 'Want another?' I asked Barbara. Her own glass was still half-full but she nodded.

I am drinking too much, I thought, as I brought back the refills. I'd never really been the kind of person who got drunk on a regular basis. But it was nice to feel the alcohol warm me and to experience the sudden detachment from the world.

Barbara was talking about her job. I couldn't believe that anyone would enjoy teaching English but she did. From the snippets of conversation I overheard in college, she was rated very highly by the students.

'I must come into your class sometime,' I said. 'Rate your skills like I do for Advanta's lecturers.'

'Oh, God, don't do that,' she said. 'I'd freeze up if I thought anyone was grading me.'

'How long will you stay here?' I asked.

'Dunno.' She shrugged. 'As long as I like it.'

'Do you?'

'Right now – yes. Maybe I'll be fed up in a few months, but it'll be summer soon and I like being here even though you could fry your feet on the pavement and you're practically a prisoner indoors.'

'I'm looking forward to that.'

'It's an inferno,' she told me. 'Really.'

'What do you do in the summer?' I asked.

'The college stays open for various classes. I have enough to do.'

'You like it, don't you?'

She nodded. 'Most of the time.'

'Lucky you.' I got up. 'Want another drink?'

'No thanks, I've only just started this one.'

'I'm getting one for myself.'

'Fire ahead. But not for me. Honestly.'

Bridget and Tomás were the only ones in the bar. They were cheek to cheek across the narrow counter. I coughed.

'Another?' asked Tomás and I nodded. He gave me a double. Not a good idea, I thought, as I walked somewhat unsteadily back to the foyer. I'd have a hangover and I didn't want a hangover. My work definitely suffered when there was an army of demolition men working in my head.

'Oh, sorry.' I bumped into someone who had emerged from the Spanish Culture show.

'Isobel!' Gabriela looked surprised to see me. 'What are you doing here?'

'I'm with a friend,' I said, trying my best to keep my eyes focused on her.

'A male friend?'

I shook my head. 'Female. From the language classes.'

'Have you been here long?'

'Not very,' I told her.

She looked at me. 'You seem to have had rather a lot to drink.'

'That's OK, isn't it?' I asked. 'As long as my work is OK it doesn't matter what I do on my own time. Does it?'

'Of course not,' she said. 'As long as your work is OK.'

'And you've told me it is.' I knew I should just shut up but I couldn't. 'You've told me lots of times.'

'I know,' said Gabriela.

'So that's all right then.'

'Absolutely.'

'And what I do after work is up to me.'

'Sure.'

'Good.'

'I will see you in the morning,' said Gabriela.

'Bright and breezy,' I told her. 'No problem.'

Bloody hell, though, I wasn't very happy about bumping into her. I had a good image at work – Isobel the cool, the efficient, the competent. I didn't want it mixed up with Isobel the drunk. I shrugged my shoulders. So what if I was drunk? It wasn't as though I got drunk that often. As long as I didn't start coming in late or taking surreptitious nips from a bottle of vodka in a brown-paper bag at the desk, it shouldn't make any difference to Gabriela.

I still wished I hadn't met her.

~

She said nothing about it the next day. I'd drunk almost a litre of water when I got home that night and had woken before the alarm in the morning. My eyes were a little bloodshot but otherwise I was fine. I put on a little extra make-up and wore my favourite Conran suit – royal-blue silk which clung to my body and gave me a very sophisticated look.

She buzzed me at eight-thirty. 'I want to go through the schedules for next month,' she said.

'I'm printing them now,' I told her. 'Can you give me five minutes?'

'Certainly, Isobel.'

I finished the printing job and brought the sheaf of papers into her office with me. She was leaning back in her brown leather chair, gazing at the ceiling.

'Here you are,' I said. 'The schedules.'

She sat up straight and leafed through them. 'Thank you.'

'There are only a couple of things I'd like to draw to your attention.' I pointed out the non-confirmed booking in a hotel and the double booking of one of the lecturers.

'But I have someone to take Mario's place for that,' I told her. 'And José is looking after an alternative venue for the hotel.'

'Fine,' said Gabriela. 'You seem to have it all under control.'

'I told you I had.' I smiled brightly at her.

She tapped her long nails on the surface of the desk. 'And you are feeling all right today?'

I feigned surprise. 'All right? Of course I'm all right.'

'You look fine,' she said, 'but I was worried.'

'Worried?'

'About you, Isobel. I was worried about you.'

'Heavens, Gabriela, why?'

'Do not play games with me,' she said harshly. 'You know perfectly well why.'

I said nothing for a moment. 'If you're worried that I had a few drinks last night, then don't be. I don't drink that often. I simply felt like it last night. I'm sure you've drunk too much from time to time, Gabriela.'

'Yes,' she said. 'But I've always had someone to look after me if I have.'

'I can look after myself,' I told her. 'I've managed pretty well so far.'

She sighed. 'I feel responsible for you, Isobel. I told Sharon I'd keep an eye on you.'

'Oh, for God's sake!' I glared at her. 'What do you think I am? A child? I don't need you or anyone else to keep an eye on me! I'm a responsible adult. And I thought you were my employer, Gabriela, not my nanny!'

For a moment I thought she was going to shout at me – fire me perhaps. Then suddenly she smiled. 'You are right, of course. And I am sorry. What you do is absolutely none of my business.'

'I'm glad you see it like that.'

'Once your work is OK.'

'Absolutely,' I said.

We stared at each other for almost a minute and then she told me that I could leave.

I walked home from work that evening. The air was warm and balmy and there was a feeling that summer was around the corner. The tourists wandered about the streets in shorts and backpacks and sat in the squares drinking beer. I liked the fact that I wasn't a tourist. I liked belonging to the city.

I bought a bottle of wine in the supermarket to have with my pasta. My diet had become incredibly healthy if you ignored the alcohol. I was existing on salads, pasta and fruit. I hadn't eaten meat in ages and I only had chips on the rare occasion I was grabbed by hunger in Sol and dropped into McDonald's. I'd lost weight but I didn't look unhealthy. I thought of joining a gym so that I could tone up my muscles as well, but that seemed too much like hard work.

Señora Carrasco, my next-door neighbour, was standing beside the lift.

'*Hola, Isobel.*' She smiled broadly at me.

I liked Señora Carrasco. She was in her mid-forties and a heavier version of Sophia Loren.

'*Hola, Teresa. Cómo estás?*'

'*Muy bien. Y tú?*' We had progressed from the formal to the friendly.

'*Muy bien tambien.*'

She beamed at me. 'Did you know there will be an exhibition of Miró paintings at the Prado next month? You must go, *Isobel*, it will be a wonderful opportunity for you.'

'Perhaps I will.'

'Oh, you must,' she said again as the lift arrived and we stepped inside. 'He is the most wonderful painter.'

I wasn't sure myself. I'd always thought Barcelona's greatest painter produced things that looked like mine when I'd been at school. But they were hard to ignore.

'I will certainly go,' I promised.

'Good.' She looked pleased.

The lift shuddered to a halt on the fifth floor. Teresa Carrasco waved at me as she let herself into her apartment.

She was right, of course. I should make the effort to see the sights of the city. It was practically criminal to live within fifteen minutes of one of the world's most famous art galleries and never to have been inside. Better for me to engage in some cultural pursuits, perhaps, than spend my nights partying with Barbara Lane and Bridget Evans. Or in avoiding the bar where I'd met Ignacio. Or in wondering would I ever see the mysterious John again.

I ate my dinner on the balcony, overlooking the city. I liked the noise of city living now. I liked the sounds of the cars and the rumble of the metro and the sudden laughter of people spilling out on the street from one of the other buildings around me.

I poured myself another glass of wine. There was something very civilised, I told myself, in living like this. A sophisticated city girl sipping wine on the balcony of her apartment. It was a pity that the block had been built in the seventies. It had all the charm of Liberty Hall. If I stayed here long enough I might move apartment. Into one of the lovely old whitewashed buildings with green shutters and wrought-iron balconies. With roses tumbling from terracotta pots and lobelia bursting from hanging baskets. I couldn't afford to rent an apartment like that yet. But one day. Maybe. If I stayed.

I finished the bottle of wine and went to bed.

Chapter 13

Three Dancers (Pablo Picasso, 1925)

Easter was late that year, almost at the end of April. The weather in Madrid was now spectacular – unbroken blue skies and temperatures climbing steadily into the high twenties. The traffic snarled its way around the main streets and a haze of exhaust fumes hung in the air. Drivers honked impatiently at anyone who had the temerity to wander into the wrong lane, or wait for more than a millisecond when the lights changed to green. More than once a volley of Spanish oaths flew through open car windows into the air.

But when the Madrileños left the city for Easter and went out into the country for the break, the traffic abated and the air quality improved.

I hadn't made any special plans for the holiday. Barbara and Bridget were going home for a few days and most of the people from Advanta had made plans. But Easter had sneaked up on me and, quite suddenly, I realised that I would be alone for a very long weekend.

I felt myself wheeze at the thought. I was afraid. Afraid of having no one to talk to, no one who cared about me. I wondered if Gabriela would allow me into the office to do some administration. It would be a good time to get some back-up work done, without the constant interruptions of telephone calls.

'Don't be ridiculous,' she said, when I suggested it. 'You need some time off, Isobel. You've been working too hard. You've got circles under your eyes.'

The circles under my eyes were because I hadn't got home until four in the morning. I'd gone to a nightclub with Barbara, whose first class wasn't until ten-thirty. She was happily sleeping it off while I nursed my hangover through the morning. Monday nights were not good nights for clubbing – it took me all week, even a shortened week, to recover.

I didn't want to press Gabriela on the idea of working over the holiday and didn't say anything more about it. But I felt panicky on Thursday when everyone said goodbye and rushed home early to involve themselves in the festivities.

~

Easter is taken much more seriously in Madrid than in Dublin. There are parades every evening as statues of different saints are carried around the narrow streets of the old city while penitents follow behind. With nothing better to do I joined the crowd in the main square – the Plaza Mayor – where a truly spectacular parade was headed by soldiers in dress uniform on horseback. They were followed by members of different religious groups dressed in flowing tunics of vibrant purples, reds and greens. As well as the coloured tunics, they wore high pointed masks and most of them walked barefoot. Someone in the good-natured crowd told me that, in older days, penitents used to beat themselves with ropes as they walked. Some of them still wore ropes around their waists – but I didn't see anyone using them for other than decoration, which was a relief. Some carried candles and some banged slowly and deliberately on huge drums.

We followed them around the streets and I was suddenly moved by the atmosphere of religion and penitence myself. I thought, miserably, that I'd been wasting my life in Madrid. That I'd been given a wonderful opportunity to start afresh and that all I'd done was turn into a drunken wretch who slept around.

I shivered in the evening warmth. I'd come to Madrid to get more in control of my life. But it seemed to me now that it had slipped out of my control even more than before.

On Sunday I took the metro to the Retiro Park where the atmosphere was light and fun-loving and I couldn't be depressed.

I loved the park. It was a huge expanse of green within the city and it was always full of people. I strolled along the path to the lake and enjoyed the distant sound of classical guitar while, in front of me, three young girls glided along on rollerblades, making skilful turns and jumps so that they almost floated in the air as their shocking pink skirts whirled around them. The guitar music wafted gently through the park, along with the laughter of the children who were watching a magic show and the occasional cries from families who were boating on the lake.

I sat on the steps overlooking the lake and watched the creaky rowboats float across the water. Behind me, a group of African men played traditional drums, the ethnic beat quirky but somehow pleasing.

I thought about Tim. I couldn't help it. The image of his face just appeared in my head and it was there before I could stop it. I wondered what he was doing while I sat here in the Retiro Park. Was he at home with the capable Laura Hart? Working with her? Or sleeping with her? I shook my head to dislodge the image of them writhing about on his bed. But, when I thought of Tim, it was nearly always of him with Laura, or with some other, indistinct woman. And I still felt jealous and hurt.

I wondered whether or not I'd ever be able to go out with anyone again. I thought, very briefly, that maybe I needed to see a psychiatrist. I couldn't unscramble my mind, put things in perspective. Sometimes, when I'd drunk a few glasses of wine and some Southern Comfort, I felt content and thought everything was OK but the feeling usually disappeared by the morning.

~

The phone was ringing when I got back to the apartment.

I flung my sweatshirt onto the sofa and picked up the receiver.

'Hello?'

'Hello, Isobel. Happy Easter.'

'Alison! How are you?'

'Great,' said my sister. 'I've probably put on about a stone today because I've been eating Easter eggs, but otherwise fine.'

I hadn't bought myself an Easter egg. That would have been pathetic.

'How's everyone at home?' I asked.

'Fine,' she said. 'Guess what! I've got good news.'

'Oh?'

'I've got a job.'

'Really? What sort of job?' I did my best to sound enthusiastic.

'In Dun Laoghaire,' she said proudly. 'I'll be working with the council. Environmental work.'

'Oh, Alison, that's great.' I was really pleased for her. She hated the shoe shop.

'Isn't it.'

'When do you start?'

'In two weeks.' She sighed. 'I can't believe I'm finally getting to do what I wanted to do.'

'Everything comes to she who waits,' I said sanctimoniously.

'Oh, shut up.'

But I knew that she was smiling.

'I was wondering,' she said slowly.

'Yes?'

'If I could come over and stay with you for a few days? Before I start work?'

'Of course you can,' I said. 'But I won't be able to take any time off myself. You might get fed up on your own.'

'You're on your own all the time, aren't you?' she said. 'Why shouldn't I be able to wander around by myself? Anyway I was only thinking of a short visit – maybe Thursday to Monday, something like that?'

'Fine by me.' I liked the idea of Alison coming to stay with me. I wanted to show someone around my home, walk confidently with them through now familiar streets, take them to see tourist sights while knowing that I wasn't a tourist.

'OK.' I paused. 'How's things?'

'The usual,' she said. 'Boring. But Ian has a girlfriend! A blonde. Absolutely stunning. Dad's mouth drops open every time she walks in the door.'

'A girlfriend!' Ian wasn't a girlfriend type of person. Occasionally, he admitted to going out with a girl but he'd never brought one home before.

'I'm sure he does it just to annoy them,' giggled Alison. 'Mum looks at her as though she's a creature from outer space. And Dad's just jealous.'

I laughed. 'So what does this beauty see in our brother?'

'Actually she's had quite an improving effect on him,' said Alison. 'He's had his hair cut and he's stopped spending all his time taking motorbikes apart. Whenever he meets her he spends ages making sure that there isn't any oil-sludge under his fingernails and dousing himself in aftershave and stuff.'

'Good God.'

'Her name's Honey,' said Alison. 'She's a beautician.'

That was too much to believe and I said so.

'Seriously,' Alison told me. 'Well, OK, she named the salon "Honey's" and kept the name for herself. Her real name is Helga.'

'Is she German?' I asked.

'No,' replied Alison. 'I think it's a family name or something. But she said that it sounds like some kind of concentration camp supervisor which isn't exactly ideal for someone who gives electro-therapy for dodgy skin, so she changed it.'

'And Ian and Honey are an item.' I grinned to myself.

'I'll get a photo and bring it with me,' my sister said. 'You'll love her!'

I went on a culture-fest the next day. So far, my trips around Madrid had centred mainly on the shopping areas or the Plaza Mayor. I'd made one visit to the royal palace, but neither Barbara nor Bridget was all that interested in sightseeing and I hadn't wanted to do things on my own. But today I took off to the Prado and to the Reine Sofia, Madrid's most famous art galleries. I got lost in the Prado which is a common enough event but I saw the Miró exhibition that Señora Carrasco had urged me to visit.

I wasn't much of an art critic, but Madrid is full of reproductions of Picasso, Dalí, Goya and Miró, so I felt as though I knew the paintings already. The Mirós were bright and colourful but I thought that Picasso's Blue Period captured how I felt.

I was hot and tired after my gallery trek, so I bought a bottle of Volvic and went to the Retiro again. I sat beneath the shade of a chestnut tree and began to read the book on Picasso that I'd bought. But it was highbrow and worthy and, quite soon, I slid the book behind my head, lay down and fell asleep.

The guitarist was playing 'Hey Jude'. It slid into my dreams . . .

I was standing in the living room of Tim's Donnybrook house, while he poured glasses of red wine and handed them to me, one after the other.

'Don't look so sad,' he said, as I drank the wine in huge gulps. 'You can start to make it better.'

I took another glass from him. 'Can I?'

'Yes. Just drink the wine. You'll be OK.'

'I don't think so, Tim. I don't think I'm OK.'

'Come to bed,' said Tim. 'Come to bed now.'

I woke up with a start and looked around in confusion. People were still strolling around the park; nobody was looking at me. But I flushed with embarrassment at the thought that I had been dreaming about going to bed with Tim, while crowds of people were clustered around a guitarist only yards away from me. I felt they could see my dreams written across my face.

I got up in a hurry, and walked quickly out of the park.

Honey was seriously beautiful. I leafed through the photos that Alison had brought and wondered how on earth someone as lovely as Honey had fallen for Ian.

'Told you,' said Alison. 'Wouldn't it make you spit?'

'I can't believe she's going out with Ian.' I shook my head. 'Is she blind or something?'

'Isobel! That's not fair.' Alison shoved another photo in front of me. 'He looks good in this, doesn't he?'

She was right. He looked great. I blinked a couple of times. When do you suddenly realise that your kid brother – whom you'd only ever known as a fearless space invader or a secret agent, who came home covered in mud from soccer played in teeming rain, who knew more about motor engines than human beings – when do you suddenly realise that he's the sort of bloke that another girl could actually find attractive?

'When he's dressed up like that,' said Alison, answering my unspoken question.

'God,' I said. 'He looks very – mature. So do you,' I added.

'You bitch!' She threw one of the brightly patterned cushions at me. 'You don't tell girls that they look mature!'

'Sorry.' I was suitably contrite. 'And if you look mature, I must look positively ancient.'

'You don't,' said Alison. 'But you're awfully thin.'

'It's just the fruit and vegetables,' I said carelessly. 'I can't seem to put on weight.'

'You're positively bony,' Alison told me bluntly. 'You need to eat more chips or something.'

'Great,' I said. '*Carte blanche* to pig out at last.'

'I mean it,' she said.

'Oh, give it a rest, Alison.' I laughed to show I didn't take her seriously. 'Stop talking about me.'

'Do you like it here?' Alison got up from the sofa where we'd been sitting and strolled out onto the balcony. I joined her. It was dark but the yellow glow of street lights hung over the city and the apartment block opposite was a checkerboard of lights.

'Yes.' I leaned over the iron rail. 'It's big and it's bustling and there are lots of people around all the time.'

'D'you find it lonely?'

'Sometimes,' I admitted. 'When I came here first especially. I felt like a stranger all the time. But I've got used to it now.'

'Made any friends yet?' she asked.

'A few,' I said. 'There's a couple of girls from Liverpool I'm friendly with. They work in the college I go to. And I've gone out with a few of the people from the office occasionally. So I'm getting into the swing of things.'

'Any boyfriends?' she asked casually.

'I thought you didn't agree with the idea of boyfriends.'

'Of getting married,' she corrected me. 'I've nothing against boyfriends.'

'Neither have I,' I said.

'So?'

I shrugged. 'Sometimes.'

'Sometimes?'

I got up and uncorked a bottle of Rioja. 'Occasionally.'

'Isobel, I don't want any more wine,' Alison protested. 'We shared two bottles over dinner. I'll have a thumping headache if I drink more.'

'Oh, come on.' I poured the wine into a glass.

'Honestly, no.'

'You're supposed to be on holiday,' I told her.

'And you have to go to work in the morning.' She grinned at me. 'I'm trying to do you a favour.'

'I'll be all right,' I told her.

She twisted a strand of hair around her finger. 'You never used to drink so much.'

'What d'you mean?'

'Wine. You drink a lot of wine, don't you?'

'It's a continental thing,' I told her blithely. 'Everyone drinks a lot of wine here.'

'But it's not like you,' she said.

'You'd be surprised.'

'Is everything OK?' she asked. 'I mean, you're all right, aren't you?'

'Of course I'm all right,' I said impatiently. 'God, Alison, you're not Mum, you know.'

She flushed. 'I know. I'm sorry. It's just that – you seem – different, that's all.'

'Of course I'm different,' I said. 'I've changed my whole life.'

'I know.' But she still looked troubled. 'I know.'

'What about Shitface?' she asked the following night. 'Do you ever think about him?'

I wanted to lie and say that he never even entered my mind. But she would have known I wasn't telling the truth.

'Not much,' I said, after a pause. 'I try not to.'

'I haven't seen him since,' she told me.

'I'd be surprised if you had.'

'I've been around Donnybrook a lot. I thought I might bump into him. Literally,' she added darkly.

'There's no need,' I said. 'I'm getting over it.'

'I'd still like to kill him.' She put her arm around my shoulder.

'Don't be daft.' But I was glad she'd said it all the same.

I brought her sightseeing. I got us lost in the Prado

despite my earlier visit. I told Alison that she was the one in the family who'd gone oricnteering, but when we'd passed the portrait of the seventeenth-century royal family for the third time, we headed for the exit.

'Too many tourists,' said Alison in disgust. 'You can't get to see the paintings properly at all.'

So we went shopping instead. I dragged her around the Corté Ingles, and then we did the more upmarket Calles de Serrano and Velazquez, where Alison bought a pair of soft navy leather shoes and a navy and white suit.

'Work clothes,' she said happily as she paid for her purchases and we went outside again. 'God, it's hot.'

'I'm getting used to it,' I told her. 'Although the temperatures in midsummer can go screamingly high. Still, I'll manage to hack it, I guess.'

'Poor dear.' Alison smiled at me.

On Sunday evening we sat in the Plaza Mayor and drank cold beers under the shade of a huge parasol.

'This is heaven,' said Alison as she leaned back in her chair. 'I could stay here for ever.'

So could I, I thought, as I, too, leaned back and listened to the sound of the guitars being played at the opposite end of the square. Children ran backwards and forwards, playing chasing over the cobblestones while their parents stood around and talked volubly, only occasionally crying 'Antonio!' or 'Cristobal!' as a child tried to run out of their watchful gaze.

The sunlight fell in slanted shafts across the square. Pigeons hopped around beneath the tables. It would be a nice place, I thought suddenly, to sit with someone you loved.

The guitarists were playing Beatles music – the ballads,

slowly and easily, and they made the music sound much more than simple tunes. There were three of them. They wore T-shirts emblazoned with paintings by Miró. They also wore the obligatory faded jeans and trainers. A throwback to flower power, I thought, except for the Reeboks.

'So why haven't you found yourself a boyfriend yet?' asked Alison suddenly.

'What?'

'Come on, Isobel. I know you. You've always got some bloke in tow.'

'Not at the moment,' I said.

'You can't pine after him for ever,' she told me.

'I'm not pining.'

'Yes, you are.'

'Don't be so bloody silly, Alison.'

'I'm stating a fact,' she said. 'Nothing more.'

'I'm not pining. I don't have a boyfriend. I do have some friends. I'm not socially destitute.'

'But it's not like you,' she said. 'And what about your weight?'

'Oh, don't you go on!' I glared at her.

'What?' She looked defensive. 'What did I say?'

'Telling me to put on weight. Barbara keeps telling me too.'

'You see!' Alison was triumphant. 'Pining.'

'Eating less,' I said. 'That's all.'

'And drinking more,' she added.

'For God's sake, Alison!' I looked angrily at her. 'Stop bloody criticising me. OK, I know I'm drinking more. But I'm not being carried home every night! I'm doing well in work. I just need something for myself, that's all.'

'But—'

'But nothing.'

'It's a few bottles of wine a day, Isobel.' She looked miserable.

'Only because you're here,' I snapped. 'I'm trying to be a good hostess.'

'No you're not.'

'Look, Alison.' My voice was dangerously low. 'Mind your own business. You're very welcome to stay with me anytime you like, but don't interfere.'

'I—' She sighed. 'OK, Isobel. I won't interfere.'

We didn't talk about me again. She had a good time in Madrid and said that she was sorry to be going home. I left her at the check-in desk of Barajas International Airport.

'Have a good flight,' I told her.

'I will.'

'And good luck with the new job.'

'Thanks.'

'And take care of yourself.'

'You too,' she said.

I hugged her. 'I'm glad you came.'

'Thanks for having me.'

'Come again.'

'I will.'

The apartment was quiet without her.

Chapter 14

Bathers of the Costa Brava (Salvador Dalí, 1923)

It got hotter and hotter. I knew now what the Madrileños meant when they called the city an inferno. The sun seemed to penetrate the stones of the buildings, the concrete of the roads and the paving slabs so that everything radiated an intense, dry heat. Although we worked an eight-to-five business day in the office, I got into the habit of snatching a siesta as soon as I got home and going out later at night when the heat wasn't as fierce.

Occasionally I went out with the people from the office, but more often it was with Barbara and Bridget. Those girls knew how to have a good time and, when I was with them, I had a good time too.

I met Ignacio again. I'd been in the bar once or twice but hadn't seen him there. I had reckoned he was just as pleased not to see me – why would he want to have a relationship with an Irish girl?

He was at the counter, sipping a San Miguel.

'*Hola*,' I said.

'Isobel!' He put the glass on the counter and stared at me. 'I didn't think I'd ever see you again. I thought, perhaps, you had gone home.'

I shook my head. 'No. But I've been very busy.'

'All the same.' His eyes were black. 'I thought I might have heard something from you. Why did you walk out on me?'

'I'm sorry,' I said. 'I know it was a horrible thing to do. I don't know why, Ignacio. I really don't.'

'Well.' He smiled. 'Would you like something to drink now?'

I ordered a Viña Sol.

'What have you been doing with yourself?' he asked. 'Having a good time?'

'Working hard,' I told him.

'Oh, dear.' He grinned at me. 'That doesn't sound very exciting.'

'It is,' I protested. 'I like the place I work.'

'Better than the Banco de Bilbao, I guess.'

'I don't know,' I said. 'I've never worked in a bank.'

I didn't know why I'd come here. I didn't want to be with Ignacio. I liked him, but I hardly knew him. My head was fuzzy.

'Would you like to go somewhere to eat?' he asked.

I shrugged my shoulders.

'There's a very nice restaurant just around the corner – Mirabelle. Do you know it?'

'No,' I said.

'I used to work there during the summer holidays.' He laughed at me. 'I'm a pretty good waiter – I've been through most of Europe's capital cities with a tray in my hand.'

I smiled at him. 'OK.'

He took me by the hand and we went to dinner.

~

I enjoyed being in bed with him. He did things that I liked. He caressed me and kissed me and ran his fingers over the base of my stomach which made me tingle. He asked me if I was happy, if it was OK for me. We twisted and turned under the single sheet and the sensations were wonderful.

Afterwards, he lay beside me and lit a cigarette.

'I don't smoke,' I said when he offered me one.

'Ah, yes. You told me the last time.'

I stared at the ceiling.

'Do you love me?' asked Ignacio.

'What?' I turned to look at him. He was smiling slightly.

'Do you love me?' he asked again.

'I—'

He grinned. 'Don't worry. I'm not expecting you to say yes.'

'What do you want me to say?'

'I don't know, Isobel. I guess I want to think that you like me. But, to be honest, I don't think you do.'

'Of course I like you, Ignacio.' I sat up and pulled the sheet up to my chin. 'You're – very likeable.'

'But you don't love me.'

'I don't know you.'

He sighed. 'Being in bed with you is very exciting, Isobel. But I am old-fashioned. I don't know how you think, but I like to have a relationship with the girls I sleep with. Are we having a relationship?'

'That's up to you,' I said.

I wasn't sure whether I wanted to see him again or not. It was very strange.

'Then would you like to meet me on Wednesday night? We could go to the movies, eat afterwards?'

'Of course,' I said again. 'Of course I would.'

~

So I met him on Wednesday night, skipping my final

language class, and the following Friday and the Wednesday after that. He was good fun, very attentive and nice to be with. But, despite the sex, which was definitely good, I didn't love him and I knew that I never would love him. I tried, I really did. I kept telling myself of all the great things that he did. But there was something missing and I didn't know what it was.

Then Ignacio broke it off with me.

'I'm sorry,' he said. 'I've had some good times with you, Isobel. But I don't think it's working.' He smiled at me to cushion the blow. 'I think you want someone different to Ignacio de Ribera.'

I stared at him. 'No.'

'But, yes, Isobel. Whoever you're looking for, whatever you're looking for – it isn't me.'

'OK,' I said sharply. 'No problem, Ignacio.' I got up and grabbed my bag. 'Nice knowing you.' And I walked home.

I wasn't as hurt as I could have been, but I felt rejected all the same. At Barbara and Bridget's next party I didn't have the enthusiasm to try and find anyone. I sat in a corner and shared my Southern Comfort with a German girl who hadn't a word of Spanish. It didn't matter. After a few drinks neither of us were talking anyway.

But I was at home in front of the TV when Julie phoned.

'How's tricks?' she asked. 'Keeping busy?'

'Busy enough,' I replied as I hit the mute button on the TV remote control.

'What are you doing?' asked Julie.

'Well, right now I'm doing absolutely nothing,' I said. 'I was dumped by my latest boyfriend.'

'What latest boyfriend?'

I hadn't told her that I'd started seeing Ignacio again. She only knew about that first night. I brought her up to speed.

'You don't sound too devastated,' she said.

'I suppose I'm not.' I poured myself another glass of wine. 'It was good while it lasted, Julie, but it wasn't the love of my life.'

'I suppose that's OK.' But she sounded hesitant.

'Oh, it is, honestly.'

'So how's work?'

'Not bad. Quite good, actually. I've been very busy and I'm glad to say that I get on well with Gabriela so everything's working out in that department.'

'Great.'

'And you?' I asked. 'How are you?'

She sighed. 'All right.'

'All right? Not great?'

'Could be better, I guess.'

'Julie, did you ring to chat about you? I've been rubbishing on about me and all the time there's something wrong with you.'

'Not wrong,' she said.

'What then?'

'I wondered if you'd like to come on holiday with me in a couple of weeks.'

'I thought you were saving your holidays for the States,' I said.

There was a blank silence. 'Julie?'

'I don't know whether I'll need them or not,' she said finally.

'Don't tell me it's all off,' I said. 'I thought everything was going well.'

'I thought so too.'

'So what happened?'

'I don't want to talk about it now,' she said. 'But it's why I need to get away.'

'The offer to come here still stands,' I told her. 'I'm due a week off and there's plenty to do. It's pretty hot, though.'

'Actually, I'd something else in mind,' she said.

'What?' I asked suspiciously.

'Des – you've met him, he's the manager in our office – has an apartment in Sitges,' Julie told me. 'He was going to go for a week in a fortnight's time but he's had to cancel. He offered it to me if I was interested. I thought you might like to join me since Sitges is in Spain so you're halfway there already.'

'Halfway is right,' I told her. 'Sitges is at least five hundred kilometres away.'

'That's nothing,' she said. 'Oh, come on, Isobel. It'll be fun.'

I wondered about that. About as much fun as our holiday in Rhodes, given the sound of her voice.

'OK,' I said. 'When is the apartment available?'

She told me and I wrote the details down on the pad beside the phone. I'd ask Gabriela about holidays in the morning.

~

Julie and I met in Barcelona airport. I arrived two hours before her and hired a bright blue Seat Ibiza for a week. Her flight was on time and she emerged into the arrivals hall in the middle of a throng of eager holidaymakers. I stood alongside the reps from hundreds of tour operators and waved frantically to catch Julie's attention.

'I hardly recognised you,' she said, finally spotting me.

'I haven't been gone that long.' I picked up her case.

It weighed nothing. Julie was one of those people who can make about six different outfits from a plain white blouse.

'But you look different,' said Julie as she kissed me on the cheek. 'You look – thin.'

'You look exactly the same,' I lied.

Julie looked terrible. She was paler than I remembered, the colour was growing out of her hair and her eyes were smudged with tiredness. Her face was gaunt and it didn't suit her.

'Don't be ridiculous,' she said. 'I look like a ghost. I was out until three this morning with one of the girls from the office.'

I grinned. At least it explained the smudges under her eyes.

'Come on,' I said. 'Let's collect the car.'

I was a bit doubtful about the car. I wasn't used to right-hand drive. I was accustomed to the traffic in Madrid as a pedestrian – take your life in your hands and run – but I knew that I'd never have the nerve to drive there. Julie said it'd be no problem, I'd catch on pretty quickly.

I almost turned the wrong way onto the motorway. I slammed on the brakes and swore loudly as a huge articulated lorry bore down on us.

'It's OK,' gasped Julie. 'We're still alive.'

'Sorry.' I reversed the car and started again. 'I think I know what I'm doing now.'

'I hope so.' She took a tissue from her bag and wiped her forehead. 'I may be depressed but I'm not suicidal.'

'Are you depressed?' I released the clutch and eased onto the road. My confidence grew a little and I picked up speed.

'Oh, you know how it is.' Julie fanned herself with

the tissue. 'I don't feel so bad now that I'm away from home.'

She lapsed into silence and I didn't press her to talk. I hate it when people try to make me talk when I don't want to and I wasn't going to force Julie's confidences. She'd tell me all about it when she was ready.

I turned on the car radio and flamenco music filled the air.

'Very authentic,' murmured Julie as she closed her eyes. 'But I hate flamenco.'

I put a Brian Ferry tape I'd brought into the cassette and we hummed along to 'Avalon'. But when he sang 'These Foolish Things' neither of us joined in and, out of the corner of my eye, I could see Julie wiping away a tear. Oh God, I thought. This could be a perfectly horrible week.

The apartment in Sitges was a couple of kilometres outside the town centre. The low-rise building was at the bottom of a hill, an olive grove to the back and pine-trees at the sides. I pulled up outside and switched off the engine.

Our apartment was on the ground floor.

'All the apartments are owned by English people,' said Julie as she unlocked the door. 'Des bought it from a bloke he knows in the UK.'

It was a small apartment – tiny kitchen area, living room, bathroom and one bedroom. The sliding-doors in the living room led onto a small, paved patio.

'It's not bad, is it?' Julie dumped her bag on a chair.

'It's fine.' I opened the patio doors and stepped outside. There was a pool outside, surrounded by sun-loungers, half of which were occupied. Late evening shadows were beginning to fall across the water and, even as I stood there, more people got up from the loungers and walked back to their apartments.

'I know it's old hat to you by now.' Julie joined me on the patio. 'But it's lovely to be in the sun.'

'I thought you were having a decent summer at home,' I said.

'Oh, it's not the same.' Julie dismissed Irish summers with a shake of her head. 'You can't sit around the pool for a start!'

As it turned out, we didn't spend that much time by the pool. We went for a walk that evening and discovered a beautiful cove with soft, cream-coloured sand and clear, warm water. We decided to go there the following morning, so after a breakfast of coffee and croissants, we went there and unrolled our towels in the semi-shade of a spindly tree.

'Why is it,' I mused as I lay down, 'that we've just got out of bed and we're preparing to go back to sleep again?'

'Because that's what you do on holidays.' Julie rubbed cream onto her arms. 'You sleep. You read. You swim. You eat.'

I giggled. 'What about "you dance all night long"?'

'I've gone past all that,' said Julie darkly. 'I'm a mature woman now.'

I snorted and she flicked some *Ambre Solaire* at me.

We lay down on the towels again.

We hadn't talked last night. We'd had a pizza at a nearby restaurant and chatted about our families and about my job in Spain, but we hadn't talked about the things that we both wanted to talk about. I knew that Julie would talk about Andy when she was ready.

She sat up suddenly and poked me in the ribs. 'Look at that.'

A boat had moored in the cove. A big, white boat with dark glass which wouldn't have looked out of place in St Tropez.

'Wow,' said Julie. 'Wonder who that belongs to?'

'Somebody rich,' I said. 'Somebody very rich.'

'One day I'll be rich.' Julie burrowed in the sand with her toes.

'Why?' I asked. 'You planning to rob the estate agent's? Or just marry into it?'

'I don't think I'll ever get married,' she said. 'I don't think I'm the marrying type.'

'I thought you were exactly the marrying type,' I said. 'Hundreds of boyfriends in your wild-child youth. Looking for something a little more serious now. And I thought you might be going to marry Andy.'

'Maybe I'm looking for something more serious.' Julie twisted her hair around her fingers. 'But Andy Jordan isn't.'

'Tell me about it,' I said simply.

She sighed. 'Oh, Isobel, I thought he loved me. I really and truly did. He was so wonderful at Christmas. He kept saying that he didn't want to go home. He told me that he couldn't imagine life without me. He bought me the most gorgeous gold chain made up of tiny interlocking hearts. What was I supposed to think?'

'Sounds pretty definite,' I agreed.

'He rang me loads of times from the States. We talked about the future, but we kind of skirted around it. So last month I asked him what he thought we should do.'

'And?'

'He suggested that I come and live with him in the States.'

'So? What's the problem?'

'Live with him, Isobel. Not marry him.'

'Oh,' I said.

'I told him I wasn't so sure about leaving home to live with him and he said that it was important that we should get to know each other more before making any long-term commitment.'

'He has a point.'

'No he hasn't.'

For a second I thought that Julie was going to cry.

'But you haven't really been together that much,' I said gently. 'Perhaps he feels that it's the distance that's making your relationship so good.'

'I understand all that,' said Julie. 'But think about it, Isobel. I'm thirty years old. He wants me to pack in my job and go to the States for three months and, at the end of it, who knows whether we'll get married or not. It's not as though we'd be spending all our time together there either. He'll be at work most of the time. I'd be rattling around Florida on my own.'

'Can't you look at it as an extended holiday?'

'No, I can't.' Julie slapped some more suncream onto her legs. 'I've got a life to live and I've got a good job at home. If he wants me to chuck it in, he's got to give me something in return.'

'You always said that you hated your job,' I told her mildly.

'Not hated,' she said. 'OK, it's not exactly the most glamorous career but it pays my wages and I like it really. Besides, Des offered me assistant manager of the Drumcondra branch.'

'Oh.'

'So, you see, I'd be giving up promotion and everything. For what? A three-month failed romance in Florida?'

'Maybe it wouldn't be a failed romance,' I said. 'Maybe you'll go to Florida and have an absolutely wonderful time and you'll end up getting married in the Church of the Seven Veils or something in Vegas.'

She laughed half-heartedly.

'I know you don't want me to say that I see his point of view. But it must be different being in love with someone a few thousand miles away. It's not exactly conducive to learning about each other, is it?' I pushed my damp hair out of my eyes.

'I know.' She sighed and burrowed into the sand again with her toes. 'And I can see his point of view too. It's just that – it's not what I wanted.'

It's not what I wanted. I'd said that to Tim when he suggested moving in with him. I knew exactly how Julie felt. And it wasn't that either of us felt marriage was the be-all and end-all of our existence. It was simply that we wanted to be sure that we were loved. To be secure in that knowledge. And without the marriage certificate it didn't seem that either of us could be.

'We're dreadfully suburban,' I said gloomily.

'I can't help it,' Julie muttered. 'I was born and raised in the suburbs.'

A girl appeared on the edge of the boat. She was tall and slender. She pulled her shining black hair into a pony-tail and stretched her arms skyward. She wore a sleek orange bathing-suit which outlined a near-perfect body. She bounced on her toes for a couple of seconds, then dived into the clear blue water sending up a spray of glittering drops.

'Bitch,' said Julie laconically.

'Come on,' I said. 'Let's get in for a dip ourselves.'

'Oh, Isobel.' Julie made a face. 'I've just covered myself in sunscreen.'

'So what?' I grinned at her. 'It'll protect you in the water.'

It was beautifully warm. I floated, my eyes closed, safely

within my depth while Julie swam parallel to the beach. When I opened my eyes and righted myself, Julie was on her return swim and the girl was back on the boat, surrounded by half-a-dozen muscular, tanned men.

'D'you think she's a film star or something?' Julie surfaced beside me.

'Pop singer maybe?' I hazarded.

'All that beefcake! On one girl. Life is so unfair.'

We sighed at the unfairness of life and went back to lie in the sun.

~

'I met Tim Malone last week.'

We were having after-dinner drinks in the bar. Julie poured the rest of her beer into a glass and avoided my startled glance.

'You what!' It came out as a strangled yelp.

'Met Tim,' she repeated. 'Not deliberately, of course.'

'Where?'

'Grafton Street. On Saturday. He was in front of me in the Banklink queue.'

'Did you talk to him?' My mouth was dry. I gulped some beer and spluttered as it went down the wrong way. I took a puff of my inhaler.

Julie watched me calmly. She'd seen this before. 'A little,' she replied, when I'd got my breathing under control.

'What did he say?'

Julie shrugged. 'Not much. He knew you'd left Delta-Print and gone abroad.'

'Did he ask?'

'What?'

'About me?'

'Does it matter?'

'Oh, Julie!' I glared at her. 'Come on.'

'He asked how you were,' she told me. 'He said that he felt terrible about everything. He said that he missed you.'

'Did he?'

'He said that he hadn't realised how much a part of his life you were and that he'd probably made a dreadful mistake.'

'You're joking.' I'd paled, I knew I had.

'I wasn't going to tell you,' said Julie. 'I didn't know whether it was a good idea or not.'

A waiter put a ceramic bowl of salted peanuts in front of us. I took a handful and began to chew.

'I wasn't talking to him for long,' Julie continued. 'Five minutes, maybe. He wanted to know about your job and how you were getting on. I told him you were doing brilliantly and that you had a new boyfriend.'

'Julie!'

'Well, what did you want me to say?' she asked. 'Anyway it's nearly true. You have got a good job. You were having a relationship even though I didn't know about it. And I can tell you something for nothing – he nearly vomited when I told him.'

'Did he really?'

'Sure did.' She took some peanuts from the bowl. 'It's the best way, Isobel. Tell them you're not interested any more, get someone new and they come running back.'

'He hasn't come running back,' I pointed out.

'No. But I think he'd like to.'

'You're just saying that.'

She laughed. 'Well, maybe I'm exaggerating a little. But he was put out when he heard about Juan.'

'Juan?'

'Your boyfriend, of course.'

'Jesus, Julie! You mean you actually told him something about an imaginary boyfriend?'

'Not a lot,' she told me. 'Just that he was a businessman and that he was crazy about you.'

'You're the one who's crazy,' I said.

'So what?' She shrugged. 'He'll never find out anyway. Might as well make him jealous.'

I laughed. I liked the idea of a jealous Tim.

'He probably knew you were spoofing,' I said.

'Hoped I was.' Julie grinned. 'But I know he was jealous. I could see it in his eyes.'

'Maybe I should've made him jealous earlier,' I said. 'Maybe it would have made all the difference.'

Julie said nothing. The sound of disco music carried on the warm breeze from the hotel near the beach.

'How d'you feel about him now?'

I sighed and gazed across the cove. The big boat had left earlier in the day, but a small fishing-boat bobbed gently up and down in the water.

'I don't know,' I said finally.

'If he contacted you now, what would you say?'

'I don't know,' I said again.

'Do you still care about him?'

I bit the nail of my index finger and pulled at the jagged edge.

'Sort of.' I looked at her. Her face was full of concern. 'It's hard to explain. I never fell out of love with him. I hated him, of course, for what he did, but that was different. And then I met him with Laura and I kind of went mad. He says that there was nothing between them and maybe it was true, but it was a question of trust. I didn't trust him, then, I couldn't. And he seemed to think that everything was OK between us. That we could carry on exactly as we had before. But we couldn't – I couldn't. I did something awful, too.'

'What?'

'He was away. California, I think. I still had the keys to his house. I let myself in and wiped his computer.'

'Isobel!' Julie looked at me in horrified admiration.

'He was working on something called Saracen 2. I deleted all the files.'

'My God,' she breathed.

'It wasn't a disaster, I'm sure he had loads of backups. But it made me feel better.'

'I bet it did.'

'I did something else, too.'

'What?'

'There were earrings in his bedroom. They weren't mine. I flushed them down his toilet.'

She looked at me open-mouthed.

'They could have been anybody's earrings,' I said defensively. 'I thought that maybe he was sleeping with someone else.'

'Perhaps he was.'

'You see.' I looked miserably at her. 'That was why it had to be over.'

'Oh, Isobel.' She took my hand. 'We're a pair of crocks, aren't we?'

'Rubbish,' I said briskly. 'We're two single women on holiday. Let's make sure we have a good time.'

We had a good time. I felt more like the old Isobel Kavanagh when I was with Julie. I didn't feel as if I had to be different, as if I had to be the life and soul of the party. And I liked it. We didn't try to get off with any of the chunky and hunky men who lurked around the beach. We went to a different restaurant each night, shared a bottle of wine, had coffees and talked.

We talked a lot. I told her about Barbara and Bridget, about Ignacio, about Stefan and about John in the executive swivel-chair.

She stared at me in disbelief.

'Are you taking precautions?'

'For God's sake, Julie!'

'Well, if you're sleeping around you should be using something.'

'I'm not sleeping around,' I said angrily.

'What would you call it?' asked Julie. 'I know I kept telling you to go out there and immerse yourself in Latin lovers. I didn't think you'd take it quite so literally.'

'I didn't,' I said. 'Only one of them was Spanish. You couldn't call Stefan – with whom, I will remind you, I didn't actually do anything – or John, Latin lovers.'

'I still can't believe it.' She waved at the waiter and ordered two more cappuccinos.

'Why not?'

'It's not exactly you.'

'What *is* me?' I asked.

'I'm not sure. But drinking and partying and sleeping around isn't.'

'I'm not sleeping around,' I repeated angrily. 'Come on, Julie! You're making it sound sordid.'

'I'm sorry.'

'I just want to have a good time,' I told her. 'Julie, I'm an adult. I'm not some stupid teenager.'

'Stupid teenagers can get away with partying all night and going to work the next day,' said Julie.

'It's not every night,' I objected. 'And I can cut it in the office. I told you – I'm efficient.'

'You don't look well,' she said.

'Look who's talking!' I glared at her. 'I hardly recognised you when you arrived.'

'I told you, that was because I'd been out the night

before. And I look OK now. You looked awful when we met. Thin face, thin body.'

'I've lost weight because I don't eat as much here,' I told her. 'Much more fresh vegetables and fruit and a lot less meat. So, quite a healthy diet in fact.'

'A diet of veggies and booze isn't much good,' said Julie.

'Stop lecturing me, Donegan,' I said. 'I don't need any more lectures from you. God, it's not as though there's much you can lecture me about. You're here to get over the creep Jordan. I'm here to get over the creep Malone. I don't think there's that much difference between us.'

'I'm not trying to get over him,' said Julie. 'I'm just trying to put a perspective on things.'

'Yes, and that's exactly what I've done too,' I said. 'I've put a perspective on my life.'

'Right,' said Julie.

'Right,' I said.

It was just as well that she was going home the next day.

~

'I'm sorry,' I said as we stood in the airport terminal.

'It's OK.' Julie was still annoyed with me.

'I mean it,' I said. 'I'm sorry.'

'Is it so hard to get what we want out of life?' asked Julie. 'I mean, I thought I had everything worked out with Andy. I really did. I thought it was all going great, even though he's American and I'm Irish and most of the relationship has been conducted over the phone! And then, suddenly, he comes up with this "live with me" suggestion. And I'm too old to decide that I'll take a couple of years out and do just that. I want to be married and to have kids and all that sort of thing.

I don't want to be footloose and fancy-free any more.' She grimaced. 'That sounds so boring, doesn't it?'

I shook my head. 'Not to me. I wanted all those things too. I always did.'

'Why?' asked Julie.

I shrugged. 'I'm not sure. Maybe it was because of my parents.' I brushed an imaginary fleck of dust from my sleeve. 'They got married very young. Mum was pregnant. She lost the baby.'

'Oh, Isobel!' Julie stared at me. 'I didn't know that.'

'It's not something my mother talks about a lot,' I said wryly. 'Anyway, I was conceived fairly soon afterwards so they had their baby after all. Sometimes, though, I think she resents the fact that I wasn't the first baby. You see, they felt as though they had to get married – well, I guess back then single motherhood was still something you didn't talk about that much. So they got married and they lost the baby, which was the reason they got married in the first place, and then I came along, but I wasn't the right baby. And I think they have always resented me.'

'Well, I think that's absolute rubbish,' said Julie firmly. 'Your mother is nuts about you. About all of you.'

'Perhaps,' I said. 'But I always felt as though I could do it better than her, Julie. I could get engaged and get married and have children and it would be perfect. Not like her.'

Julie stared at me. 'That's crazy, Isobel.'

'I know,' I said. 'But it's how I felt. So, when it all went pear-shaped, I guess I just lost my head completely. I wasn't better than her after all.'

'But it's not a question of being better than anyone,' said Julie. 'It's not a competition, Isobel.'

'I know,' I said again. 'But I always felt it was.'

'You nutter.' She grinned at me, then hugged me.

'You'll find someone, Isobel. And, I suppose if you're having fun in the meantime, you'll enjoy waiting.'

'Yes.' I smiled back at her. 'And you'll find someone too, Julie. Better than Andy Jordan.'

I waved goodbye to her and went home.

Chapter 15

Woman Struggling to Attain the Unreachable
(Joan Miró, 1954)

There was pandemonium in the office. I could hear Gabriela shouting at someone as I stepped out of the lift. It was very unlike Gabriela to shout. She got heated sometimes and her words poured in a torrent of incomprehensible Spanish, but she rarely lost her temper with any of us.

I sat down at my desk just as she stormed out of her office.

'Oh, Isobel,' she said, her voice dripping with sarcasm. 'So nice of you to turn up.'

I stared at her, my mouth open. I was five minutes late.

'It's wonderful to think that I am not the only person, the one person in this office who realises that we need to be here to make money. That if we are not here there is no business.' She stalked down the corridor.

'What on earth is wrong with her?' I asked Magdalena, who had followed Gabriela out of the office.

'José was in a motorbike accident last night,' said Magdalena. 'He broke his leg and he's in hospital. Maria has the flu. Sofia rang in to say that she has food poisoning.

And we've just discovered that the hotel where tomorrow's conference was supposed to be wasn't booked.'

'Oh.' I made a face at Magdalena. 'Is José OK?'

'He's fine. Not a scratch, apart from the leg.'

'That's good. But not so good about the conference.'

'Not so good at the best of times,' she said. 'But a nightmare this week because of the trade exhibition.'

I'd forgotten about the trade exhibition. A gathering of Spanish manufacturers all showing their goods in a major exhibition that would have the hotels full and space at a premium all week.

'But didn't we confirm the booking with them?' I asked.

'Normally we do,' said Magdalena. 'Luis is supposed to do it. I don't know what happened. It wouldn't matter so much, there'd usually be somewhere else even at this short notice, but this week it's a disaster.'

'Don't we have space here?'

'Not enough,' she told me. 'You know our biggest room only holds twenty. There are fifty people booked in for our conference.'

'No wonder Gabriela's thrown a fit,' I mused.

'She'll throw more than a fit if she has to cancel,' said Magdalena glumly. 'She already blames all of us. Especially José, who was in charge of the thing, but since he's in hospital there isn't much she can do. Luis was supposed to do the confirming, but not the actual booking. He hasn't arrived yet so she's doubly annoyed.'

'Have we tried alternative venues?' I asked.

'She's already been on to a dozen hotels, but none of them have availability,' Magdalena said.

Just then, Gabriela walked back into the office. I could see that she was barely keeping her temper in check.

'Well?' she asked, looking at Magdalena. 'Any bright ideas?'

Poor Magdalena looked miserable. First into the office this morning, she'd taken the brunt of Gabriela's anger.

'I have an idea,' I said tentatively. 'A hotel that might have space.'

'Well, don't stand there,' snapped Gabriela. 'Check it out.' She went into her room and slammed the door behind her.

'Time of the month,' said Luis who'd just walked into the office.

'Oh, Luis, that is a terrible thing to say.' Magdalena looked at him furiously. 'And you won't be saying it when she's firing you because she has to cancel the presentation tomorrow.'

'What!' Luis was aghast.

'I rang the hotel this morning to query something. It turns out that you never confirmed the booking. That's your job, Luis. If we don't find an alternative venue quickly, you'll be surplus to requirements,' said Magdalena. 'And I won't be crying for you. You spend too much time chatting up the girls in the office and not enough time doing your job.'

She flounced off to her desk and left me standing in the middle of the office while Luis rummaged frantically through the filing cabinet.

I sat at my own desk and looked up the number of the Hotel Lux. I hadn't been there for a few weeks. I was trying to see less of Barbara and Bridget and their crowd because, no matter what resolutions I made, I always got drunk when I was out with them. Since my holiday with Julie, I'd decided that I'd gone a bit too far in the reinvention of Isobel Kavanagh and that I should be more sensible. Sometimes it seemed the right thing; at other times (like when I was at home on my own) it seemed stupid.

I skimmed through the phone book. Advanta had never

used the Lux before, but there was always the chance it might have a room.

'I'm not sure that we have a room to suit you exactly,' said Señor Murillo, the manager, when I finally got through to him. 'But we do have a function room and it is available tomorrow.'

'Don't book it for anyone else,' I said. 'I'll be there in fifteen minutes.'

I jumped up from the desk and popped my head around Gabriela's door. 'Don't panic just yet,' I said. 'I'm going to check out a place. I'll be back in an hour.'

'Isobel, if you find me somewhere, I'll give you a raise.'

'I hope you mean that,' I said.

I got a taxi outside the office and reached the Lux in a few minutes. It was silly to feel that I had to run up the flight of steps into the hotel, but I did anyway.

Señor Murillo shook my hand. 'It is an emergency, yes?'

'Yes,' I said.

'We will see if the Lux can help you.' He looked at me curiously. 'I have seen you here a number of times before, have I not?'

I smiled at him. 'I drink in the bar sometimes.'

'Ah, yes.' He nodded. 'You have a friend who is a friend of Tomás Medina.'

'That's right.' I was surprised that he knew. But maybe that's why he was the manager.

He led me along a narrow corridor. 'Don't be worried that you are being brought into the worst part of the hotel. This leads to an annexe we had built two years ago.'

'No problem.' But I was worried. The businessmen wouldn't like to think that they were being shunted into the basement.

'Here we are.' Señor Murillo opened a double door. 'Will this suit you?'

It wasn't perfect, but it would certainly suit. There was just about room for fifty people. Chairs were stacked neatly around the walls.

'Do you have projection equipment?' I asked. 'And microphones?'

Señor Murillo nodded.

'And would you be able to provide lunch?'

He looked at me quizzically. 'What sort of lunch?'

'Nothing complicated,' I assured him. 'Cold meat salad, perhaps?'

He looked at his watch as though every second counted. 'We can manage something.'

'It's important that it's good quality,' I said anxiously. 'It doesn't have to be extravagant, but not poor quality.'

'The Hotel Lux never compromises on quality,' he told me pompously.

'OK.' I looked around the room again. It would be all right. 'Can I phone my office to confirm?'

'Certainly.'

I took my mobile phone from my jacket pocket. 'Gabriela?' I'd rung her direct line. 'It's me, Isobel. I have a place for us.'

'Really?' I didn't think she believed me. 'With enough space? With everything we need? With catering?'

'Yes, yes and yes,' I said.

'How much will it cost?' she asked.

'I haven't discussed that yet,' I said. 'I wanted to know what your limits were.'

'You know how much it usually is,' she said. 'I'll leave it up to you.'

'OK. I'll be back shortly.'

'Isobel?'

'Yes?'

'Well done.'

'You can say that after I find out the price.'

Señor Murillo had walked to the end of the room while I made the phone call.

'Señor?'

He turned to me.

'How much will you charge to hire the room all day and to provide me with a projection screen, perhaps a projector, microphones and a lunch for fifty people?'

'You expect me to tell you that straight away?'

'Not straight away,' I said. 'But I need to decide very quickly.'

'And if you don't decide very quickly?'

'Señor, you know and I know that I'm not in a strong bargaining position. But I am also in the position that I have other business I can do with your hotel. If you are interested.' I shrugged to show that I didn't care about the other business. 'It might not be of interest to you, I understand. But . . .' I left the sentence hanging in mid-air.

He grinned at me. 'Come to my office. We will see what we can work out.'

It took twenty minutes to arrive at an acceptable price. It was more than we would normally pay for a venue and lunch, but not horrifically more. I thought that Gabriela would be pleased.

She was. She put her arms around me and told me that I was worth more than anyone else in her office. That the day she had decided to employ me was the best decision of her life. That I was the most sensible person that she had ever met. That I had intelligence. I would go far. If I applied myself – who knows?

'Thank you,' I said, when I had finally extracted myself from her embrace.

'No, it is important that I tell you these things,' she

said, her hand still resting on my shoulder. 'I know I am sometimes difficult to work with. I know that, Isobel. But you continue to work for me and I will reward you.'

I cleared my throat. 'You mentioned something about a rise.' I tried to sound offhand.

'Yes, I did.' Gabriela nodded vigorously. 'There will be extra in your salary this month.'

'Thanks,' I said again, although I wondered exactly how much the extra would be. Still, I felt a great deal of satisfaction knowing that it was me, Isobel, who'd sorted out the crisis. It proved that I was able to do things, that I was as good at business as the rest of them.

Luis took me to lunch. 'To thank you,' he said. 'She would have fired me. It was all my fault.'

'These things happen,' I said as I dipped my chicken into some mayonnaise. 'Although I'm sure it shouldn't have.'

'I thought I'd confirmed with them,' he said. 'I was sure I had. I thought I'd even seen the fax.' He shook his head. 'But it was a mistake.'

'Never mind,' I comforted him. 'It's sorted out now.'

'She absolutely chewed me up,' he said morosely as he picked at his fish. 'She doesn't like it if things go wrong.'

'Can't blame her,' I said. 'And with so many people off work this week, things were even worse. Plus the trade exhibition.'

'I know.' He sighed. 'I thought I was going to be fired.'

'Cheer up.' I laughed. 'You just have to do something wonderful to redeem yourself.'

He rubbed his forehead. 'If she ever trusts me again.'

'Don't be so melodramatic,' I said. 'Of course she'll trust you again.'

'It was a genuine mistake.'

'Luis.' I put down my knife and fork. 'Can you just shut up about it now? Everything is OK.'

We went back to the office. Gabriela was at a meeting. Magdalena grinned at me as I walked to my desk. 'Congratulations,' she said.

'Congratulations?'

'You've saved the day, Isobel! Gabriela was singing your praises earlier.'

I was uncomfortable. 'I just thought of a place,' I said. 'It wasn't anything great.'

'You thought of the right place,' said Magdalena. 'Well done.'

'Thanks.'

I still felt uncomfortable. I'd felt clever earlier, but, in reality, all I'd done was book a hotel. It wasn't exactly brilliant stuff. Still, I supposed, if it meant that Gabriela was happy, it was a good thing. I pulled a file towards me and started to work again.

~

'It'll be fun,' said Barbara on the phone to me that evening. 'Come on, Isobel, we haven't seen you in ages.'

'I know,' I told her. 'I've been busy in work.'

'It's not a party,' she said. 'Not on a Thursday night. We're just inviting a few people around for drinks. It'll be more sophisticated than falling around the apartment drunk as skunks.'

I laughed. 'OK, what time?'

'About nine.'

'See you then.'

~

There were about twenty people in the apartment when I

arrived. 'Great to see you.' Barbara kissed me, continental style, on each cheek. 'You're looking fantastic.'

I knew I looked better. I was still eating loads of fresh fruit and vegetables, but I'd had a lot of early nights since I'd come back from Sitges and I'd cut back on my drinking. I was wearing an old pair of jeans that had been slightly tight around the waist a couple of years ago but were now nicely loose, and my silk top was cropped so that my nicely tanned, flat stomach was on display.

I handed over a bottle of Southern Comfort.

'D'you want some of this, or will you have wine to start?' asked Barbara.

'I'll stick to the Southie,' I told her. 'Don't want to mix my drinks!'

She laughed and poured a measure. 'Do you know everyone?'

I knew some of them. I sat on the sofa and chatted to a girl who gave art appreciation classes at the college.

When I'd finished my drink, Tomás handed me a cocktail which I eyed suspiciously.

'I made it myself,' he said. 'You'll like it.'

I did.

'Ladies and gentlemen.' Barbara stood on a coffee-table. 'Can we have a bit of silence for a moment.'

The hum of conversation ceased. 'Thank you,' she said. 'Most of you are probably wondering why we have gathered here tonight. If it had been my choice, it would have been tomorrow night but, unfortunately, Señor Medina is working tomorrow night. And he is the one who has an announcement to make.' She smiled at Tomás. 'It's all yours.'

'*Señors y Señoras.*' Tomás cleared his throat. 'As you

know I have been going out with a wonderful lady for the past few months. It suddenly occurred to me that I was very lucky to have her. And I didn't like the idea that one day she might decide to go back to England. So, I thought, what can I do about this? And the answer was very simple – marry her! I asked her how she felt about it, and she said that it sounded a pretty good idea to her.' He grinned at us all. 'And so, tonight, I want to tell you all that Bridget and I are engaged to be married.'

We clapped as he took a jewellery box out of his pocket.

Bridget stood beside him and he slipped the ring onto her finger. I felt a lump the size of a tennis ball in my throat. We clapped again. Everyone clustered around them to give them good wishes and Bridget held out her hand so that we could see the sparkling diamond on her finger.

'I'm really pleased for you,' I croaked. 'And the ring is lovely.'

'Isn't it?' She beamed at me. 'D'you want to make a wish, Isobel?'

'Oh, I don't—'

'Go on!' She handed it to me. 'Only not for a husband, you know.'

'I know.' I grinned unsteadily at her. 'I'll wish for a rich mother-in-law. That's the form, isn't it?'

She laughed. 'Regretfully, Señora Medina isn't rich. But I love Tomás just the same.'

'I'm glad.' I slid the ring onto my finger and turned it anticlockwise three times.

I didn't wish for anything.

~

I drank a few more of Tomás's prize-winning cocktails

and then left. It was around midnight and the streets were still teeming with people. The city deserved its reputation as an enjoyed city, I thought, as I crossed the street. Everybody in Madrid liked to have a good time.

Tomás and Bridget. I hadn't imagined that they'd get engaged. I thought Bridget was like Barbara – enjoyed partying and meeting people and having a good time. I didn't think she was the settling-down sort.

Maybe we all are, I thought. Deep down, maybe everyone just wants to find someone and set up house. Despite all the opportunities to do other things. To have great careers. To travel the world. Maybe it's just inbuilt in us.

I shivered even though the air was warm. Oh God, Tim, I thought, why don't you love me any more?

I was going to cry. I didn't want to cry. Not for Tim, not for anyone. But I couldn't help it.

'Isobel?'

I looked up.

'Isobel?'

I wiped away the tears. Of all the people I didn't want to meet, Luis was as high up on the list as it was possible to be.

'Hello, Luis,' I said.

'Are you all right?'

'I'm fine,' I said. 'Honestly.'

'You seemed upset.'

'Not really.' I smiled weakly. 'A friend of mine got engaged. That's all.'

Luis laughed. 'And are you crying because she is engaged to be married or because you are not?'

That was a bit close to the bone. I winced.

'Isobel?'

'I don't know why I'm crying, Luis. It's a woman thing.'

'You are crying because you do not like your life in Madrid,' said Luis. 'And you know you should do something about it.'

'There's nothing wrong with my life in Madrid,' I said spiritedly. 'Just because I don't want to fall into bed with you.'

'Why not?'

'Because I work with you.'

'So? Why is that a problem?'

'It just is.'

'That's not much of an answer.'

'It's all you're getting.'

I shook my head. The cocktails, despite their apparent innocence, had made it fuzzier than I thought. I stumbled. Luis caught me by the arm. 'I'm fine,' I told him. 'Leave me alone.'

'If you tell me why you were crying.'

'It's none of your business, Luis.'

'Oh, come on, Isobel.' He held my arm more tightly. 'We are friends. You saved my job. Why were you crying?'

'Because—' I sighed. 'Because I was once engaged to be married myself and because we decided – no, Luis, *he* decided to call it off.'

'Oh.'

'Exactly.'

'And you are upset because now your friend is engaged and you are not.'

'I don't know,' I said irritably. 'I don't know why I'm upset.'

'Come back to my apartment,' said Luis. 'I will make you some coffee.'

'I don't need coffee.'

'But you might need company.'

'I don't think so.'

'Humour me,' said Luis.

~

I hadn't realised how close by me he lived. The block was older and the apartments more spacious. Luis lived on the third floor.

'Sit down.' He waved me towards a battered old sofa. 'Make yourself comfortable.'

I sat down.

'You can turn on the TV or the music centre if you like,' he called from the kitchen.

But I liked the silence. I closed my eyes.

'Isobel?' Luis's voice came from miles away 'Are you all right?'

'Mm?'

'Are you all right?'

I opened my eyes. His face was close to mine, his eyes dark and concerned. I reached out and touched him. 'Mm,' I murmured. 'I'm fine, Luis.'

'Good.' He didn't move as I pulled him closer to me.

'Come here,' I complained. 'How can I kiss you if you're so far away?'

'Do you want to kiss me?' asked Luis.

'I do,' I told him.

'Sure?' But he was closer to me now.

'I want to kiss you.' Our lips were only millimetres apart. 'Oh, Luis, I want to kiss you.'

'I guess I was wrong when I thought you might only like women,' murmured Luis.

~

Luis Cardoso made everyone I'd ever slept with until now seem like an amateur. We kissed for what seemed like hours. Then he lifted me onto his shiny teak dining-table and made love to me. After that, he carried me into his bedroom and made love to me again.

'*Oh, Isobel, mia Isobel,*' he murmured as he held me close to him. 'You are the best, the most wonderful, the most loving.'

'So are you.' I nuzzled close to him. 'So are you, my darling, wonderful, gorgeous Luis.'

I woke up at half-past seven. Luis's arm was wrapped around me. My head was pounding, my mouth was dry.

And I knew I'd made another, terrible mistake.

Chapter 16

Personages in the Night (Joan Miró, 1949)

I got out of the bed as quietly as I could. Luis mumbled something then rolled onto his side. I stood beside the bed, holding my breath in case he woke up. But he didn't. I exhaled slowly.

I couldn't believe it. I'd gone to bed with Luis and that was the last thing in the world I'd wanted to do. I had to work with Luis. I had to see him every single day. I couldn't just walk away from him and pretend it hadn't happened.

What on earth had I been thinking of? What had possessed me (apart from Luis in an utterly fantastic way)? I needed my head examined. I tiptoed around the bedroom, picking up my clothes from where I'd thrown them in wild, abandoned passion the night before. I retrieved my bra from the wall-light – I don't know how it had got there. I remembered tiptoeing like this around Ignacio's apartment a few months ago. Julie was right. It was sordid.

I would be late for work. Luis would be late too unless his alarm clock went off pretty soon. I understood now how it was that he arrived looking such a mess. He obviously left getting up until the last possible moment.

The alarm still hadn't gone off by the time I sneaked out of the apartment and ran down the stairs. An army of pile-drivers marched through my head. I felt sick.

I hoped Luis wouldn't wake up for ages, that I'd manage to get into the office before him, that I'd have thought of what I was going to say to him. I'd no idea what I was going to say to him.

The creaky, useless old lift in the Edificio Gerona was out of order again. I'd get fit, I thought, running up and down the stairs of Madrid's apartment blocks. I undressed as I moved through my apartment, into the bathroom and under the (cold) shower.

My nipples stood out like little doorknobs as the icy water cascaded over me. I shivered. It serves you right, I told myself. You stupid, stupid bitch.

I liked Luis. You couldn't help liking Luis. But I didn't love him and, despite the wonderful sex, I knew I'd never love him. This wasn't the kind of situation that works so well in the movies – where the unkempt, casual friend who's always around when the heroine needs him turns out to be the love of her life – a fact she never realises until the final frame even though the rest of us have known it from the moment he's walked onto the screen. It just wasn't like that with Luis.

And, oh God, everyone else in the office would know about it and I didn't want them to. Luis would boast about me the way he boasted about everyone else. I wondered, fleetingly, what had happened to his girlfriend, Maria. But I didn't care about Maria, I only cared about me.

Isobel the idiot. Isobel the fool that had joined the list of Luis's conquests. Isobel Kavanagh, the girl without a brain.

If I hadn't drunk those bloody cocktails I might have been OK. What in heaven's name was in them? I rubbed the towel vigorously over my body. One minute I'd felt fine. The next, I was an emotional wreck. And then I'd turned into some kind of rabid nymphomaniac. I blushed as I remembered crawling over Luis's body, doing things with him that I'd never done before. I groaned and pulled a comb through my hair. No time to dry it. I rummaged through my wardrobe. It'd have to be my red linen suit and white blouse. I hadn't done any ironing in ages and the white blouse was the only one left. And I hated the white blouse.

Gin, I remembered suddenly. There'd been gin in the cocktails and I'm one of those people who normally get depressed when they drink gin. There must have been an anti-depressant in there too. I certainly hadn't been depressed when I sat astride Luis on top of his polished, teak dining-room table.

My head was still thumping. The metro was crowded. I was nearly half an hour late for work.

'Good morning, Isobel.' Luis was at his desk, hair uncombed, suit crumpled.

'Good morning, Luis.' I felt the colour stain my cheeks.

'How are you this morning?'

'Fine. Thank you.' I marched past him, stopped at the water dispenser and filled a paper cup, then sat down at my desk.

'Hi, Isobel.' Magdalena dumped an armful of green folders on my desk. 'You're late.'

'I know.' I glanced involuntarily at my watch. 'Was Gabriela looking for me?'

Magdalena grinned. 'You're lucky. She's at the Lux looking in on the conference and deciding how much of a raise to give you.'

'Good.'

'Where were you last night?' she asked.

'Last night?' I felt the blush start again and had to

force myself not to look in Luis's direction. 'Oh, my friend Bridget got engaged. You know the girl from the college?'

'The one who is going out with the barman from the hotel?'

I nodded. 'That's the one. So we had some drinks in her apartment to celebrate.'

'I wish I could drink as much as you and still make it into the office,' said Magdalena. 'If I'd been out drinking last night I wouldn't be arriving only half an hour late today.'

'I didn't drink that much!' Did everyone in Advanta think of me as a lush? I'd cut down on my drinking, for God's sake. And I'd never really drunk that much in the first place.

'You'd had quite a few when I met you.'

Magdalena turned at the sound of Luis's voice. 'You met Isobel last night?'

'Yes,' said Luis. 'And she wasn't terribly steady on her feet.'

'Oh, I was fine.' I couldn't meet his eyes. Just couldn't.

'Were you? You could have fooled me.'

'I probably fool you all the time,' I said sharply, and Magdalena laughed.

She'd guess, of course. If she hadn't already guessed. I opened my desk drawer to get some paracetamol but the little bubble pack was empty. I rubbed the side of my nose and closed my eyes.

'Here.' Luis stood beside me and offered me a couple of capsules.

'Tylenol,' he said. 'Go ahead.'

'Thanks.'

He sat on the edge of the desk.

'I'm busy,' I said. 'I was late in today.'

He grinned. 'So I noticed. I wasn't.'

'I had to go home and shower.'

'I didn't bother,' said Luis. 'So much more memorable that way.'

'Luis!' I knocked over the remainder of my water. It spilled across the desk and dripped onto the floor.

'Oh, fuck!' I cried.

The others in the office looked up in surprise. Luis said nothing but began to mop the water with a tissue. I looked up and caught Magdalena gazing at us speculatively.

'Clumsy this morning.' Luis threw the sodden tissues into the wastepaper bin.

'Tired,' I said.

'I'm not surprised.'

'Luis,' I said. 'Would you please go away?'

'But why?' He smiled at me. 'Gabriela, the slave-driver, is out of the office. I am not busy. I have time to sit and talk to you, *mia Isobel*.'

'I don't have time to talk to you,' I snapped. 'And I'm not your Isobel.'

'*Oh, mia Isobel!*'

'Luis. Please.'

He shrugged. 'What is wrong, Isobel? If I said nothing to you then you would complain that Luis Cardoso doesn't care about you. That he is happy to get you into his bed but—'

'Luis, for God's sake!'

Magdalena was still watching us. One or two of the other staff were watching us too.

'Luis, I'm sorry, but I don't have time to discuss this now,' I said loudly. 'Perhaps you could talk to me about it after lunch?'

'Anything you wish, *mia Isobel*,' said Luis. 'Anything you wish, anytime you wish.'

He walked back to his desk again and I opened one

of the green folders. But I hadn't a clue what any of the paperwork was about. It was just as well there wasn't a seminar today. I could sit at my desk and stare empty-headed at files and it wouldn't make much difference.

Oh God, I thought, what had I done with my life? I didn't feel like me any more. I didn't feel like the Isobel who cycled along the seafront, letting the wind tangle my hair and bring colour to my cheeks. I didn't feel like the Isobel who made wedding dresses for friends and who'd hand-sewn four hundred and twenty pearls onto her own dress. I didn't feel like the Isobel who ate tea and toast with her sister at midnight while we talked about her career prospects. I felt like a stranger.

And wasn't that what you wanted? I asked myself fiercely as I drew a line through a memo. You wanted to be a different Isobel and you are a different Isobel.

So what's the bloody problem?

I rubbed my temples. My head felt as though it was going to explode.

'Isobel?' I looked up. Magdalena stood in front of my desk holding a cup of coffee. 'I thought you could do with this.'

'Oh, Magdalena, thank you.' I took the cup from her. 'You're right. It's just what I need.'

She pulled up a chair and sat down. 'Are you all right?' she asked.

'Apart from the headache, I'm fine.'

'You look awful, Isobel.'

'Don't you start.'

'Pardon?'

'People are always telling me I look awful.' I smiled at her, but my smile didn't reach my eyes. 'They tell me I'm too pale, or too thin, or that I've black bags under my eyes.'

'Do they?'

'Sometimes.'

'You're pale today,' said Magdalena. 'But you've been thin since I've known you. And, yes, you have black smudges under your eyes.'

'A true friend.' I sighed. 'I know I must look terrible today.'

She pulled the chair closer. 'Isobel?'

'Yes?'

'I know it's rude of me to ask. But did you and Luis—?'

'You're right,' I said. 'It's none of your business.'

She flushed. 'I'm sorry.'

I said nothing.

'I'd better get back to work,' said Magdalena eventually. 'But if you need to talk about anything . . .'

'Why would I need to talk about anything?' I closed one file and opened another. 'There's nothing to talk about.'

She sat in silence for a moment then got up and walked away.

~

My headache grew worse. My eyes hurt. I read endless reports on lecturers and seminars and didn't understand a word of them. At twelve o'clock I got up from my desk and went to the ladies'. My stomach was churning and, although I was hot, I was shivering too. I wondered if I was actually sick, whether I was getting the flu or something which might explain why I felt so bad. I leaned my head against the coolness of the wall-tiles and then, suddenly, lunged for the nearest cubicle and threw up.

Being sick makes me wheeze. It's because you're

coughing and spluttering and you can't breathe properly. For a moment or two, I thought I was going to die. But there was no point in using my inhaler yet, because I knew that I hadn't finished throwing up. My stomach was still on a roller-coaster.

The door to the ladies' opened just as I vomited again.

'Isobel!' Gabriela was beside me in an instant. She'd arrived back at the office a little earlier, delighted at how the conference was going. 'Isobel! Are you all right?'

I couldn't speak. I wished it had been anybody but Gabriela.

She ripped some paper towel from the container and handed it to me. 'I'll get you some water.'

I'd finished being sick. I flushed the toilet, put down the lid and sat down. Now my head was pounding worse than ever and my hands were shaking. I was fighting for every breath too.

Gabriela returned with a paper cup of water. I took a sip and then gasped at her, 'Can you get me my handbag? I need my inhaler.'

She nodded and disappeared again. I rinsed my mouth out with water.

When she came back with the bag I took a couple of puffs of the inhaler and, almost immediately, began to feel better.

'Is this a bad attack?' she asked, her voice full of concern. 'I did not realise you had asthma, Isobel. I didn't think it made you ill like this.'

It was a great excuse, but there was no point in excuses.

'It's not the asthma that made me sick,' I said. 'Being sick has made me wheeze.'

'And what has made you sick?' she asked. 'Have you

been feeling unwell for a while? Was it something you ate?'

She was being very tactful, I thought. 'No, Gabriela.' There was no point in lying to her. 'I'm really sorry,' I said. 'Really, really sorry.' And then I started to cry.

I didn't mean to cry. Gabriela said nothing, she just tore off some more paper towel.

'Do you want to talk about it?' she said, after the tears had stopped and I'd blown my nose.

'Oh, no. It's OK, Gabriela. Honestly. I'm fine now.'

'Don't be absolutely ridiculous,' she said sharply. 'You are not well, Isobel.'

'But I am,' I said.

The door to the ladies' opened and both of us looked up. Sofia stared at us in amazement.

'Can you use the toilets on the other floor?' asked Gabriela.

Sofia nodded wordlessly and closed the door again. Oh God, I thought, it'll be all around the office in a minute. Isobel Kavanagh is crying in the toilets and Gabriela is watching her. And Luis would hear about it and he'd think it was because I'd fallen for him or something. Oh God. Oh shit. Oh fuck, fuck, fuck.

'Would you like some more water?'

'No thanks, Gabriela. I feel OK now.'

'I think you'd better tell me about it.'

I shook my head slowly. The pain bounced around my skull.

'Isobel?' I looked up at her. 'I want you to tell me.'

It wasn't any of her business, I thought furiously. It was nothing to do with her.

She waited patiently.

'I'm sorry,' I said again. 'I shouldn't have come in today.'

'Not if you felt this ill,' said Gabriela.

I wasn't going to tell her, but suddenly I did.

'I've made such a mess of things,' I said. 'Oh, Gabriela, I'm such an idiot.'

'Isobel.' She looked at me carefully. 'Are you pregnant?'

I stared at her. I'd never thought that anyone would think of it as a possibility. But of course here I was, head down the toilet and wailing that I'd made a mess of my life. In her shoes, I'd have probably thought the same. But I knew I wasn't pregnant. I'd made sure of that.

'No.' I smiled wanly at her. 'I'm not pregnant.'

She sighed, and I realised it was with relief. 'I just thought—'

'I realise what you must have thought. I'm sorry.'

'Well, it can't be that bad, can it?'

I supposed not. God, if I'd been pregnant – it was too much to even contemplate.

'So, do you want to talk about it anyway?' asked Gabriela.

I smiled again, a little less wanly this time. 'Not really.' I pushed my damp hair out of my eyes. 'Or maybe I should.'

'I think you should,' said Gabriela firmly. 'I've noticed that you haven't looked well lately, Isobel. I thought maybe it was just a lot of late nights, you know. But it's more than that?'

'It's a lot of stupid things,' I said. 'You'll think me a horrible person, Gabriela.'

'No, I won't.'

'You will. Because I am a horrible person.'

'Tell me why.'

I sighed. 'When I came to Madrid, I thought I would be a different person. When I was younger and living at home I had lots of boyfriends but I was a sensible sort of girl. Then I met Tim. I was crazy about him, Gabriela.

I couldn't wait to marry him! So when he called it off – I was devastated. I thought my life had come to an end.' I was silent for a moment. Gabriela watched me, but said nothing. 'I was so unhappy at home that I think everyone was sick of me. Barry Cleary was sick of me. It was Sharon who thought I should work abroad. I think it was because I was driving Barry insane. So I came here, Gabriela, and I thought that I could be different. That I should go out every night and have a good time and nobody knew anything about me. And that's what I did. I met a guy in a bar near the apartment and went out with him for a while. I went to lots of parties with the girls from the college. I know I drank too much but I felt better when I was drinking. More lighthearted. Last night I went to an engagement party. I drank cocktails. I never drink cocktails. I got upset – stupid, I know, but I kept thinking about Tim and our wedding and everything and I left the party because I knew I was going to cry. So I was walking home and I met Luis.'

'Luis?' she interrupted me. 'Luis Cardoso? Our Luis?'

'The very one.'

'Oh, Isobel!'

'Don't say "oh, Isobel".' I made a face at her. 'He was so nice to me, Gabriela. He brought me to his apartment and made me coffee and he was – oh, nice and kind and—'

'—you went to bed with him?'

'I couldn't help it,' I said. 'It just seemed the right thing to do.'

'And you've been sick because—?'

'Because I drank too much and because he came and sat on my desk and called me "*mia Isobel*" and because I know everyone in the office will know about it and I feel like such a fool.'

Gabriela shrugged. 'Claims about Luis are exaggerated,' she said. 'Yes, he has been with some of the girls in the office. He seems to be the sort of person who can get away with it! Everyone stays friendly with him afterwards.'

'Very continental,' I said.

She laughed. 'We are, perhaps, less analytical about it. Anyway, maybe you'll want to go out with him again.'

'No,' I said. 'I like him, Gabriela. But he's not my type.'

She made a face. 'Alfredo wasn't my type. But I still knew that he was the one I'd marry.'

'You knew it straight away, you said. But I don't feel that with Luis.'

'Not everyone knows,' said Gabriela.

'I like him,' I said. 'But that's all. And it's not one of these likings that suddenly turn into mad passion. Besides – he's slept with half of Madrid.'

Gabriela chuckled. 'He'd like you to think that.'

'Even so.'

'Are you feeling better now?' she asked.

'I guess so.'

'You shouldn't have come in today. You could have stayed in bed.'

'In Luis's bed?' I said.

'Perhaps not.'

We both smiled.

'But you should go home now, Isobel. There is nothing exceptional scheduled for today. Go home and have a good sleep and you'll feel better by tomorrow.'

I stood up. My legs were shaky.

'I'll order a taxi,' said Gabriela. 'Don't bother going back to your desk. Go into my office and wait there.'

'Thank you,' I said. 'You've been really good to me, Gabriela.'

'What are friends for?' She smiled and gave me a hug.

~

I crawled into bed. My head was thumping, my legs shaking and my breathing was ragged. I'd taken too many puffs of my inhaler and my heart was racing. I felt awful. I wished I was at home in Sutton, where Mum would be sympathetic and bring me cups of weak tea (although, to be honest, I wouldn't have been able to keep it down), and would fetch me cool, damp towels for my aching head. I would have killed for a cool, damp towel right then. The apartment was like a furnace because I didn't leave the air-conditioning on during the day.

I alternately baked and shivered under the sheet. Maybe I *was* getting the flu. Maybe it was nothing to do with cocktails and Luis and humiliation. But I knew that it had everything to do with cocktails and Luis and humiliation.

Eventually I fell into a dreamless sleep.

I was awakened by the sound of the apartment buzzer. I sat up slowly in the bed and shook my head experimentally to see how the headache was. Almost gone, which was good, and I didn't feel sick any more either. Although my legs were still shaky.

I padded into the living room and pressed on the intercom. 'Who is it?'

'It's me, Luis.'

'Luis!'

'Yes. Can I come up?'

'Oh – um – yes, Luis. Of course.'

What else could I say? I pulled on a pair of jeans and a T-shirt and ran my fingers through my hair. I just about had time to wash my mouth out with Listerine when he knocked at the door.

'*Hola*, Isobel. How are you feeling?' His eyes showed nothing but concern.

'Hi, Luis. Come in. I'm much better, thanks.'

'What was it?' he asked. 'Something you ate?'

I shrugged. 'More likely something I drank.'

'Were you very drunk last night, Isobel?'

'I think so.' I smiled faintly. 'I didn't realise it at the time.'

'Poor Isobel.'

'It's my own fault,' I told him. 'I should have had more sense.'

'And maybe more sense than to have come to my apartment?'

'Definitely more sense than that, Luis.'

'I knew you'd been drinking, Isobel. And I'm sorry. I shouldn't have gone to bed with you.'

'As far as I recall it wasn't just the bed,' I said dryly, although the memory of making love on the table was making me squirm.

'It was very good nonetheless.'

'Luis!'

'It's true,' he said. 'You are a very exciting, sexy woman, Isobel.'

'Please, Luis.'

'So what is the problem?'

'I shouldn't have slept with you, Luis. I don't love you.'

'That's not much of a reason.'

'It is for me.'

'But you have slept with other men since you have been in Madrid.'

Oh, God, I thought. Exactly what does he know about me?

'I—'

'No matter, Isobel.'

'Luis, I'm sorry. Honestly.'

Why was I apologising to him?

'It doesn't matter, Isobel. It was a great experience.' He grinned. 'For you too, I hope.'

I blushed. 'Yes.'

'And we are friends?'

'I suppose so.'

'In that case, tell me about it.'

'About what?'

'About the man you ran away from. The Irishman.'

'Does there have to be one?'

'Oh, come on, Isobel. Everyone knows that there was something!'

'Did Gabriela—?'

'Gabriela said nothing. But we're not stupid.'

So much for the Isobel with no history. And so much for my reinvented self – the self I didn't much like anyway. I told him about Tim and me and the wedding. And I didn't care that he regarded me with sympathy afterwards.

'I am not surprised you came to Madrid,' he said. 'We are much nicer men here!'

I laughed, although it hurt my head. 'You are.'

'Isobel, I will not try to get you into bed again. Maybe, in time, you might wish to. If so, I will be here. But I will leave it up to you.'

'Luis, please don't get offended when I say that it'll be a long, long time before I get into bed with anyone again. As long as it'll be before I drink alcohol again.' I stood up and went to the cupboard under the sink. There were six bottles of Rioja in the cupboard. I put them into a cardboard box, along with a bottle of Southern Comfort and a bottle of vodka. 'Take these, please,' I said as I handed him the box. 'I really don't even want them in the apartment any more.'

'You don't think that you have become a little extreme over this?'

'No,' I said. 'I came here to be a different person, Luis, and I became a different person. But I don't like her very much. So if I get rid of these, I get rid of her. Do you understand?'

'I understand,' he said. 'And I hope you get better soon, Isobel.'

'So do I,' I said.

And, when I closed the apartment door after him, I sat down and began to get better.

Chapter 17

Combinations (Salvador Dalí, 1931)

It had been a beautiful day in Madrid. I didn't really want to leave but I'd promised to come home for Ian's birthday in October and I didn't want to break my word. Not that Ian would have cared either way, I suppose, but I knew Mum would be disappointed if I said I wasn't coming. And part of me wanted to see them all again even though another part of me dreaded it.

The plane had begun its descent into Dublin airport. We'd already been told that it was cold and raining and now we were being bumped around as we flew through the heavy clouds. I clutched my armrest and wished that I liked flying.

We shuddered our way downwards, eventually landing with a welcome thud on the runway. The rain splattered against the windows of the plane.

'*Bienvenidos à Dublin.* Welcome to Dublin,' said the stewardess.

'Right,' I muttered as I undid my seatbelt. 'Welcome home, Isobel.'

The airport was crowded. I'd never seen so many people in it before. I looked around for Mum or Dad, but it was impossible to identify anyone in the throng.

'Isobel!' I heard my name before I saw my sister. She was waving frantically at me. I pushed my way through the crowd and hugged her.

'Welcome home,' said Alison. 'I was afraid I'd never be able to see you.'

'I didn't see how I'd pick out anybody in this lot.' I pushed her away from me. 'And I wasn't expecting you.'

'The central heating packed up at lunchtime,' she said. 'Dad is at home supervising the repair-men.'

I shivered at the thought of the house without central heating.

'They've promised it'll be fixed,' said Alison, 'although I don't hold out much hope.'

'You'll certainly feel the cold a lot more,' I told her, 'with your hair like that.'

She grinned at me. 'D'you like it?'

'It's wonderful,' I said. 'You look great.'

She did. She'd had her hair chopped short at the back and full at the front and looked a hundred times more sophisticated than she'd done the last time I'd seen her. She wore black jeans, black boots and a black leather jacket with a smoke-grey fur collar.

'And you've learned to drive too,' I said.

She shook her head. 'Haven't got that far yet. I was going to get lessons but the evenings were too dark and it was raining too much so I thought I'd wait until the spring.'

'Then how are we going to get home?' I asked.

'Peter's driving,' said Alison simply.

'Peter?'

'My boyfriend.' She looked defiantly at me.

'Great,' I said calmly although I couldn't wait to see a boyfriend that Alison deemed worthy enough to drag to the airport on a wet and windy autumn night.

He was waiting for us near the exit. He was tall and fair-haired, with piercing blue eyes.

'If you had his children people would think you were Scandinavian,' I murmured when she pointed him out to me.

'Isobel!' She punched me gently in the side. 'I'm not having his children. Don't be stupid.'

She walked up to him and kissed him on the cheek. 'This is Isobel.'

'Hello,' I said.

'Hi.'

Alison linked her arm to his. 'Sorry we took so long. There were thousands of people in there.'

'So I see.'

Taciturn, I thought. It was hard to imagine Alison staying with someone taciturn.

'Would you like me to take your case, Isobel?'

And chivalrous. Well, that was a definite advantage.

'That'd be great.'

'I wouldn't offer,' said Alison. 'She packs bricks in her case.'

'It's OK.' Peter picked it up. 'No problem.'

I was impressed by him. The case weighed a couple of tons.

The rain pelted against the walkway in sheets of water.

'Where did you meet him?' I asked as he paid for his parking ticket.

'Works with me,' said Alison.

'You're not serious!'

'Of course I am.'

'An office romance!' I laughed. 'Alison Kavanagh, the feminist champion, in an office romance.'

'It's not a romance,' she said sharply. 'It's a relationship.'

'That's OK then.' I smothered a smile but Alison didn't notice. She was watching Peter.

He hauled my case into the boot and I clambered into the back seat.

'When did you get your hair cut?' I asked Alison. 'You seem to have left rather a lot of it back here on the seat.'

Peter laughed and Alison giggled.

'That's not hair,' she said. 'At least, not from me. Peter has a Labrador. She sheds.'

'Oh.' I picked clumps of golden fur from my tartan jacket.

'I'm sorry,' said Peter. 'If I'd known I was going to be giving you a lift I'd have cleaned it out a bit. But Alison sprang it on me.'

'Oh, Alison.' I sighed. 'I could've got a taxi, you know.'

'It's no problem,' Peter assured me. 'We were going out tonight anyway.'

'I don't think you would have chosen a night at the airport,' I remarked.

'You'd never have got a taxi tonight,' said Alison. 'Not in this weather.'

I pulled my jacket more tightly around me. I was cold. And the sound of the rain against the windows made me shiver. I thought of my friends in Madrid and how they'd be crowded into Leon's Tapas Bar or eating dinner in one of the millions of cheap and cheerful restaurants they frequented and I missed them.

~

The central heating was fixed. The hallway was warm. Not very warm, but warm enough. Mum rushed at me almost before I'd crossed the threshold and folded me into her arms.

'Welcome home, darling!' She patted me on the head like a baby. 'It's wonderful to have you back.'

'Thanks,' I mumbled into her blouse 'It's nice to be back.'

'I was afraid your plane would be delayed,' she continued. 'The weather is so awful.'

'It was a bit late,' I admitted. 'But it was good of Peter and Alison to hang around for me.'

'That's OK.' Peter stood in the hall.

'Come in and have a cup of tea, Peter,' said Mum. 'Isobel's right. You were very good to pick her up.'

'I didn't mind,' said Peter.

'Well, take off your jacket and warm yourself inside,' said Mum. 'The heating's been on for about an hour. I was very worried about it. I thought we'd end up wrapped in blankets and eating our dinner in front of the oven for warmth.'

~

It was strange to be back under their roof. Odd not being in control of my own life. Not being able to lounge around in a T-shirt and nothing else. Not feeling as though I could grab the remote control and turn on whatever programme I liked.

Ian's girlfriend, Honey, called around later that night. She was every bit as beautiful as her photographs suggested, and very intelligent. Ian was besotted by her and I could hardly blame him.

Alison was equally besotted by Peter Gaffney. It was funny to see her face flush whenever his name was mentioned and to discover that she had an entire new wardrobe of sophisticated clothes that she wore when she went out with him.

Ian in love with Honey. Alison in love with Peter. And me, the older sister, far too wise to be in love with anyone.

~

Ian's party was much better fun than I expected. He'd hired out a room in the local pub and a live band which played seventies hits.

'They're humiliating me,' groaned Alison, nodding in the direction of our parents. 'Dad thinks he is John Travolta.'

'They're having a good time,' I said. 'I think this was a great idea.'

'Oh, Ian's into everything retro these days.' Alison giggled. 'Actually, you're right. It is a good idea. The songs are hilarious!'

'Having fun?' asked Ian as I knocked back a bottle of Ballygowan.

'I haven't had as much exercise in ages,' I told him. 'I'm danced off my feet.'

'You look great.' He grinned at me. 'Alison said you looked like shit when she went to visit.'

'She exaggerated,' I told him.

'She said that you were miserable and that you were drinking too much and eating nothing.'

'She exaggerated,' I repeated.

'Really?'

I sighed. 'I was a bit dodgy for a while, I suppose. I guess I just felt sorry for myself and miserable about everything. But I'm back on track again now. And I'm fine, Ian. Honestly.'

'I believe you,' he said quickly. 'I told you – you look great.'

I was wearing a pair of black jeans that fitted like a second skin and a gold-coloured top that I'd made the previous week. I'd had my hair done before I left Madrid and I knew I looked good. It had been very important for me to look good.

'Ian!' Honey waved at him. 'Come and dance. It's Abba!'

He smiled at me and followed her onto the dance floor. They were a perfect couple.

~

I sat down at a table near the bar and watched Ian and Honey, Alison and Peter, Mum and Dad as they gyrated to the music. I was glad they were having a good time. Especially Mum and Dad. It was a long time since I'd seen them out enjoying themselves. If I ever thought about my parents' marriage – and I rarely did – I guess I just thought that they cared enough about each other to stay together. I remembered them having a row when I was small. I was in bed, supposed to be asleep. But I hadn't been able to sleep. And then I'd heard raised voices downstairs and I'd tiptoed onto the landing to listen.

'I married you, wasn't that enough?' Dad had demanded. I shivered and pulled my pyjama top around me. I couldn't hear what Mum replied.

'It wasn't my fault,' he said, and his tone was halfway between anger and concern. 'It could have happened to anyone.'

And then I heard my mother and her voice was a wail. 'But it happened to me! I lost my baby. It happened to me.'

I'd run back to the bedroom and pulled the covers over my head. I hadn't known about the lost baby then, about the reason they'd married. And when I found out, years later, I knew that I'd get it right myself. When I got married it would be to the right man, the man who loved me for myself.

~

'You OK?' Dad sat down beside me.

'I'm fine.'

'You're looking wonderful.'

I smiled. 'Thanks.'

'We've been worried about you.'

'Why?'

'Oh, the way you left, Isobel. Because you were unhappy.'

'Not with you,' I said.

'But unhappy.' He put his arm around me. 'I hated seeing you so miserable.'

'I didn't like it much myself.' I snuggled up to him. 'But I'm over it now, Dad. It's all behind me.'

'And do you like the new job?'

I sat up straight again and nodded. 'They're really good to me. Gabriela's so kind. And the others are friendly.'

'When will you come home?'

'I don't know,' I said. 'Eventually, I suppose.'

'There's no one over there, is there?'

I shook my head.

'Not like you,' he said.

'What d'you mean?'

'Not like you to be without a boyfriend.'

I grinned at him. 'I'm enjoying it.'

'Really?'

'Really.' I kissed him on the cheek. 'I've discovered that I don't need a boyfriend to feel cared about.'

'Of course not,' he said, 'we care about you.'

'I know.' I leaned my head on his shoulder and we sat in companionable silence while the band played 'Mama We're All Crazee Now'.

I rang Julie the next day.

'How was the party?' she asked.

'Pretty good. We didn't get home until four.'

'How's the head?'

'Fine.'

'Fine?'

'Absolutely fine. I had a couple of beers and then went on to Ballygowans. So I was OK this morning.'

'That's good.'

'Julie,' I said. 'I mean it. I'm fine.'

She laughed. 'I believe you. When are you calling around?'

'Tonight?'

'Tonight is great.' She cleared her throat. 'There's just one thing, Isobel.'

'What?'

'I'm not on my own.'

I looked at the receiver in puzzlement. Of course she wasn't on her own. At the very least her parents were there too.

'Your parents?'

'I don't mean them, you dope!' she exclaimed. 'God, Isobel, sometimes you're thick.'

'Well, I don't—' Suddenly the penny dropped. 'Andy?'

'Who else?'

'When did he arrive?'

'The beginning of the week. He arrived on the door-step, Isobel.'

'Completely unexpected?'

'Completely. I couldn't believe it.'

'And did he expect you to welcome him with open arms?'

Julie laughed. 'Not exactly. He was sheepish about it really. He brought me a teddy-bear.'

'A teddy-bear!'

'Yes. A huge one. It had a box attached to it.'

'And what was in that?' I asked.

'Another box.' She giggled. 'And another, and another. Until down to the smallest box.'

'Julie!' I knew what was coming.

'It was the most beautiful ring, Isobel. So I tried it on.'

'And are you still wearing it?'

'Of course I am,' she said. 'I love him.'

She looked absolutely radiant. Her hair, nut-brown, almost her natural colour, gleamed in the hall light. Her dress was black silk.

'Looking sharp,' I said. 'Here.' I presented her with some handmade chocolates I'd bought in the Duty Free.

'Oh, Isobel, thank you.' She kissed me on the cheek. 'Come on in.'

'Let me see it.' I grabbed her left hand.

The engagement ring was beautiful. It was a solitaire diamond and it glittered and sparkled on her finger. It was almost as beautiful as my engagement ring had been.

'It's gorgeous,' I breathed. 'Absolutely gorgeous.'

'Thanks.'

'So where is he?'

'In the living room,' said Julie. 'We were watching TV.'

Andy's shoes were upturned carelessly on the carpet and he was half-sitting, half-lying on the sofa. There was a glass of beer and an open newspaper beside him. He swung himself upright when I walked into the room.

'Isobel! It's lovely to see you.'

'Hi, Andy.' I smiled at him. 'Congratulations.'

'Thanks, Isobel. I think I'm very lucky.'

'So do I,' said Julie.

'What made you decide?' I asked.

'I couldn't live without her,' said Andy simply.

Julie beamed.

'Oh, Andy,' I said. 'That's incredibly corny.'

'I know. But it's true.'

'And when did you realise that?'

He thought about it for a moment. 'In work one day. I was sitting at my desk working on a paper and I couldn't concentrate. I kept thinking about Julie. And I knew that I'd be mad to let her go.'

Julie beamed again. 'So he came over to get me.'

'I didn't ring because I was afraid she'd argue with me.' He grimaced. 'Our last conversation hadn't been easy. So I thought I'd surprise her and come over. Hell of a job getting a flight.'

Julie took up the story. 'I was doing my hair and nobody else was in. I'd just started to dry it when the doorbell rang – and there he was.'

'Dripping wet and shivering with cold,' added Andy.

'And a huge teddy-bear, also wet and probably cold.'

'I think you felt sorrier for the bear than me,' said Andy ruefully.

'Well,' Julie grinned at him, 'he did look kind of forlorn.'

'I knew you'd be a sucker for the bear!'

She laughed and turned back to me. 'And Andy looked at me – it was like in a book, Issy— He said that he loved me—'

Andy looked embarrassed. Julie gave him a good-natured push. 'Well, you did. And he asked me to marry him.'

'That's the most romantic thing I ever heard,' I said.

'So I stood looking at him and I couldn't speak,' continued Julie. 'And then he handed me the teddy-bear and the box with the ring.'

'Did it fit?' I asked.

'Isobel!' Julie looked pained.

Andy laughed. 'It's a bit loose. We're getting it sized tomorrow.'

'I don't want to give it to them,' said Julie.

'I'm really delighted for you both,' I said warmly. 'When is the happy day?'

'Next summer,' Julie told me. 'Andy's going to Prague for three months in the New Year and he'll be back and forward to the States for a while after that, so June or July will be the earliest we can reasonably do it.'

'You could always nip in to the register office before then,' I said.

'Isobel Kavanagh! Can you imagine my mother's face if I didn't have a huge, white, fairy-tale wedding?'

'I guess she wants the works?'

'Of course she does,' Julie said. 'She's been waiting for my wedding since I was born! Besides, Andy's family are Greek, after all. They're into big, family affairs.'

'Are they all coming over to Ireland?' I asked.

'I don't know,' said Andy. 'I haven't told them yet.'

'What!!'

He looked sheepish. 'I've told my parents – they expected me for Thanksgiving and I won't be back by then, and Ari knows too, but not the rest of the family.'

'His parents are disappointed he's not marrying a Greek girl. Or an American girl. But they said that maybe Irish was next best.'

I laughed. 'It'll be a great day.'

'I hope so,' said Julie. 'Sit down, Isobel, for goodness sake. Do you want a drink?'

'Southern Comfort would be nice,' I replied. 'A small one, Julie, with lots of ginger.'

She made a face. 'Ruining a good drink.'

'Where's the rest of the family?' I curled up in the big armchair near the fire.

'Visiting Danielle,' said Julie. 'You know what she's like – loves entertaining. She's been watching one of those TV cook programmes and she wants to experiment on them. I'm in her bad books because I said that you were calling around. I told her that Andy and I would visit later in the week. I just couldn't cope with the idea of my parents, my sister, three brothers and their assorted families in one house.'

'Would have been a good introduction for you, Andy,' I remarked.

'I wouldn't have minded.' His tone was brave. 'I like families.'

'So do I,' said Julie. 'But *en masse* the Donegans can take a bit of getting used to.'

We sat back and she turned up the volume on the TV. *True Lies* had just started. It was one of my favourite Arnie movies. And Andy said that Jamie Lee Curtis had the most perfect body in the world.

I sipped my drink and helped Julie demolish the top layer of a box of Ferrero Rocher while Arnie saved Jamie Lee and possibly the free world as well.

'Brilliant,' pronounced Julie when it was over. 'Totally implausible, of course—'

'Never.' Andy grinned at her.

'Not Arnie,' she said. 'Nor the plot. I'm talking about Jamie Lee's stomach. No woman can have a concave stomach after the age of about seventeen!'

'I didn't even have one then,' I muttered. 'And I've blown any chance of looking concave by eating all those chocolates.'

'In that case a slice of fruit cake won't do any more damage,' said Julie. 'Come into the kitchen with me,

Issy. I'll make some coffee. You'll be OK here on your own, won't you, Andy?'

'I'll simply count the moments until you return,' he told her solemnly.

Julie spooned Costa Rica into the filter. The diamond glittered in the kitchen's spotlights.

'It's a fabulous ring,' I told her. 'Really it is.'

She smiled with self-satisfaction. 'I know. I'm so lucky, Isobel. I can't really believe it.'

'You didn't think of saying to him that you had to think things over?' I asked.

'Are you mad?'

'Because you said that to me when we were in Sitges. "If that shit ever calls me again I'll get someone to tell him that I need to think about talking to him".'

'He didn't telephone,' she reminded me. 'He came in person.'

I took three cups out of the cupboard. 'I suppose he did.'

'And I do love him.'

'I can see that,' I said. And I could. It was in all the little things. The way they shared a look, a private understanding, the way they thought of themselves as one unit. I'd felt like that when I was with Tim. I knew what she meant. The pain grabbed me so suddenly that I almost cried out.

'I'm just nipping up to the loo,' I said.

'Sure.' She placed slices of cake onto a gold-rimmed plate.

I sat on the toilet seat, bent over, my head resting on my knees. The pain that I felt wasn't the pain of losing Tim, it was the pain of jealousy. I couldn't believe that I felt like this. Jealous. Of my best friend. Jealous because she loved someone and he loved her and because I was alone. It was so stupid. So childish.

I was over Tim. I was over all that stuff. I shouldn't feel like this.

But I couldn't help it.

If it had worked out then maybe by now I would have had a child of my own. We would have been a family. Tim and Isobel Malone and our baby. You fool, I told myself, sitting upright. A child of your own and you're behaving like a baby yourself. Snap out of it, Isobel.

Someone once told me that envy was the most wasteful of emotions. I reminded myself of that as I sat down with Andy and Julie and tried to make myself not care.

Chapter 18

Pierrot & Guitar (Salvador Dalí, 1924)

I sat under the shade of a tree in the Retiro Park and leafed through *Hola!* I read *Hola!* to improve my Spanish, not for the gossip and the pictures of the Infanta Elena on the beach in Corsica. If there were pictures I was interested in, they were the ones of Leonardo Di Caprio, looking tanned and healthy as he went to a film première. He's too young for you, Isobel, I told myself mournfully. Too young and too far away.

I yawned. I'd been out with Barbara and Bridget the previous night and it had been late when I got back to the apartment. I didn't go out with them very often any more, but we still got together occasionally and last night had been to celebrate Bridget's pregnancy.

Pregnant, I thought. This time last year she didn't even know Tomás and now she was having his baby. Tomás and Bridget lived in an apartment on the other side of town. I'd been there a few times since they'd married. It had been a shock the first time I'd gone. I'd been used to the chaos that was the apartment she'd shared with Barbara – dirty dishes piled into the sink, mounds of ironing heaped into an armchair and knickers hanging over the shower-rail to dry. But her apartment now was absolutely gorgeous. It had polished wooden floorboards, brightly coloured rugs that she'd brought back from their honeymoon in Mexico and modern furniture that could have looked out of place in the old-fashioned building, but somehow didn't. Every time I came back to my apartment I felt as though I'd stepped into some tacky time warp. The furniture was too big and too heavy, the floor tiles were old and needed to be replaced and I didn't have any meaningful knick-knacks lying around that would underline my sense of style and sophistication.

The apartment was boring.

Barbara had suggested I move in with her when Bridget got married, but I'd declined. There weren't as many parties these days, but I didn't think it would be a good idea to live with Barbara. Besides, I was used to living on my own now.

A warm breeze rustled the leaves on the tree. Quite suddenly, winter was over and the cold air had given way to the unexpected warmth. The Madrileños were still bundled up in coats and hats, but I wore jeans and a sweatshirt and didn't care that they probably thought I was a tourist.

The park was crowded. Everyone had taken advantage of the warmth to get out into the air. Balloon sellers and popcorn sellers, guitarists and flautists, families and couples all jostled for position on the pathways.

I lay back on the dry grass, put the magazine behind my head and closed my eyes.

I felt very peaceful. I wasn't wishing to be somewhere else, or wishing I was someone else or wishing that my life had turned out differently. I listened to the sounds of the guitar and the laughter of the children and felt the warmth of the gentlest of breezes caress my face, and I felt completely and utterly at ease. It was as though my whole life had been working towards that one moment when everything was exactly as it should be and nothing could be more perfect. I smiled to myself and drifted into half-sleep.

When I sat up again, the guitarists had stopped playing and the children had gone. It was after four but still warm and I was thirsty. And hungry too, I thought, as my stomach rumbled in a very unladylike way and reminded me that I hadn't had anything to eat since eight that morning.

I got up and brushed the grass from my jeans. I ran my fingers through my hair and made my way out of the park. There was a small café near one of the exits. I hadn't felt the slightest bit hungry all day – now, in sight of the café, I felt as though I'd faint if I didn't get some food inside me quickly.

I sat down at a terrace table and ordered coffee and tortilla. Very few other souls were hardy enough to sit outside but I wanted to get the last of the sun. Crazy when, in a few weeks, I'd be doing my best to stay out of it!

The waiter brought the coffee and the tortilla. I took *Hola!* out of my bag and glanced through it again.

I finished my coffee, ordered another, and sat back in the chair. The feeling of peace and tranquillity was still with me. I hadn't felt this good in weeks.

A couple of middle-aged tourists stopped outside the café and unfolded a huge map of the city. They twisted and turned the map until they were satisfied that they knew where they were.

'I *told* you, Gerard.' The woman, thin and angular and wearing a shocking-pink trouser-suit, looked at him impatiently and tapped the earpiece of her sunglasses against her teeth. 'We should have turned *left* when we came out of the park. Now we've gone miles out of our way.'

'Well, it seems bloody silly to me.' Gerard's face was flushed. 'Why did the sign point *this* way to the art gallery?'

'It probably wasn't the same gallery,' said the woman.

'Oh, for God's sake!' Gerard puffed out his chest. His stomach ballooned over his pale grey trousers. 'How many art galleries can they have? The bloody Prado, whenever you think of Madrid you think of the bloody Prado.'

'You're putting me off going to see it,' said his companion.

'Don't be stupid,' said Gerard as he rearranged his camcorder more comfortably across his shoulder. 'We're here, so we'll go and see it. But I bet it's no great shakes. All these places are the same. People talk about them as if they matter, but they don't really.'

Gerard dismissed one of the world's most famous art galleries with a wave of his arm as he and his female companion walked purposefully down the street. If it's Saturday, it must be Madrid, I thought.

I glanced at my watch. I'd been sitting in the café for almost an hour and I supposed that I should do the decent thing, pay my bill and leave. I opened my bag to get out my purse.

I'd brought my deep, capacious duffel bag and it was almost impossible to find things in it. I couldn't find my purse. At first I panicked, visualising myself having to tell the waiter that I'd no money and imagining my now colloquial Spanish deserting me completely as he decided to report me to the police. But I knew that I was being silly – my purse was in my bag, nestling in the folds of the denim fabric.

Only it wasn't. I took out a dog-eared book, my bottle of *Allure*, my keyring, my bottle of Factor 6, my lip salve and some old postcards that I'd bought when I first came to Madrid but had never sent to anyone. There was no sign of my purse.

I clamped down the feeling of panic. All I had to do was remember exactly what I'd done that afternoon, where I'd put the purse. I hadn't needed any money for the metro because I had a multi-journey ticket. I hadn't needed any money in the park either because I'd simply sat under the tree. But I must have brought my purse with me. I never left it behind.

Underneath the bag, I thought suddenly. Maybe I'd slipped it into the little compartment at the base of the bag. I did that sometimes, to keep things safe. I didn't remember doing it with the purse, but I could have done. I unzipped it frantically but the only thing the compartment under the bag contained was a bright pink Tampax container. No purse.

Shit, I thought. Shit, shit, shit.

I put my belongings back into the bag but rummaged around fruitlessly for another couple of minutes before thumping it to the ground in annoyance.

'*Perdone*.'

I looked up. The man standing beside me was smiling slightly. '*Hay un problema?*'

'No.' I smiled brightly at him. '*No problema*.'

He furrowed his brow. 'You are English?'

'No,' I said again.

'*Española?*' He looked at me in surprise.

'No.' I really didn't want to be involved in this conversation.

'*Americana?*' He grinned.

'No,' I said firmly. '*Soy Irlandesa*.'

'Oh.' He smiled at me. 'I have been to Ireland. It is a nice place.'

God, I thought wearily, not now.

'Yes,' I replied. 'It is a nice place.'

'And you are on holiday here?' He sat down on the seat opposite me.

'No,' I said. 'I work here.'

'Really? Do you like Madrid?'

'Very much,' I replied. I wished he would go away. 'If you'll excuse me,' I continued. 'I have to go.'

'Where?' said the Spaniard. 'You don't have the money to pay your bill.'

I stared at him in dismay.

He laughed at me. 'But of course you don't. I see you making the pantomime. The pieces out of your bag. Your book. Your perfume – nice perfume. Your keys.' He shrugged. 'It is not difficult to see that you have no money.'

'I must have lost my purse.' It sounded feeble, even to me.

'But of course.' He smiled. 'No girl would come into a café and order a meal for which she cannot pay.'

I gasped. Did he think that I was actually some sort of criminal? Did he think that I made a habit of going into places and running off without paying?

'I assure you, I thought I had my purse with me.' I sounded like an old maid.

'Easy mistake,' he said. 'And I'm sure the owner will understand.'

I bit my lip. I was sure that the owner wouldn't.

'So.' He smiled at me again. 'You have a problem.'

'I can explain it to the owner,' I said helplessly. 'It isn't so much money after all.'

'But the tourists, they try this all the time,' said the Spaniard.

'Don't be ridiculous.' I looked angrily at him. 'They don't.'

'All the same.' He shrugged again. 'Perhaps you should let me pay your bill and save some unpleasantness.'

I'd guessed that was coming. 'It's quite all right,' I said pertly. 'I can give *el Señor* my name and my address and I will come to him tomorrow with the money.'

'I suppose so,' he said. He raised an eyebrow. 'But it would be easier for me to pay for you.'

I sighed. 'I couldn't possibly allow you to do that.'

'Why not?'

'Because I don't make a habit of allowing strange men to buy me things,' I said sharply.

He laughed. A real laugh. The laughter made him seem less threatening and more like a helpful stranger. I realised that he was younger than he'd first seemed – his early thirties perhaps? It was hard to tell for certain. His eyes were hidden by a pair of fashionable sunglasses. His skin was olive, his hair black and he was certainly attractive. Not quite my long, lean man, he was too broad-shouldered for that – but there was something about him . . . I blinked to stop myself thinking about him like that. He wore jeans, a sweatshirt with a print of a Joan Miró painting, and had a tan leather jacket around his shoulders.

'You sound like someone from a nineteen-sixties movie,' he said. 'Audrey Hepburn perhaps. Although you do not look fragile enough for Audrey Hepburn. But you have the same kind of eyes.'

I almost smiled. 'Don't be stupid.'

'I'm not being stupid,' he said. 'You are the one who's being stupid. Come on.' He raised his hands expressively. 'Let me pay for your snack and you can go home. *No problema.*'

'I really don't think—'

'I know I'm a strange man.' I knew he was mocking me. 'But I will properly introduce myself to you and then I will not be so strange.' He held out his hand to me. 'Nicolas Juan Carlos Alvarez,' he said. 'But my friends call me Nico.'

I took his hand and shook it. His grip was firm and decisive, his palm dry.

'It's very nice of you to make the offer, Señor Alvarez. But I really think—'

'Don't think,' he said. 'Just act.'

I looked at him doubtfully. 'I would repay you, of course.'

'Of course. But quite unnecessary.'

'I didn't do this deliberately.'

'Why would you?' he asked. 'You could not be sure that someone like me would be at hand.' He took off his sunglasses and his brown eyes twinkled at me.

It was like a jolt, the sudden surge of physical attraction that hit me. I felt my stomach heave as though I was in a lift that had suddenly gone down. My mouth was dry. I couldn't believe that this was happening to me. I swallowed a couple of times and looked down at the table.

'So, it is OK. I will pay for you.' His voice seemed to come from miles away.

'OK,' I croaked.

He motioned to the waiter who, eyeing me curiously all the time, brought my bill.

'Is that it?' Nicolas looked at me in amusement. '*Dos cafés y una ración de tortilla?*'

'I wasn't very hungry.' I glanced at him, unwilling to look him in the eye.

Suddenly he was serious. 'You *are* working here?' he asked. 'You are not a student with nowhere to go?'

'Of course not,' I said impatiently. 'I'm telling you the truth when I say that I forgot my purse. Or lost it, perhaps, in the Retiro Park.'

'You were in the park today?' he asked.

I nodded.

'Me too,' he said.

'Good for you.' I wished that the waiter would take the money so that I could leave.

'So.' He sat back in the seat and looked at me apprais-ingly. 'What is your name, *Irlandesa*?'

'*Me llamo Isobel*,' I told him.

'*Isabella*.' He rolled the name around in his mouth, making music out of each syllable. '*Isabella*.'

'No,' I corrected him. 'Isobel.'

He smiled slightly. '*Isabella* is prettier, *Irlandesa*.'

'Whatever.' I shrugged

'OK,' he said. 'And what are you doing here in Madrid, *Isabella*?'

The waiter returned and I sighed with relief. Nicolas took out a wallet and overtipped hugely.

'I must be going,' I said. 'It was very good of you to help me out like this, Señor Alvarez, and I'm extremely grateful. I'll send the money to you here.'

'Don't be absolutely ridiculous,' he said and his voice was angry. 'I don't want you to repay me. It is only a portion of tortilla after all!'

'OK.' I didn't want to argue. 'Then can I say thank you very much and goodbye?'

He looked at me for a moment and then smiled. 'Of course. It was very nice to meet you, Isabella.'

'And I'm glad you were here to save me from being arrested,' I said. I slung my bag over my shoulder. 'I must get home now. *Adiós*.'

'*Adiós*.'

I walked down the street without turning back. But I knew that he was watching me. I could feel his eyes on me until I turned the corner into the shade.

~

The purse was sitting on the darkwood table. I still

didn't remember leaving it there. I shook my head at my absentmindedness and opened it to check that I actually had money in it. A small bundle of notes was squashed into the front compartment.

I filled the coffee pot with water and lit the gas. Now that I was at home, alone, I felt safe from any sudden surges of physical desire and I thought that perhaps I had been rude to Nicolas Alvarez. But it was because he was so attractive, because I'd been so surprised by my own reaction. So I'd lashed out, even though there was no need. Because he wasn't trying to pick me up – there was no need for me to flatter myself like that. He'd seen me obviously distressed, having lost my purse. He'd assumed I was a tourist and he'd decided to help.

And I'd behaved childishly. Because I was attracted to him. Not in the way I'd been attracted to the men I'd slept with in my early days in Madrid. Not even in the way I'd been attracted to Luis Cardoso. But in a mind-numbing, electric-shock, scary kind of way. The way I used to be attracted to men. The way I'd first been attracted to Tim Malone.

I shivered. I wasn't interested. Really I wasn't. Nor was I ready. In fact, I didn't think I ever would be ready again. And I was right not to be ready. I had my career to think about. My high-flying career with Advanta Training.

Gabriela had been negotiating to buy a computer company. The owner, Alejandro Juncosa, was still running the company, but Gabriela had assigned Luis and me to work with him. We had a great deal of freedom and responsibility and I loved it. I wasn't going to blow it all on the first man that made me go weak at the knees.

I turned on the TV and flicked through the stations until I reached Sky News. The weather forecast for Spain was warm and sunny. Of course it was warm and sunny. It was that time of year.

He was attractive, though. I could see him quite clearly in my mind's eye. I felt my heart thud again.

No, I said out loud, I wasn't really attracted to him. I was just lucky that he got me out of a tight spot.

I wondered if he went to that café often, if he spent much time in the Retiro Park. He'd been there today, at the same time as me. I wondered what sort of things he liked. Music, perhaps. Did he enjoy the sounds of the classical guitar like I did? Books – but he wouldn't be the sort of man to enjoy gothic tales like *Rebecca* or the very English Jane Austen. He'd like heavy metal and Dean Koontz. Or maybe not. There was the Miró sweatshirt to consider. A man who wore Miró emblazoned across his chest might be an artist at heart himself.

Isobel, I told myself, you are completely insane. Anyway, Miró's art was modern. Nicolas Alvarez could like Miró and Meatloaf.

I went to bed early that night. I decided that I needed my sleep. The strain of working late every evening because we were currently so busy was obviously beginning to tell.

Every Monday we had a meeting. Gabriela, Magdalena, Alejandro and either Luis or myself got together in the light wood-panelled board room back on the Castellana. Luis and I took it in turns to go to the meeting. When it was about accounts, Luis went; when it was about future courses, I went along.

This morning it was my turn. We went through the courses scheduled for the summer, talked about the successes and failures of the spring agenda and discussed the advertising strategy for the rest of the year.

'Oh, and there's another thing.' Gabriela gathered her

papers together. 'We have a table at the industry awards on Friday week. So keep that date free in your diaries.'

I tapped it into my personal organiser. Since buying out Alejandro's firm, we'd become more technology-minded, and we all had electronic organisers. Sometimes I wished I could have kept my battered Filofax, but I had to admit that the organiser was more useful. I could download information from it into my personal computer in the office and I didn't have to thumb through pages and pages of scribbled writing to find things. But I was slower at keying in information than I'd be at simply writing it down.

My diary was getting full for this month. Social butterfly, I told myself as I snapped the organiser shut.

I wondered if I'd have time to make myself a dress for the awards night. I usually made my own evening clothes because at five-foot-one so many off-the-peg dresses didn't fit me properly, but I'd be under a lot of time pressure. I wanted to look good for the dinner, though. It was important for the company.

~

I went shopping for material the following evening. Because of the siesta during the day – and even though the department stores stay open the whole day through – many shops stayed open until eight or nine in the evening. After work I hurried along to a fabric shop where I was now quite well known, and bought myself a swathe of deep red, almost maroon, silk.

'It will look wonderful on you,' the sales assistant assured me as she wrapped it in tissue paper.

'I hope so,' I said.

'Oh, absolutely.' She slid the material into a carrier bag. 'And I hope you have a good time at your dinner.'

'Thanks.' I took the bag and walked into the evening sunlight.

'Hi, Isobel!' It was Barbara, laden down with shopping.

'Good God,' I said. 'Buying up the city?'

'New season,' she explained. Barbara was a shopaholic. She couldn't pass by anything that said new without at least trying it on.

'What did you buy?'

'Oh, nothing much. Couple of Mondi skirts. Lovely Max Mara trousers. Fabulous Fendi cardigan.' She was also a designer-label freak.

'Fancy a coffee?' I asked her. 'I was going to catch the last of the sun in the Plaza Mayor and listen to the guitarists.'

'Lovely,' she said, so we headed off for the square.

'*Dos cafés*,' ordered Barbara as she sat back in her chair. 'Oh, God, Isobel, my feet are killing me.'

'What d'you expect?' I asked severely. 'You're walking around in totally unsuitable shoes.'

She laughed. Her shoes were high-heeled and designed for style rather than comfort. 'I know. Still, one must look good, you never know when it might be important.'

'You never know when you might need to sprint down the road either,' I said.

The waiter put two black coffees in front of us.

The Plaza Mayor was filling up. A swarming crowd of football supporters, wearing the rival strips of Madrid's two big clubs, Atletico Madrid and Real Madrid, surged into the square. They were hurling good-natured insults at each other and waving flags. The guitarists, outnumbered, abandoned their music.

'I'd forgotten about this game,' commented Barbara. 'Although how I could when the newspapers have been talking about nothing else for weeks is beyond me.'

'Real will win,' I said confidently. 'Two nil.'

Barbara sighed. 'I couldn't care less.'

'You should go to a match,' I told her. Magdalena, who loved football, had brought me to see Real play a couple of times, and – to my surprise – I'd enjoyed myself.

'The only team I'd ever watch is Liverpool,' said Barbara. 'And even then it's a sacrifice.'

We watched the brightly coloured throng surge through the square.

'*Isabella!*'

I looked around.

'*Isabella!! Qué tal estás?*'

I sat up straight in the chair. Barbara looked at me curiously.

Nicolas Alvarez was carrying a guitar. He wore dusty jeans, the Miró T-shirt and a pair of worn leather shoes.

'You know him?' Barbara eyed me speculatively.

'Not really.'

He stood in front of me. 'How are you?'

'Fine,' I said. 'Thank you.'

His eyes flickered to Barbara who smiled at him.

'This is a friend,' I said. 'Barbara Lane.'

'Pleased to meet you,' he said. 'Nico Alvarez.'

'Pleased to meet you,' said Barbara. 'Would you like to join us? We were just about to order a beer.'

'Thank you.' He pulled up a wicker chair and sat down beside us.

'Are you going to the football?' I asked.

He shook his head. 'No. But there's no point in continuing to play when the plaza has been invaded.'

'Was that you playing the guitar?' asked Barbara. 'It was wonderful.'

'Not just me,' he told her. 'There are three of us. We play sometimes here, sometimes in the park. Sometimes we are very lucky and play at a party or in a hotel.'

I wondered how many times it was him I'd heard play in the park.

'Brilliant,' Barbara said. 'I'd love to be able to play an instrument. And I must have heard you and your pals hundreds of times.'

'Probably,' he said ruefully. 'We play a lot.'

'Isobel, why haven't you introduced me to Nico before now?' Barbara looked innocently at me. 'You know I'm crazy about guitar music.'

I knew nothing of the sort.

'I only met him recently,' I said. 'And I didn't know that he was a musician.'

'Not all the time,' he told me. 'Unfortunately I have also a day job. I work in a pharmaceutical company.'

'That's OK,' said Barbara. 'No musician should have to starve for his art these days.' She beamed at him again. I was getting tired of her beams.

'So did you find your purse?' asked Nico.

I nodded. 'Yes, I'd left it at home. And I'm glad we met because it gives me the opportunity to repay you.' I pulled some money out of my purse.

'Not at all.' Nico waved the proffered notes away. 'You can buy me the beer instead.'

'But—'

'I insist. It was my pleasure to rescue you.'

'Rescue?' Barbara looked at us.

'I was in one of the cafés near the park,' I explained. 'I'd forgotten my purse. Nico paid for me.'

'How chivalrous,' murmured Barbara.

'That's me.' Nico grinned, showing perfect white teeth.

'So tell me.' Barbara moved her chair closer to his. 'Do you give lessons?'

'Pardon?'

'Music lessons. Do you teach people how to play?'

'Oh, no. I don't think I would be good at that.'

'You could be,' she said. 'If you've never tried—'

'I don't have the patience,' he told her.

'That's a shame.' She looked disappointed. 'I would have asked you to teach me.'

I looked at her in astonishment. Barbara learn the guitar! I couldn't believe her.

'If you want to learn I will find out about a teacher for you,' said Nico.

'That's very good of you.' Barbara smiled again.

I wished I could think of something to say but my mind was a complete blank. I'd been totally taken aback by Nico's sudden appearance, and I was shocked to find that, even though he looked hot and scruffy and quite unlike the suave Madrileño of before, I still felt the surge of physical attraction.

'You have been shopping?' His question was directed at both of us.

'Yes,' Barbara answered. 'Spending too much money, as always.'

'And you, Isobel?' He looked at me. 'You had your money with you this time?'

'Yes,' I said.

'What did you buy?'

'Nothing much.' I shrugged. 'Material for a dress I'm going to make.'

'A dressmaker.' He raised an eyebrow. 'I didn't think you were a dressmaker.'

'Only sometimes,' I said. 'Like you only play music sometimes.'

The corner of his mouth twitched. 'And is the dress for you or for someone else?'

'For me.'

'A special occasion?'

'Not really. Work.'

'Where do you work?' he asked.

'A training company,' I answered. 'Nothing very exciting.'

'And you?' He turned to Barbara.

'I teach English at a private college,' she told him.

'Your Spanish is excellent,' he said.

'It should be.' She grinned. 'I feel as though I've lived here for ever.'

'Where do you live?' he asked.

I wondered whether Barbara should tell him. After all, we knew nothing about him. Mum's warnings about crime-filled foreign cities suddenly echoed in my mind. But Barbara had already given him her address. 'Why don't you call in and have coffee sometime?' she asked.

'That's very kind,' he said. 'Do you live there also, Isobel?'

I shook my head.

'Where do you live?' he asked.

It would be rude not to tell him, but I still wasn't sure. 'Edificio Gerona.' The name of the apartment block was suitably vague. There were probably hundreds of Edificio Geronas in Madrid.

Nico glanced at his watch and finished his beer. 'It was very good of you,' he told us. 'But I must go.'

'Don't forget, call in to see me,' said Barbara.

'Of course.' He smiled at her.

I sighed.

'What a gorgeous man,' she breathed as he disappeared into the crowd. 'Why didn't you tell me about him before?'

'Because there was nothing to tell,' I said. 'I bumped into him. He paid my bill. He was very nice. That's it.'

'Isobel!' She looked at me in exasperation. 'I know you've been a bit on the quiet side these last few months but I can't believe you'd pass that one up.'

'Oh, come on, Barbara. He's a scruff.'

'You don't mean that,' she told me shrewdly. 'You're just saying it. You must know that he's the sexiest man to walk the streets of Madrid.'

'I admit that he's attractive,' I said. 'But I think you're getting carried away.'

'I hope I am,' she said. 'In those arms. No problem.'

I laughed. 'You're mad.'

'Not at all,' said Barbara. '*You* are for letting me meet him. I think he's absolutely fantastic.'

'Barbara, you've only spoken to him for about five minutes,' I objected.

'I only need five seconds. And that's rich coming from the girl who—'

'Barbara, please!' I interrupted her.

'Oh, come on, Isobel. Admit it. You're thinking about what it would be like with him!'

'I'm thinking nothing of the sort,' I said sharply.

She made a face but said nothing. I drained the cold dregs of my coffee.

'*Do* you fancy him?' She looked at me questioningly.

'He's attractive, I admit that.' I tried to grin at her. 'But I'm off men at the moment, Barbara. I'm much too busy in work.'

'Oh, work,' she said dismissively. 'There are much more important things in life than work!'

~

There was no point in being interested, I told myself, as I lay in bed that night. I didn't want any more one-night stands. And a man as attractive as Nicolas would have had hundreds of one-night stands, I was certain of that. The next time I got involved with someone I wanted to be sure it was for ever. And, since nobody could be sure, I wasn't ever going to get involved.

It was easier that way. Much easier.

Chapter 19

Still Life with Bread and Fruit Bowl (Pablo Picasso, 1909)

The good thing about my office in the building where Luis and I worked since the takeover of the computer company, was that it had a tiny bathroom en suite. This meant that I could have a shower in the middle of the day when it got uncomfortably warm or that I could shower and change before going out in the evenings whenever I was working late.

I worked late on the day of the awards dinner. We all did, because it was the last day of a three-month course which had been hugely successful.

I stood in the blue and white bathroom and wrapped my towel around me. I should have been thinking about the dinner but I was thinking about Nico Alvarez. I was annoyed with myself for thinking about him, as though I was sixteen again with a crush on someone totally unsuitable. But I just couldn't get Nico out of my head. Maybe it was just pique because Barbara had thrown herself at him. Maybe I just wanted to see if I could still attract men. But that was stupid and childish and thinking that way made me more annoyed than ever.

I was fastening the clasp of my pearl necklace when Luis knocked on the office door. 'Are you dressed?' he called.

'Of course.'

'Shame.' He poked his head around the door. 'Oh, Isobel, you look lovely.'

'Thank you.' I turned around to show him the dress. I was pleased at how it had turned out. The deep red silk fell in gentle folds around me and the colour flattered my skin tone.

'I know that I'm not much good at clothes,' he said. 'But that's very pretty.'

'I'm glad you like it.'

'I wish my clothes looked half as well,' Luis complained. 'I can't seem to get anything to hang right on me.'

'Idiot,' I said, and straightened the jacket of his tux so that it didn't look as though he'd just slung it on.

'Thank you,' said Luis. 'Shall we go?'

We walked out into the warm evening air. It seemed a pity that we would have to go inside again.

We were late arriving at the hotel. Gabriela was in the foyer, wineglass in her hand, chatting to a number of men.

'Sorry we're late,' said Luis as she caught his eye. 'We took a taxi and the traffic was terrible.'

'You should have walked,' said Gabriela. She detached herself from the group and we strolled further into the hotel. 'I was so bored listening to them! Where's Alejandro?'

'He had to go home first,' I told her. 'He said he'd be here soon.'

'OK.' Gabriela tapped on the edge of her glass. 'You all know the people at our table – Juan Perez, Alberto Martinez, Stefano Santiago and Salvadore Costa. They're our best clients so I want you to be very nice to them.'

'Of course we will,' I told her. 'And I promise not to say a word when Alberto tells me that I have breasts like soft round peaches.'

'Isobel! He didn't say that, did he?'

'Not to me personally.' I grinned at her. 'He was on the phone to someone in his office and I heard him say it. He mentioned the *Irlandesa pequeña* so I knew it was me he was talking about.'

Luis laughed and Gabriela smiled hesitantly. Just then, Alberto arrived and I had to struggle to keep a straight face.

Alejandro and Magdalena arrived just as we were getting ready to go in for dinner. Like Luis, Alejandro wasn't much of a man for business suits, but unlike Luis his tuxedo fitted him perfectly and he'd gelled his black wavy hair so that it stayed neatly in place instead of flopping around his face as it normally did.

'He looks great, doesn't he?' I hissed at Magdalena as we were sitting down.

'Yes,' she said primly.

'I didn't notice how attractive he was before. Very sexy!'

She flushed and unfolded her napkin.

I stared at her, realisation dawning. 'Magdalena! Are you and Alejandro—?'

'Not exactly.'

'Then what, exactly?'

'Isobel!' She looked pleadingly at me. 'I don't know. He asked me if I'd meet him for a drink before the dinner. I said OK.'

'You little witch.' I grinned at her.

'It might be nothing.' Magdalena shrugged but her eyes twinkled.

What was it about working in an office, I wondered, that made people throw themselves at each other? At least I'd never gone out with anyone I'd worked with. Luis didn't count. That night had been a total aberration. And besides, he was still going out with Maria Turo.

It was a boring evening. I listened to the speeches and heard people congratulating themselves and each other and I thought that I'd fall asleep.

Then they announced the winner of the 'Businessperson of the Year' award and we were all amazed to hear Gabriela's name.

She was too. I always thought that people knew they'd won awards in advance so that they had time to prepare a speech and thank everyone in the company, but Gabriela was completely taken by surprise. She blinked a couple of times and looked around as though there might be another Gabriela Suarez in the room. Then everybody at our table started to clap and Gabriela walked up to receive a magnificent cut-glass bowl.

'I am honoured,' she said, her voice shaking. 'And this award is so totally unexpected.' She grew in confidence as she stood there. 'I started my company fifteen years ago and I employed one other person. Now, we have over twenty people working with us full-time and we have many others on seasonal contract work. I am delighted that the hard work of all these people is being recognised and that the name of our company is so well respected. It gives me great pleasure to accept this award on behalf of everybody connected with us. Thank you very much.'

We all stood up and applauded her again. It was very emotional, even though a few minutes earlier I'd been thinking what a load of rubbish all these awards were. Photographers took pictures of Gabriela shaking hands with the mayor and with other business people and she was beaming with pride when she came back to the table.

'Congratulations!' Our clients were thrilled to be at our table.

'Well done, Gabriela!' Luis kissed her on each cheek.

'Wonderful,' I said.

'You are superb,' Magdalena told her.

She put the glass bowl in the centre of the table. I was pleased to discover that it was Waterford crystal.

A waiter appeared with a bottle of Dom Perignon and fluted champagne glasses. We toasted Gabriela and the company and our clients and ourselves and I was proud to be part of it all.

~

'I'm just sorry that Alfredo couldn't be here,' said Gabriela later that evening as we sat around the table relaxing. Most of the clients had gone home, a few still hung around the bar. 'He would have been so proud.'

'Why didn't he come?' asked Luis.

'He hates this sort of thing,' she replied. 'He hates wearing suits and dressing up and being nice to people.'

'Don't blame him really.' Luis had undone the top button of his shirt and his bow tie hung around his collar. 'It's unnatural to get dressed up like this.'

'But I'm sure he'll be disappointed when you get home and he realises he missed it,' said Magdalena.

'I guess so.' Gabriela refilled her glass with champagne. 'Yes, you are right, Magdalena, he will be disappointed.'

'That's why it's better to go out with someone in business yourself,' said Magdalena. 'So that they know how things work.'

I caught her eye and she looked away in confusion while Alejandro sipped champagne, completely unperturbed.

'Alfredo knows,' commented Gabriela darkly. 'That's why he doesn't come.'

'I suppose you don't go to vets' conventions,' said Luis.

'He's never asked me.' Gabriela sounded amused. 'And he's never invited his patients to dinner either!'

We laughed at the thought of cats and dogs sitting around Gabriela's highly polished mahogany dining-table.

'Oh, I am so tired!' Magdalena leaned back in her chair and closed her eyes. 'It has been a very busy week.'

'You're right,' Alejandro agreed with her. 'Tomorrow night I'll be sitting in front of TV and nothing will make me move.'

'Me too,' said Gabriela.

'I'm cooking dinner for Maria,' said Luis. 'But then I think we'll just watch a video. If she's expecting a lot from me she'll be very disappointed.'

'She won't be the first girl you've disappointed.' Magdalena grinned and nudged him in the ribs.

'That's very unfair,' said Luis. 'I've never had a complaint!'

'What about you, Isobel?' asked Gabriela. 'Have you anything exciting planned for tomorrow?'

'I need to go shopping,' I said. 'We've been so busy lately I've been living on frozen dinners from the supermarket. And the apartment is a mess. So I'll be very domesticated and tidy it up.'

'How awful for you!' Luis made a face at me. 'Shopping and tidying your apartment.'

'I know it's dull,' I said. 'But it has to be done.'

'Thank goodness I have someone to do it for me,' said Gabriela. 'I really couldn't face wandering around the house with a duster and polish after a night like tonight.'

I grinned at her. She'd drunk lots of champagne as people came up to the table and toasted her again and again. Her face was pink and her eyes were bright.

'So you can sit back and savour your fame,' I said.

'I can't exactly sit back.' She made a face. 'I'm taking the children to see their grandparents tomorrow. My brother will be there with his children too. It will probably be manic.'

'Poor thing,' teased Magdalena.

'That's what you get for being married with children,' I said lightly.

'Oh, I don't know,' said Alejandro. 'I think it might be nice to be married with children.' He glanced at Magdalena and she knocked back her glass of wine.

I looked at my watch. 'I think I'd better go,' I told them. 'I'll see you on Monday. Congratulations again, Gabriela.'

She smiled at me. 'Have a nice weekend, Isobel. And part of the congratulations go to all of you too. I wouldn't have won without your support.'

~

I'd been tired at the hotel but now I was wide awake. I opened the patio door and stood on the balcony of my apartment. The city was almost quiet – I could hear the hum of cars in the distance and the occasional shriek of laughter that wafted on the night air. I wondered who was laughing, what was funny.

I thought of Gabriela and how pleased she'd been about the award, even though she'd tried to be nonchalant about it. It must be wonderful, I mused, to be so successful. So talented and beautiful and happy and brilliant. And to have a husband that adored her and children that she loved. If anyone could have it all, Gabriela did.

I wished I could be like her. I wished I had her determination and her drive. I wished I knew the secret of her success.

I pulled a shapeless white T-shirt over loose emerald-green jersey shorts and slipped into a pair of flat canvas shoes. I looked at myself in the long mirror in the hallway of the apartment. I wasn't at my best this morning.

I'd drunk very little at dinner the night before. A few glasses of wine and a glass of champagne. And lots of water. I'd even had more water before I'd gone to bed. But I'd slept badly and had woken up at six in the morning wheezing and coughing. The wheezing had eased after a couple of puffs on my inhaler, but I hadn't managed to go back to sleep. And now I looked tired. I should make the effort, I thought. I should change into something smarter and then I'd automatically feel better. Slap on a bit of make-up too, maybe, even though I never wore make-up on Saturdays. But I couldn't be bothered. It was only the supermarket after all.

I grabbed my inhaler and shoved it into the pocket of my shorts. My breathing was OK now, but I still didn't feel quite right and I didn't want to get caught out gasping for breath on the side of the street. I never thought about my asthma until it bothered me. And it had bothered me so rarely since I came to Madrid that now, when I wheezed even a little, I noticed it more than ever. Come on, I told myself as I picked up my bag, get on with it.

'*Hola, Isobel!*' Señora Carrasco waved at me as I walked out of the apartment. '*El ascensor – no functiona.*'

I groaned. The lift was always breaking down. And the fifth floor was just that little bit high for trekking up and down the stairs. I took it slowly and my breathing was OK.

Once I was outside I felt better. I walked on the shady

side of the street to the corner shop where I always did my shopping. I liked the corner shop. It was a little family-owned supermarket and the husband and wife were very friendly. Señora Ferrer smiled at me as I walked in.

It was blissfully cool and dark inside. I'd made out a shopping list but, typically, I'd left it sitting at home on the table. I wandered along the aisles, putting things into my wire shopping basket at random, trying to remember what I actually needed. Bathroom stuff, bread and water, I had to get water. That was important. I put a couple of litre bottles into the basket. I stopped at the fruit and vegetable display. My consumption of fresh fruit had gone down lately. Fruit was a good idea. And vegetables. I could make myself pasta and vegetables tonight and have some fruit for dessert.

I picked up a shiny purple aubergine and turned it around in my hand.

'*Hola, Isabella.*'

I turned around so quickly I made myself dizzy. I stumbled for a moment and Nico Alvarez caught me by the arm. 'Are you OK?'

'Yes,' I said. 'Yes, I'm fine.'

'Are you sure? You are very white.'

I smiled at him, a feeble smile. 'Only because I've been out late.'

'Oh,' said Nico. 'Anywhere nice?'

I put the aubergine into my basket. 'Dinner.'

'I see.'

'With the people from work. It was a business dinner.' I wondered as I talked why I felt the need to explain to him.

He nodded. 'And *you* had a good time?'

'It was OK,' I said.

I added peaches, plums, a bunch of black cherries and

a huge green watermelon to the basket. It was too heavy to hold.

'Let me,' said Nico.

He put the fruit into brown-paper bags and weighed it.

'Are you going to eat it all yourself?' he asked.

'Not tonight,' I said faintly, shuddering at the thought.

He grinned at me. 'Just as well.'

I queued at the checkout. I wished I hadn't bought toilet rolls and deodorant. They were such personal types of purchases it was embarrassing to see them moving slowly along the little conveyor belt.

I packed my shopping into my straw basket. The watermelon didn't fit.

Nico took the basket and the watermelon from me.

'I can't ask you to carry them,' I protested.

'You did not ask,' said Nico. 'I'm carrying them anyway.'

I didn't object. Anyhow, I wasn't sure I wanted to. I trailed behind him as he walked back to the apartment. He knew exactly where he was going.

'Edificio Gerona,' he said as we arrived.

'The lift – *no functiona*,' I said. 'And I live *en el quinto piso*.' I was gibbering.

'I'll bring them upstairs.' Nico had already started to climb them and, once again, I followed him.

Señora Carrasco was polishing the number on her apartment door. She beamed at me and at Nico. I was sure that she'd launch into conversation but she said nothing beyond an interested hello.

I pushed open the apartment door. Nico stood outside.

'I suppose you should come in,' I said. I knew I didn't sound very welcoming.

'It's OK.' Nico put my shopping in the tiny hallway. 'I will be going now.'

'Thank you for carrying the things for me.' I didn't know how to behave, that was the problem. I didn't know what to say, what to do.

'It was no trouble,' he said.

'All the same—'

'I got you at a weak moment.' He smiled at me.

'I – maybe.'

'Anyway, you have everything you need?'

'Yes. Thank you.' I smiled feebly at him. 'I'm glad I bumped into you.'

'Bumping into me twice was accidental.' He grinned. 'A third time? I don't think so. I came looking for you.'

'Looking for me?' I stared at him.

He pushed his hands into the pockets of the loose trousers he wore. 'You were already halfway down the street when I saw you. I called, but you didn't hear me.'

'Sorry,' I said. 'I was in a dream. Why did you come looking for me?'

'I thought, perhaps, you might like to come out with me.'

I blinked. He'd come looking for me. To ask me out. I swallowed hard. I couldn't go out with him.

'It's very nice of you, but—'

'But what?'

'But I'm not going out with anyone right now.'

'That's convenient,' said Nico. 'It means you can come out with me and not feel badly about it.'

'No,' I said. 'I mean, I'm not going out with anyone at all.'

'Why?' he asked.

'It's just – I don't think – I'm not ready to go out with anyone.'

'You're not ready?' He looked at me curiously. 'In what way are you not ready, Isabella?'

I didn't know what to say. I couldn't say I wasn't ready

because I didn't want to get involved with someone. Least of all him because I was attracted to him. It sounded ridiculous.

'Oh, Isabella, I won't bite, you know. Perhaps you would like to come to dinner with me. Or we could go to the movies together. Or have coffee. Would you like that? Just coffee?'

I swallowed. I wanted to say yes but I was afraid.

'What is the matter?' he asked gently. 'What are you afraid of?'

'Nothing,' I said. 'Nothing. I'm not afraid.' I laughed. 'Why would I be afraid? I'd love to have coffee with you.'

'This evening?'

'I can't this evening,' I said hastily. 'I've things to do. Not this evening.'

'Tomorrow then?'

I stared at him.

'That is OK?' he asked.

'Yes,' I said. 'Tomorrow is OK.'

'Perfect.' Nico Alvarez smiled at me. 'I will pick you up tomorrow. Eight thirty?'

'Yes,' I said. 'Eight thirty.'

'Excellent. I will go now, Isabella, and leave you to unpack your shopping. Unless you wish me to help?'

'No,' I said hastily. 'No, I can manage. Thank you. I'll see you tomorrow.'

'*Hasta pronto*,' said Nico and kissed me, quickly, continental-style on both cheeks.

I stood in the centre of my apartment, surrounded by shopping, and held my hands to my burning face.

Oh God, I whispered to myself, please let me not make another mistake. Please.

Chapter 20

The Enigma of Desire (Salvador Dalí, 1929)

The girl in the Irish pub was singing 'Nothing Compares 2 U' in the haunting style of Sinéad O'Connor. She held the mike so close to her lips that I could hear each intake of her breath. The melody plucked at my heart and sent shivers down my spine.

'Are you cold?' asked Nico.

I shook my head. 'No. I'm fine. Thank you.'

He smiled at me. 'OK. What would you like to drink, Isabella?'

'A fruit juice would be nice,' I said. 'Orange.'

'*Zumo de naranja*? Are you sure?'

'Yes. Absolutely.'

'OK.' He went up to the bar and left me sitting at the wooden table in the corner.

The pub was crowded. Old metal Guinness signs decorated the walls alongside ads for Tullamore Dew and Jameson. Pottery jars and glass bottles, cream, brown and green, were ranged on high shelves and one wall was given over to a mural of the Lakes of Killarney. The atmosphere was vibrant and the crowd was young.

'I like this place.' Nico placed my glass of juice carefully on the table in front of us.

'I've never been here before,' I said.

'No?' He looked at me in amazement. 'But it is very popular with the Irish people.' He laughed. 'With the Spanish people too!'

'I don't know many Irish people here,' I told him. 'And I usually go to a tapas bar or pavement café with my friends from work.'

'I see.' He took a sip from the pint of Guinness he'd brought back for himself.

'Do you like it, Nico?' I asked curiously.

'Yes,' he said. 'I've been here a number of times before. And I always drink the Guinness. I must have Irish blood, Isabella.'

'My name is Isobel,' I reminded him.

He was silent for a moment and I couldn't think of anything to say to fill the gap.

He'd picked me up from the apartment half an hour earlier and we'd caught the metro to the pub. We'd hardly spoken on the journey. He'd said that I looked beautiful (which was an exaggeration because I was wearing my black jeans, a black cotton top and a light jacket and looked neat, not beautiful); I'd said that I was pleased to see him. And then we travelled in silence to the pub.

Silence didn't seem to bother him. He hadn't made any effort to talk to me then and he wasn't rushing to speak now either. I wondered if he was already regretting his invitation.

The girl finished singing and everyone applauded.

'She was very good,' said Nico. 'A wonderful voice.'

I nodded my agreement. 'It would be nice to have a voice like that.'

'Do you sing, Isabella?'

I laughed. 'No. I can empty a room in ten seconds when I sing.'

'Do you play an instrument?'

I shook my head. 'The only thing I can play is my CD.'

'That's a pity.'

'I like music,' I assured him. 'I'm just no good at it myself.'

'Who is your favourite composer?' asked Nico.

My favourite composer, I thought wildly. I didn't know any composers. I knew bands – Oasis or Blur or the Cranberries – but I couldn't differentiate between Beethoven or Bach. In fact I couldn't think of a composer's name besides Beethoven or Bach.

'Isabella?'

'I don't really have a favourite composer.'

'I will compose something for you, then I can be your favourite.'

I smiled uncertainly. 'Do you compose a lot?' I asked.

'Not exactly.' He ran his fingers through his hair. 'I'd like to be a really good composer, but I don't think I ever will be. And I will admit this to you, *mia Isabella*, but please don't tell anyone else – I compose to make money.'

'But I thought you had a job,' I said. 'You told me before you worked in a pharmaceutical company.'

He nodded. 'The music is a hobby.'

'So you compose songs for your hobby?' I looked at him with interest. 'And you get paid for it? Modern songs?'

He looked uncomfortable. 'No. Not songs.'

'What then?'

'Music for advertising.' He made a face. 'You know, for TV or radio.'

'You mean jingles?'

He nodded. 'Yes. Jingles.'

'Really?' I was intrigued. I'd never thought about anyone sitting down and writing an advertising jingle before. 'Would I have heard them? Are they famous?'

'I cannot say famous,' he said. 'But you have probably heard one.'

'So, Nico, which? Which did you compose?'

He sighed. 'The one for Cocoramba coffee.'

I stared at him. 'Really?'

'Yes.' He looked at me and rubbed his chin. 'You see, not very good.'

'I wouldn't say that,' I told him carefully. 'It certainly sticks in your mind.'

'You see.' He sighed. 'You don't like it.'

I grinned. 'I suppose there's a different set of rules for advertising jingles, Nico. I'm not supposed to like it. Just supposed to remember it. And I do. When I hear it in the morning I can't get it out of my head!'

'I know,' he sighed. 'It was like that when I wrote it. But the company liked it. I have done another one.' He looked at me hopefully. 'I think it is better.'

'Do I know it?' I sat back.

'It's for a perfume,' he said. He cleared his throat, closed his eyes and hummed. The tune was sweet and light.

'That's lovely,' I said.

'Thank you.'

'I mean it. It makes me think of – oh, summer and flowers and birds swooping through the air.'

He smiled. 'I am glad you said about the birds. The perfume is called *Drina*. Short for golondrina.'

'There you are.' I looked at him triumphantly. 'You've succeeded as a composer. I thought of the images you intended. Your music's exactly like a swallow in flight.'

'And what about you?' he asked. 'What do you like to do, Isabella?'

I shivered suddenly. I didn't know what I wanted to tell Nico Alvarez about myself.

'Oh, there's nothing exciting about me, Nico. I don't

do anything creative like play the guitar and write advertising jingles.'

'But you are here in Madrid, not at home in Dublin,' he said. 'Why are you here? For work only? Because you like Spain? Do you have a boyfriend here? Or is there someone waiting for you in Ireland?'

'A lot of questions,' I said.

'You don't have to answer them.' He drained his pint. 'Would you like another drink or would you like something to eat?'

I glanced at my watch. It was nine o'clock. Far too early to eat dinner in Madrid. And I hadn't agreed to go to dinner.

'Another juice would be nice,' I said.

'You would not prefer a glass of wine?'

I shook my head. This was a date, sort of. I didn't want to drink wine and suddenly become mellow and relaxed and start thinking that it would be nice to drag Nico into bed. I didn't trust myself not to think like that when I'd been drinking.

'OK, no problem.'

~

'Here you are.' Nico returned with the juice and another pint of Guinness.

'Thank you.'

He sat beside me, closer to me this time, but forced closer because the pub was even more crowded now.

'Is this really like pubs in Ireland?' he asked.

I looked around and nodded.

'And which do you prefer? This or a tapas bar?'

I shrugged. 'At different times I like them equally.'

'Do you ever get homesick?'

'Why would I get homesick?'

'Family, friends?'

'I talk to my family on the phone,' I said. 'And I've plenty of friends here.'

'It is not easy to find out about you, Isabella.'

'What do you want to find out?' I asked. 'I'll tell you anything you want to know.'

Suddenly he leaned towards me and brushed my hair from my eyes. I jumped.

'I want to know who has treated you so badly that you react like that.'

My heart was hammering in my chest.

'Nobody,' I said. 'And you startled me.'

'I startled you?' He looked at me. 'I moved a piece of your hair, Isabella. I didn't do anything to startle you.'

'Well, you did.' I was shaking and I could feel my lungs begin to tighten. I picked up my bag and took out my inhaler.

'You have asthma?'

'What do you think?' I said tartly, when I'd taken a puff and released my breath slowly.

He grinned. 'I'm sorry. That was a silly question.'

I couldn't help smiling myself, even though I still felt shaky.

'It is bad, the asthma?'

I shook my head. 'Not really. And much better since I came to Madrid.'

'So that's why you are here,' said Nico. 'A health cure.'

'It's not that at all.'

'OK, Isabella. I will stop asking you about things you don't want to talk about.'

We sat in silence. Neither a companionable silence nor a cold silence. Just the absence of talk. I listened to the female singer begging someone to 'Unbreak her Heart'.

Other people had suffered real pain in their lives. Other

women had been beaten by their husbands or betrayed by them. Other women had a right to be unhappy or to recoil when a man pushed hair out of their eyes. I was simply being silly.

'Would you like to go somewhere to eat?' asked Nico.

'Now?' I asked.

'I'm hungry now,' said Nico. 'But if you don't want to, it's not a problem.'

I wanted to but I was afraid to.

'Perhaps not tonight,' he said as I remained silent. 'Perhaps we can leave it for another evening.'

'Perhaps,' I said.

He smiled at me. 'Come on, Isabella. I will take you home.'

The evening air was warm but the breeze was cool. I shivered slightly and buttoned my jacket.

'Soon it will be summer,' Nico remarked, 'and you'll be longing for a cool breeze.'

'I know.' I felt better in the open air. 'But I love the heat, Nico.'

He grinned. 'It's the dry air that's good for your asthma.'

'Actually it's hardly troubled me at all lately,' I said. 'Only if I drink too much.'

'Is that why you drink orange juice?'

I shook my head. 'I just didn't feel like drinking anything stronger tonight.'

'Why?' he asked as we turned onto the main road. 'Were you afraid of what I might do to you if you drank too much?'

'No,' I said. 'I'm not afraid of you.'

'That's something.' He caught me by the hand and dragged me across the street. Horns blared as we reached the opposite pavement. 'Afraid of me now?' he asked. 'Since I nearly got you killed?'

'Terrified.'

He turned towards the metro station.

'I thought I'd walk home,' I said.

'Are you sure?'

I nodded.

'OK.' He fell into step beside me.

'You don't have to walk with me if you don't want to,' I told him. 'I mean, I'd like you to walk with me, but not if it takes you out of your way.'

'I want to walk with you,' he said. 'And I can get a taxi home.'

'Where do you live?' I asked.

'Near the Atocha station.'

'Oh, Nico, that's miles out of your way.'

'It's no problem, Isabella.'

~

I liked being with him. People looked at him, I could see that. Women looked at him. He was incredibly attractive. And I couldn't help feeling attractive beside him. I wondered what it would be like to make love to him. Better than the nights with Ignacio. Better than with Stefan. Better than on the swivel-chair with John. Better than Luis. Better than Tim?

I felt myself flush as I thought of Tim. How was it that when I least wanted to remember him, I couldn't help thinking about him? And hating him. And still wishing that I'd married him.

'Edificio Gerona.' Nico stopped outside the apartment building.

'Thanks for walking with me,' I said.

'My pleasure.'

I couldn't ask him in for coffee. I just couldn't.

'Do you think you'll catch a cab easily?' I asked.

'I'm sure I will,' said Nico. 'Or I can get the metro. There's a station just around the corner.'

'Yes,' I said. 'I know.'

We looked at each other in silence.

'Thanks for a lovely evening,' I said.

'Would you like to meet again?' he asked.

'If you like. Yes.'

'I would like to see you, Isabella. When would suit you?'

I needed time. Time to sort out how I felt about this. 'Next week?'

'OK,' said Nico. 'Next week. Only this time I will take you to dinner.'

'All right.' I smiled at him.

'Give me your telephone number,' he said. 'And I will call you.'

I opened my bag and took out a business card.

'*Isobel Ka – van – agh.*' He struggled with my surname. '*Administration Manager.*' He grinned at me. 'An important person, Isabella?'

'It sounds more important than it is,' I said.

He laughed. 'And this is my card.'

'*Nico Juan Carlos Alvarez*,' I read. '*Sales Director*. That sounds very important.'

'We are all sales directors,' he said. 'So I am not very important either.'

'But you are a composer,' I reminded him. 'Not really a sales director at all.'

'And I will compose a song for you,' he told me. 'I promise.'

'Promise me one thing,' I said.

'Anything, *mia Isabella*.'

'Don't compose anything like the jingle for Cocoramba coffee.'

He laughed. I laughed. And we laughed together.

Everyone from the computer division of Advanta had now moved back to the offices on the Castellana. I liked it there, although I'd grown used to the freedom that working away from Gabriela had brought. Still, it was more convenient to be in the same building. I picked up some reports and brought them into her office.

'I've brought the September lists.' I put the papers on her desk. 'It looks good. But we overlap by one day here—' I pointed it out to her, 'so I think the best thing to do is to get Alejandro to do that day in the office and let Manuel do the course with Crédit Agricole.'

'Have you spoken to Alejandro?' asked Gabriela.

'Not today,' I replied.

'I have.'

'Oh?' She was annoyed about something, I could see that.

'He is leaving us,' she told me.

'What!' I stared at her.

'He feels too constrained here.' Her lips were thin lines of fury. 'He thinks that we are too organised! That it is too planned! I tried to tell him that we are a big company, that we have to be organised, but it is falling on deaf ears with him. He wants to go and write new programs or something silly like that.'

'I see.'

'I thought I was doing him a favour keeping him with the company,' she said. 'Even though he was not always the best person for the job. I know that he prefers doing to training. But his company was a training company! I don't understand it.'

'Maybe he just needs to work on his own,' I told her. 'Maybe that's the sort of person he is.'

'Bah!' She shook her head. I hid a grin. Gabriela's anger was legendary around the company but it rarely lasted. She was the sort of person who got into a complete fury for a while and then forgot about it. She never harboured a grudge, it wasn't in her nature.

'Anyway,' she said more calmly. 'It is not necessarily a bad thing. It gives me the opportunity to change things around again which is something I wished to do.'

'Good,' I said.

'So how do you feel about being the manager of our computer-training division?' she asked.

I stared at her. 'Me? You want me to be the manager?' My voice came out as a squeak.

'Why not?' she asked. 'You know about it. You get on well with people. The clients like you.'

'But me—' I opened and closed my mouth.

'Yes, you.'

'But what about Sofia, or Magdalena, or Luis?' God, I thought, Luis would be furious.

'Isobel, I have chosen you,' said Gabriela. 'Now it is not the usual thing when you have been offered a job to tell the boss that there are three other people in the company who would do it better.'

'I didn't say they could do it better,' I said hastily. 'I just thought . . .' My voice trailed off.

Gabriela smiled. 'I think you will do a good job,' she said. 'And I know that the others will be pleased for you.'

I certainly hoped so. I didn't want to be stabbed in the back.

But when Gabriela made the announcement later in the day, they all congratulated me.

'You deserve it,' said Luis and he sounded as though he meant it.

'Congratulations.' Magdalena kissed me on both cheeks,

although it was Magdalena that I'd been most worried about. I always considered her to be Gabriela's right-hand woman.

'You don't mind?' I asked her privately later.

She smiled at me. 'Not at all. I like working with someone, Isobel, but not being the person in charge. With you, I think it is different. You like telling people what to do.'

Did I? I hadn't noticed. I'd never told people what to do in Delta. Sometimes I'd had to tell them what Barry wanted them to do, but that was entirely different. I hadn't made any decisions myself. But Magdalena was right. I enjoyed working on my own initiative. I grinned to myself as I thought about that. I now had the one key attribute that all employers want – *Must be Able to Work on Own Initiative.* I liked knowing that the ultimate responsibility for getting things right ended with me. I was happy doing things my way.

God, I thought, maybe I've turned into a career woman! Isobel Kavanagh, who'd only wanted to get married and have children, had turned into somebody else without even realising it. I'd reinvented myself after all, but not in the way I'd thought.

I moved into Alejandro's office, changed the pictures to Picasso and Miró, bought some fresh flowers for the vases and sat behind his desk. Power, I thought madly. Power at last!

The strangest part of all was having my own personal assistant. Well, Nina wasn't exactly *my* personal assistant, but she was an office worker who was assigned to computer training and who took my messages when I was out and checked with me before she did anything. So it was almost like having someone looking after me. Nina brought me cups of coffee during the day, although I never asked her to. I didn't like the idea that she felt she should make me coffee. But when I said that to her she told me not to be stupid, she was making some for herself too.

It was Nina who put through the call from Nico.

'It's a man,' she said, 'with a lovely sexy voice, Isobel! And he said it was personal.'

I waited for a moment before I took the call. '*Isobel, dígame.*'

'Hello, Isabella. It's me. Nico.'

'Hi, Nico.'

'I am calling to see if dinner on Saturday night would be OK?'

It sounded pretty good to me. Saturday nights were often lonely nights.

'Where will I meet you?' I asked.

'I will collect you, Isabella.'

'Please don't bother,' I said. 'It's a long way for you, Nico. Tell me somewhere in the centre of the city and I'll meet you there.'

'I'll meet you at Sol metro,' Nico said. 'What time would you like to eat?'

I hadn't quite got into the habit of eating as late as some of the Madrileños. 'Would ten o'clock be OK?'

'Of course,' he said. 'I will see you then.'

'OK,' I said. 'Thanks for calling, Nico.'

'My pleasure, Isabella. Ten o'clock. Saturday.'

'*Adiós,*' I said.

I sat and stared at the computer screen in front of me. My screensaver was a picture of George Clooney. Nico Alvarez made George look plain.

'Hi, Isobel.' Magdalena walked into my office and sat down. 'Are you busy?'

I shrugged. 'Not really. I've got lots of things to do but I can't seem to get to grips with any of them.'

'I know what you mean,' she said. 'I feel very carefree this afternoon.'

'Because Gabriela is in Barcelona.' I grinned at her and she made a face at me.

'Not entirely.'

'Do you want something in particular?' I asked. 'Or just a chat?'

'Nothing special,' she said. 'But I wondered, would you like to come out with us for Sofia's birthday? I thought it would be nice to have a girls' night out. She'll be thirty – she says it's a crisis birthday.'

I laughed. 'Once you get past twenty-one, they're all crisis birthdays. When did you plan to go out?'

'Saturday is the only night we can all make it.' She sighed. 'Everyone seems to be doing so many things these days.'

'But I can't go on Saturday,' I said blankly.

'Can't go?' Magdalena looked at me in astonishment. I was always complaining that my weekends were boring. 'What are you doing on Saturday, Isobel?'

'I – I'm going out already.' I felt my cheeks begin to redden as Magdalena watched me. 'I have a prior commitment.'

'A prior commitment? Like what?'

'I'm going to dinner,' I said.

'Isobel!' Her eyes sparkled. 'With a man?'

'Well, yes, with a man.'

'What man? Who?'

I couldn't help smiling. 'His name is Nico Alvarez. He works for some drugs company and he plays the guitar in his spare time.'

'And is he attractive?'

I thought about Nico, about his black hair and his almost black eyes and his square-cut jawline.

'Oh, yes, Magdalena. He's attractive.'

'Why didn't you tell us before?' she demanded. 'Come on, Isobel. Tell me about him.'

'There isn't much to tell.' I sat back in my chair. 'I met him in a café. Then I met him accidentally in the Plaza Mayor. And he asked me out.'

'And this is your first date?'

'Actually no,' I admitted. 'I went for a drink with him last week.'

'For goodness sake! And you told no one.'

'What was there to tell?' I shrugged. 'It was just a drink.'

'Oh, Isobel, you are so – so Irish! You could have told me about it. I could give you tips on how to be with Spanish men. How to make them love you.'

I laughed. 'I don't want him to love me, Magdalena!'

'But why not?' she asked. 'Everybody wants someone to love them.'

'True,' I said. 'But I want the right person to love me.'

'Maybe this Nico is the right person. You'll have to tell me everything about Saturday night. Where are you going?'

'I don't know yet,' I said.

'Well, don't go to Fernando's because that is where we'll be with Sofia. It wouldn't do to have us cramping your style.'

'Indeed it wouldn't,' I agreed as the phone rang and I picked up the receiver. 'Indeed it wouldn't.'

Chapter 21

Ma Jolie (Pablo Picasso, 1914)

I woke up early on Saturday morning. The sun was barely creeping from behind the building opposite, spilling weak light into the apartment. I pulled the sheet around my head and tried to go back to sleep but it was impossible. I kept thinking about Nico and our date.

I rolled out of bed and pulled on a long white T-shirt. Now that the nights were warmer, I didn't wear any night-clothes in Spain. I poured myself some orange juice and walked out onto the balcony. I loved standing on the balcony, looking out over the city. I wondered if Nico was awake. I leaned over the rail and peered in the direction of the Atocha station, as though there was the remotest chance I could see it!

There was the entire day to get through. I told myself I should just laze around and be relaxed and lovely by ten o'clock that evening, but I wasn't able to laze around. I attacked the apartment, cleaning it so thoroughly that every surface shone. But the smell of disinfectant and wood-polish made me sneeze so violently that I had to go out for a while simply to clear my head.

The city was vibrant and awake. Tourists and Madrileños strolled around the streets and sat out beneath the striped awnings of pavement cafés. It felt good to be alive and good to be part of it.

I window-shopped as I walked, enjoying the feeling of the sun on the back of my neck. I was glad to be here.

I turned a corner and stopped in shock. I had almost walked into a wicker chair outside a café, and, looking inside, I could see Luis Cardoso sitting opposite a stunning blonde. And while I watched, Luis leaned towards her and brushed her cheek with his fingers in a gesture that was both intimate and provocative.

I glanced at my watch. It was only ten o'clock.

Luis looked out of the café window and saw me. I flushed with embarrassment as he raised his hand in a wave and gestured me to come inside. I shook my head. He spoke quickly to the girl in front of him and came out to see me.

'Isobel, this is a surprise!'

'More of a surprise for me,' I said tartly. 'Who's that?'

He looked at me. 'My companion, you mean?'

'Yes, your companion!' I almost spat the words at him.

'Isobel, what on earth is the matter with you? I am with a friend. There is no need for you to react like this.'

'What about Maria?' I asked. 'Does she know you're with a friend?'

'I am no longer seeing Maria,' said Luis evenly. 'So I am perfectly entitled to see whoever else I choose.'

'Oh, Luis.' I felt my face redden again. 'I'm sorry.'

'You know, Isobel, you have the strangest ideas about men and women.' Luis sighed. 'You seem to think that we should all be joined to each other by the hip. And if we have a relationship with someone, then it must be for ever or else it is a personal tragedy. I went out with Maria for a time. It was a choice whether we would stay together or not. We decided not. *We* decided, Isobel, not *I* decided. And so I am now going out with Anna.'

'Is she Spanish?' I looked over his shoulder to where the blonde was lighting a cigarette.

'No.' He grinned at me. 'She is Danish. And she is gorgeous, is she not?'

'She's incredibly gorgeous,' I said.

'So I am a lucky man.'

'Again,' I said.

He laughed. 'Oh, Isobel. You take it all so seriously.'

'I didn't once,' I reminded him.

'Yes, you did.' He smiled at me. 'You, Isobel, were serious even when you tried to have your fling. You did it with such determination.'

'You are a bastard, Luis.' But I said it with amusement in my voice.

'And you are a lovely person, Isobel. But you still need to relax a bit. Take life as it comes—'

'I know, I know,' I interrupted him. 'You've made your point, Luis.'

'Good,' he said. 'So I can go back to my lovely Anna now?'

'Absolutely,' I told him. 'Have fun.'

'We've had that already,' he said calmly as he walked back inside the café.

Was Luis right? I wondered as I showered that evening. Did I take everything too seriously? Had I taken it all too seriously – Tim and me and everything that followed? Did it matter so much, after all?

There was a green canopy over the door of Quixote with the name written in gold – a huge, flourishing Q and the rest of the letters trailing after it. The restaurant had been open for about six months and was the sort of place where you looked at the prices and then checked again because you couldn't believe that food could cost so much. I'd never eaten here before, just peered at the menu in its little glass case on the wall outside. I wished Nico had chosen somewhere cheaper and less formal. Thank God, I thought, that I'd decided against my bright pink denim dress and had worn the soft cotton in muted browns and burnt sienna instead.

The *maitre d'* met us at the door and smiled at Nico. 'Nice to see you,' he said and I wondered how often Nico entertained here. We followed him down a steep flight of stairs into the basement of the building.

There were only ten tables in the room, each in a small alcove beneath the vaulted ceilings. In each alcove was a mural of a Spanish building – the cathedral at Seville, the royal palace at Madrid, Gaudì's house in Barcelona. We were led across the highly polished marble floor to sit beneath a picture of the train station at Atocha.

The waiter handed us menus. I looked at mine and suddenly wasn't hungry at all. I was nervous again and annoyed at myself for being nervous.

'Pardon?' Nico looked up at me.

'Nothing,' I said. 'I was just thinking out loud.'

'What will you have to eat?' he asked.

'I think I'll have the Caesar salad to start,' I told him. 'And the *pollo asado*.'

'I hope you like anchovies,' said Nico, 'because the Caesar is laced with them.'

'That's OK,' I said.

'Good.' He smiled at me. 'I'm an anchovy fan too, but you'd be surprised at how many people hate them.'

'What are you going to have?' I asked.

'The *gambas mimosas* are nice,' he said. 'They are cooked in a slightly hot sauce. And I will have the *pollo con almendra*.'

We closed the menus and almost immediately the waiter returned to the table.

'How are you, Nico?' he asked. 'When will we see you here again?'

A bit rich, I thought, considering he was here now. I wondered, again, how often Nico came here. They were treating him like an old friend. Maybe the jingle-writing sideline made him a lot more money than I'd thought.

'I'm not sure, Tonio,' said Nico. 'How is the new guy doing?'

'He plays the piano.' The waiter nodded towards the instrument in the corner of the room. 'But, to be honest, I think Guillaume prefers the guitar.'

'I hope so,' Nico grinned. 'Perhaps he'll give me a call again soon.'

'He will be here later tonight,' said Tonio. 'He had to leave for about an hour, but he'll be pleased to see you, I'm sure.'

'I won't go until he returns,' said Nico. 'So, if he's late it will cost me in wine.'

Tonio laughed. 'What can I get you to eat?'

Nico gave our orders while I mulled over the conversation he'd had with the waiter. So Nico played the guitar here sometimes. How many jobs did he have? The pharmaceutical company, the jingle-writing, playing the guitar in the Plaza Mayor – and maybe in restaurants too! It was a wonder he'd found time to take me to dinner at all.

'I played guitar for them at weekends when this place opened first,' said Nico when the waiter had left. 'Fridays and Saturdays. It went well, I think, but then I had to go to the US for a month on business and the owner brought in a piano-player. This is the trouble with the entertainment industry! You've got to be available all the time.'

'But you think he might give you the guitarist's job back?'

'Maybe.' Nico took one of the soft bread-rolls from the basket in front of us. 'It would be nice.'

'You like playing the guitar in public?'

'I'm a show-off, yes?'

'No,' I shrugged. 'But I must have heard you so many times and not known it was you. In the park, in the square—'

'I hope you enjoyed it.'

'It was beautiful,' I said and suddenly felt embarrassed.

'Thank you,' said Nico simply.

'I don't know where you get time.' I began to butter a roll. 'With your sales job and your jingle-writing – it seems impossible.'

'You're right,' said Nico. 'One day the time will come when I must choose between them all.'

'And what will you choose?'

'I don't know yet,' said Nico. 'I don't know what the most important thing for me is.'

Tonio, the waiter, reappeared with the wine that Nico had ordered and filled our glasses.

'Cheers,' said Nico, in English.

'Cheers.'

The wine was cold and I shivered.

'Are you cold?'

'No,' I said. 'I'm fine.'

'So.' He smiled at me. 'How long do you think you will live in Madrid?'

'I don't know.' I shrugged. 'I've been here over a year now and the time has flown by – I haven't decided.'

'But you will definitely return to Ireland?'

'Sometime. It's my home.'

He nodded. 'You have a big family?'

I told him about them. Strangely, talking about them to somebody else seemed to make me appreciate them more. I didn't say that my mother drove me crazy, or that Dad didn't understand me; nor did I tell him that Alison and I sometimes fought like cats and dogs or that I'd once ripped up Ian's homework in a fit of rage. I made us sound idyllic.

'It would be good to have family like that,' he said as he took another bread-roll.

'Tell me about yours.'

'Oh.' He picked at the roll. 'My family are doctors. My mother is a doctor at the Sta Maria Hospital, my father is also a doctor there. My sister is studying to be a doctor. My brother qualified last year.' He laughed shortly but there was no amusement in it. 'I am the odd one out.'

'But you work in a pharmaceutical company,' I said. 'So you have an interest in medicine too.'

Tonio arrived with our starters.

'*Gracias*,' I murmured as he slid the plate in front of me.

'I trained to be a doctor,' said Nico when Tonio had left. 'But it wasn't what I wanted to be. I thought it was – well, with a family of doctors you nearly always think like that – but it just wasn't what I wanted to do. So I quit.'

'And how did your family react?'

'How do you think?' His eyes were dark. 'They were not amused.'

I grinned at him. 'None of us ever do things the way our parents expect. They've got over it now, though, I suppose. And they must think that the jingle-writing is great!'

'That's a joke, yes?' He looked at me curiously. 'You do not mean that.'

'Of course I do,' I said. 'You wouldn't have been a good doctor. But you are a good musician. And you're still doing something in the medical world too. They must be pleased.'

'They don't exactly see it like that,' said Nico. 'They think I am wasting my time and my brain. And they hate the fact that I am working in a pharmaceutical company!'

'Oh.' I looked blankly at him.

'They think I should be a doctor and stop wasting my training for profit.'

'I suppose that happens in families where there is a tradition of one profession,' I mused. 'But they'll get over it.'

'I don't think so,' said Nico. 'I am the eldest. They think my life is unsuitable.'

'That's stupid,' I said. 'Wait until you're a famous musician. Then they'll be thrilled to pieces.'

He smiled. 'Thank you. I don't think I will ever be a famous musician, but it's nice that you think so. Tell me about you.' He ground black pepper over his food. 'Have you made many friends?'

'Yes,' I nodded. 'I went to a language class two nights a week when I came here first and I made some friends there. The people in the office are nice too. We go out together sometimes.'

'But you miss your family,' said Nico.

'You're big into family,' I said.

'It's a continental thing.' He shrugged.

'My sister came to visit me. We had a good time.'

'And have you seen our art galleries and our museums and our palaces?' he asked.

I laughed. 'We traipsed around everything when she came. And I go to the Prado sometimes.'

'Have you gone to the bullfight yet?' he asked.

I looked at him in horror. 'I certainly have not. I couldn't possibly go to a bullfight. I'd be on the side of the bull!'

He laughed at that and filled my glass with Rioja. 'Very foreign.'

I felt more comfortable with him now. I liked the way his eyes crinkled when he smiled and the way his mouth twitched at the corner when I said something that amused him. I liked the way he put his head to one side when he was considering a point and the way he shrugged in a very continental manner when he was dismissing something. I felt myself relax in his company, as though I'd known him for a long, long time.

We didn't have a dessert – I was too full of roast chicken and mushrooms and baby peas. The owner, Guillaume, came to our table and spoke to Nico about playing guitar again some weekends and then he sent over some sambuccas which we knocked back in one mouthful.

I was vaguely light-headed by the time we left the restaurant. The streets were still full of people. Nico took my hand and I moved closer to him, enjoying the feel of his body beside me.

'Have you ever been there?' he asked as we walked past the Convento de las Descalzas Reales.

'The Convent of the Barefoot Royal Nuns.' I smiled at him. 'How could I not go there? It sounded so intriguing.'

'And did you like it?'

'It made me think,' I said, 'that back then women had a lot more power than they have now. Secret passages to the royal palace. Goodness knows what sort of plots they were involved in. And all those paintings and icons!'

Nico laughed. 'You're not meant to think like that. You're supposed to be surprised that it is still a real convent.'

'It *was* interesting,' I said. 'But I bet the past was much more exciting.'

'Would you like another coffee?' he asked.

'If I have more coffee I'll never be able to sleep tonight,' I said. 'But a hot chocolate would be nice.'

'The San Gines?'

I smiled. 'It's a weakness of mine.'

The Chocolateria San Gines was one of my favourite places in Madrid, tucked in among the narrow cobbled streets of the old part of the city. Once, the nuns made the heavy chocolate drinks, now the people behind the counter were probably students, but the quality of the chocolate was superb and chocolate was one of my greatest weaknesses.

I asked for a cup of chocolate and Nico grinned when it was placed in front of me with a pastry stick to dip in it. The liquid was thick and syrupy and clung to the pastry stick. I made appreciative sounds as I ate it while he looked at me in amusement.

'I haven't been here in ages.' I looked at him defensively.

'Such a pity when you seem to like it so much.'

'I know.'

'Why have you been depriving yourself?'

'None of my friends like it as much as me.' I wiped away the chocolate that I'd somehow managed to get onto my nose.

'Your chin also.' Nico picked up the white paper napkin and wiped it away.

'Thank you.' I looked into his eyes as he did it.

'My pleasure.'

I almost said 'No, mine' because I'd liked the way he'd done it – gentle and possessive all at once. I liked him. My heart thudded deep in my chest. I liked him a lot.

He looked at his watch. 'Perhaps I should take you home now,' he said.

I looked at my watch too. 'It's getting late.'

'Sure,' he said. 'Let's go.'

We were quiet in the taxi. I couldn't think of anything to say, and he didn't seem to want to talk. We reached the apartment much too quickly. We got out of the taxi and Nico paid the driver.

'Would you like a nightcap?' I asked, conscious that I was nervous and that my voice sounded shaky.

He smiled. 'Not tonight. Maybe another time.'

I blinked at him. 'Are you sure?'

He nodded. 'We have had a good time, yes? If I come to your apartment now, it might not be such a good time.'

'I—'

'But I would like to see you again, if that's OK.'

'Yes,' I said. 'That's OK.'

'I will telephone you later in the week perhaps.'

'I'd like that.' I scrabbled around in my bag for my keys. 'I had a lovely evening.'

'I too.' He put his arms around me and kissed me.

His kiss was different from Tim's. His skin was smoother and I didn't feel the rasp of a growing beard. His touch was firmer – he held me so tightly I thought I might break. He broke off and looked at me.

'I'll call you next week,' he said.

'OK.' I smiled at him. 'Thanks for a lovely night.'

'Thank you too, Isabella.'

I sat on the balcony and looked over the lights of the city. I couldn't sleep. I'd had a wonderful time with Nico. He'd been warm and caring and courteous. He hadn't wanted to hop into bed with me. (Although a tiny part of me wondered was that a good thing or not.) I'd liked being with him. He'd been – comfortable. I touched my lips where he'd kissed me and wondered if I could fall for him.

He called on Monday and we met for lunch. He'd like to meet me that evening, he told me, but he couldn't because he was playing the guitar with his friends at a birthday party. This was paid work, he said, not like busking in the Plaza Mayor, and they never turned down real, paid work. It made them feel like genuine musicians and they loved it.

We went to the movies on Tuesday night, to dinner again on Thursday, we met for lunch on Friday and he brought me to the Prado on Saturday – so that I could see the more wonderful works of art and not get lost.

He held my hand as we walked through the lofty rooms together, surrounded by history and feeling at peace. Afterwards we went to the Retiro Park and he took me out in a boat. I trailed my hand through the water and pretended that the lake wasn't crowded with shrieking teenagers hell-bent on capsizing someone. Then we went for tapas and he took me home. I nearly invited him in but I didn't and he didn't say anything. He kissed me on the cheek and said he'd call.

~

Gabriela knew that there was someone. She said she could see it in my eyes and in the way that I smiled. She had watched my smile taking me over day by day, she said, and she was happy to see it.

'You have fallen in love with him?' she asked one afternoon as I went through a report with her.

'Not exactly,' I told her. 'I can't fall in love with someone in a week.'

'No?' She looked quizzically at me.

'Come on, Gabriela,' I said. 'It's all very well for people to fall in love straight away in books or in the movies, but it doesn't work like that in real life.'

'Oh, I don't know.' She shrugged her shoulders. 'I met Alfredo on a Friday night and I knew by the Monday morning that I wanted to marry him.'

'I don't want to marry Nico.' I laughed. 'But he's done great things for how I feel.'

'In that case, I am glad.' Gabriela smiled at me. 'I like you, Isobel. I want you to be happy in Madrid.'

'I *am* happy,' I said and meant it.

~

I went to my favourite fabric shop and bought the material for another dress. Julie and Andy were getting married in six weeks' time and I wanted to wear something special. She'd asked me to be a bridesmaid, but I refused.

'I'm far too old,' I objected. 'You're supposed to get young, virginal things as bridesmaids.'

Julie chuckled. 'If it comes to that, I'm far too old to be getting married in a long – *long*, Isobel – white dress and a veil. But Mum wants it and I suppose I do too, in a way.'

'What about Danielle?' I imagined Julie's older sister would want to be involved.

'She's going to be matron of honour,' said Julie. 'Oh, Isobel, are you sure you wouldn't like it? I think it'd be fun.'

'I'm sure it would. But I'd feel a bit of a moron in a peach and pink creation with silk flowers in my hair. Julie, you know I'd do anything for you but—'

'I understand,' she said. 'Just don't say I didn't ask.'

I'd never say that, she knew. But I couldn't have been a bridesmaid for Julie, walking up the aisle after her. As it was, I dreaded her wedding. I tried not to think about my abandoned nuptials but I couldn't help it. I could see my dress again, the four hundred and twenty pearls glistening, but I resolutely put the picture to the back of my mind.

I picked a deep mauve for my dress. The colour suited me and the material was rich and easy to work with. I kept it plain and fitted with a skirt that finished just above my knee and I knew that it looked simple but elegant.

'That is beautiful,' said Magdalena one evening when she saw it hanging on my dressmaker's dummy. 'It will look so lovely on you.' We were going to the movies later.

'Thanks.' I tidied up my threads and put them away.

'Your friend will go to live in America?'

I nodded. 'We talked about it the last time we met. I'm glad we're still friends, even though we're so far apart.'

She nodded. 'You will have a good time at home?'

'Oh, I hope so.' I grinned at her. 'We'll go out and have lots of fun and make exhibitions of ourselves.'

'And what about Nico?'

'What about him?' I asked.

'He will not go with you?'

I flopped onto the sofa beside her. 'I didn't ask him, Magdalena. And it would be reading something into things with him that just isn't there.'

'I thought you loved him, Isobel.'

I shrugged. 'What's love? I don't know. I like him a lot but I don't want to bring him back home and parade him around as though we're next on the marriage machine.'

'Oh, Isobel, you make it sound awful.'

'I'm sorry.' I stretched my arms above my head. 'I didn't mean to. It's just that people misinterpret things and I don't want that to happen. And I don't know Nico very well yet either.'

She looked at me curiously. 'You have not been to bed with him?'

'Magdalena!'

'It's a fair question.'

I blushed. 'No, I haven't.'

'Why?'

'I don't know.' I stared at the ceiling. 'I suppose mostly because he hasn't suggested it.'

'You could suggest it,' said Magdalena.

'I don't want to,' I said. 'I don't want to be the one to change things.'

'You don't like him in that way?' she asked.

I thought of him, his lean body, his strong arms and his dark, dark eyes. Of course I liked him in that way! I'd be insane not to.

'It's not as simple as that,' I said lamely.

'I think it's odd, Isobel. Is he gay?'

'Magdalena!' But then I thought of the incredibly good-looking Ari Jordan, soon to be Julie's gay brother-in-law.

'It's a reasonable question,' she said. 'You've been out with him a dozen times and he hasn't even suggested going to bed. I'd be worried, Isobel.'

'I'm not worried,' I said. 'And I'm perfectly happy the way things are.'

Barbara Lane was very pissed off about my relationship with Nico. She complained that she'd been the one to say that she fancied him and that I'd more or less told her to go ahead and meet him if she wanted. And the next thing she knew, she said accusingly, it was me, Isobel, who was dating him. I told her not to be silly and took her and Bridget to hear him play. It was a tourist show at one of the hotels and I warned them in advance that it might not be exactly the sort of thing they'd like. But I promised that Nico, Emilio and Juan were worth listening to. The girls were scathing about the flamenco dancers, they liked one of the singers, they thought that the magician was very good but – like me – they were enthralled by the guitar music.

'They're wonderful,' whispered Barbara as she poured mineral water into her glass. 'Really good.'

'The piece they're playing now was composed by Nico,' I said proprietorially. 'He's a brilliant composer.'

'It's pretty good,' agreed Bridget. 'Pity there isn't really a commercial market for music like this.'

'I know.' I shelled some pistachio nuts. 'He doesn't think they'll ever make it as musicians, but he's thrilled to get this work. He asked his parents to come and listen but they wouldn't.'

'Why not?' asked Barbara.

I told her about Nico's family of doctors and their

belief that he was wasting his talent fooling around with the guitar and writing commercial jingles, despite the job with the pharmaceutical company.

'But he has talent as a musician,' protested Bridget.

'And as a jingle-writer,' I giggled. 'He did the tune for Cocoramba coffee.'

'Oh, not that awful thing!' exclaimed Barbara. 'If you hear it first thing in the morning it's stuck in your head all day long!'

'That's the one.' I laughed. 'But he's done the jingle for *Drina* perfume as well.'

'That's not bad,' she said. 'But he's lucky I don't stand up and announce that he's to blame for the coffee ad.'

'Please don't,' I begged her, because it wasn't outside the bounds of possibility that she might. 'They'd never get another night's work.'

Barbara made a face at me. 'Oh, OK. But only because this music is nice and your Nico is an absolute hunk.'

I blushed. 'He's not my Nico.'

'You mean he's free?' She looked at me archly. 'I can make my move if I want to?'

'I didn't mean it quite like that,' I said.

'You see.' She smiled triumphantly. 'Your Nico.'

'I wouldn't mind someone like that,' said Bridget. 'He's the best-looking bloke I've seen in ages.'

'Oh, come on.' I grinned at them. 'I think you two are getting carried away. Besides,' I looked accusingly at Bridget, 'what about Tomás?'

'What about him?' She shrugged her shoulders and shifted in the seat. 'I love him. He's the father of my child. But he's not as desirable as Nico.'

'Don't be ridiculous. Tomás is fantastic.' I stared at her. 'And look at Nico! He's tall, I'll grant you that – and it's not exactly an advantage for a five-foot-one girl going out with a six-foot-tall man – but he's too thin to be a hunk and his face isn't exactly right.'

They looked at me in silence. 'Isobel,' said Barbara. 'You know exactly what we mean. He oozes sex.'

'Do you think so?' I asked, because I thought so too.

'Stop pretending,' said Bridget. 'You know he does. So,' she sipped her drink, 'how is it?'

'What?'

'The sex.'

I stared into my drink for a moment. 'I don't know yet,' I admitted as I looked up again.

'Isobel!' They both looked at me as though I had two heads. 'You haven't slept with him yet?'

'Good God,' I said sharply. 'I don't have to sleep with every man I meet.'

Barbara arched her eyebrows. 'Really?'

'Give me a break,' I said. 'Things were different then.'

'They certainly were,' she said lazily. 'A man a night, I thought, Isobel.'

'It wasn't like that.'

'Close, though.' She sipped her drink and looked at me appraisingly. 'Does Nico know about your past life?'

'Oh, don't be bloody silly,' I said. 'And you're making it sound sordid.'

'It was a bit, though, wasn't it?' asked Barbara.

'I can't believe you're saying things like this.' I was furious with her. 'I just can't believe it.'

'Leave her alone, Barbara.' Bridget put her hand on her friend's arm. 'Don't tease.'

'Who's teasing?' But Barbara smiled at me. 'Sorry, Isobel.'

'It's OK,' I said but the night was ruined. I felt uncomfortable when Nico came and sat beside us. I was annoyed by the way Barbara simpered and smiled at him while Bridget watched her in amusement. I was cranky and offhand with Nico when he took me home. And I knew I wouldn't ask Barbara or Bridget to come out with me ever again.

Chapter 22

The Signal of Anguish (Salvador Dalí, 1936)

Nico rang me at work. I hadn't seen him in over a week. Both of us had been busy, both working late. I was tired but I hadn't minded the work. He was both tired and irritable because he hated working late in the company since it curtailed his music time. He'd only rung once since the night I'd brought Barbara and Bridget to hear him play and I was afraid that he'd gone off me. I was surprised at how desolate that thought made me feel.

'Isabella?' He never called me anything else. At first I'd wanted him to call me Isobel, but Isabella was warmer, more loving. Although, I thought, as I rested the receiver between my shoulder and ear so that I could continue updating computer files while I talked, although why I wanted him to be loving was a mystery. I wasn't ready to be loved.

'Hello, Nico.'

'How are you today, Isabella?'

'I'm well.' I made a face at the computer which had managed to lose next month's lecture roster. 'And you?'

'I'm well too,' he said. 'Except I'm afraid I cannot go to the cinema with you on Saturday night after all.'

'Why?' I asked. 'Do you have a job?'

'Yes, but not guitar. I've been asked by the company to spend some time in our office in Seville.'

'Seville!' I stopped searching the computer for the lecture roster and held the phone receiver properly. 'Seville! For how long?'

'I'm not sure, *mia Isabella*. A few weeks. I have to be back here by August anyway. After that, who knows?'

'Do they want you to move there permanently?' I was surprised at how disturbed I felt about that.

'No. At least, I don't think so. There is a temporary position there and they want me to fill it. It's at a more senior level than I am now.'

'So they're talking about promoting you. That's great, Nico. But I didn't realise you cared so much about your job! I thought music meant more to you than work did.'

'Isabella, I have to be realistic. I've made some money out of music but not much. This is a good opportunity for me. I have to go.'

'And you'll be back in a few weeks?'

'*Claro*. I'm sorry, it was unexpected. I will miss you, Isabella.'

'But why do you have to go before the weekend?' I knew I sounded petulant.

'I start there on Monday morning. I need to check into the apartment there. Get myself organised.'

'Well, have a good time,' I said. I was surprised about this sudden move and uneasy at the way he'd sprung it on me.

'Would you like to come out with me tomorrow night?' he asked. 'We could have dinner at Quixote perhaps?'

'If you like.'

'Isabella, if you are busy that's fine. Don't trouble yourself on my account.' His voice was cool.

'Nico, I'm sorry.' I was annoyed with myself. 'Of course

I'd like to have dinner with you tomorrow night. And it's not so bad. I'll be in Ireland for some of the time you're away.'

'Of course,' he said. 'At your best friend's wedding.'

'So I'll have lots to do,' I told him.

'And you won't miss me at all,' he said.

~

Alison picked me up at Dublin airport again. She wore a lightweight linen suit and looked very efficient.

'Came from the office,' she explained. 'We had a meeting with some county officials today. Usually I wear jeans and a jumper to work.'

'You look great,' I told her. 'Is Peter with you?' She was still going out with Peter – it was her longest-lasting relationship ever.

She shook her head. 'He's gone to the pub with the officials.'

'Sorry if I dragged you away.'

'No problem.'

I followed her to the car park. She was driving Peter's car.

'He lent it to me,' she explained. 'I'm on his insurance so you don't have to worry.'

'I wasn't worried,' I said as I heaved my bulging suitcase into the boot. 'Though I think it's very sweet that he has you on his insurance.'

'Sod off,' she said companionably and slid into the driver's seat.

Mum was delighted to see me. You'd think I'd been away for years instead of months. She hugged me and kissed me and held me away from her so that she could make critical appraisal.

'You look well.' She sounded surprised.

'Thanks.'

'No, Isobel, I mean it. You've put on some weight since Christmas.'

'I put on some weight *at* Christmas,' I told her darkly. 'All that pudding and cake.'

'Well, I thought you needed it,' she said. 'You were very pale.'

'No, I wasn't.'

'Girls, girls.' Alison put her arm around our shoulders. 'Little birds in their nest shouldn't quarrel.'

'We're not quarrelling,' I said. 'We're debating. How's Ian?'

'Out,' said Alison.

'With Honey?'

She made a face. 'Not sure. It's got a bit ropey with Honey these days.'

'That's a pity,' I said.

'Ian's far too young to tie himself down.' Mum filled the kettle and took cups out of the cupboard.

'True,' I said. 'Men aren't mature enough to get married until they're in their thirties.'

There was an awkward little silence. Marriage hadn't been discussed in the Kavanagh household since my ill-fated nuptials.

'And what about you, Alison?' I asked lightly. 'Any chance of you tripping up the aisle?'

She blushed furiously and shook her head. I said nothing. I wondered whether she'd ask me to make her a wedding dress.

Julie was in a panic. Her room was a disaster area – clothes, books, half-opened boxes and black refuse sacks littered the floor. I picked my way through the debris.

'It's not debris,' she told me. 'It's my stuff. And wedding presents.'

'Are you bringing all that to the States with you?' I pointed at the heap of boxes stacked against the wall.

'Some of it.'

'Julie,' I peered inside one of them, 'this is full of stuffed toys.'

'Of course it is.' She looked defensively at me. 'It's Yellow Teddy and Raggy Doll and Walrus.'

'Yellow Teddy and Raggy Doll and Walrus?' I raised an eyebrow.

'I have to bring them, Isobel. I've had them since I was a baby. I couldn't possibly sleep if they weren't in the room with me.'

'And this?' I took a small green beret out of the box.

'It was part of my first school uniform.'

'And you want to bring it with you?'

'Why not?'

'No reason.' I grinned at her. 'I don't have my first school uniform and I certainly didn't bring any of it to Madrid with me.'

'I like keeping things,' she said. 'I can't help it.'

I sat on the edge of her bed. 'How's everything going?'

'Oh.' She ran her fingers through her newly styled copper curls. 'It's a nightmare. You've no *idea* how much preparation—' Her voice faltered as she looked at me. I'd tried not to let my expression change but something of my thoughts must have been mirrored in my face.

'I'm sorry, Isobel,' she said. 'That was so thoughtless of me. I didn't mean—'

'It's OK,' I said. 'It doesn't matter.'

'But—'

'Honestly, Julie. Besides, there's another man in my life now. I couldn't be happier.'

'Really?'

'Really.'

'The bloke you told me about? The musician bloke?'

I nodded.

'Have you gone out with him much?'

'A fair bit,' I admitted.

'So tell me about him.' She moved a pile of half-folded jumpers from the bed and sat down beside me. 'What's he like?'

I didn't know what to say. 'He's nice,' was all I could come up with.

'Nice!' She said it with derision. 'You don't say "nice" about a boyfriend. He can be a lot of things – hunk, sexy, attractive, intelligent, a bastard – but not nice.'

'But he is, Julie. He's kind and considerate and brings me to places I like . . .' I shrugged. 'He treats me well.'

'Doesn't sound like it's a very passionate relationship.'

I thought of the night before Nico went away and the chaste kiss that he'd planted on my forehead even though, at that moment, I'd wanted to pull him into my arms and keep him there. Julie was right. It wasn't a very passionate relationship.

'I'm not ready for passion,' I told her.

'Oh, Isobel.' She looked anxiously at me. 'Is it my fault? I know I said some awful things about the fact that you'd been to bed with other blokes, but—'

'Julie, it's nothing to do with that,' I said. 'Honestly.'

'But if there's no passion, why do you go out with him?' she asked.

It wasn't passionate now. But there could be passion. If we wanted it.

'Oh, he's easy to be with. Easy on the eye too.' I laughed.

'As long as you're happy.' But she sounded doubtful.

'When does Andy arrive?' I changed the subject.

She forgot about Nico. 'Tomorrow,' she said. 'I told

him it was silly to arrive the night of my hen party, but he said he'll stay in and watch TV.'

'Where's he staying?'

'With Danielle.' Julie got up and began packing more clothes into the cardboard boxes.

'Are you looking forward to it?' I asked.

'Which?' She put one box on top of the other. 'The wedding or the move?'

'Both.'

'I'm excited about the wedding,' she admitted. 'I can't believe that I'm actually going to do it. I keep thinking that something terrible might happen—' Her hand flew to her mouth and she looked at me aghast. 'I'm sorry,' she said again.

'It's OK,' I assured her. 'And nothing will happen to spoil your day. Unless we manage to get you completely drunk tomorrow night and chain you naked to a lamppost or something. Andy might change his mind if something like that happened.'

'You wouldn't,' she said.

'Wouldn't I?' But I laughed.

~

There were ten of us at Julie's hen night, although I only knew her sister Danielle, and two mutual friends of ours, Siobhán and Christine.

We went to Thunder Road. It was like being in the Hard Rock Café in Madrid. We ate burgers and drank pitchers of beer and were all a little drunk by the time we left.

Temple Bar was crowded. It was a warm night and most people wore T-shirts and shorts or jeans. I was the only person in a sweatshirt. It wasn't warm enough for me to go bare-armed.

'Where to now?' asked Christine.

'I'm going home.' Danielle looked at her watch. 'It's nearly one o'clock.'

'Early!' Julie was scathing.

'For you, maybe, but I can't keep my eyes open,' said Danielle. 'I'm exhausted. I was up at five this morning with Elaine. I need my rest.'

'OK.' Julie kissed her on the cheek. 'Will you get a taxi all right?'

'Oh, sure,' said Danielle. 'If I can't get one, I'll call Ray. I have my phone with me.'

'OK,' said Julie again. 'I'm glad you came.'

'Goodnight,' said Danielle. 'Don't do anything too outrageous.'

'Who does she think I am?' asked Julie plaintively. 'The whore of Babylon or something? We're just out for a good time.'

'Well, let's get on with it,' said Siobhán. 'How about Eamonn Doran's? That's supposed to be a good spot.'

'OK.' Julie didn't care. She followed Siobhán slightly unsteadily down the street.

I wasn't too steady myself. I caught the heel of my shoe in a loose paving-stone and almost ripped my foot off. Shit, I thought as I tried to wrestle my expensive Spanish leather shoe free.

'Allow me.' Although I couldn't see him, I knew him instantly. I gave the shoe another tug and it came free. I fell backwards, landed with a thump and looked up into the surprised face of Tim Malone.

We stared at each other for a moment.

'Isobel!' he said finally. 'What on earth are you doing here?'

'What does it look like?' I asked. 'Rescuing my footwear.'

'I thought you were abroad,' he said. 'Spain, I heard.'

'I'm home for a week,' I told him. 'I'm going to Julie's wedding.' I slid the shoe back onto my foot. 'Remember Julie?'

'Of course,' he said. 'I met her not so long ago.' He eyed me speculatively. 'And she's getting married.'

'Yes,' I nodded. 'An American guy. She's moving to Florida after the wedding.'

'The emigrant society is back,' said Tim. 'You and Julie both.'

'Don't be silly.' We stood looking at each other for a moment. 'I'd better go,' I said briskly. 'We were headed to Eamonn Doran's.'

'They didn't wait for you,' said Tim.

'That's because they didn't notice,' I told him. 'But I'd better catch up with them now.'

'I'll walk with you.' He fell into step beside me before I could say anything.

It felt strange to have him so close.

We walked in silence. He didn't seem to want to talk and I couldn't think of anything to say. I was confused. I couldn't believe that Tim, my Tim, was beside me. He'd been in my mind for so long, sometimes to the front of it, lately pushed to the back of it, but he'd always been part of me. A part I thought had gone for ever. How could he be here now?

We turned into Crow Street. I saw Christine disappear into the pub.

'They'll be looking for me.' I broke the silence.

'No they won't,' he said confidently.

'They will. I'm going into the pub.'

'Fair enough.' Tim caught me by the arm. 'I'll come in for you in fifteen minutes.'

'Don't be silly,' I said.

'Isobel.' He was still holding my arm. 'Isobel, I need to talk to you.'

'There's nothing to say, Tim.'

'Maybe you don't want to listen to me, but I need to talk to you, Isobel.'

I wanted to talk to him. Of course I did.

'OK,' he said. 'You go ahead into the pub. I'll come in shortly. You don't have to come with me.'

I stood looking at him. 'Go on,' he said.

I walked away from him and into the pub.

It was crowded. I pushed my way down the stairs where the music pounded and bodies gyrated. Dry ice pumped from vents in the walls.

The girls were clustered around the bar.

'What happened to you?' demanded Julie over the noise of the music. 'We looked everywhere for you.'

'My heel caught in a paving-stone.' I wasn't going to tell her about Tim. Not yet.

'What d'you want to drink?' she asked.

'A beer. Any beer.' I looked around. Would Tim follow me here? Would I want him to?

'Wake up.' Siobhán prodded me in the side and handed me a bottle of Miller.

'Thanks.' I took it absently. What did he want to talk to me about? There wasn't anything he could say to me. I wished the music wasn't so loud. Time was when I liked it to be very loud, all-encompassing, blocking out everything but the sound, but I wanted to think now and I couldn't think.

The girls had started to dance. Julie's eyes were closed as she moved her head from side to side. She probably wouldn't notice if I left. I moved in time to the music and drank beer from the bottle.

He appeared fifteen minutes later. He might have been there longer, I didn't know.

'Isobel.' I couldn't hear him over the noise but I knew what he was saying. 'Are you coming with me?'

I couldn't see Julie, she was at the centre of a throng of people. I looked around. The girls were all engrossed in the music and themselves. They wouldn't notice if I left.

'Well?' Tim mouthed.

I nodded. I wanted to know what he had to say.

'Come on.' He put his hand on the small of my back. 'There's a coffee house open down the street. We can talk there.'

It was quieter outside but the street was still thronged with people. It was more like half one in the afternoon than half one in the morning.

'When is Julie getting married?' asked Tim.

'On Friday.'

He steered me around the corner and into the coffee shop. It was small, only half a dozen tables with red and white checked oil-cloth on the tables and rickety wooden chairs which rocked when you sat down on them.

'Cappuccino,' he told the waiter who hovered beside us. 'Isobel?'

'The same.'

It wasn't as nice as the chocolate at the Chocolateria San Gines, but it was hot and comforting. I looked closely at Tim.

His hair was shorter, neater. His face was slightly fuller. He wore a denim shirt and jeans. But he hadn't changed much at all.

'You look wonderful,' he said.

'Thank you. So do you.'

He laughed. 'I look wrecked.'

'No,' I said. 'No, you don't.'

He dropped two cubes of brown sugar into his cup. 'I was out with some friends tonight. Last thing I wanted, really. I'd been looking forward to an evening in front of the telly.'

'That's not like you,' I said.

'Oh, it is really.' He stirred his coffee. 'I spend more time in front of the telly now than I used to.'

'Why?'

'Age.' He grinned at me. 'I'm in my thirties now, Isobel. I've got to be sensible.'

I smiled. 'You'll never be sensible.'

'I suppose you're right.' He continued to stir his coffee. I wished he'd drink some of it. The stirring was driving me crazy. I spooned some of the froth from mine and sipped it.

'So what have you been doing with yourself, Isobel?' He finally put the spoon in the saucer. 'I couldn't believe it when I heard you'd gone abroad.'

I shrugged. 'I was bored here. I'd been thinking about changing jobs for a while, then the opportunity in Madrid came along, so I took it.'

'I never imagined you'd do anything like that.'

'Like what?'

'Move away from home. I always thought you were such a home bird, Isobel. I really was surprised.'

'You didn't know me very well after all.' I stared at him.

'I thought I did,' he said.

I said nothing.

'Tell me about the job.' He smiled at me. 'Is it very interesting?'

'It's not bad. We're a training company. We do seminars and training courses for middle and senior management. We organise in-house training schedules for big companies. I work in our computer-training division. I'm the manager, in fact!' I could barely keep the triumph out of my voice.

'I never thought you had it in you.'

'Neither did I,' I confessed. 'But I'm glad I had.'

'So I did the right thing,' said Tim.

'Right thing?'

'When I suggested that we postpone the wedding.'

'You broke my heart,' I said shakily. 'You know you did.' I gulped at the coffee.

'I'm sorry,' said Tim gently. 'I truly am, Isobel. If I could have changed anything I would have.'

'Oh really.' My eyes were bright. 'What would you have changed?'

'I would have married you,' he said.

It was one of those moments when time is suspended. The waiter walked across the room in slow motion. A girl laughed at one of the other tables and the sound seemed to hang in the air for ever. My heart flipped over in my chest.

'Don't be silly.' My words were a croak.

'I'm not being silly,' he said. 'I'm stating a fact.'

I picked up my bag and rummaged around in it. I grabbed my inhaler and took a puff.

'How's the asthma?' he asked.

'Not bad most of the time,' I replied. 'The air in Madrid suits me better. It's drier than here.'

'I thought, perhaps, it was me made you wheeze,' said Tim.

'No.'

'I meant what I said.' He drained his cup and signalled to the waiter for a refill.

'I don't understand,' I said.

He leaned back in the chair. 'Remember when I wanted the wedding postponed? I told you that it had all got too much for me. And it had, Isobel. I was in a heap over it. It seemed like every single day there was something else to do, something else to worry about, something else to distract me. And I kept thinking "Will it be like this for ever? Will Isobel always be running my life?" I panicked, Isobel. That's all.'

'You told me that you felt trapped.'

'I did,' he said. 'I felt as though I had no control over anything any more. It was awful.'

'But if you loved me—' I broke off, unable to finish the sentence.

'I *did* love you,' he said. 'I lost sight of *why* I loved you, that's all. When we finally decided it was over, it was like a weight off my shoulders.' Tim looked apologetically at me. 'I was so relieved. I felt that I'd got my life back again. And I had a good time. I went out with my friends, I went out with the people from work, I stayed up all night whenever I wanted to keep going with a project and I didn't have to worry about how you felt or that I was meant to be seeing you or anything like that. So everything was great for a while.'

'And then?'

He ran his fingers through his hair. 'And then – then I missed you. At first I thought it was simply because I'd run out of things to do. I thought that I was being stupid. I knew that you wouldn't want to have anything to do with me anyway. So I went out with a few girls. Nothing serious. But none of them was you, Isobel. And I got more and more upset about what had happened and how I'd treated you. I couldn't believe I'd done what I'd done. It was as though I was a different person. So I rang your office one day, and they told me that you'd left.'

'That must have surprised you,' I said.

'I was astonished,' he admitted. 'I couldn't believe it. I assumed you'd have stayed with Delta. So I asked them where you were and they said you'd gone abroad. I couldn't believe that.'

I smiled faintly. 'It was hard to believe myself.'

'I didn't know what to do. I decided that you'd obviously made a serious decision about your life but

I couldn't believe that you wouldn't want to come back some day. I rang your house.'

'Did you?' I looked at him in surprise. 'Nobody told me.'

'They wouldn't,' he said wryly. 'I spoke to your sister.'

'To Alison?' I was amazed. 'She never said.'

'I didn't think she would,' said Tim. 'She told me that you had a fabulous job in Spain and that you wouldn't have the slightest interest in hearing from me and that you'd made a great life for yourself and would I kindly hang up because she was expecting a call.'

'Wow.'

'She was pretty adamant,' said Tim.

'She didn't breathe a word of this to me.'

'Well.' He made a face. 'She never liked me anyway. I suppose she thought I'd try and lure you back from Spain or something.'

I laughed. 'You'd have a hard job.'

'Would I?' he asked.

I fiddled with the catch on my bracelet. 'I like Spain.'

'I suppose it's much more exciting living there than here.'

'Nothing to do with excitement,' I said.

'And have you made friends there?' asked Tim.

I looked at him. 'Of course I have. I'm not a hermit. The people I work with are a great bunch, and I made some other friends from a language study course.'

'Boyfriends?' he asked with studied casualness.

'On and off,' I replied, equally casual.

'Julie told me you had a boyfriend. I met her ages ago. I thought she enjoyed breaking that piece of news. But I suppose it's to be expected. A girl like you wouldn't be without one for long.'

'A girl like me?'

'Attractive, beautiful, desirable.'

I laughed. 'You're getting carried away, Tim.'

'A bit, perhaps.'

'A lot.' I drained my coffee and looked at my watch. 'It's getting late.'

'I suppose so.'

'My eyes are closing,' I told him.

'There wasn't any other woman, you know,' he said.

I coughed. 'What?'

'You thought it had something to do with Laura Hart, didn't you? It hadn't, Isobel. I swear it.'

'I believe you.' I could see her again, sitting in his back garden, in the pink T-shirt, looking beautiful.

'Honestly. It's like I said. It was the whole wedding thing.' He took my hand and I jumped. He held it more closely, twined his fingers between mine. 'It had become a nightmare. Who to ask, who to leave out. Hotels, menus, bands. All that sort of stuff. And it seemed so crazy.'

'It's OK, Tim. It doesn't matter any more.'

'But it wasn't just that.' He sighed. 'I felt as though I was being used.'

'What!?'

'I know, it sounds stupid. But you talked about the house and the things you wanted to do to it, and how easy it would be to get to work from Donnybrook and how we could still live there if we had a child – and I thought – this girl doesn't love me, she just loves the things I can give her.'

'Tim!' I freed my hand from his grasp and stared at him in horror. 'You can't believe that.'

'I believed it at the time,' he said.

'No.' I was aghast. 'I never felt as though you were a provider of things, Tim. I loved you.'

He held up his hands in a gesture of despair. 'I just wasn't sure any more.'

'You make it sound terrible,' I said. 'Maybe I *was* terrible. I didn't mean to be. I suppose I did talk about the house. I wanted it to be our house, not just your house. I never meant—' Suddenly I couldn't talk any more. A tear rolled out of my eye, down my cheek, and landed on the table.

'Oh, Isobel.' He reached out to me. 'I'm so sorry.'

I took a tissue from my bag and blew my nose. 'It's OK.'

'It's not OK,' he said. 'I've ruined our lives.'

I wiped my eyes. 'Don't be silly,' I said shakily. 'My life is fine, thanks.'

'But you're not married to me,' he said. 'And I regret that very much.'

'Do you?' I didn't think he meant it.

'More than anything.'

I swallowed. 'It's a bit late now, Tim. I have a job abroad.'

'You were right to take the job,' said Tim. 'But I wish you'd stayed.'

'And pass up the chance of a Spanish lover?' My tone was light but inside I was a mess. I couldn't believe that I was here, with Tim, having this conversation. I couldn't believe that, after working so hard to rebuild my life, to change everything, I was sitting face to face with him and he was able to make me feel exactly as I'd done when I first went out with him. I wasn't free of him, despite what I'd hoped. There was still something between us. I closed my eyes.

'Thinking of him?' asked Tim.

'Who?'

'Your Spanish lover?'

Isabella, querida. It was as though he'd just whispered the words into my ear. *Isabella, querida*. Passion that was there but unshared. Barely spoken.

'No,' I said tautly.

'Good,' said Tim. He paid the waiter and grinned at me. His boyish, devil-may-care grin. 'So what are we going to do now?' he asked.

'I'm going home,' I said. 'I told you I was tired. I'm going to fall asleep any minute.'

'I didn't mean now, this minute,' said Tim. 'I meant – now, generally.'

'I don't know,' I told him. 'I'm going back to Madrid after Julie's wedding. Lots of work on my plate. And I bet you've got some hot-shot project coming up.'

'Isobel, it was important, us meeting like this.'

'Oh, Tim, maybe it was, but things are different now.'

'But do you feel differently?' He touched my cheek. 'Or do you only think you do?'

His fingers burned into my cheek. I was immobile. The waiter placed the bill on the table.

'We need to meet again,' said Tim.

'Yes,' I whispered.

'We've got to talk.'

I nodded.

'We have to make sure that we reach the right decisions.'

'I know.'

'I've never stopped loving you, Isobel.'

Oh God, I thought, maybe I'd never stopped loving him either.

Chapter 23

The Beautiful Bird Revealing the Unknown to a Pair of Lovers (Joan Miró, 1941)

Julie and I went to the Berkley Court for breakfast on the morning of her wedding. We arrived there at nine o'clock, dressed down in jeans and T-shirts and probably doing nothing for its five-star reputation. It had been Julie's idea. She thought it would be a good way to start the day. We ordered bacon, sausage, eggs, tomatoes, toast and croissants.

'I'll burst out of my dress,' said Julie mournfully, as she dipped toast into the runny yolk of her egg. 'But I'm so hungry and it'll be ages before we get anything else to eat.'

I was hungry too, and amazed at Julie's casual approach to the big day.

'But what's left to do?' she asked when I said so. 'I have to turn up at the church at three o'clock. That's six hours away. My hair appointment is for noon. I'm doing my own make-up. This is a nice, restful way to start the day.'

I agreed with her. 'Has everyone arrived safely?' I asked.

She nodded. 'Mr and Mrs Jordan got in last night. They're staying at the Marine. So is Ari. There's a cluster of other relatives and friends of the Jordans but most of them have made their own arrangements for staying and I don't know much about it. Nor,' she added as she popped some sausage into her mouth, 'do I care.'

'I wish I'd been as laid-back as you,' I told her.

'But I wasn't a few days ago,' said Julie. 'Remember when you called to the house? I was in a total panic then.'

'Still—'

'Still, what?' She looked at me curiously. 'What's the matter with you, Isobel? You've been acting funny all morning.'

I buttered some toast. 'Nothing.'

'Is it the whole wedding thing?' Her voice was full of concern. 'Maybe I shouldn't have involved you so much. Maybe it was wrong of me to ask you to do a reading. Maybe—'

'Julie!' I forestalled a litany of maybes. 'It's nothing to do with your wedding. Honestly.'

'All the same,' she said. 'I can understand how you might feel – upset about it.'

'I'm not upset.'

'Well, there's something wrong.'

I gazed around the dining room. Mostly businessmen having power breakfasts, I guessed. Dressed in sharp suits and neat ties, briefcases by their sides. Sometimes I had breakfasts like that, in the Lux or the Sheraton or the Hilton. Not very often, but sometimes.

'Isobel?' Julie looked at me. 'What's the matter?'

'I met Tim,' I told her.

She stared at me. 'Tim?'

'Tim. Tim Malone. My ex-fiancé. Remember him?'

'I know who you mean.' Her voice was sharp. 'When did you meet him? Why did you meet him?'

'The night of your hen party. By accident.'

She put her knife and fork on her plate. 'I knew you'd disappeared. We were looking for you. I thought you'd just got tired but I couldn't understand why you hadn't said goodnight.'

I felt uncomfortable. 'I know. I'm sorry.'

'But, Isobel. *Tim.*'

'It was an accident,' I assured her. 'When we came out of Thunder Road I caught my heel between a couple of paving-stones. He was there.'

'How was he there?' she demanded. 'How did he know to be there?'

'He didn't know,' I said. 'Of course he didn't know. It was one of life's little coincidences.'

'Oh, Isobel.' She sounded even more concerned. 'What did you do?'

'Nothing,' I said calmly. 'He asked me out for a cup of coffee. I didn't really want to go, but he was very insistent.'

'Is that where you were when everyone else was in Eamonn Doran's?' she demanded.

'I *was* there for a while. But he said he'd come and get me. And he did.'

'So you had coffee. What did you talk about?'

'This and that,' I told her. 'My job. Spain. Things like that.'

'It's good that you had lots of great things to tell him,' said Julie. 'Did you tell him about Nico?'

I shook my head. 'No point.'

'Isobel! Of course there was a point. At least that way he knows he can't just waltz back into your life.'

'He wasn't waltzing back into my life,' I protested.

'I hope not. So did you tell him to sod off?'

'I didn't say anything like that, Julie. I listened to him.'

She looked grimly at me. 'Listened to him?'

'He apologised for everything,' I said. 'He felt badly about it all. Did you know he rang the office looking for me? And the house?'

'Of course I knew,' she said. 'Alison told me.'

'Alison did?' I stared at her.

'She was worried he'd try to contact you,' said Julie. 'So we promised each other not to tell him exactly where you were.'

'Oh, for God's sake!' I looked at her in anger. 'What did you think I was? Some sort of Victorian heroine who'd swoon at his feet or something? How dare you decide something like that?'

'We were thinking about you, Isobel,' she said. 'Honestly.'

I couldn't be angry with her for long. Besides, I probably would have done the same. 'You might have told me.'

'We thought – well, you were getting better, Isobel. We didn't want you to be messed up by a phone call from Tim Malone.'

'I wouldn't have been.' I pushed my plate away.

'So what are you going to do?' asked Julie.

'Do?'

'About Tim.'

'Nothing much.' I was offhand. 'I might meet him before I go back to Spain. I don't know.'

'Be careful, Isobel.' She looked worried. 'He made mincemeat out of you before. Don't let him do it again.'

'I won't.' I smiled at her. 'You're getting all steamed up over nothing, Julie. Honestly you are.'

But she didn't look convinced.

The church looked wonderful. So did Andy Jordan, as he

stood at the altar, tall and handsome in a black tux. Ari was beside him, whispering into his ear. Julie's brother Joe showed me to a pew on the bride's side. I smelt the familiar smell of the church, the polish, the flowers, the religious smell, and felt almost peaceful. It was hard to think that a couple of years ago it would have been my wedding. It should have been Tim waiting at the altar, it should have been posies of peach and white at the end of each pew instead of the red and yellow which were there now. It should have been the Conrad instead of the Marine. It should have been the pearl-covered dress that had taken so long to make and had ended up in ribbons. Alison had discovered it under the bed after I'd gone to Madrid. This morning she'd told me that she'd bundled it up with the rubbish and thrown it away.

'I felt really bad about it, Isobel,' she said. 'But what else could I do? And I didn't want Mum to find it and start sobbing about how that bastard had ruined her daughter's life.'

I shrugged but it was hard to think that all my work and all my dreams had ended up on a rubbish tip.

Alison poked me in the side. 'You'd never guess he was gay, would you?' she whispered in a carrying tone that made the people in the pew in front of us turn around.

'They'll think you mean Andy.' I shook with laughter. 'They're horrified already.'

'It's such a waste,' she said mournfully. 'They're both so good-looking.'

'I know.'

'Is he going out with someone?'

'I don't know,' I said. 'But he's definitely gay, Alison, there's no point in you thinking you could change that.'

'I'm not thinking anything of the sort,' she said. 'Besides, I have my own love life worked out, thanks very much.'

'You and Peter?'

She shrugged. 'We get on well together. We like the same things. We laugh at the same jokes. Why not?'

'Will you marry him?'

'I might.' She looked at me defensively. 'I'm not sure yet. We won't rush into anything. I might live with him first.'

'God.' I thought about Alison living with Peter Gaffney. 'Can you imagine how Mum'll react?'

'That's what's holding me back,' she said glumly.

There was a stir at the back of the church and Julie arrived wearing a long, white, frothy dress that took up half the aisle.

'She's certainly gone for it,' murmured Alison.

But she looked lovely. I tried not to feel jealous as she walked serenely by, I tried not to feel somehow less of a person when she smiled at me. I tried to be joyful and happy when she exchanged vows with Andy and I did the second reading in a strong voice, confidently speaking about love and devotion as though I knew what it was all about.

When would Tim phone me? Since I'd met him two days before, I'd jumped each time the phone had rung so that Mum looked at me strangely and asked who I was expecting to call. I'd said Gabriela, that there had been a problem at work just before I left, but I knew that she didn't believe me.

I hadn't told them about meeting Tim. I hadn't even intended to tell Julie. I glanced at Alison. She'd have a fit if she thought I'd met him. She'd go absolutely berserk.

Julie and Andy signed the register and we all went out into the sunlight. It was a perfect day, the kind of day I'd wanted. People wished them well, kissed Julie, shook Andy's hand. Cherry-blossom floated down from the trees and caught in her hair.

'Hi, Isobel.' Ari Jordan came over to me. 'How are you?'

'Very well, thanks. And you?'

'I'm well too.'

'How's the chiropractic going?'

'Great,' he said. 'I was at a course in Australia a couple of months ago. Learned a lot of good stuff.' He winked at me. 'Met an absolute hunk of a lifeguard on Bondi Beach.'

'Ari!'

'It was a short-lived thing,' he said.

'Is there anyone long-term in your life now?' I asked.

He shook his head. 'But I'm hopeful. How about you?'

'No,' I said, trying to keep the thoughts of Tim out of my head.

'Did you ever hear of what happened to the shit who dumped you?'

'Oh, Ari,' I protested, 'he wasn't that bad.'

'Worse, from what I recall,' said Ari. 'You were distraught on that holiday in Rhodes. I felt so much for you.'

'That was nice of you.'

'Andy tells me you moved to Europe.'

I nodded. 'I'm working in Madrid now.'

'Any nice men there?'

'Lots.' I grinned at him.

'I meant for you.' He looked offended.

'I know,' I said. 'And yes, I've dated as you'd put it, a couple of times.'

'Only a couple?'

'A couple of guys more than a couple of times.'

'That's good.'

'Yes,' I said.

'Any of them serious?'

I thought of Nico as he waited in the reception area of the office for me. Leaning against the wall. Dressed in a suit because he was meeting other suits, as he put it. Tall, dark, handsome. Oozing sex, as Barbara put it.

'No,' I said.

'Good,' said Ari. 'You need to get around a bit.'

'Hi there.' My sister joined us. 'You must be Ari. I'm Alison.'

'Wonderful to meet you,' said Ari and turned his charm on her.

I wandered around the church grounds. When I'd thought of Nico I'd experienced the pain of missing him. But Tim crowded my thoughts too. I wasn't sure how I felt about them both. I tried to tell myself that it didn't matter, that I wasn't involved with either of them, that it was all academic. But I couldn't believe myself. I sat on the stone wall and watched as the photographer did his work.

Our table was top-heavy with women. Siobhán, Christine, Alison, myself, a girl called Natalie from Julie's office and only a couple of men, both from her office too. Their names were Mark and Jim and they insisted that they were thrilled to be surrounded by women.

'I'm sure they are,' whispered Alison. 'What about us? That's more to the point.'

'You shouldn't be eyeing up men,' I scolded. 'What about Peter?'

'What about him?' She grinned at me. I must have looked surprised because she made a face. 'I'm only joking, Isobel. My God, but you've lost your sense of humour.'

'No, I haven't,' I said crossly. 'I just—' I sighed. Maybe

she was right. I couldn't find anything to be light-hearted about today. I tried all the time. I'd done my best at the church and afterwards when we were having drinks – but I couldn't get into the spirit of things and my mind was a mass of contradictions.

During the ceremony I'd thought about Tim. I'd visualised us standing in this church together, exchanging vows and I'd shivered inside. But outside, in the glow of the afternoon sun, I'd thought of Nico and wished that he wasn't in Seville. And that I'd given in to passion before he'd left.

I hated them both for making me feel like this. I hated myself for being a fool.

I sat at the table and took a puff of my inhaler. I'd been dancing for half an hour without a break and I was exhausted. The girls were still going strong, but I needed to sit down and catch my breath. Besides, my feet were sore. I didn't mind sitting there on my own, I needed the rest. But Julie saw me and hurried over.

'Are you OK?' she asked.

'Of course.' I slid the inhaler back into my bag. 'I'm knackered, that's all.'

'Are you enjoying yourself?'

'It's a great day,' I told her. 'Really great.'

'It's going well, isn't it?' she said in quiet satisfaction. 'Wasn't the church lovely?'

I nodded.

'I thought Dad's speech was a bit long.'

'No it wasn't.'

'He shouldn't have said that about the night of my Debs'.'

'Julie, you never told me that you'd asked two men to your Debs'.' I laughed at her.

'I didn't,' she said vehemently. 'Dad was exaggerating. It was a mix-up, that's all.'

I laughed again. 'At least Andy now thinks you're some kind of hot stuff.'

'He knows I'm hot stuff.' She dissolved into laughter. 'And I'll be even hotter when we get to the States.'

'Are you looking forward to it?'

She nodded. 'Yes, I am. I know I'll probably get homesick, but I think I'll be able for it. After all, Isobel, if you could do it, so can I.'

'Madrid is closer to home than Florida.'

'None of it is that far away these days.' She smiled. 'And you have to come and visit. Very soon.'

'I will.'

She got up. 'I'd better circulate. There's loads of old aunts that I haven't even talked to yet.'

'Go ahead,' I said.

'Sure you're all right?'

'Of course.' I waved her away. 'Besides, here comes Jim from your office. I can chat to him. Now go. Circulate.'

She kissed me on the head. 'Talk to you later.'

Jim sat down on the chair she'd vacated. 'She looks great, doesn't she?' he asked.

'Fabulous,' I said.

'Such a nice girl, too,' he said. 'Des was very disappointed when she handed in her notice.'

'I didn't see him here.'

'He's at a different table. One with couples.'

I grinned. 'I'd noticed we were at an unescorted table. And that you guys seemed to have got the better part of the bargain.'

'Only if we get the best girl.'

'I'm disappointed in you.' I grimaced. 'Very sexist.'

'Not at all,' he said with injured innocence. 'A statement of fact.' He drained his glass. 'Can I get you a drink?'

'No thanks. I'm fine.'

'Well, would you like to dance?' He looked invitingly at me.

The music was slow now. The band was playing 'Moonlight Serenade'.

'Why not?'

Jim wasn't a good dancer. He stepped on my toes twice in as many minutes.

'I'm sorry,' he said after the second time.

'It's OK.'

'I've never been much good at this. My mother says I've two left feet.'

'Don't think about it,' I told him. 'Just move with the music.'

'So you're living in Spain,' he said.

'Yes.'

'Do you like it?'

'Yes. Madrid's a nice city.'

'Good place to live?'

'I think so.'

'Would you ever come back?'

I shrugged within the circle of his arms. 'Maybe.'

'Are you going to dance with him all night or can I butt in?' Mark tapped me on the shoulder.

'I don't mind.' I looked from one to the other.

'My turn,' said Mark.

Jim grinned at me and disappeared towards the bar.

'You wouldn't want to believe anything he tells you,' said Mark.

'Why?'

'He's a pathological liar. Does it to impress women.

Has he told you he's the one that really runs the office yet?'

I looked up at Mark. 'I thought Julie was the one who really ran the office.'

He laughed. 'You're probably right.' He held me closer to him. 'You're a good dancer.'

'So are you.' He was better than Jim, anyway.

'And you live in Madrid?'

I nodded.

'Like it there?'

'Yes.'

'Ever think of coming back?'

'Sometimes.' I smiled. 'Not often.'

'That's a shame,' said Mark. 'When do you go back?'

'Day after tomorrow.'

'Would you like to come out with me tomorrow night?'

I stopped and stared at him. 'Me?'

'Yes, you.'

'Tomorrow night?'

'Yes, tomorrow night.'

'But you don't know me.'

'I talked to you over the meal. Julie's talked about you before. And I'd like to get to know you.'

'It's very kind of you. But I don't think so.'

'Just a drink, something to eat?' He looked hopefully at me.

'No, Mark. Thanks all the same. But I've things to do tomorrow.'

'Oh, well.' He shrugged. 'It was worth the chance.'

The music speeded up again and I said that I wanted to sit down. He left me at the table and disappeared in the direction of the gents. I shook my head as I thought of a date with Mark. I couldn't understand why he'd asked me.

It was warm in the hotel. I needed some air.

It was still warm outside too. Other couples wandered around the hotel gardens, or sat in clusters on the grass. I walked along the gravel path towards the sea, then sat on the edge of the grass and watched a ship slowly cross the horizon.

I was lonely. I ached inside and I didn't know why. I wanted to cry when I should have felt glad for Julie and for Andy. I was sick at myself for the envy that I knew I felt. I got up and walked back to the hotel but I couldn't go back inside feeling like this.

I walked through the grass, leaned against a huge tree and closed my eyes. If only I was back in Madrid.

'Mark McCrory, someone will see us.'

'No, they won't.'

I recognised Mark's voice and opened my eyes again. I couldn't see him, or Christine (whose voice I also recognised), but I saw the leaves of the huge rhododendron bush rustle slightly and heard a giggle.

'Mark!' It was a suppressed cry.

I slid down into a sitting position behind the tree trunk. I was afraid to walk away in case they'd see me.

'Oh, Mark! Yes!'

Bloody hell, I thought. He's not doing it with Christine in the bushes. He can't be.

'I've always wanted to, Christine. You know that.'

He *was* doing it to her in the bushes.

'Oh, Mark.'

'I mean, why haven't we got together before?'

She groaned.

'God, you're beautiful,' he said.

I was glad he'd got over the disappointment of me turning down his date.

'My God, you're huge.'

I had to get out of here. Even if they did see me.

Anyway, they wouldn't see me. They had far greater things on their minds.

~

Mrs Donegan cornered me as I walked inside.

'It's great to see you again, Isobel.'

'You too. Doesn't Julie look wonderful?'

'She was always a pretty girl.' Mrs Donegan looked mistily at her daughter. 'I hate to think of her going so far away.'

'It's not that far,' I said.

'America.' Mrs Donegan sighed. 'People used to go to America and never come home.'

'That was a long time ago,' I reminded her. 'And it's only a six-hour flight these days. Besides, you can phone. Or fax. Or e-mail.' I grinned. 'Any of those wonderful ways of modern communication.'

'I can't even use the microwave properly,' said Mrs Donegan ruefully. 'So I don't think I'll get very far with the e-mailing. However that works.'

'You need a computer,' I told her.

'Well, there you are then,' she said. 'We certainly don't have one of those. And even if we did, I'd be afraid to switch it on. I'm not technology-minded.'

'You don't think you are,' I said, 'but computers are all around us. Electronic thermostats, your video recorder—'

'That's another thing I can't use,' she said. 'I'll stick with the phone, I suppose. Tell me, Isobel, how are you getting on in Spain? Do you miss home?'

I suppose she wanted reassurance that Julie would miss home, but that she'd cope.

'Sometimes,' I admitted. 'But it's good fun being abroad.'

'Do you get lonely?'

'Of course,' I said. 'But not all the time. I've lots of friends.'

'I'm glad,' said Mrs Donegan. 'I'm glad you worked things out after that terrible time you had.'

There was a lump in my throat. I wished people weren't always so sympathetic. Even now. 'Oh, I got over that a long time ago,' I told her cheerfully.

'That's good.' She patted me on the shoulder and looked around the room. 'We must find a new man for you, Isobel.'

'Oh, no,' I said hastily. 'I'm happy.'

'The very person.' She beamed at Mark McCrory who'd just walked into the ballroom. He was on his own. I kept a straight face with difficulty.

'Mark, Mark, this is Isobel.' Mrs Donegan waved at him.

'It's OK, we've met.' I smiled briefly at Mark. 'I'm sorry, I must go and powder my nose. See you later, Mrs Donegan.'

I fled into the foyer. The band began to play 'I Will Survive'.

I hated weddings. Truly I did.

Chapter 24

The Persistence of Memory (Salvador Dalí, 1931)

I didn't sleep very well that night. My breathing was uneven and I lay on my side while thoughts whirled around in my head like paper in the wind. I thought of how lovely Julie had looked, of her obvious delight in Andy Jordan. Of Mark and Christine. Of Alison and Peter Gaffney. Of Luis. Of Nico. Of Tim. I took another puff of my inhaler. My asthma was much worse since I'd come home.

I tried not to think of Tim but I couldn't help it. I despised myself for suddenly allowing him to take over my semi-conscious mind, for being so close to me again. I heard the dawn chorus begin at five o'clock and the milkman arrive at six. I lay in bed, eyes open, and stared at the tear in the wallpaper where I'd once stuck a poster of Michael Hutchence. I grieved for what had happened to him and I ached for the girl I'd once been.

I got up and wrapped my dressing-gown around me. I went downstairs, put on the kettle and played around with a bowl of cereal. I wasn't hungry.

I didn't do much that day, just sat in the garden and read Mum's Agatha Christie books. I'd read them all when I was younger and I still remembered whodunnit which made a mockery of my engrossed reading.

Mum joined me for a while. It was peaceful sitting there and I should have been able to allow the warmth of the sun and the powerful fragrance of the roses to lull me, but I couldn't. When the phone rang, I jumped a mile.

But Mum had already got up to answer it.

'No one,' she said when she came back out with a glass of orange juice for me. 'We've had more wrong numbers in the last two months than you'd believe. We reported it, but it's a waste of time. We've got the same number as some shop in Cork, but people keep forgetting to put the area code in front of it.'

I finished *Murder on the Orient Express* and started *Death on the Nile.* Alison wandered out with a cushion and her Walkman. 'Don't wake me,' she instructed, as she slid the headphones over her ears. 'I'm exhausted.'

The phone rang before she sat down. 'It's probably Peter,' she said. 'I'll get it.'

It was a wrong number too. 'I'm not getting up if it rings again,' she warned. 'Peter will have to learn that I need my sleep.'

It rang again about half an hour later.

'I'll get it this time,' I said. 'I need to fetch another drink anyway.'

'Thank God you answered at last,' said Tim Malone. 'I really didn't want to hang up again. Your mad mother would have decided that it was a nuisance call and phoned the police.'

'That was you earlier?'

'Of course it was me,' he said. 'Who else would it be?'

'I don't know,' I said. 'I'm sure lots of people ring this house. Alison has a good social life, Ian has friends, so has Mum. And Dad. Not that many people ring here for me.'

'Don't be facetious,' he told me.

'I'm merely stating a fact.'

'OK, OK. I rang to find out what time you can meet me tonight.'

'Meet you?'

'Of course, Isobel. I meant what I said the other day. We need to talk.'

'Why?'

'Because there's a lot of things we need to say.'

'I thought you'd said it all.'

'Well, I did,' said Tim. 'But I need to know how you feel, Isobel. I need to meet you. Please.'

He'd never said please to me before.

'Oh, Tim, what's the point? It's too late.'

'The point is that there are things in our lives that need to be sorted out. It's never too late.'

'My life is sorted out,' I said desperately.

'Maybe,' said Tim. 'And if it is then I promise to leave you alone and never contact you again. But we have to be sure, Isobel. We owe it to ourselves.'

'Do we?'

'Yes,' said Tim firmly.

My hands were sweating. I wiped each palm on my denim shorts. 'What do you suggest?'

'I'll be in town tonight. There's a new pub on Dawson Street. It's got atmosphere and, if you don't like me, at least there are other good-looking men swarming around.'

I laughed. '*Other* good-looking men?'

'Good-looking men,' he said. 'Not me.'

'Modesty was always one of your strengths,' I told him.

'Not this time,' he said and I could almost believe him. 'Honestly, Isobel. Not this time. Not about this.'

'I don't want to meet you in a pub,' I told him. 'We always used to meet in pubs. Besides, I don't know the new pubs anymore.'

'What would you like to do?' he asked.

I was silent.

'Tell you what,' he said. 'To prove how serious I am about this, I'll pick you up. I'll face the lion in its den, ring your doorbell and pick you up.'

I shuddered at the thought of Tim ringing the doorbell.

'No,' I said. 'Don't do that.'

He thought for a moment. 'I'll meet you in Fitzers. We can go for a drink afterwards if you like.'

'OK.'

'Eight o'clock.'

'OK.'

'See you then, Isobel.'

I still couldn't believe I'd agreed to meet him.

~

'But I thought you'd stay in tonight.' Mum was upset. 'It's your last night.'

'I promised some friends I'd meet them,' I told her. 'I didn't realise it mattered to you.'

'Of course it matters,' she said sharply. 'You're my daughter. I like having you here.'

I put my arm around her. 'I'm sorry. But I've made the arrangements now.'

'Oh, it doesn't matter,' she sighed. 'You young people have to do your own thing. Not hang around with doddery old women like me.'

'Mum!' I looked at her in exasperation. 'You know it isn't like that.'

She looked sulky.

'And I'm not a young thing,' I reminded her. 'I was thirty this year.'

'You don't look a day over twenty,' she said spiritedly.

'Oh, thank you.' I hugged her again, and kissed her on the face. 'There are times when I love you, Mum.'

'You can't placate me like that,' she said, although there was amusement in her voice. 'Go on, have a good time with your friends.'

'See you later.' I picked up my bag and hurried out of the house.

I was early. I decided against going to the restaurant straight away because I didn't want to sit there waiting for Tim. He was dreadful about time-keeping. He rarely turned up on time for any of our dates, usually arriving fifteen to twenty minutes late, with no real excuse. I wasn't going to let that happen tonight. I would be late myself.

I sat overlooking the cricket pitch at Trinity College and allowed the evening sun to warm my shoulders. When I closed my eyes I could almost imagine being in the Retiro Park. Someone was playing a guitar. I opened my eyes again. It was a young girl, chestnut hair tumbling around her shoulders. Not Nico. I laughed at myself, then shivered as I thought of Nico. I was going insane, I knew I was.

Tim was already at the table when I arrived. I sat down opposite him and smiled tentatively.

'You look lovely,' he said.

'Thanks.' I hadn't worked that hard at it tonight. Jeans,

a white blouse and a blue jacket. No make-up, just a touch of mascara and some lip-gloss. Simple jewellery. Nothing that screamed at him that I'd spent ages thinking about what to wear, how to look.

'Would you like something to drink?' he asked.

I shook my head.

'Sure?'

'Positive.'

I hid behind the menu and looked at the jumble of letters.

'What do you want?' asked Tim.

'Penne.' I said the first thing I could see.

'Nothing more substantial?'

'I like pasta,' I said.

'OK, fine.' He signalled the waiter who hovered near the bar.

'Thanks for coming out tonight,' said Tim, when he'd given the order. 'I wasn't sure that you would. I'd have understood if you hadn't, Isobel, but I needed to talk to you.'

I picked the leaves off the rose in the vase in front of me.

'I said it the other night and I meant it.' Tim frowned. 'I made a big mistake, Isobel. The biggest.'

I swallowed the lump that had come into my throat.

'Afterwards I wondered what had happened to me. I was so happy with you. I loved you. I wanted to marry you.' He shrugged. 'I can't explain it other than what I've already said. I panicked.'

I didn't know what he wanted me to say. I tore the rose leaves in half.

'If I could change it, I would,' said Tim.

'You can't change things,' I said. My voice echoed around in my head as though someone else had spoken. 'Things are different now.'

'How different?' asked Tim.

I blinked a couple of times. 'I have a new life. A new country. New friends. New job.'

'Does that mean you've turned your back on everything here?'

'No.' I cleared my throat. 'But you can't expect me to want to give up everything I've worked for.'

'And what is that exactly?' asked Tim.

'I told you. I've a responsible position in our company. I'm well-paid, Tim, and I have an interesting job. I have a good life in Madrid. It's a nice city. I've made a lot of friends.'

'Is there someone special?'

'I have a boyfriend,' I said, hating the word which sounded so young and childish. 'He treats me well.'

'What does he do?'

'He's a musician.'

'Isobel!' Tim stared at me. 'For God's sake! What does a musician earn?'

'He also works in a pharmaceutical company.'

'I suppose that's something,' said Tim. 'But a musician, Isobel. One of these refugees from the sixties types? Or a Nigel Kennedy clone?'

'He was born in the sixties,' I told him. 'Hardly a refugee. And Kennedy plays the violin. Nico is a guitarist.'

'Then it's flower-power nostalgia,' said Tim. 'Honestly, Isobel.'

'What?' I glared at him. 'Just because he doesn't fit your ideal of what a man should be? A techno whiz-kid or a company clone?'

'No. Nothing like that.' He looked apologetically at me. 'I didn't mean to imply – I'm sorry, Isobel.'

'Nico is a decent, caring bloke and I'm very fond of him.'

'But do you love him?' asked Tim.

'I don't know,' I said finally.

'Then you don't love him,' said Tim decisively. 'If you did, you'd know. You knew that you loved me, didn't you?'

'I thought I loved you,' I said. 'But then again, I thought you loved me.'

'*Touché*,' said Tim as the waiter placed our food in front of us.

I swirled my pasta around in the cream and mushroom sauce. There were so many things I shared with Tim. I couldn't just forget about them all, forget about him. The time when we'd been caught in a thunderstorm and we'd stood on the beach at Sandymount clutching at each other while the rain pummelled the sand and the waves crashed onto the shore. The time we'd gone to Galway and got a puncture and Tim had let go of the spare wheel which took off down the road so that he'd had to sprint after it. The time his mother told me that she didn't think I should wear such a see-through blouse and Tim had told her not to be such a silly old cow and that I was absolutely gorgeous. And the ordinary times. Watching TV together. Walking down the street together. Being part of each other's lives.

'Isobel, I loved you more than I ever loved anyone before.' Tim put down his fork and looked straight into my eyes. 'And I was the worst kind of asshole to do what I did to you. I can understand if you absolutely hate me and never want to see me again. I *know* all of that, Isobel. I know I'm a selfish, self-centred, opinionated fool. I *know*. I know I let things get so out of hand that I made an idiot out of you as well as myself. I appreciate how you felt, even though you might never believe that. All I'm asking now is that you give me a chance. You don't have to commit to anything. Just give me a chance, that's all.'

'A chance at what?' I asked. 'We can hardly have a relationship while I'm two thousand miles away.'

'Think about me,' he said. 'I could come to Madrid for a few weeks. You know how it is – I can bring my laptop and work just about anywhere. I wouldn't impose myself on your life, Isobel. I just think we had something really special and I don't want to let it go without being absolutely sure that it's already dead.'

His eyes glistened. I'd never brought a man to the brink of tears before.

'Let me think about it,' I said after a while. 'I'm very confused, Tim. I don't know how I feel.'

'I understand that,' he said. 'Absolutely.' He beamed at me. 'I care about you a hell of a lot, Isobel.'

'I care about you too,' I said.

~

We went for a drink in the latest trendy pub afterwards. It was crowded, hordes of people spilling onto the pavement with their bottles of beer. It reminded me of Spain. We sat on the edge of a terracotta planter and observed life as it went on around us. Our shoulders touched. I could feel the heat of Tim's body through my blouse and it was achingly familiar. Every so often I trembled and I didn't know why. Each time, Tim asked me if I was OK and each time I said yes, fine thanks.

'My bum is sore,' he said after we'd been there for about half an hour. 'We'll have to go somewhere else.'

I looked at my watch. 'I'd better go home,' I told him. 'My flight is in the morning.'

'Plenty of time.' Tim grinned at me. 'Come on, a night-cap and then I'll drive you home.'

'I don't want another drink here, Tim.'

'I wasn't thinking of here,' he said. 'I thought we could go back to my place.'

I stared at him. 'No.'

He caught me by the hand. 'Do you hate me that much?'

'It's not that.' I bit my lip. 'Be realistic, Tim. If we go back to your place, sooner or later – well, sooner or later—' I broke off.

'I'll try and have my evil way with you?' he supplied.

'Sort of.' I looked at him. 'I can't imagine that you wouldn't, Tim.'

'You've a lot to learn about me,' he said. 'I've changed. I truly have. And of course I want to make love to you, Isobel. From the moment I saw you tonight I wanted to get you into bed. But I won't. Because I want you to believe in me. And I'm not going to mess up what little trust you might have left for the sake of a quick—'

'Tim, please!'

'So come back,' he said. 'I'll be a model of good behaviour, have some coffee to make sure that I can drive you home safely, and then you can see that I'm a reformed character.'

'I wish you'd stop talking about yourself as if you were some dissolute bastard,' I said in irritation. 'You'd swear that you went around doing nothing but breaking girls' hearts. It wasn't quite like that, was it?'

'I just feel so badly about things,' he said. 'I keep thinking that you must hate me.'

'I'd have hated you more if you'd gone through with it and then decided that it was a big mistake,' I told him.

'Really?'

'Of course.' I spoke decisively although it was the first time I really believed it myself. 'It would have been much worse, wouldn't it? We'd have been married and it would all have gone wrong and we'd have been twice as miserable.' I smiled at him. 'God, Tim, I would have hated to get married and have it all go wrong.'

'You're an incredible person, Isobel Kavanagh.'

'I know.' I drained my bottle of beer.

It was easier in Tim's car somehow. We didn't speak, but he put a tape of classical music into the deck and I let the soothing sound wash over me, relaxing me. I wondered if he'd chosen that tape specially for me. Tim's taste was more heavy metal than Vivaldi and I couldn't believe he'd changed that much in a couple of years. It showed that he'd made an effort though – when we'd gone out together before, the window would have been down and Led Zeppelin would have blared from the speakers. I leaned my head against the edge of the seat and closed my eyes.

'Tired?' asked Tim.

'Not really.'

'Sure?'

'Just – chilling out,' I said.

It was very strange to walk into his house again. I'd never expected to be there, to sit on the well-remembered sofa with my legs curled up in front of me while Tim went into the kitchen to make coffee. It felt odd. Right and yet – not right. I shook my head.

The engraved silver picture-frame caught my eye and I got up to look at it. I remembered the night that the photograph had been taken – the night of our engagement. I looked self-satisfied then, I thought, my eyes smiling into the camera, my arm possessively around Tim's shoulder and my ring glittering on the third finger of my left hand.

'I didn't like to hide it away.' Tim walked back into the room carrying two cups of steaming coffee. 'I hope you don't mind?'

'It seems funny to remember it now.' I took a cup from

him and sipped the coffee. 'I got pretty blitzed that night as far as I remember.'

'You and me both.' Tim smiled ruefully. 'And Greg phoned at an ungodly hour the next morning for me to go in to the office.'

'Poor you,' I teased.

'I was sick three times,' he told me.

'I remember,' I said. 'You called around to the house that evening and told me that it was as well you only got engaged once.' I bit my lip as soon as the words were out.

'I'm sorry.' Tim placed his coffee cup on the mantelpiece and put his arm around me. 'I'm really sorry, Isobel.'

I didn't know whether to let him hold me. Part of me wanted him to – part of me ached at feeling his arm around me again. But I was afraid. Afraid that the emotions would come back and no matter what Tim said, I just couldn't fall in love with him again. It would be too easy and it would hurt too much.

He kissed my hair. 'I keep saying and doing the wrong thing, don't I?'

I lifted my head to look at him. 'It's too much, Tim. I can't cope. Not now.'

'Sometime?'

'I don't know.'

'You have to let me prove to you that I love you.'

'Why?'

'Because I'll never forgive myself if you don't.'

I leaned against his chest as I'd done so many times in the past. It was wonderfully normal to be with him again. And it gave me a huge sense of – satisfaction, I suppose, to realise that the man who'd dumped me at the altar still loved me. I'd gone away, I'd rebuilt my life, I'd put him to the back of my mind, and now he wanted me again. It was a feeling of power that I'd never experienced before. But I was still afraid. I broke free from Tim and sat on the sofa again.

He sat beside me and hit the remote. Sky News was showing us the weather – high pressure over Europe, projected temperatures of 24° in Dublin, 34° in Madrid.

'It must be like a cauldron there,' said Tim.

'Sometimes,' I admitted.

'But you like it?'

'It's home.'

He reached out and took my hand. 'Really?'

'For now.'

'You know, this should have been your home,' he said. 'If I hadn't been such a jerk.'

I swallowed. 'But it's not.'

Tim squeezed my hand. 'It still could be.'

'No, it couldn't.' I slipped my hand from his and stood up. 'It couldn't, Tim. I have to go.'

He handed me my jacket and picked up the keys of his car.

~

The porch light was still on when I got home. I opened the front door as quietly as I could and walked gently into the kitchen. Ian and Alison were sitting at the table, a pot of tea and an apple-cake in front of them.

'Midnight feast?' I asked lightly.

'No,' said Alison.

'Can I have some?'

'If you like.' Ian took a mug from the wooden tree and filled it for me.

'Thanks.' I sat down.

'Did you have a good time tonight?' asked Alison.

'Not bad.'

'Where did you go?'

'Something to eat. Then for a drink.'

'Who with?'

I stared at her. 'Is this some sort of inquisition? I get the impression that you're being a mother surrogate here. What's the problem?'

'I just wanted to know who you were out with tonight,' she said. 'That's all.'

'Why?'

'I didn't realise it was a secret.'

We glared at each other.

'It isn't a secret,' I said.

'It was him, wasn't it?'

'Him?'

'You bloody well know, Issy.'

Ian broke into the conversation. 'It was that shitbrain Malone.'

I stirred my tea. 'I met Tim, yes.'

'For God's sake, Isobel!' Alison looked at me in despair. 'What on earth are you doing going out with him?'

'I wasn't "going out with him",' I said. 'At least, not in the way you're implying. I met him for something to eat and a drink. That's all.'

'But, Isobel, he broke your heart!'

I smiled serenely at her. 'When you're a bit older you'll understand that time is, as they say, a great healer.'

'Oh, cut the crap,' she snarled.

'Look,' I pushed my cup away, 'I met Tim a couple of days ago and he invited me out. It was a no hard feelings thing, that's all. So I don't see what you're getting all het up about. If it didn't bother me, it shouldn't bother you. And I don't know why you feel the need to question me about it. And how the hell did you know I was meeting him anyway?'

'Julie.'

'Julie!'

'She told me you'd met him.'

'Jesus wept.' I sighed. 'You and Julie spend far too much time worrying about me and not enough worrying about yourselves. On her wedding day too! The fact that I met Tim Malone and have arrived home in a perfectly sane and healthy manner should, I hope, reassure you that I haven't lost my mind or anything. It was a perfectly reasonable and rational meeting. Old friends. That's all.'

Alison looked disbelievingly at me. Ian didn't look at me at all.

'That's all,' I repeated.

'I don't want him to upset you,' muttered Ian.

'It's very good of you to care, but there's no need.'

'Yes, there is,' he said. 'You're my sister.'

'Mum would love to hear all this.' I laughed. 'Her three children looking out for each other. I seem to recall that she would have enjoyed a little sibling harmony when we were younger.'

Ian smiled slightly. Alison stabbed at the apple-cake.

'Honestly,' I said. 'I'm fine.'

'Don't let him mess you around, Issy,' Alison pleaded.

'I won't,' I told her. 'Nobody will mess me around. I promise.'

Chapter 25

Landscape with Two Figures (Pablo Picasso, 1908)

'Pretty good.' Gabriela closed the brochure and put it into her folder. 'The winter courses should be well booked up this year.'

'We've had advance bookings already,' I reminded her. 'And a lot of the people who did the beginner's courses with Alejandro a few months ago are booking in for intermediate courses now.'

'I'm very pleased with the way things have gone,' said Gabriela. 'And I'm particularly pleased at how hard you have worked, Isobel.'

'Oh, I enjoyed it.' It was true. Although my personal life had become more confusing by the day, my professional life was great. I was very happy working with Gabriela, much happier than I'd been at Delta. I liked coming up with new ideas for courses, or ways of making old ones more up-to-date and interesting. I loved meeting people and my job gave me more than enough opportunities to do that.

'Would you like a quick drink before going home?' Gabriela glanced at her watch.

'Sure. Let me just check my voice-mail.' I went into my office and listened to my messages. The third was from Nico.

'*I am going mad, not being able to talk to you*,' he said. '*I am tired of speaking to your machine, Isabella. I know it is more than a month since I came to Seville and I'm sorry that the job is taking so long. But I will be home soon. I miss you.*'

I miss you too, I thought as I gathered up my belongings and put on my lime-green jacket. I miss you a lot. I hadn't realised how accustomed I'd become to Nico being around. To having coffee with him in the Plaza Mayor. To going boating in the Retiro Park. To strolling around the shops with him while he clucked disapproval at the prices of clothes and then urged me to buy the most expensive thing anyway. And especially to sitting with him in the Chocolateria San Gines while he watched in amusement as I tackled the almost solid cups of chocolate.

Gabriela and I strolled downstairs together and into the newly-decorated reception area – all shiny marble tiles and a fountain in the centre. A man got up from one of the modern metal seats.

'Tim?' I looked at him in astonishment.

'Hi, Isobel.' He wore a light-coloured suit, white shirt and olive-green tie. 'How's it going?'

'Tim,' I repeated, not quite believing it was him.

'Yes, it's me.' He grinned at me and kissed me formally on each cheek. '*Buenos días.*'

'What on earth are you doing here?' I asked.

'Waiting for you,' he said.

'This is a friend?' Gabriela was watching us.

'Yes.' I turned to her. 'I'm sorry. I should have introduced you. Gabriela Suarez, Tim Malone. Gabriela is my boss, Tim. Tim is a – an old friend, Gabriela.'

'Tim,' she repeated. She raised an eyebrow at me. '*Tu novio*?'

I nodded. '*Sí.*'

'It is good to meet you.' She shook Tim's hand. 'I have heard about you. I was just leaving. I will see you tomorrow, Isobel.'

'But, Gabriela—'

'Don't worry,' she called over her shoulder. 'I'm catching the metro.'

Tim and I stood in reception and stared at each other.

'I can't believe it,' I said again. 'What are you doing here, Tim?'

'Is that any way to treat your long-lost fiancé?' he asked. 'I told you. I came to see you.'

'But here?'

'I had to come to Madrid anyway,' he explained. 'Well, Greg Roberts could have done it but when I heard Madrid . . . I had to come, Isobel. Obviously.'

'Obviously.'

Tim put his hand around my shoulder and steered me out into the street. I blinked in the fierce light of the sun and scrabbled around in my bag for my sunglasses.

'I've never been here before.' He looked around. 'Nice, isn't it?'

'I like it.' I put on the sunglasses and felt better now that Tim couldn't look directly into my eyes. 'How long are you staying?' He'd picked up a grey canvas bag at reception which I guessed contained clothes.

'Until Sunday. Tonight, tomorrow night and then a flight home Sunday morning. I wanted the afternoon one but it was full.'

'Where are you staying?'

He made a face. 'I didn't book anywhere. And don't look at me like that, Isobel – it was just I wasn't sure where to stay. You can recommend somewhere to me.'

'The Lux is handy,' I told him. 'It's near the centre of things.'

'The Lux it is then,' he said cheerfully and swung his bag over his shoulder.

I could have asked him to stay. Maybe it would have been the right thing to do. But how could it be when I only had one bedroom and one bed? I wasn't ready for anyone to share that bed.

'You OK?' he asked.

'Yes.'

'Have I ruined your weekend?'

'No. Not at all.'

'How about the Spanish boyfriend? I won't mess that up, Isobel.'

'He's not here,' I said absently.

What would I have done if he was? I cursed Nico for being away.

'Thanks for replying to my messages,' said Tim.

I laughed. He'd sent an e-mail every day since I'd returned to Spain. I usually replied before I went home. This morning's message had been jokey, light-hearted, with no hint of his impending visit.

'What were you planning on doing here?' I asked him.

'It depends on you,' said Tim. 'I want to take you out. Wine you. Dine you. Do all the things that I've wanted to do with you. Just be with you again, Isobel.'

'But if I've already got plans?'

He shrugged. 'No problem. Do your own thing. I can always meet Mario and Felipe. I'd prefer not to, but there's plenty for me to do if you're busy.'

'I'm not busy,' I said.

'Good.' He smiled at me. 'Let's have a great time this weekend.'

I brought him to the Lux. Señor Murillo was standing in the foyer. '*Hola, Isobel.*' He shook my hand and kissed me. 'How are you?'

'Very well, thank you.'

'Are you here for business or pleasure?' he asked.

'I'm not quite sure.' I indicated Tim. 'This is a friend of mine. I wondered if you would have a room for him. Until Sunday morning?'

'But for you, of course, Isobel. Let me see what we can do.' He checked the computer on the desk in the corner. 'A single room?'

'Yes,' said Tim.

'No problem. If you will give me some details then we can code a key for you.'

I sat down while Señor Murillo organised a room for Tim. I still felt guilty that I hadn't asked him to stay with me. But it would have been too much.

'Room fifty-five.' Tim came over to me with the plastic keycard. 'I'll just sling my gear there and then we could go somewhere?'

'Tim, I need to get home first. Change. You know.'

'But—' His eyes met mine. 'Of course. I'm sorry, Isobel. Do you want me to pick you up later?'

I shook my head. 'I'll meet you here. Say – an hour and a half?'

'Jesus – what are you going to do?' He grinned broadly. 'Dye your hair? Have liposuction?'

'Do you think I need it?'

'God, no.' He looked horrified. 'That was a joke, Isobel. Honestly.'

I smiled. 'I know. I'll see you back here. There's a little bar just to the left.'

Tim nodded. 'Come here often, do you?'

'We use it for conferences,' I said.

'See you later.' He kissed me only this time it was less formal.

'Yes.' I rubbed my cheek. 'See you later.'

I walked back to the apartment. I couldn't believe he'd come here. Not Tim. Not chasing after me. Tim had never chased after me. As far as I could remember, I was the one who'd always done the chasing. From the night I'd met him in Howth until the day I'd handed back the ring, I was the one who'd gone looking for him. I was the one who'd sat beside the telephone willing it to ring. I was the one who'd seethed when his job took him to the States or the UK or Japan while I waited at home. I was the one who'd always been there whenever he wanted. But this time he'd had to come to me. I smiled to myself as I walked up the stairs to the fifth floor.

I was like a teenager on her first date. I tried on and discarded my pink dress, my blue dress, my green dress and my red dress. I put on my tight denim jeans and a bright yellow top but decided that, if we went to eat anywhere, I'd explode out of the jeans. I put on a pair of wide cotton trousers and a matching top but I thought they made my hips look too expansive. I tried my green skirt and cropped blouse, but I'd put on weight since the last time I'd worn that outfit and a ridge of skin poked out of the gap between the blouse and the skirt. They'd said I was thin when I'd first come to Spain, but I wasn't thin now! Fifteen minutes before I was to meet him I was still standing in front of the mirror in my bedroom wearing nothing but my bra and pants. The phone rang. I swore softly.

'*Isabella, querida.*'

Oh, shit, I thought. Not now.

'Isabella, I haven't once managed to talk to you.' Nico sounded peeved. 'I have called but you have not replied.'

'That's not true, Nico. I called back the number you left, but it's a mobile phone – sometimes there was no signal, sometimes it was in use.'

'Bloody Carlos,' snapped Nico. 'He keeps borrowing it.'

I grinned. 'Well, I did call you.'

'It's so long since we talked, Isabella. Not since you went to Ireland. I needed to hear your voice.'

'It's good to hear you too, Nico.' I glanced at my watch.

'How was your friend's wedding?'

'It was fun,' I said. 'It was like all weddings.'

'Not much fun,' said Nico. 'I hate weddings. All fuss.'

That sounded chillingly familiar.

'I had a good time,' I told him.

'And your family?'

'They're fine.'

'But you will not go back to Ireland yet? You will stay in Madrid?'

'Of course,' I said.

'I am glad.' His voice softened. 'It is lonely here without you, Isabella.'

'Is it?'

'Yes. There is nobody to sit with in the evening. No one to talk to. No one like you.'

'You're probably having a great time without me!' I laughed.

'No,' he said seriously. 'I am not. But the work is good, I enjoy that.'

'I'm glad.'

'So what are you doing tonight?' asked Nico.

I cleared my throat. 'I am going out with some friends,' I lied. 'With Barbara and with Bridget.'

'Oh.' He paused for a moment. 'Anywhere nice?'

'I don't know,' I told him. 'We're meeting in the Lux. Actually, Nico, I'm a little bit late.'

'I'm sorry,' he said. 'I didn't mean to make you late.'

'No. That's OK.' Suddenly I didn't want him to hang up. 'Really, Nico. I'm glad you called.'

'I am glad I called. I thought you might decide you were an *Irlandesa* after all.'

'I'll always be an *Irlandesa*, Nico. But I'm a *Madrileña* too.'

He laughed. 'Take care of yourself, *querida*. I will be back next week.'

'Take care of yourself, too, Nico.'

'*Buenas noches.*'

'Goodnight.'

I replaced the receiver. I was shaking. Then I looked at my watch again, pulled on the green dress which was the nearest, and hurried out to meet Tim.

I don't know why I felt so guilty. I met him in the Lux's tiny bar and we walked to Cactus Charlies, a burger and beer restaurant which I frequented with the girls when we didn't go to the Hard Rock Café. I didn't want to go to the Hard Rock with Tim.

We sat at a corner table and ordered burgers and chips. Burgers and chips were my favourite comfort foods and I felt the need for comfort. Tim insisted on ordering wine too, although I didn't want to drink alcohol.

'Oh, come on,' he urged. 'It won't kill you.'

'It's not that. I'm tired. Wine will make me sleepier. You don't want me to fall asleep on you, do you?'

'That's not in the game-plan.' He grinned at me.

What *was* in the game-plan? I wondered. What, really, did Tim think could or would happen between us? And what did I want to happen?

'—in the end he agreed that I was right and we changed the configuration and it worked.' Tim beamed at me as he finished the story I'd been half-listening to.

'You got your own way,' I said.

'I always get my own way,' said Tim.

'Do you?'

'Always.' He looked me straight in the eye. The waiter put the food on the table.

'So, that girl I saw you with is your boss?' Tim poured a fountain of salt onto his chips.

I nodded. 'Gabriela Suarez.'

'Great legs.'

'Tim!'

'Well, she has. Good-looking woman for her age.'

'What age is she?'

'Forty-ish?' He looked at me quizzically.

'Fortyish.' I smiled. 'Her husband's a vet and she has two gorgeous children.'

'Do you still want children?'

The question stunned me. I gulped some wine. 'Sometime. Not yet.'

'You told me once that a woman should have children before she's thirty.'

'I think it was my mother who said that.'

'I don't think I was talking to your mother about parenthood.'

'Anyway, not yet,' I repeated.

'But you still want them?'

'Of course.'

'I thought maybe you'd changed your mind.'

'Why?'

He shrugged. 'So many changes, Isobel. Your life, your job. Everything about you is different. Especially here.'

'What's different?' I asked.

He sat back in the chair. 'You're better-looking—'

'Oh, Tim!' I interrupted him. 'That's a ridiculous thing to say.'

'But true,' he continued. 'Maybe it's the weather or something. But you look healthier – I haven't seen you use your inhaler at all yet. At home you'd have squirted it at least once by now. You're more confident—'

'Huh,' I interrupted him again.

'More decisive.'

He hadn't seen the ritual of choosing what to wear.

'More – desirable.'

'Tim!'

'It's true,' he said.

'You keep saying all this stuff to me.' I pushed my unfinished food away, 'as though there's some reason that I should fall into your arms and say "Great, I've reached your standards" and everything would be OK.'

'I'm sorry,' he said. 'I didn't mean it like that. And although I think you've changed, it's only in some ways. You're still the same Isobel. And still the Isobel I fell in love with.'

'And out of love with,' I reminded him.

'No,' he said. 'I never fell out of love with you. I just wasn't sure about everything. That's completely different.' He refilled his wine glass. 'Women seem to think that men don't feel anything. That we make decisions simply because it's convenient to do something at a particular time. But I felt a lot of things for you, Isobel, and I didn't just switch off when you decided that you wouldn't wait for me.'

I said nothing. Rocky Racoon blared out of the loudspeakers.

'Do you want to go?' asked Tim.

I nodded.

I let him pay the bill. We walked out onto the crowded streets.

'Would you like to go for a drink?'

I shook my head.

'A walk?'

'No, thanks.'

'What would you like to do?'

'Nothing.'

'Isobel.' He turned me to face him. 'Don't be mad at me.'

'I'm not,' I said. 'Really I'm not. I'm just – confused.'

He put his arm around me. 'Don't be,' he said. 'Don't be.'

We strolled back to the Lux. I thought he might want to walk me back to my apartment and I didn't know what to say, but instead he ushered me into the hotel and into the bar.

'One drink,' he said. 'And you can have mineral water if you like.'

I ordered a Southern Comfort.

We sat in the uncomfortable armchairs – low, rounded, straight-backed. Tim picked the dry-roasted peanuts out of the Bombay Mix on the table.

'Will you come out with me tomorrow?' he asked.

I laughed. 'You sound like a kid asking a friend out to play.'

'Will you come out to play with me tomorrow,' he asked mockingly.

'If you're good.'

'Of course I'm good.'

'Where d'you want to go?'

'I suppose you're bored with touristy things, are you?'

'No.' I grinned. 'I've only seen some places. But there's lots to see if that's what you want to do.'

'I'll let you choose,' said Tim. 'I'd like to spend the day with you.'

'Sure.' I drained my glass. 'But I'd better go now.'

He reached out and caught me by the hand. 'You don't have to.'

I didn't move. I could feel a pulse beating at the base of my throat.

'I do,' I said.

'You could stay here,' said Tim.

I slid my hand out of his. 'No, I couldn't.'

'I'm not forcing you,' he said.

'Good.'

'I just want you to.'

'Maybe.' I stood up although my legs were shaking. 'But I can't, Tim.'

'Somebody better at home?' He laughed but his eyes were serious.

'No.'

'Sure?'

'Certain.'

'I'll walk you back to your apartment.'

'I'd rather you didn't,' I told him. 'It's not far but I'll get a taxi. There's a rank outside the hotel.'

'I'd really rather go with you. That is, if you insist on going in the first place.'

'I insist on going and I insist on going alone.' I smiled at him. 'You're right – I am much more decisive. I'll call you tomorrow.'

'OK,' said Tim. 'But I'll see you to your cab.'

There were plenty of taxis lined up outside the hotel.

'See?' I said. 'Easy.'

'Take care, Isobel.' He kissed me, very quickly, very gently, on the lips.

'Goodnight,' I said as the taxi pulled away from the kerb.

I hung up all my dresses when I got home. I cleansed, toned and moisturised my face. I sat on my balcony, wearing an ancient T-shirt, and I stared across the jumble of buildings at the neon sign that said *Hotel Lux.*

I rang him early the next morning.

'What time is it?' he asked sleepily. 'God, Isobel, it's only eight o'clock.'

I laughed. 'Up early, to bed late – but a siesta in the middle of the day, Tim. That's how it works here.'

'But I didn't have a siesta yesterday,' he complained.

'You will today,' I promised. 'It's going to be scorchingly hot. You won't be able to do anything but sleep by midday.'

'Want to bet?' he asked.

'I'll meet you in an hour,' I told him.

'OK,' he said. 'Why don't we have breakfast together?'

So we did. Orange juice and croissants in the Lux's dining room. The waitress fawned over Tim although I couldn't understand why. Then he smiled at her and I did understand because when he smiled at me like that I went weak at the knees.

'Have you planned our itinerary?' he demanded.

'I didn't want to make it too difficult for you,' I laughed. 'You've got to go to the Prado and you've got to see *Guernica*. If you don't, people will think you're a complete philistine. And you have to have a drink in the Plaza Mayor. And then we can go to the royal palace – you'll like that, Tim. There's an old armoury and dispensary there. Also,' I looked at him, 'if you want a busman's holiday there's a computer software exhibition you could go to.'

'Ah.' He looked at me guiltily. 'I knew about the exhibition. That's why Greg said I could come. Softsys is showing Crusader, Saracen 2 and Grail. I don't have to go as an exhibitor, but I said I'd drop in and see how the guys here were getting on.'

'I guessed,' I told him. 'What time?'

He shrugged. 'Doesn't matter.'

'Would you like to do that first?'

He looked sheepish. 'If you don't mind. Get it out of the way.'

I kissed him on the forehead. It was completely natural, spontaneous, and he grinned at me. 'I can read you like a book,' I said.

Actually the exhibition was interesting. I left Tim at the Softsys stand while I wandered around some of the others. I picked up leaflets on a whole range of new software ideas and some nifty little office gadgets too. I spent ages looking at a clothes-design program and wondered if I should buy it for myself. I realised that I was now very computer literate and I could understand Tim's fascination, although I couldn't imagine how anyone could actually sit down and write a program that could cope with such a wide range of tasks. They had computer games too – so realistic that you could almost believe you were flying a fighter jet or piloting a submarine.

After about an hour I collected Tim and dragged him along to look at paintings. I was pleasantly surprised when he, too, looked at *Guernica* in shocked amazement and told me that he always thought it was in colour.

'Mad as a hatter,' he proclaimed as he looked at the smaller, detailed sketches of the painting that Picasso had done. 'How could you think up something like that?'

'It's no different to you dreaming up a complicated software package,' I said. 'Creative, artistic.'

'You're mad as a hatter too.' Tim put his arm around me and pulled me closer to him.

It was hot by the time we reached the Plaza Mayor. We sat down under the shade of a yellow umbrella and I stretched my feet out in front of me.

'It's the shuffling along that makes them tired,' I said as I wriggled my toes. 'Walking at a decent pace doesn't do half as much damage.'

'I do quite a bit of walking these days,' said Tim. 'Hill walking mainly.'

'Good God.' I looked at him in surprise. 'I thought the most energetic thing you did was walk to the Chinese takeaway.'

'You underestimate me,' he said. 'Always willing to try new things, that's me.'

I smiled and closed my eyes. The square was crowded with tourists – this time of the year the Madrileños disappeared out of the city. But the tourists were here in force, clicking their cameras and soaking up the sun.

A guitarist was playing 'Sad Lisa', the notes of the melody drifting through the still air. I opened my eyes. But it wasn't Nico sitting in the square plucking at the guitar strings. I don't know why I thought it might be.

'When does everything close down for siesta?' asked Tim.

I looked at my watch. 'Fairly soon.'

'Do the bars and restaurants close too?'

'Don't be silly,' I told him. 'Not when there are tourists around.'

'It's nice here, isn't it?' He leaned back in the cane chair and put his hands behind his head. 'Peaceful.'

'Yes.'

'I don't think I could live here, though.'

'Why not?'

'Too hot,' he said. 'Too bright. Too dusty.'

'Oh, Tim. That's ridiculous.'

'No.' He sat up straight again. 'I'd miss the unpredictability of the weather at home. The days when it starts out horrible and cold and then the sun suddenly breaks through the cloud and it's beautiful.'

'Dank, misty, grey Novembers,' I said.

'Crisp, clear, multi-coloured Octobers,' he returned.

'Dank, misty, grey Augusts,' I grinned.

'Sitting in St Stephen's Green watching the ducks.'

'I'll bring you to the Retiro,' I said. 'Although that's more like the Phoenix Park really.'

'Come home, Isobel,' he said suddenly.

I didn't reply. We sat in silence for a while.

'You were probably right about the siesta,' he said eventually. 'My eyes are closing. I should get back to my room for a while.'

'OK.'

We caught the metro to the Lux. I wanted to stay on for my station but Tim dragged me with him.

'Don't worry. I'm not going to do anything to you.' He kept a firm hold of my wrist until we were inside the hotel. 'A siesta means resting, doesn't it? Come with me.'

'With you?'

'To my room,' he said.

'Oh, Tim.' I picked at the edge of my bag. 'I don't think—'

'Nothing will happen,' he told me.

'It's not that.'

'What then?'

I shrugged. 'I don't know.'

'Please, Isobel. It's not really a single room. There are two beds, you can lie on one, I'll lie on the other. But we've only got today and I want you to stay with me.'

I knew it was stupid but I went upstairs with him anyway.

The rooms in the Lux were surprisingly big and beautifully decorated. Tim's had mint-green carpet, matching curtains and contrasting bedspreads.

He lay down on the bed nearest the window and closed his eyes. I lay on the other one.

'Come here,' he said.

'No.'

'Isobel, please.'

'Tim, what's the point?'

'I want you near me.'

I sighed and got onto the bed beside him. He put his arm around me and I flinched.

'Isobel.' He sounded hurt. 'I won't eat you.'

'Sorry.' I moved closer to him.

He stroked my hair, the side of my face, the base of my throat. I knew I was crazy, I knew where it would lead, but I couldn't help myself. Tim was my ex-fiancé, after all, it wasn't as though I'd come up to the bedroom of a complete stranger. It wasn't like other times, completely meaningless. Tim was familiar, comforting. We had shared so much together. He pulled me still closer to him.

'Remember the time in your house?' he murmured as he undid the buttons of my light summer blouse.

I giggled. Everyone had been out. We'd been in my bedroom. I hadn't bothered to lock the door, I knew that nobody was expected home. Then, just as I was beginning to be swept away by the joy of making love to Tim, the door had creaked open. I'd frozen, mid-groan. Tim – well, it wasn't Tim's finest hour either. And then Sooty, next-door's cat, had stalked across the bedroom floor, his tail a damn sight more erect than Tim was right then. I'd burst out laughing, but Tim hadn't found it funny. At the time. He was laughing now as he remembered.

'No cats here,' he whispered.

He kissed my neck, moving down between my breasts.

'I thought you said you wouldn't eat me.' I was trembling with desire.

'I lied,' said Tim.

I went to the airport with him the next day. He kissed me, hugged me, told me he'd be in touch. I said, great, I'd wait to hear from him. I waited until he'd gone through the departure gate before I left.

I wished I hadn't slept with him. In a long list of stupid things, it was the stupidest thing I'd ever done. Part of me had loved it – being back with him, hearing him say my name over and over again, knowing how to bring him to the brink and then moving back – having power over him. And as he'd made love to me, I'd thought that he was mine again and I felt incredibly powerful.

But now I wasn't sure. That was Tim's legacy to me – never to be sure. I didn't know if I loved him all over again, or whether it was just a physical thing. He said he loved me, he told me hundreds of times, but I couldn't be certain. He'd told me that two years ago.

Yet I'd felt so at home with him. The way he moved. The way he did things that I loved. Everything about him.

And when I was at home again I could still smell Tim's smell and hear Tim's voice and I felt incredibly alone and unbelievably guilty.

Chapter 26

Night (Joan Miró, 1957)

The e-mails from Tim were there most mornings when I got into the office. He told me he sent them from his home computer just before he went to bed. So that you're my last waking thought, he'd said.

Today's message was a poem. I looked at it in astonishment. A poem! From a man whose favourite reading was *PC User* and whose favourite books were by Robert Ludlum!

Come live with me, and be my love,
And we will some new pleasures prove
Of golden sands, and crystal brooks,
With silken lines, and silver hooks.

I remembered it from school. It was John Donne and I'd never expected that anyone would send it to me in later life, so proving our English teacher right when she said that poetry was useful. Useful to Tim, perhaps, but I didn't know how to feel about having poetry sent to me, least of all by Tim. Come live with me and be my love – I'd been down that path already!

I looked at the words on the screen for a moment then simply typed *thanks* and sent that as my reply.

When I got home that evening I changed into a T-shirt and shorts, opened a bottle of San Miguel and sat on the balcony. I'd no plans to go out, I wanted to be on my own for a while. I read my book while the sun slid lower in the sky and the lights came on in the apartments around me.

The phone rang. I didn't want it to be Tim. I couldn't cope with Tim right now.

'Isabella.'

'Nico.'

'How are you, *querida*?'

'I'm fine. How are you?'

'I'm at home. I arrived an hour ago. I would like to see you.'

'That would be nice.' I'd wondered when Nico would reappear, wondered how I'd feel.

'It's OK if I come to your apartment? Say – half an hour?'

I hesitated.

'Isabella?'

'Yes, Nico. Of course.'

'I will not stay long. I have lots of things to write up. But I cannot go to bed without seeing you, Isabella.'

'OK,' I said.

'Isabella – everything is all right?'

'Of course,' I told him. 'Everything is fine.' I replaced the receiver and leaned my head against the patio window.

It was exactly half an hour later when he called. I'd changed into a cotton top and trousers.

'Hi.' I opened the door and let him in.

He crushed me into his arms. 'I thought I'd never get home.'

'You're squashing me.' But I laughed.

'Sorry. It seems so long since I've seen you.'

'A month.'

'A lifetime,' he declared. 'Here is a present for you.' He handed me a bottle of wine and a box of handmade chocolates.

'Oh, Nico, thank you.'

'I thought of you without anyone to take you out for chocolate and so I had to do something about it.'

I hadn't brought Tim to the Chocolateria San Gines. He didn't like chocolate anyway.

'Thank you, Nico,' I said again.

'So.' He held me at arm's length. 'You look tired, Isabella. You have black circles under your eyes.'

'Have I?'

'Yes. And you are pale.'

'I feel OK.'

'Sure? It is not the asthma? Or hay fever?'

'No,' I said.

'Good.' Nico kissed me gently on the lips.

What's happening to me? I asked myself, as I returned the kiss with an intensity that truly shocked me. How can I kiss Nico like this when I've just slept with Tim? This was all wrong.

'Do you want some wine?' I asked breathlessly when we came up for air.

'If you like.'

'I'll open this.' I picked up the bottle he had given me. 'I like Faustino.'

'OK.' Nico sat down. 'It's good to be back.'

I watched him for a moment, then I opened the bottle and poured the wine into glasses.

'You're supposed to say it's good to have me back,' he said.

'Of course it is.' I handed him the wine. 'Would you like a chocolate?'

'No, Isabella. They are for you.'

I sat on the sofa beside him.

'What have you been doing while I was away?' he asked.

'Well, I went home,' I said. 'That was a week. And I worked.'

'No play?'

'Oh, I went out a few times.'

'Anywhere nice?'

I shook my head.

'Did you miss me?' asked Nico.

'Naturally,' I replied.

'We are playing guitar tomorrow night,' he told me. 'Do you want to come along?'

'If I'm not working late.'

'Working late! Oh, Isabella, don't say that you have to work late. I thought we were both finished with working late.'

'Not yet,' I said. 'We're extremely busy right now.'

'The committed career woman,' he said. 'Try and come, *mia Isabella*.'

'Of course I'll try,' I said, more gently. 'Where are you playing?'

'The Meridien. Nine o'clock. We've never played there before – Juan and Emilio were very worried in case I wouldn't be home in time! Why don't you bring your friends?'

'Maybe.'

He reached out for me and held me close to him. He ran his fingers gently down my arm. I couldn't believe the way I was feeling. I looked up at him. The passion was there, easy to read. He slid the cotton top from my shoulders.

'From the moment that I left, I wanted to come back,' he told me. 'I have never felt about a woman the way I do about you, Isabella.'

I swallowed. I didn't love him. I *couldn't* love him.

He kissed me so gently. Tenderly, his lips soft, his body hard. Should I say yes to this? I wondered wildly. Or should I think of Tim and remember that he said he loved me.

'Are you all right?' asked Nico suddenly.

'I – I'm – of course.'

'And this is OK with you?' He moved his fingers from the base of my throat to the swell of my breasts. Desire exploded within me. And suddenly I wanted him for no other reason than he was there and he loved me and I wanted him to love me.

~

He was a wonderful lover. Part of me had thought that he wouldn't be, and that was why he hadn't tried to get me into bed before now. I didn't compare him with anyone as he covered my body in kisses. I couldn't even think when he moved inside me. I had never before abandoned myself so utterly to another person. My mind was completely blank and the only thing that mattered in the world was the closeness of him, the scent of him, the feeling of him.

Afterwards I didn't feel guilty. I didn't feel as I had after any of the others. It had been too great an experience for that. But I had no idea of where I went from here.

~

'Are you busy tonight?' I asked Magdalena next morning.

'Not really.' She laughed. 'I was going to go to my exercise class. But if you have an excuse to put it off, that's great!'

'You don't need to exercise,' I said. 'You're fine the way you are.'

'Thank you, Isobel. But I have put on nearly half a kilo in the last few months and I want to lose it.'

'Abandon your class tonight,' I said. 'And come with me to hear Nico play.'

'Nico!' Her eyes glinted. 'He is back in Madrid, your Nico?'

'Of course he's back in Madrid,' I said irritably. 'That's why I'm going to hear him play.'

'And have you seen him yet?'

I blushed. I couldn't help it. I could feel the colour start in my cheeks and rush to my forehead.

'Isobel!' Her eyes glinted even more.

'What?'

'When did you see him?'

'Last night.'

'And did you give him a warm welcome?'

'What do you think?' I asked.

'I think you must have given him a very warm welcome indeed to look like that.' She grinned at me.

'Oh, Magdalena,' I sighed. 'I didn't mean to, you know.'

'Does it matter?' She looked at me curiously. 'Is everything all right, Isobel?'

'To be honest, I don't know.'

The phone on my desk rang. 'Señora Mantilla. How are you? Can I help?'

Magdalena made a face at me. Señora Mantilla was one of our most difficult clients. 'Good luck,' she mouthed and slipped out of the office.

I was busy all day. Gabriela had gone to Barcelona again

but had managed to leave one of her computer disks behind. Although she was good at running the company, our boss was not the world's most computer-literate person. Eventually we managed to download the disk onto her computer, but not before she'd done her best to try and wipe her presentation from the hard disk.

'I don't know why I bother sometimes,' I muttered to Luis, who'd prepared the disk Gabriela had left behind. 'I think she does it to make life more difficult.'

'Of course she does,' he said seriously. 'It's a test, every time.'

'It bloody better not be,' I told him. 'I don't need her testing me.'

'You're very irritable,' said Luis.

'I'm sorry,' I sighed.

I wanted to sit back and listen to the music that night but Magdalena insisted that I tell her everything that had happened with Nico. And with Tim. Gabriela had told her about Tim's arrival in Madrid.

'To be honest,' said Magdalena, 'I thought you'd tell me about it, Isobel.'

'I would have,' I said. 'But it didn't seem important.'

'But your ex-fiancé.' She looked at me. 'It's something worth telling, Isobel.'

'I wanted to forget about it,' I said.

'Why?'

The audience clapped as Nico, Emilio and Juan walked onto the tiny stage. They looked great in their flowing white shirts and skin-tight black jeans.

Magdalena nudged me. 'Who is that one?'

'Emilio,' I told her. 'He's nice.'

'But your Nico is the best-looking of all, no?'

Of course he was. Easily. My Nico. I shivered.

'I wish I could play like that,' said Magdalena enviously. 'It's so lovely.'

Haunting, I thought. I watched Nico as his fingers moved over the strings of the guitar. As they had over me, I remembered, and it had been so wonderful. I felt the desire fizz up inside me again. It was as well that nobody could read my thoughts or see the images that ran through my head.

When they finished they received a rapturous applause. They smiled at the audience, bowed once and retreated behind the tiny stage.

'Will they join us?' asked Magdalena.

'I think they play again a little later,' I said. 'And then they'll join us.'

'So tell me,' she topped up our glasses from the bottle of wine, 'what is the story about you and Nico?'

'There's no story,' I said. 'Honestly.'

'How can you say that, Isobel. I saw the way you looked at him.'

I flushed. 'And how exactly was that?'

'As though you belonged to him.'

'Well, I don't. And he doesn't belong to me. If I've learned one thing over the last few years, it's that people don't belong to each other.'

'But you love him?'

'God, Magdalena, I just don't know.' I looked miserably at her. 'I don't trust how I feel about anything any more.'

'Maybe you think about it too much,' she said. 'Maybe you shouldn't try to analyse how you feel.'

'I think I have to,' I said. 'I left Ireland because of Tim. You know the story, Magdalena.' (Everyone in Advanta knew the story by now.) 'And when I came here first I just wanted to have a good time. Although I didn't really enjoy having a good time! Then I met Nico. And he's one of the nicest people I know. But I didn't think he loved me. Cared for me, yes. But love – it's a different thing. So I went home for my friend's wedding and I met Tim again.'

She sipped her wine as she listened to me. Her eyes never left my face.

'And he told me that he loved me and that everything had been a mistake and that he wished he'd married me.'

'Isobel!'

'And I told him that it was far too late, that I had a new life. But he sent me messages. And Nico was in Seville.'

'Oh, Isobel.'

'And then Tim arrived in Madrid. He was like a limpet. He was with me all the time.'

'So you slept with him?'

I nodded. 'I didn't want to. Well, maybe I did. That's the whole thing, Magdalena, I just don't know any more. So he went back to Ireland and he rings all the time and tells me he loves me. Then Nico came back from Seville and he arrived at my apartment with wine and flowers and—'

'You slept with him,' said Magdalena in a matter-of-fact tone.

'God, Magdalena, I feel awful.'

'But you have slept with other men in Madrid.'

'How much do you know about me?' I asked her. 'I mean, is my entire life the subject of office gossip or something? Does everyone know every mistake I've ever made?'

'Luis told me,' said Magdalena.

'Luis. I might have known.'

'He cares about you a lot,' she said.

'Oh, really.'

'Yes. He likes you. He thinks you have courage.'

'Why?' I laughed harshly. 'Because I did what he did? Slept with people I didn't care about?'

'That's unfair,' said Magdalena.

'Why are you defending him?' I asked.

'I'm not defending him,' she said. 'I'm defending you. Who says you didn't care about the people you slept with?'

I stared at her and suddenly wanted to cry.

'Come on, Isobel,' she said. 'It's not so bad.'

'It feels like it is,' I said.

'You don't have to care about anyone if you don't want to,' she said. 'You can sit at home every evening and watch TV if you like. There's no rule that says there has to be a man in your life.'

'I know,' I said glumly. 'But I can't seem to keep them out of it.'

~

Nico and the others played once more, then came to the table and sat with us. I introduced him to Magdalena and she told him that the music had been magical. Then, unashamedly, she turned her attention to Emilio.

'Did you enjoy it?' asked Nico.

'The music? I always enjoy it,' I told him. 'You have an incredible gift, Nico.'

'*Gracias.*' He smiled mockingly.

'I mean it. You should chuck the company and take up music full-time.'

'But I cannot do that, Isabella. I have to earn my living, you know.'

'And you don't think you could earn it from music?'

'I don't think so.'

'In spite of the jingles?'

He made a face. 'The jingles are not music.'

'But with them and with the nights you play—'

'I still would not make enough, Isabella.'

'For what?' I asked. 'You're an independent person. You don't need to make a lot of money.'

'Perhaps.' He looked at me oddly. 'But perhaps one day I will need the money. When I have a family of my own.'

I could feel myself shaking. I wanted to get out of this conversation. Quickly.

'Oh, musicians don't settle down,' I said as lightly as I could. 'Everybody knows that.'

'Isobel, would you like another drink?' Magdalena rescued me.

'A *café solo* would be nice,' I answered gratefully.

'And you, Nico?'

'*Un vaso de vino tinto, por favor.*'

'Do you want something to eat?' I asked.

He shook his head. 'I'm not hungry. I'll have *tortilla* when I go home.'

'OK.' I felt snubbed even though he'd been perfectly friendly.

I sipped my coffee while the others laughed and talked. I felt as though I wasn't really here, as though I was watching myself. Isobel Kavanagh, in Spain. With friends. Trying to say the right thing. But did she really fit in?

'Are you all right, Isabella?' Nico turned to me.

'I'm fine,' I said. 'Why?'

'You seem distracted.'

'A little,' I told him. 'It was a busy day today.'

'Would you like to go home?'

If I said yes, would he want to come with me? Would he want to make love to me again?

'Maybe I should,' I said finally. 'I can hardly keep my eyes open.'

'Come on.' Nico stood up. 'I will talk to you guys tomorrow. And it was wonderful to meet you, Magdalena.'

'You too.' She smiled at him. '*Buenas noches.*'

'*Buenas noches,*' said Nico and I together.

~

We walked in silence to the Edificio Gerona. I couldn't think of a single thing to say. Nico didn't seem to feel the need to say anything.

The lift was broken. I was breathless when we got to the fifth floor and had to fish around in my bag for my inhaler. Nico watched as I puffed at it.

'Is it allergic, your asthma? Or psychological?'

'Both, I suppose.' I unlocked the apartment door.

'And you have had it all your life?'

'Yes.'

'Anybody else in your family suffer?'

'Not in my immediate family,' I told him. 'But my mother's sister, Rachel, wheezes too.'

'It doesn't affect you too badly.'

'Only when I'm under pressure,' I said. 'If I've had to rush. If something smells very strongly.' I shrugged. 'It's not important.'

'What is important to you, Isabella?'

'Nico, stop acting like a doctor. Would you like me to make you some *tortilla*?'

His dark eyes glinted. 'How domesticated!'

'I will make some if you're hungry.'

Why did everything we said sound as if we were talking about something else? Why did I feel so off-balance tonight?

'OK, Isabella.' Suddenly he smiled. 'I will risk your homemade *tortilla*.'

I broke some eggs into a bowl and began to whisk

them. Nico turned on the TV. They were showing *ER*. I heated some oil in a pan and poured the eggs into it.

'That smells great,' said Nico.

I flipped the omelette over, sprinkled it with basil and oregano, then slid it onto a plate.

'*Tenga*.'

'*Gracias*.'

I spooned coffee into the cafetière. I'd never be able to sleep tonight, I thought. All this caffeine running through my body.

The phone rang and I jumped.

I picked up the receiver.

'Did you like my poem?' asked Tim Malone.

I glanced at Nico who was eating the omelette and reading the newspaper. 'Very unlike you,' I told Tim. 'But yes.'

'I'm trying to be unpredictable,' he told me. 'I want you to be surprised by me.'

'I was always surprised by you.' I smiled slightly.

'I just rang to say that I miss you,' he said. 'And that the sentiments in the poem – well, it's how I feel.'

'Oh, Tim!' I hadn't meant to say his name but I couldn't help it.

Nico glanced up from the paper.

'I want you to know how much I love you,' said Tim. 'And how much I miss you. And how much I want you to come home.'

'I really don't think it's a good idea to talk about this now.' I moved away from the sofa, closer to the window.

'Why not?'

'It's late.'

'Am I boring you?'

'No.'

Nico was reflected in the glass. His head was bent over

the paper as though he was concentrating deeply on the news. But he couldn't have been. I know I'd have been eavesdropping if I was him.

'You must know how I feel, Isobel. And you know you feel the same way. You know you do! Otherwise you never would have come to the room with me and—'

'Tim!'

'What are you hiding from?' he asked. 'God, I know I treated you badly. I've spent the last couple of years realising that. But that doesn't mean that I can't make up for it, Isobel. Honestly.'

'I know,' I said, although I knew nothing of the sort. 'But I don't want to talk about it now.'

'All right.' He sighed. 'I'll phone you tomorrow.'

'OK.'

'Sleep well, Isobel.'

'You too.'

'I'll be thinking about you.'

'Really?'

'I'm always thinking about you.'

'Goodnight,' I said and put the receiver down.

I poured out the coffee and handed a cup to Nico.

'*Gracias*,' he said. 'Who was on the telephone?'

I shrugged. 'An old friend.'

'Is this an old male friend?' asked Nico casually.

'Yes.'

'A good friend?'

'Once.'

'I see.' He sipped his coffee. 'Did you see in the newspaper that there will be a strike on the metro next week? That will be trouble, don't you think?'

'I didn't notice it,' I said. 'When will it start?'

Nico rustled through the paper. 'Monday morning. I will have to get up early for work.'

'Me too,' I said brightly. 'I'm going to see some clients

on the other side of the city. I must leave myself plenty of time.'

Nico drained his cup. 'I must go,' he said. He looked at me for a moment. 'You are tired, Isabella?'

'I – yes.'

'That is a pity.' He reached out and touched my face, very gently. 'Perhaps you need a good night's sleep.'

'Perhaps.'

He kissed me on the lips, but it was a casual kiss. 'I will telephone you.'

'Yes. Please.'

'Take care, *querida*.'

'You too,' I said.

Chapter 27

Girl Seated Seen from the Rear (Salvador Dalí, 1925)

It was a bad-hair day, one of those days when lots of little things conspire against you so that you feel as though God has singled you out for special, irritating attention.

My alarm clock didn't go off so I was late getting up. My hairdryer cut out with a loud bang, a flurry of dust and blew the fuses in the apartment. I missed the metro by seconds as I clattered into the station, my still-damp hair swinging around my face.

It didn't stop in the office either. Nina rang in sick, I lost the file of our October students and I knocked over a cup of coffee and ruined the memo I'd just printed. I was cursing grimly to myself when Gabriela walked in.

'Hi, Isobel.' She looked flustered. 'Sorry to barge in on you, but I'm having a crisis.'

'You too?' I finished mopping the coffee from my desk and threw the tissue into the bin.

'Rosa has chicken pox,' said Gabriela. 'And I think Julio will get it too. I came in because I had a meeting this morning, but I've got to get back home again. Rosa is feeling sorry for herself and I have to stop her scratching her spots.'

'Poor thing,' I commiserated.

'But I need you to do me a favour.' Gabriela put a folder on my desk. 'I was supposed to go to Barcelona tomorrow – you know, the conference on corporate training? I can't go now. I'd like you to go instead.'

'Oh.' I looked at her blankly.

'Is this a problem, Isobel?'

I shook my head. 'Not at all.'

She smiled with relief. 'I was afraid that you were going to refuse.'

'How can I refuse?' I grinned at her. 'You're the boss.'

'Yes, but—'

'It's OK, Gabriela. Honestly.'

'You will like Barcelona,' she said. 'It is a pretty city.'

'I won't have much time to see it.' I glanced at the schedule for the conference.

'Oh, you can stay for the weekend if you like,' said Gabriela. 'I was booked in for tomorrow and Thursday, but if you want to stay for Friday and Saturday, that's OK.'

'Perhaps.'

'Whatever you like. I've really got to go.' She looked anxiously at her watch. 'Silvia is looking after them but they can be hell if they're sick.'

'Go,' I said. 'Don't worry about anything.'

She smiled at me and disappeared. I wiped a spot of coffee from the keyboard.

Two days in Barcelona would be nice although Nico would be pissed off at me. We were supposed to be going to dinner tomorrow night. He wouldn't be all that understanding if I cancelled.

Since the night we'd made love our relationship had changed. Of course it had to change, but it hadn't changed for the better. I felt guilty for having slept with him even though I desperately wanted to sleep with him again. But I was still getting the e-mails from Tim and I kept thinking of Tim every night when I went to bed. And Nico didn't try to make love to me again. I think – but I'm not sure – that I was offended by that! It was as though I hadn't been good enough for him.

There was a barrier between us and it wasn't entirely of my making.

I sighed and reached for the phone.

'Alvarez.'

'Hi, Nico, it's me. Isobel.'

'*Hola, Isabella.*' He was casual.

'I called because I can't go to dinner with you tomorrow night.'

'Why not?' It sounded as though he was only half-listening to me.

'I've got to go to Barcelona for Gabriela.'

'Lucky you,' said Nico.

'It's only for a couple of days. I'll be back by the weekend.'

'Whatever you like.'

'I'm sorry,' I said. 'I was looking forward to dinner.'

'Were you?'

'Of course I was.'

'It doesn't matter,' he said. 'You can call me when you get back.'

'Nico?'

'Yes?'

I sighed. 'Nothing.' I replaced the receiver. It had been a very unsatisfactory telephone call.

~

The conference finished on Thursday afternoon. Despite Gabriela's assurances that there would be no problem in staying over, I wanted to leave Barcelona. For an unknown reason I was caught in a black depression and I didn't have the heart to go sightseeing. So I stuck to the original timetable and caught the seven o'clock flight back to Madrid.

The arrivals hall was crowded but I saw Nico straight away. Tall and dark and with an indefinable something that made him stand out from the crowd. My heart contracted as he smiled at me.

'What are you doing here?' I asked. 'How did you know I was coming back tonight?'

'I rang your office,' he said simply. 'Nina told me.'

'It was good of you to come.'

'I wanted to.' He lifted my bag from my shoulder. 'Allow me.'

I was glad to let him take it. It was getting heavier by the second.

'I brought the car,' said Nico.

He rarely drove his car; Madrid was not the type of city you drove in for pleasure.

'Come on.' He opened the door for me. I moved a dozen CDs and a sheaf of music out of the way and got in.

'Did you enjoy the conference?' Nico drove like all Spaniards – fast.

'Yes.' I clutched at the arm-rest in the door as we hurtled around a corner.

'I thought it would be very boring.'

'Mostly it was,' I admitted. 'But there were some interesting bits.'

'Worth missing dinner for?'

'Don't get at me, Nico.'

'I'm sorry.' He sped through amber lights and I closed my eyes tightly.

'Here we are.'

I opened my eyes again. We weren't anywhere near my apartment.

'I thought we could have dinner tonight instead,' said Nico.

'Where are we?'

'This is my home,' he said as he got out of the car.

We were on a tree-lined avenue. Small villas and low-rise apartment buildings stood side-by-side.

'This block is where my apartment is. I am on the top floor.' It was only three stories high. Brightly coloured flowers climbed the whitewashed walls and each balcony was dotted with terracotta pots bursting with blossoms.

I followed him up the cream and brown marble stairs to his apartment. The interior walls of the building were hung with reproduction Picassos and Mirós. On each stairway a huge cactus plant thrust out of a glazed urn.

'At least the apartment hasn't burnt to the ground.' Nico unlocked the door. 'Come in.'

The living room of Nico's apartment was at least twice the size of mine and his balcony reached around two sides of the building. The interior walls were apple-white and covered with old theatre prints. The table in the dining area was pale wood and a huge blue and red porcelain bowl of fruit was in its centre. The apartment was surprisingly stylish for a man who lived on his own. I couldn't help comparing it with the mess that had been Tim's house. I doubted very much that Nico had ever left an empty takeaway carton on the beautiful dining-table.

'I'm not the best cook in Madrid.' Nico stood beside me. 'But I do my best for you, Isabella. There is a chicken cooking in the oven – I hope – and I have prepared vegetables also.'

'Oh, Nico, thank you,' I said.

'When I eat for myself, I usually send out for food.' He smiled sheepishly. 'Not good, healthy food. Pizzas and burgers usually.'

'Very nutritious,' I said.

'But I have made a special effort for you,' he promised. 'I hope you like it.'

'Of course I will.'

Tim had never cooked for me. Tim had never made a special effort for me. Maybe the new Tim had a *cordon bleu* qualification and would slave over a hot cooker for me whenever I wanted. I pushed thoughts of him to the back of my mind.

Despite his protestations, Nico was a surprisingly good cook. I enjoyed the meal and I was almost content lying in the curve of his arm on his comfortable grey sofa afterwards.

'You are very special to me, Isabella,' he whispered as he curled my hair between his fingers. 'Very special.'

He kissed me. I loved the way Nico kissed me. I followed him into his very masculine bedroom and we made love with a strange kind of desperation that matched my mood and that made him hold me tighter than he ever had before.

'Stay the night with me,' he murmured. 'There is no need for you to go back, is there?'

There wasn't. I didn't have to go into the office the next day if I didn't want to. I would, of course, but I didn't have to be at my desk at the crack of dawn. And I wanted to stay with Nico. I wanted to burrow into the bed beside him and lie in the warmth of his arms. I wanted so much, yet I didn't know exactly what I needed. And, yes, when we were locked together, then I felt special.

~

He was already out of bed when I woke up the following morning. I could hear him whistle to himself as he clattered around in the kitchen. I slid out of bed and grabbed a discarded T-shirt which hung over the back of a chair. I looked at myself in the mirror. My eyes were dark smudges in a pale face. Nico's T-shirt, smelling of *Polo*, was long and almost reached my knees.

The aroma of freshly brewed coffee enticed me into the kitchen. Everything was clinically clean here too. The worktops were grey stone, the sink was polished chrome and the cooker was a very businesslike unit built into the pale wood surrounds.

'*Café solo*?' He handed me a tiny cup.

'*Gracias.*' I sipped the coffee and looked around with interest. There was a photograph on the wall of the kitchen and I moved closer to it.

It showed Nico standing in front of a detached two-storey villa. His parents were on one side of him. He had his arm around the girl on his left and she looked up at him, adoration in her eyes. She had creamy skin, a perfect face, and long black hair that almost reached her waist.

'Who's she?' I asked casually.

'That's Carmen,' he said, equally casually.

'Is she a relative?'

The question was so silly that I was surprised he took it seriously. He shook his head. 'She was a friend of mine.'

'A close friend?'

'She was a girlfriend, Isabella. We went out with each other for a long time.'

'And did you love her?' I asked.

He was silent for a moment and sipped his coffee carefully. 'Who knows?'

'Either you loved her or you didn't.' My tone was petulant.

'I loved her for a time,' he said.

'You look very happy in that photograph.' I peered at it more closely. 'When was it taken?'

'Last year,' said Nico.

So last year, when I had been nursing a broken heart, Nico had been in love with the girl in the photograph. Carmen. Maybe he'd made love to her in this apartment, in the same bed as he'd made love to me. Perhaps he'd cooked her *pollo con ajo*, as he'd cooked it for me. I supposed he'd whispered '*Carmen, querida*' to her as he'd murmured '*Isabella, querida*' to me.

And why shouldn't he? I hadn't known him then; God knows I'd had a love of my own to worry about. And yet I felt a sudden stab of jealousy and its intensity shocked me. I'd never expected to feel like this. The coffee was bitter in my mouth.

'Why did you split up?' I asked.

'For goodness sake, Isabella!' He looked at me in annoyance. 'It's only a photograph.'

'I know what it is.'

'Well, then.'

'But it's a photograph of your ex-girlfriend.'

'So what?'

'There's something odd about a man who keeps a photo of his ex-girlfriend hanging in his house.' Suddenly I thought of Tim and our engagement photo on his mantelpiece and I blushed furiously. But Nico didn't notice my flaming face.

'Isabella, you're being silly.'

'I'm not.'

'Yes, you are. I don't like it when you act like a child.'

'Don't talk to me like that.' I glared at him.

He turned away and rinsed his coffee cup. I watched

him, angry and upset. He took a diary from a shelf and looked through it. It was clear to me that he didn't want to talk to me. That the subject of Carmen – *Carmen querida* – was too sensitive.

'Do you mind if I have a shower?' I asked finally.

He glanced up from the diary. 'Go ahead.'

I stalked into the bathroom. The water in the shower was so hot that I nearly lost a layer of skin. I got dressed and walked back into the living room. Nico was flicking through some brochures.

'I'd better go to work,' I told him.

'OK,' he said. 'I'm meeting some clients, I won't be in the office today.'

'Thank you for dinner last night.'

'*De nada.*' He barely looked up from his work.

'Will you call me?'

'I'm playing in Quixote tonight. Tomorrow perhaps?' He turned over a page.

'Sure. Tomorrow.' I picked up my bag. 'I'll get the metro to the office.'

He stood up. 'I'd carry it for you, but I am late already.'

'It's OK.'

He smiled slightly. 'Have a good day, Isabella.'

'Sure.'

He kissed me on the cheek. 'I'll call you.'

~

I stood in the metro station, jostled in every direction by *Madrileños* hurrying to work. I was hurt by Nico's sudden indifference and upset by the evidence of his previous girlfriend. And I didn't know why I was so upset. And I didn't know what to do next. And I didn't know what I wanted to do next.

Friday night in Madrid. I sat on the balcony and listened to the sound of the traffic, the sudden blaring of a car horn, people calling to each other. I went inside and got my briefcase. I took out the notes I'd made at the conference. I read about training schedules, conference organisers, hotel facilities, in-house programmes, expert lecturers. I sat with the sheaves of paper on my lap and I didn't move, even when my stupid tears smudged the print so that I couldn't read any more.

The telephone woke me the following morning, dragging me from the fitful sleep I'd finally fallen into. A headache pounded at the top of my head.

'*Hola*,' I croaked.

'Isobel? Is that you?'

'Alison.' I blinked a few times and looked at my watch. 'What are you doing out of bed at nine o'clock on a Saturday morning?'

'It's only eight here,' she said. 'I had to phone you. It's awful news. Granny Behan died last night.'

'What?' I blinked again.

'Last night,' repeated Alison. 'Granny Behan died.'

'How's Mum?'

'Oh, OK – ish,' said Alison. 'You know.'

'What happened?'

'Heart attack, I think. Her next-door neighbour always calls in on Friday nights. When Granny didn't answer the door she got worried and phoned. Dad went over. Granny was dead in her armchair.'

'Oh, God.'

'The funeral's on Monday.'

'I'll be there,' I said. 'Is Mum up yet?'

'No,' said Alison. 'She was very upset last night. Dad made her drink some brandy and she's asleep now.'

'I'll phone later,' I said. 'I'll let her know about my flight.'

'I can't believe she's dead.' Alison sounded suddenly bewildered. 'One minute she's alive and one minute she's dead. It doesn't seem possible.'

'No.'

'I'd better go. I've got to do things. I'll wait to hear from you later.'

'OK,' I said. 'Thanks for ringing.'

'Sorry to muck up your weekend.'

I hung up and sat on the sofa.

We weren't a very close family. We'd visited Granny Behan when we were children, of course, but she wasn't a story-book granny – she wasn't plump and welcoming with grey hair and glasses. Granny Behan had been a tall, angular woman whose bones had stuck in you. She wasn't the sort of granny who'd play chasing around the back garden or allow you to mess up her furniture. Granny Behan had treated us like miniature adults and, when we were in her house, that was how we behaved. But whenever there was anything wrong, when we'd fallen or hurt ourselves, or when Mum needed to go somewhere, Granny Behan had always been there to look after us.

'Those dreadful children,' she'd say, looking at us from soft brown eyes that belied her stern appearance. And she'd bandage us, tell us not to be silly, no need for tears and give us her encyclopaedia to look through.

I hadn't seen Granny Behan the last time I was in Dublin. I regretted not having made the effort now. Caught up in my own world I hadn't thought of her. Poor Gran. Poor Mum.

I reached out for the phone. I needed to talk to Nico. He'd understand. He'd comfort me.

But I only heard the shrill ringing at the other end. Nico wasn't there.

Chapter 28

Weeping Woman (Pablo Picasso, 1937)

The sky was blue and cloudless but a cool breeze rustled through the leaves of the trees in the graveyard and I pulled my cotton jacket more tightly around me as we prayed for Granny Behan.

Mum threw clay onto the coffin, a dull thud followed by the sound of pebbles sliding on the polished wood. We turned away and walked to the cars.

'She had a long life,' said Mum later, as we dispensed tea and sandwiches back at her house. 'And she'd be glad to go quickly.'

People always said that. Maybe it was true.

'I wish I'd seen her again.' Rachel stood beside my mother. She was pale and subdued, quite unlike her usual cheerful self.

'She knew you were thinking about her,' said Mum.

'But I wasn't.' Rachel stirred her tea. 'I wasn't thinking about her at all.'

'Of course you were,' said Mum determinedly. 'You just had her to the back of your mind, that's all. With family, you're always thinking about them. They're with you all the time.'

Mum was a great believer in family.

'It's just so hard to believe.' Rachel's eyes watered. 'So quickly.' She took her tea and walked out to the garden.

'Always dramatising.' Mum handed me a cup. 'Drink this, Isobel, you look shattered.'

'Headache,' I muttered.

'Take something for it.'

'I did.'

Mum looked at me quizzically. 'You all right?'

I nodded. 'I'm OK.'

'Working too hard,' she said.

I smiled wanly. 'No, not really.'

Tessa Blaney, one of Mum's friends, joined us. 'Why don't you have a nice cup of tea yourself, Helen,' she said gently. 'You could probably do with it.'

'I will, when I see to everyone else.'

'Let me worry about them for a while. Go on, Helen. Have a bit of a sit down.'

She nudged Mum away from the teapot and made her take a cup of the steaming brown liquid. 'It'll do you good.'

'I suppose so.' Mum went and joined Rachel in the garden.

They looked very alike sitting on the low stone wall together. Mum's hair was greyer, but they had the same features, the same expressions, the same way of half-raising an eyebrow when they were talking to each other. Family.

'And how are you, Isobel?' asked Tessa. 'I hear you're doing really well over there in Spain.'

'Not bad, Mrs Blaney.'

'Are you having a good time?'

'Oh, yes. Fine.'

'Job's going well?'

'Yes.'

'And tell me, have you met any nice young man over there?'

I smiled at her. 'There's lots of nice young men over there.'

'Any one in particular?'

There had been, of course. But Nico hadn't answered his phone at all on Saturday. And I wasn't going to go to his apartment and start ringing the bell.

'Sometimes,' I compromised.

'Well, isn't it great to be young and have men dancing attendance on you?'

'I wouldn't know,' I said.

Tessa Blaney laughed. 'Don't lie to me, Isobel Kavanagh. I can tell there's someone.'

I smiled again and my head hurt. I wished Tessa would go away. I wanted to be on my own.

'Isobel!' Ian beckoned to me across the room. I excused myself from Tessa. 'Thought you were looking particularly trapped,' he said.

'I was.'

'Are you OK?' he asked. 'You look dreadful.'

'Thanks!'

'I don't mean it like that.' He shrugged. 'You're awfully pale, you know.'

'I'm fine,' I told him. 'Headache, that's all.'

'This bloody thing would give anyone a headache.' He looked around. 'All these people! Who'd have thought Granny knew them all?'

'I don't suppose she did,' I said. 'Lots of them are Mum's friends. They've come to offer support.'

'Support!' He snorted. 'Support in eating sandwiches and drinking tea. Or whiskey.' He nodded in the direction of Tessa's husband who held a crystal glass filled with an overgenerous measure.

'Why not?' I asked. 'They came to the funeral. Probably

the last thing they wanted to do today. The least we can do is give them something to eat and drink.'

'Are you getting sensible?' asked Ian. 'Or have you just become a bit of an old woman?'

'Sod off,' I said companionably and he put his arm around my shoulder and squeezed me.

Ian's Honey had come to the funeral Mass but she'd gone back to work directly afterwards, explaining that she hadn't been able to get a stand-in to take her appointments.

It was all back on again with Honey, apparently. 'Can't seem to live without her,' Ian had told me. 'Something about her, Issy.'

'The fact that she has legs up to her armpits,' I had teased gently.

Alison and Peter sat side-by-side. They looked completely natural together and right for each other, two fair heads bent close, engrossed in their own world.

'Are you sure you're OK?'

I'd sighed without realising it and Ian was looking at me anxiously.

'I wish people would stop asking me that,' I said crossly. 'There's nothing wrong with me.'

'Mum says that they work you like a slave in Madrid.'

'What would she know?' I asked. 'And they don't. Besides, I like it.'

'Alison told me that you had a boyfriend there.'

'On and off,' I said.

'Not serious then?'

I looked at my brother. I'd never discussed relationships with him before. Not really. I'd always thought of him as too young, even when he'd sympathised with me about Tim and then later, when, with Alison, he'd warned me about getting involved with him again.

'Not serious,' I said.

'But you look – sad.'

'We're at a funeral, Ian. It's supposed to be sad.'

'Not this bit,' said my brother. 'This is where people laugh and tell stories.'

'You're dreadful,' I told him. 'Really dreadful.'

But he was right. Under the influence of the whiskey and the tea, people were chatting easily, smiling, even joking a little. Mum and Rachel were talking animatedly now, Rachel using her hands to illustrate some point and Mum mimicking her.

Why did I feel as though I was frozen inside? Why did I want to go home to Sutton, throw myself on the single bed and wrap the duvet around me as I'd done when I was a teenager? Surely the ache that I felt now, that indescribable ache for no reason, surely that was a relic of teenage angst and had no place in the life of someone who was thirty?

A successful, career-woman thirty.

With no one to put his arm around her as Peter did around Alison. Or no one to confide in as Ian did with Honey. Or no one to laugh with as Andy and Julie did.

Don't be so bloody stupid, I told myself viciously. You are an independent woman. Being married is no longer the aim of your life. And if you need a hug and a kiss right now you only have to call Tim Malone. He'd be happy to oblige. You wouldn't even have to ask.

The hum of conversation continued. I still felt as though I was trapped in my own world, cocooned from everyone else. I talked to people I hadn't seen in a long time – Ursula Walsh, Gran's next-door neighbour, who'd always seemed very old to me but now, inexplicably, looked younger than her fifty-five years; Paddy Reynolds, who owned the butcher's shop in Sutton, the only place Gran ever bought meat and the only place Mum ever bought it either; Cliona Hughes, the lecturer at the

English literature evening class that Gran attended. I hadn't known Gran was going to English literature classes – she was seventy-seven, what more could she learn? But Cliona Hughes said that Gran was a wonderful woman – sparky – and an inspiration to the class. She would have been sparky, I supposed. She'd always been more sparky than comfortable.

It was stupid to miss her now, when I hadn't seen her in so long. I washed cups and plates and stacked the dishes neatly in the pine cupboard beside the sink. Then I poured myself a Southern Comfort from the bottle on the table. I'd introduced Gran to Southern Comfort, five or six years ago. She'd loved it. I gulped back the drink and allowed it to warm me.

I wanted to go home. I was tired of being surrounded by people. I needed some quiet.

'Go ahead,' said Ian when I muttered to him that I could do with a bit of solitude. 'I'll keep an eye on Mum.'

'Do you mind?'

He shook his head. 'You look really tired, Issy. And you've got to go back to Spain tomorrow night.'

I smiled feebly at him. 'Jet-setting, that's me.'

'Go and have a sleep,' he advised. 'I won't tell Mum you've gone.'

'Thanks.' I kissed him on the shoulder which was as high as I reached on Ian these days. 'See you later.'

I walked back along the seafront, not caring that the breeze was still cold. I was nearly knocked down by half-a-dozen children rollerblading at high speed along the cycle track. I thought of the rollerbladers in the Retiro Park who didn't go for speed, just intricate jumps and spins and loops. But for the first time ever the thought of sitting in the park didn't cheer me up. All I wanted was to fall asleep and be somewhere apart from the day-time world.

But I couldn't go to sleep. I lay in my bedroom and counted sheep but I stayed wide awake. I tried breathing slowly and evenly but only induced a fit of coughing. I pulled the quilt around my shoulders and burrowed under the pillow but I could still hear the birds in the tree outside the window and the sound of children laughing as they played on the road outside.

I got out of bed again and went downstairs. I took the washing in off the line. I sat in the garden. I pulled a few weeds. Then I went inside and phoned Softsys.

'Just a moment,' said Shauna brightly when I asked for Tim Malone. She'd hesitated for a second, trying to place my voice, but couldn't remember me. I didn't give my name, said it was a personal call.

'Hello.'

'Hello, Tim?'

'Isobel? Isobel, how lovely to hear from you.'

'Thanks.'

'Are you OK? You sound a bit funny.'

'I'm at home, Tim. I came home for my grandmother's funeral.'

'Oh, Isobel. Your mum's mother?'

'Yes.'

'I'm sorry.'

'Me too.'

'Is your Mum OK?'

'Oh, I suppose so.'

'How long are you staying?' he asked.

'Not long,' I told him. 'I'm going back tomorrow afternoon.'

'That's not much of a break.'

'It's all I have time to take.'

'You sound fed up,' he said.

'I am.'

'Where are you now?'

'At home.'

'Your mum's?'

'It's the only home I have.'

'Do you want me to come out?' he asked.

I hesitated.

'Would you like to meet me?' he amended.

'Yes.'

'Well, do you want me to come out there, or will you come into town?'

I didn't know what I wanted.

'I'll come out there,' said Tim. 'You're obviously in shock, Isobel.'

'I shouldn't be in shock,' I said. 'She was my grandmother, after all. It's not as though it was Mum or Dad.'

'It's a shock all the same,' said Tim firmly. 'I'll be out in half an hour.'

Half an hour. Nobody would be back from Granny Behan's in half an hour. I washed my face and put on some foundation. I couldn't meet Tim looking pale and wan although it seemed somehow irreverent to apply eye-shadow and mascara, even if the eye-shadow was terracotta and the mascara colourless.

I waited in the front room until I saw his car pull up. I went outside straight away.

'Hi there.' He held out his arms and folded me to him.

'Hi.' I leaned against his shoulder. The comfort I wanted. The comfort I needed.

'Come on,' said Tim. 'Let's go.'

He drove up the hill of Howth and parked at the summit. He didn't speak during the drive, didn't try to ask me anything.

'Here.' He handed me a waxed jacket from the back seat of the car. 'It's chilly.'

'What about you?' I asked.

'I've got a jumper.' He grinned at me. 'Besides, I'm a man. We don't feel the cold.'

We walked precariously through the gorse and furze until we came to a clear patch and sat down overlooking the sea.

'It's beautiful, isn't it?' Tim's words encompassed the glittering water, the bright blue sky, the golden flowers around us and the wheeling, screeching gulls overhead.

'Yes.'

'More beautiful than Spain?'

'Different,' I said. I shivered.

'Are you cold?'

'Not really. This jacket's lovely.'

'Do you miss this in Madrid?'

'What?'

'The sea. The smell of it, the taste of it in the air.'

'Tim!' I looked at him. 'That's very lyrical.'

'I like the sea,' he said defensively. 'I'd hate to live somewhere land-locked.'

I smiled. 'I know. I like it too, although I've never quite got to grips with it like lots of the people around here. I don't do yachting or racing or even swimming very much.'

'It must be strange in Madrid, to know it's so far away.'

'If you go to the Palacio Real you can look over the approach to the city,' I told him. 'On a hot day it shimmers and shifts so that you can almost believe it is the sea.'

'Not quite the same thing,' said Tim.

'No.'

'And what other ways do you fool yourself in Madrid?' he asked.

'What!'

'I'm sorry.' He didn't really sound it.

'Don't get at me, Tim. I'm not in the mood.'

He hugged me. 'I didn't mean to get at you.'

'No?'

'No.'

I leaned against him again and closed my eyes. He was right about the sea. I missed it. I missed places that I'd known all my life, places that had meaning for me, where I'd grown up, learned about growing up. Madrid had been an escape for me, but had it served its purpose?

'Do you like my messages?' he asked.

'You must have to do a lot of work to send me poetry,' I murmured lazily.

'You inspire me,' he said.

'Don't be bloody stupid.' But it was nice to hear him say things like this. I wondered if he really loved me. It was as though he did, but – never sure, I thought to myself, never sure with Tim.

'I love you, Isobel.' He broke into my thoughts. 'Truly I do.'

'Oh, Tim.'

He kissed me. Slowly, surely, exploring me as though he'd never kissed me before. He ran his fingers through my hair, caressed my cheeks, held me tight.

'I want to be with you.' He held me away from him. 'I want to put my mistake right.'

I stood up. The wind buffeted me. Tim jumped up and steadied me.

'I was OK,' I told him. 'I'm not going to be knocked down by a gust of wind.'

'How do I know that?' he asked.

'I'm not that fragile,' I replied.

We stood side by side.

'I mean it, Isobel,' said Tim. 'I love you. I want you to marry me.'

He looked so earnest, so loving, so sincere. He was here with me when I needed him. He understood how I felt.

'Why?' I asked.

'Because we were meant for each other.'

I raised an eyebrow.

'And I've missed you.'

'Have you gone out with other people?' I asked.

He looked uncomfortable.

'I don't care,' I said hastily. 'I've gone out with other people myself. I just want to know.'

'A few girls,' he said. 'They didn't mean anything.'

'Did they know that?'

'Pardon?'

'Nothing.'

'We're a good team, Isobel. We can make it work.'

I stared out over the sea. 'What if it all gets too much for you again?' I asked.

'It wouldn't,' he said.

'How d'you know?'

'I just do.'

The sun sparkled off the water below us.

'Are you sure?'

'Of course,' he said.

'I'd have to get a job here,' I mused.

'You can have babies if that's what you want.'

'Tim!' I looked at him. 'I never wanted to marry you just to have babies.'

'But you want them?'

I thought of Gabriela's black-eyed children. 'Yes,' I said.

'So do I,' said Tim. 'I've thought about that a lot. When you talked about it before, it made me feel even more trapped. But now I feel differently.'

'Do you?'

'Absolutely. I reckon I'd be a good dad. Pretty nifty at the computer games, anyhow.'

I grinned at him. 'Competitive git.'

'We'll have wonderful children,' he told me.

Tim was giving me my life back. The one I always thought I'd have. I wanted it now. I really did.

'OK,' I said.

'OK what?'

'OK, I'll marry you.'

'Oh, Isobel.' He hugged me so hard that he squeezed all the breath out of me and I had to take a puff of my inhaler.

I didn't say anything to my family that night. It wasn't the right time. But I caught the DART into town next morning and met my fiancé.

'I hope this is OK.' He took a blue velvet box out of his pocket.

'Tim!' I opened it cautiously. My engagement ring sparkled at me. My first engagement ring.

'I kept it,' he said. 'I couldn't bring myself to go back to the jeweller with it and I—' He shrugged.

'Thought it might come in useful one day.' I slipped it on to my finger and watched the sun glitter against the stone.

'No,' he said.

'You weren't keeping it for me.'

'I don't know why I kept it,' he said honestly.

I smiled at him. 'It's lovely. It was lovely two years ago and it's lovely now.'

'I couldn't think of a more appropriate one. I wondered if it was quite right, giving you the same ring again, but I reckoned if you didn't like it you'd throw it back at me and we'd be back to square one again.'

I laughed. 'I never threw it at you.'

'You probably wanted to.'

'Maybe.'

He kissed me. 'I've got to get back to work. I know it's not the thing when you've just got engaged for the second time, but I do have a project bubbling and Greg is going mad for me to finish it.'

'All right.' I didn't mind. 'Do you want to drop me at the airport later?'

He hesitated for a second.

'It doesn't matter if you can't.'

'No. I want to. What time?'

'Four.'

'D'you want me to pick you up at home?' He looked apprehensive.

'I have to tell them,' I said. 'We might as well get it over with.'

'I wish you didn't have to go back today,' he said irritably. 'We can't talk things over properly. And we should get it all organised.'

'You sound like I used to.'

'*Touché*.'

'But you're right. We've just decided on this without thinking it through.'

'We don't need to think it through,' he told me firmly. 'We'll get married as soon as you tidy things up in Madrid. A winter wedding would be nice, don't you think?'

'I'm imagining me with goosepimples in a white dress,' I said. 'It's not a very attractive picture!'

'You'll be beautiful no matter what time of the year. I think the best thing would be for me to come to Madrid in a few weeks' time. Help you pack your stuff, that sort of thing. Have a pre-wedding holiday. We can settle on things then.'

'OK.' I was happy to let him take over.

'OK.' He kissed me again. 'I'll have to go, Isobel. I'm really sorry. I'll pick you up at four.'

'Fine. I'll go home and break the happy news.'

'Don't look so glum about it!'

'I'm not glum.' I smiled at him. 'I'm very, very happy.'

My family's reaction was more muted than I'd expected. Well, there was only Mum and Dad to react – Alison and Ian were at work.

Mum was sitting at the kitchen table looking through the sample memoriam cards that had flooded through the doorway as soon as Gran's death had been announced. I thought it incredibly ghoulish and intrusive of companies to send them, but it seemed to give Mum a focus. She was reading the rhymes out loud.

'I know this probably isn't the best time,' I said as I sat down beside her. 'But I have some news.'

'News?' Her eyes were still far away.

'Good news,' I said brightly.

'I could do with good news.' She shuffled the cards together as though they were playing cards.

'I'm getting married.'

She stared at me.

'I'm engaged,' I said.

'Engaged? Who are you engaged to?'

I moistened my lips. 'Don't get mad at me.'

'I'm not mad.'

'Tim Malone.'

'What?' She blinked a couple of times. 'You're engaged to Tim Malone?'

'Yes.'

'But, Isobel—'

'I know what you're going to say and you're right. I had my doubts too. But I met him when I came home for Julie's wedding and I've been in touch with him ever since. We both realise that we still love each other and we want to get married.' Why did I sound so defiant?

'Well, Isobel, if it's what you want.' She looked more bewildered than ever.

'It's what I want.'

'But what about your job in Spain? I thought you loved that job. I thought you loved Madrid. I thought you had a boyfriend in Madrid.'

Isabella querida. But not when I needed him. And how come my mother was suddenly so enthusiastic about my life in Spain?

'Not a serious boyfriend,' I told her. 'And, yes, I like my job. But I need to think about my future. It's not in Madrid, Mum. It's here. Living here in my own house and raising my own family. That's what I want.'

'And you think you'll be happy with him?'

'I know I will.'

'You thought that before.' She looked anxiously at me.

'I know. And we got it all wrong.' I put my arm around her. 'But we'll get it right this time, Mum. I know we will.'

'I only want you to be happy.' Her eyes filled with tears. 'It's important, Isobel.'

'I know.' I held her close to me while she cried for her mother and I felt more grown-up than I ever had in my life before.

~

Tim called at exactly four o'clock. He looked nervous.

'Come in.' I opened the hall door wide.

'Your dad isn't standing there with a hammer, is he?'

I shook my head. 'They're in the kitchen. Ian and Alison are at work.'

'I can't say I'm sorry to miss Alison,' he said.

'Don't be so scared.' I squeezed his arm. 'She doesn't mean to snap.'

'I'm not convinced about that,' he said darkly.

He followed me into the kitchen.

'Hello, Mr Kavanagh. Mrs Kavanagh.'

'Hello, Tim.' Dad stood up. 'I wasn't expecting to see you in this house again.'

'To be honest, I wasn't expecting it either,' said Tim. He looked very boyish. 'But I'm glad I came to my senses and I'm glad Isobel understands me.'

'I hope she doesn't have to do too much understanding!'

'Not at all.' My fiancé was extremely polite. 'I think we've worked through our difficulties and I'm really looking forward to settling down with her.'

'Just don't hurt her again,' said Dad gruffly.

'I'll never hurt her again,' said Tim.

'When are you going to get married?' Mum had asked me this already.

'Isobel will decide,' said Tim. 'She has to go back and sort things out in Spain and when she's ready, I'm ready. But I don't want to rush her.'

'I hope you're doing the right thing.' Her glance took in both of us.

'I know we are,' said Tim.

'We'd better go.' I picked up my bag. 'It wouldn't do for me to miss the flight.'

I kissed my parents goodbye and followed Tim to the car.

'Nightmare,' he breathed as we drove away.

'What d'you mean, nightmare?'

'Meeting them. I was afraid your dad might kill me.'

'They're not that bad.' I laughed.

'Who knows?' asked Tim. 'They probably blame me for everything.'

'Tim, it *was* all your fault.'

'You see?' But he was smiling. 'I knew you'd blame me.'

It was lovely to have him kiss me goodbye. To have someone who didn't want me to go. To feel the warmth of his embrace, the scratch of his five o'clock shadow as I sat on the plane. To know that he was waiting for me.

It was wonderful to know that he was waiting for me again.

Chapter 29

Girl Standing at the Window (Salvador Dalí, 1925)

I stood in the queue at the taxi rank outside the terminal building and felt a trickle of sweat slide down my back. The sky was blue-grey, thunder growled in the distance and the air was humid, difficult to breathe. I shook my inhaler and sucked on the mist. It didn't help all that much – it was like being in a sauna and I could never stay in a sauna for more than five minutes.

The taxi was air-conditioned. I sat back and gratefully breathed in the cool air. I had a headache again, made worse by the oppressive humidity. I rubbed my temples and closed my eyes. The taxi driver took the long way around to my apartment but I didn't care. Sometimes I'd argue with taxi drivers who took the long way around, but not today. Today I was too happy to argue, despite my headache and despite my wheezing lungs. Today was the beginning of the rest of my life. I held out my hand and turned it so that the diamond ring caught the sudden shaft of sunlight that had filtered into the taxi. Isobel Malone, I said to myself. Exactly as it was meant to be.

The thunder was closer. I paid the fare and hurried into the apartment building. The lift – working – glided up to the fifth floor.

Señora Carrasco was painting her front door.

'*Hola, Isobel.*' She waved the paintbrush in friendly greeting. 'Where have you been?'

'I was at home,' I told her. 'In Dublin. My grandmother died.'

'Oh, Isobel.' She placed the paintbrush carefully on the tin of paint and came over to me. 'I'm so sorry.'

'It's OK,' I said. 'She was old.'

Señora Carrasco hugged me. 'But it is a sad time, nonetheless.'

'Yes.' I took my keys out of my pocket.

My neighbour eyed me curiously. 'Are you all right, Isobel? You look very pale.'

'It's the weather,' I said.

'Yes.' She grinned. 'I do not like the storms. That is why I am painting inside.'

I laughed. 'I do. But only when it starts properly – thunder, lightning, rain!'

'We need some rain,' agreed Señora Carrasco.

'Well,' I smiled at her. 'I'd best get inside, tidy up.'

'Isobel!' She caught me by the hand. 'Isobel – you are wearing an engagement ring!'

'Yes.' I smiled at her again. 'I'm engaged to be married.'

She stared at me. 'I did not know. That is wonderful news – your friend is a very sexy man.'

I blushed, then shivered. 'I think you are mixing things up, Señora. You have not met my fiancé.'

'But—'

'I am marrying an old friend from Ireland.'

'I am surprised.' She regarded me thoughtfully. 'Your other friend spent so much time with you.'

I blushed and said nothing. Neither did she.

I opened my apartment door. 'I've got to go. I've things to do.'

'OK.' She walked back across the hall. 'No problem.'

'I—' But she'd picked up the paintbrush again. I shook my head. It didn't matter to me what she thought. Nothing mattered to me other than the fact that I was engaged to Tim again. And that I knew that he loved me.

I had a lukewarm shower and wrapped a robe around me. It was almost dark in the apartment now, the clouds overhead heavy and dark.

The phone rang and startled me.

'Hello, Isobel,' said Tim.

'Hi.'

'How're you doing?'

'Fine, thanks.'

'I just rang to say that I miss you.'

'Oh, Tim. And I miss you too.'

A clap of thunder broke almost overhead and I jumped.

'What was that?' asked Tim.

'Thunder,' I said. 'There's going to be a massive storm tonight. The sky is almost black and I can hardly breathe.'

'You're all right though?'

'Of course.'

'Well, I just rang to say I'm thinking of you.'

'And I'm thinking of you too.'

'Take care, Isobel.'

'You too, Tim.'

I hung up and walked onto the balcony. A flash of lightning lit up the sky, tearing it in half as it cut its way earthwards. A moment later peals of thunder rolled one after the other, crashing overhead. The lightning struck again. I stepped back towards the shelter of the apartment. I loved thunderstorms but I'd never seen anything like this before – huge, jagged bolts of lightning and thunder so loud that it seemed to surround me. God moving furniture around, Mum had told me when I was small, and I believed her until one day I asked, if he was God, why didn't he lift it instead of dragging it across the sky and making such a noise?

The next lightning flash was almost on top of the Hotel Lux. The next peal of thunder seemed to be overhead. Then, suddenly, an eerie silence. It seemed as though the whole city was waiting for something, holding its breath. And then the rain came. Cascading out of the sky, falling in great sheets of water, like a tidal wave hitting the beach. There were no individual drops of rain, just one flood of water, pouring onto the balcony so that I was soaked; there was far too much water to be drained away through the little outlet in the concrete surround. I reached behind me and closed the patio door. I was wet through already so I might as well stay where I was but there was no need for the apartment to be flooded. I leaned over the balcony and watched the water race in torrents down the street, crashing into cars and swirling around lampposts. It was wonderful.

I thought I heard a knock on my apartment door but I wasn't sure. The noise of the storm was so great that it blotted out everything else. I went back into the apartment and peered through the spy-hole in the door.

Nico stood outside, a bunch of flowers in his hand. I caught my breath and stood, immobile, dripping rain-water onto the tiled floor. How had he got in? I wondered. There was a security system in place so that people couldn't come in the entrance door without somebody buzzing them in. But someone had let Nico in. And he must know that I was here. I bit my lip. I wasn't quite ready to face Nico yet. To tell him about Tim.

He rapped on the door again. He knew that I was here; he would be able to see the light. I had to let him in. I opened the door.

'Isabella!' He strode inside. 'Isabella, where have you been?' He almost embraced me, but didn't. I was too wet for anyone to hug.

'On the balcony,' I said lightly. 'Watching the storm.'

He stared at me. 'I didn't mean just now. I meant for the past few days.'

'I had to go home,' I told him. 'My grandmother died.'

'So it was true,' he said.

'What d'you mean – it was true?'

'I rang your office, of course. But the girl who told me said it in such a way that I thought, perhaps, she was lying.'

'Oh Nico, don't be so bloody silly.' I shivered in the wet robe.

'You are cold.'

'Of course I'm cold,' I said. 'I was standing in the rain.'

'Why would you do that?'

I shrugged.

'Are you all right, Isabella?'

'Absolutely.' I shivered again. 'I'll get dressed.'

'Not because of me.' He smiled and my heart skipped a beat. He had a wonderful smile.

'I'll get dressed.' I walked into the bedroom and closed the door behind me.

I was freezing. I pulled on a pair of jeans and a cotton jumper. My hair hung in rats' tails around my face. I rubbed it with the towel and ran a comb through it. I sprayed *Allure* behind my ears, then replaced the bottle on my dresser with a bang. What was I thinking of? Perfume for Nico! Why?

My ring was on my bedside locker. I left it there. I would tell Nico tonight, of course, but I didn't think it would be a good idea to waltz into the living room flashing my diamond at him.

He'd left the flowers on the table and opened the

patio door again. It had stopped raining, but the balcony was still awash with water. Nico stood at the door, looking out.

'Hello again,' I said.

'Why did you bother?' he asked.

'Bother?'

'The jeans, the jumper. I liked you the way you were.'

'I was cold.' I undid the cellophane wrapping from the flowers.

'Is everything all right, Isabella?' He stepped back into the apartment and wiped his feet on the mat. 'Were you very close to your grandmother?'

'I liked her,' I told him. 'It was a shock to hear that she'd died.'

'You should have called me,' he said.

'When?'

'When you heard the news.'

'I did,' I said shortly. 'You didn't answer.'

'Poor Isabella.' He put his arms around me and I could feel the beating of his heart. 'I'm sorry. I should have telephoned you before now.'

'No.' I pulled away from him. 'I'm glad you called around, Nico. I wanted to talk to you.'

He held me at arm's length. 'To talk to me?' He laughed. 'That sounds very serious, *mia Isabella*.'

'I suppose it is,' I said. I sat down on the sofa and he sat in the chair opposite me, looking at me from big brown eyes that, tonight, were almost black.

'I met a friend when I was back in Dublin,' I began nervously. 'An old friend.'

Nico raised one eyebrow but said nothing.

'We'd been friends for a long time,' I said. 'We loved each other.'

Nico sat back in the armchair and looked at me speculatively.

'Well, to be honest, Nico, we were engaged to each other.'

'Engaged?'

'To be married. Obviously.'

'Obviously.'

'But we split up. That's – why I came to Madrid, really. To forget about him.'

'But you did not forget?'

'I – put him to the back of my mind,' I said.

'You did a good job,' said Nico. 'I never realised that there was someone at the back of your mind.'

'Nico, I—'

'When we made love together, I didn't know that you were trying to keep your fiancé to the back of your mind.'

'Nico—'

'When we went out together, I didn't know that I was there to help you forget.'

'Nico—'

'When I called you *querida* I didn't realise that it meant absolutely nothing to you because there was someone else.'

'Nico, it wasn't like that.'

'Oh?'

'No.'

We glared at each other for a moment.

'I care for you a lot,' I said lamely.

'Thank you.'

'But – well, where was it going, Nico? It wasn't as though we were going to get married or anything. It wasn't as though it was for ever.'

'Why?'

'Oh, come on,' I said. 'Sure, you called me *querida*. Sure, you made love to me. Sure, we were together and it was wonderful. But I was never the person you really cared about. I'm an *Irlandesa*, I'm not the girl you'd marry!'

'Since when has marriage become so important to you? What about your job – your great career?'

'It's not the most important thing.'

'You told me it was.'

'No, I didn't. I said it was important to me. But I wanted to get married someday. I was ready to get married before, but it didn't work out. I'm ready to be married now.'

'But not to me.'

'You don't want to marry me,' I said. 'I know I'm not the girl you want. Or the girl your family wants. Try Carmen.'

'Carmen!' He stared at me. 'I do not love Carmen.'

'You loved her,' I said. 'I could see that. You probably still love her. Why else would you keep a photograph of her in your apartment?'

'Don't be absolutely ridiculous.' He stood up. 'You are upset about a photograph! I can't believe I'm hearing this, Isobel.'

He'd called me Isobel. He never called me Isobel.

'I'm sorry,' I said. 'I like you a lot, Nico—'

'I'm flattered.'

'—but it isn't for ever, is it? And with Tim it will be for ever.'

'Tim,' he said. 'He has phoned you, hasn't he? He phoned you one night when I was here. So you didn't just meet him when you went home, did you?'

'It's a bit more complicated than that,' I said.

'I did not believe you were this kind of girl,' said Nico. 'You go out with me, make love to me, share things with me. And then you tell me that you are going to marry someone else!'

'If I'd thought it mattered—'

'What?' he asked. 'If you'd thought it mattered – what? You allowed me to care for you and to make love to you. If a man had done this to a woman – had told her it was over and he was going to marry someone else you would think he was a pig. But it's OK for you to go out with me when you feel like it and then decide that you want to go home and marry this, this – Tim.'

'Oh, stop it!' I cried. 'You're twisting things around!'

'Am I?'

'Yes. And you never once acted as though you wanted anything more permanent. We were friends, that's all.'

'Is that what you think?'

I said nothing. I was close to tears.

'Is it?' he demanded. 'Is that the way I have treated you?'

'Please, Nico.'

'Oh, do not start to cry.' He looked at me in disgust. 'It is a thing women do, cry. When things are happening that they don't like – they cry.'

'Nico—'

'And I am supposed to say that it doesn't matter, because of your tears. Well it does matter, Isobel. It matters to me. I cared about you, I loved you, I thought you loved me. OK, so I was wrong. But don't cry to pretend that you are hurt. Don't insult me like that.'

I bit my lip.

'So it is over between us,' said Nico. 'I am sorry, Isobel. Perhaps I should have dragged you to bed on our first date together. Perhaps that would have put things into context for you. Perhaps you would have felt better about it that way. But I didn't think you were ready. I thought there was *something* – I didn't realise it was *someone*. I wanted to make love to you so much, Isobel. And I didn't. But when we did – it was wonderful. I thought it meant as much to you as it did to me. I'm sorry if I was wrong.

I'm sorry that I didn't know I was only a substitute for the man you want to marry! You were ready to sleep with me, though, when you felt like it. It is a strange thing for a man to feel used. Still, no matter. You have got what you want. You have made him jealous enough to marry you!'

'It wasn't like that.' I almost choked on the words. 'I swear it wasn't, Nico.'

'I admire you,' he said. 'I admire the way you can suddenly switch from one person to another. It is a wonderful talent you have, Isobel.'

'Nico, I told you I was engaged to Tim before,' I said desperately. 'But we didn't simply split up. There was less than a month to go to the wedding. He got cold feet. We postponed the wedding. Then we decided that we wouldn't get married at all. He was afraid of marriage then. I came to Madrid to forget about it – start all over again. And you helped me. I care about you a lot. But I can't be sure about how I really feel with people any more. Or how they feel about me. Not one hundred per cent, absolutely sure. Except Tim. I can be sure of Tim because we've been there already. So I know everything will be all right. He won't let me down a second time.'

'Isobel.' Nico rested his hands on my shoulders and I jumped. 'What are you saying? That you are marrying this man because he dumped you once and you can be sure he won't do it again? That is the craziest thing I've ever heard.'

'But I loved him,' I said. 'I still love him.'

'Are you sure?'

'Absolutely.'

'One hundred per cent?'

'Yes.'

He let me go again. 'I do not understand,' he said.

'You're a man,' I told him. 'How can you understand?'

He shook his head. 'You are marrying someone who has treated you badly before. Are you out of your mind?'

'No.'

'Isobel – would you change it if I asked you to marry *me*?'

'Nico, please don't say things you don't mean.'

'How do you know I don't mean it? Do you want me to change my mind now? Would that make things easier? You are being very silly, *querida*.'

'*Don't* call me that,' I said sharply.

'I am sorry,' he said. 'And I am sorry you want to end it like this.'

'Me too,' I whispered. 'Truly, I am. But, Nico, let's face it. You're a good-looking man. You can pick any girl you want. Barbara Lane, for instance. She's crazy about you. Magdalena told me that you were the sexiest man she'd ever seen. Women will fall at your feet, Nico.'

He stared at me. 'Do you think that is the person I am?' he asked. 'That I want for women to fall at my feet? Do you understand me at all?'

I felt terrible. 'I'm sorry.'

'You are so caught up with how *you* feel, Isobel, that you haven't thought a single bit about how *I* feel. You think that because you have fallen in love with your Tim again that I can just forget about you by going out with someone else. It worked for you, of course.'

'Please stop, Nico.' I pushed a strand of damp hair from my forehead. 'I didn't mean—' But I'd run out of words.

We stood looking at each other. The water gurgled on the balcony. The thunder still rumbled, faintly, in the distance.

'I will go,' he said finally. 'I hope that you will be very happy, Isobel.'

'Thank you,' I said faintly.

He stopped at the door. 'If I had thought you wanted

to be married – if you had once made me think that way – I would have asked you, Isobel. Perhaps it is as well I did not.' He went out and slammed the door behind him.

I stood in the centre of the room. My head was pounding and I could hardly breathe. I wrapped my arms around me and hugged myself tightly. That was the worst scene of my life. Worse than when Tim had dumped me. Worse than telling people that the wedding was off. Worse than anything. Because I'd hurt someone I never wanted to hurt.

Nico had told me he loved me. But what else does a man say when he has just taken you to bed? I like you? You're OK? Hey, you were wonderful? They don't all tell you that they love you, but it's one of the phrases. Tim had told me that he loved me after the first time. I hadn't believed him then. It takes more than a roll in the sheets after all.

I picked up the flowers from the table. Roses. Nico liked bringing roses. Red were his favourite. These were orange, bursting with colour and with scent. But my asthma was still troubling me and I was afraid to sniff them.

I walked onto the balcony, still with the roses in my hand. There was no sign of Nico.

It's not fair, I thought. He didn't understand. I cared about Nico. Maybe I loved Nico. But I had to marry Tim. That was the way things were. I looked at the flowers. He always brought me flowers. He was a very generous man. But he talked nonsense and he knew what to say to make me feel bad. I wished, now, that I'd never met him. My fingers tightened around the roses then I suddenly hurled them over the balcony into the darkness below. I leaned over and watched them as they were washed away, faint splashes of colour in the blackness of the rainwater that coursed down the street.

Chapter 30

Illumined Pleasures (Salvador Dalí, 1929)

I got up early the next morning. I dusted my face with powder – there were dark circles under my eyes and my cheeks were pale. I wondered if I had a serious illness. The headache was still there, not as blinding as it had been, but enough to make me wince in the glare of the morning sun. There were traces of the thunderstorm in the city – the leaves that had been ripped from the trees were now in sodden masses at the side of the road and murky puddles lurked in the gaps between the paving-stones. But the air was clear and I didn't need my inhaler to ease my breathing.

I walked into the office building, very conscious of the glittering ring on my finger, but I didn't meet anyone on my way into my room and I was glad about that. I felt slightly uncomfortable at the thought of telling them about my engagement. Mostly, I felt uncomfortable about telling Gabriela. She was more than just a boss to me, she'd taken an interest in me, given me opportunities that I'd never had before, and I hated the idea of repaying her by leaving.

Our morning meeting was in the boardroom. I brought a notebook and a folder although I didn't need either of them. We sat around the circular table while Gabriela, having offered her condolences about my grandmother, talked about next year and the new courses she had in mind. We'd landed a contract for a telephone company which had recently changed all its computer software so she wanted me to draw up a plan for their in-house training. I nodded. She hadn't noticed the ring yet – nobody had because I'd kept my hand under the table.

She handed around new brochures. 'Let me know what you think.'

It was my moment. I reached out and took one. The lights reflected off the diamond and it glittered furiously.

It took a few seconds for people to react.

Luis noticed first. 'Isobel! You are engaged!'

Even though I was ready for it, I blushed.

'Isobel!' Gabriela stared at me. 'You never told me.'

'It was a bit sudden,' I explained.

'But when did you do this?' she demanded. 'You were in Dublin the last couple of days. Where did you get the time?'

'I met him while I was there.'

She looked at me blankly. 'But I saw Nico yesterday morning. He was in the Plaza Mayor.'

I stared at her. 'I'm not engaged to Nico.'

'What?' Luis looked at me, his face showing puzzlement.

'I'm engaged to Tim,' I said.

'Tim?' It was Magdalena's turn to look blank. 'Tim?'

'Your ex-fiancé!' Gabriela still stared at me.

'Not ex any more.' I giggled nervously.

'But what about Nico?' asked Luis.

'Nico knows about it,' I said.

'I thought you were still going out with him,' said Gabriela.

I said nothing.

'Does this mean you're going back to Ireland?' Magdalena asked.

'I – eventually – yes.'

'When?' Gabriela sounded businesslike.

'I'm not certain.'

'When do you plan to get married?'

'We didn't set a date. It was all rather sudden.'

'Certainly it was sudden,' said Luis. 'I can't believe it, Isobel.'

'Why not?'

'I thought you hated him.'

'Not hated,' I said.

'But – he was so bad to you.'

'That's in the past. And he was right to do what he did. Maybe not when he did it, but these things happen.'

'All the same—'

'Please,' I interrupted. 'I'm engaged to be married to Tim. I hope you'll all come to the wedding.'

Gabriela smiled at me. 'Of course,' she said. 'But we'll be sorry to lose you, Isobel.'

'I'll be sorry to leave,' I said as I bent my head over the new brochure.

'I meant that,' I told her later as we sat in her office. 'I feel really bad about leaving the company.'

'If it's what you have to do,' she said.

'I think it is.' I twirled the ring on my finger. 'I love him, Gabriela. I can't help it.'

'So what are your plans?'

'He wants to get married as soon as possible. But I wanted to sort things out here first. Stay with you until you are sure who you want to replace me. I think we'll get married in January.'

'Three months, more or less,' said Gabriela. 'That is not far away.'

'No.'

'And your Tim, he would not like to live in Madrid?'

I shook my head. 'He wouldn't like the weather. He likes four seasons, not two.'

Gabriela laughed. 'I understand. I hope you'll be very happy, Isobel.'

'I hope so too.'

She clipped some papers together. 'I didn't realise you and Nico had split up.'

I blushed. 'We hadn't exactly,' I admitted. 'Although things had become a little uncomfortable between us.'

'So – he didn't know you were seeing Tim?'

'Gabriela, you're making it sound as if I was doing something terrible. I know it seems as though I was stringing Nico along, but it wasn't like that, honestly.'

'He must be feeling hurt.'

'I should have done things differently,' I said. 'But he'll get over it. It's not as though I was the only girl in his life.'

'There was someone else?' Gabriela looked surprised.

'Not exactly.' I shifted in my seat. 'But he still has a photograph of his previous girlfriend in his apartment and I'm sure he still cares about her.'

'That doesn't mean he didn't care about you,' said Gabriela.

'It wouldn't have worked,' I told her. 'Honestly, Gabriela. I know it was great at first, but we've had some awful rows in the last few weeks. I've made the right choice.'

'I didn't know it was a matter of choice between them.'

I shrugged. 'It wasn't. But, Gabriela, Tim was there when I needed him. When Gran died and I felt so badly, Tim was there to comfort me and care for me.'

'And where was Nico?' she asked.

'I don't know,' I told her. 'I phoned to tell him, but he wasn't around. We had a very easygoing relationship that way.' I smiled at her. 'Now I'd better go and phone Felipe Caruana. I promised him I'd call about his in-house training programme.'

'OK.' Gabriela pulled a brochure from the pile in front of her.

I was halfway to the door when her voice stopped me. 'Isobel?'

'Yes?' I turned around.

She looked anxiously at me. 'Don't take this the wrong way. But are you sure you're doing the right thing?'

Was I doing the right thing? It was easier to be objective about it in Madrid. And I knew I was being objective. Tim loved me – he'd proved that he loved me. Nico said that he loved me but that didn't mean anything. Marriage was more than love, it was a partnership. Tim and I could be that partnership because we'd been through trust and mistrust and we understood each other. I didn't always understand Nico. He looked at life in a different way to me. It was part of his foreignness, part of what attracted me to him, but you couldn't build a life on differences. And we were very different. At the end of the day, despite the pharmaceutical company, despite the jingles, despite saying that he'd marry me, I knew that Nico was a free spirit. He wasn't the marrying type. I thought maybe it was more his pride that was hurt when I told him about Tim. A macho man like Nico – even a sensitive, guitar-playing, art-loving macho man – wouldn't be all that pleased about being dumped by his girlfriend.

I turned onto the Calle Don Alvaro. The days were getting shorter. The streetlights glowed in the dark.

Back in the apartment, I sat down in the armchair and pulled the phone toward me. Julie would understand.

'Tim Malone!' Her voice squeaked. 'You're marrying Tim Malone!'

'Why not?'

'Isobel, he treated you like shit!'

'No, he didn't,' I protested. 'He wasn't ready to marry me and he said so. I wouldn't call that treating me like shit.'

'You're out of your mind!'

'No, I'm not.'

'You said once that you could never be sure of him again,' she said.

'You said once that you never wanted to speak to Andy Jordan again,' I pointed out.

'I know.' She sounded worried.

'Don't worry about me,' I told her. 'I know what I'm doing.'

'Do you?'

'Absolutely.'

'When's the wedding?' Her tone was lighter.

'January, I think.'

'And what about your job?' she asked.

'I'll try to get something when I go home,' I said. 'But Tim and I want to start a family.'

'Is this what it's all about?' she asked. 'Having children?'

'No, it's not.' I twirled the ends of my hair. 'But I've

always wanted a family, Julie. And Tim is ready now. He wasn't before.'

'So now that he's ready he'll marry you.'

'Kind of.'

'But your life has changed,' she said. 'You're not the same person.'

'Of course I am.'

'Last time we talked you'd been promoted and you said that you were a businesswoman and proud of it!'

'I was. I am. But there's more to life than work, Julie.'

'I know.' She still sounded worried. Why was everyone so damned worried about me? Why did they think that I didn't know what I was doing?

'What happened to Nico?' she asked.

And why did they all ask about Nico? It wasn't as though we'd been going together for years. It wasn't as though Julie had even met him!

'Nico's fine,' I told her. 'We just weren't for ever, that's all.'

'Why?'

'I don't know why,' I said. 'I just know.'

'If you're sure.'

'I'm sure.'

'That's OK, then.'

'Will you be at the wedding?' I asked.

'Of course,' said Julie. 'I wouldn't miss it.'

'Thanks, Julie.'

'What are you thanking me for?'

'I thought you might not be able to come.'

'Are you out of your mind?' she asked comfortably. 'It's your wedding, Isobel. I would have been there the first time so I'll definitely be there the second. How could I miss it?'

'Will Andy come?'

'If I tell him to,' she chuckled.

'How is he?'

'Wonderful,' she said.

'Everything OK in the USA?'

'I love it here,' she said. 'I love the people and I love the life.'

'Are you working yet?' She hadn't been last time I called.

'Not so's it counts,' she admitted. 'I'm doing some part-time work in a car salesroom. Not exactly me, but it keeps me occupied. To be honest, Isobel, we're hoping to start a family soon ourselves.'

'Really?'

I could almost see her shrug. 'Gotta start sometime.'

'Good luck.'

'Thanks.' She laughed. 'We're having fun trying anyhow.'

'I bet you are.' I thought of Andy Jordan, lean and muscular.

'It's funny.' She laughed again. 'All the times I desperately hoped that I wasn't pregnant and now I want to be.'

'Well, don't let me keep you from it,' I told her.

'He's at work,' said Julie. 'But don't worry, I'll hop on him when he comes in.'

'You're lucky,' I said. 'You and Andy are so perfect for each other.'

'We work at it,' she said. 'We're not always perfect, Isobel. Nothing is.'

'Rubbish.' I laughed. 'Tim and I will be perfect. I promise you.'

'I hope so.'

'We will,' I said. 'I'll give you a call when we've got a definite date for the wedding, Julie.'

'OK,' she said. 'Thanks for ringing. And congratulations – again.'

'Thanks.'

'Take care.' She rang off.

~

I turned on the TV and picked up my book. Even though I didn't want to watch TV, I liked having it on for company. It was lonely living by myself. I'd done it and I'd learned a lot but I missed having people around me. It would be nice, when we were married, to sit side-by-side with Tim on the sofa watching TV in companionable silence. Sharing things. That's what it was about, after all. Sharing. And one day we'd have our own children sitting with us. I grinned to myself at my suburban dream. A perfect family. Whereas what would probably happen would be that we'd have two kids who wore rings through their lips or belly-buttons or whatever the current fad would be, while they complained to each other that we didn't understand them. But it was nice to dream the dream anyhow.

~

I went shopping at the weekend. I bought six pairs of shoes in a small shop off the Serrano because I could never find shoes in Dublin to fit me. The sales assistant thought all her bonus days had come at once when I brought them all over to the cash desk. One of the pairs was white, the softest of leather with a spindly heel. I thought that, whatever sort of wedding dress I eventually got, the shoes would look wonderful with it. I bought a newspaper and went into a small café where I skimmed through the stories and ate luscious pastries. I intended to diet when I got back to Dublin, but I wasn't going to start now.

'Hello, Isobel.' I glanced up from the paper. Barbara Lane stood beside my table.

'Barbara!' I hadn't seen her since the night she'd come to hear Nico play. 'How are you?'

'I'm fine.' She pulled out a chair. 'Mind if I join you?'

'Not at all.' I'd been furious with her that night but now it didn't matter at all. My life had changed and what Barbara thought or did made no difference to me whatsoever.

'Any news?' I asked as she sat down.

She shook her head. 'Life's been very boring lately. You?'

I smiled at her and held out my hand.

'Oh, Isobel.' She gasped. 'It's absolutely gorgeous.'

'Thanks.'

'When did you—?'

'Last week.'

She smiled ruefully. 'I always knew it. You said you didn't fancy him, that it was just a fling, but I always knew it wasn't.'

For a wicked moment I thought of letting her believe that I'd got myself engaged to Nico Alvarez. But common sense took over.

'I *did* fancy him but it *was* just a fling,' I said. 'I'm engaged to Tim.'

'Tim!' She stared at me in astonishment. 'Tim – your boyfriend? That Tim?'

I grinned. 'That Tim.'

'But – why?'

'Why do most people get engaged?' I asked.

'It's just that—' She broke off and signalled a waiter. '*Dos cafés, por favor.*'

'I love Tim,' I said simply. 'And I want to marry him.'

'But what about Nico? When did you split up? Because I was sure I saw you with him only a couple of weeks ago. In the Plaza Espana.'

'You might have done.' I shrugged.

'So—'

'It's quite simple. *Gracias*,' I said to the waiter who put the cup of coffee in front of me. 'I had to go home. I met Tim. We decided we still loved each other. I got engaged.'

'I'm shocked.' She dropped a lump of brown sugar into her coffee. 'I really am.'

'Why?'

'I just thought that you and Nico – oh, I suppose I was making a mountain out of a molehill. It's just that you were different with him, Isobel. And,' she looked at me from beneath her fringe, 'I was jealous of you.'

'Jealous?'

'Oh, don't pretend.' She stirred her coffee vigorously and splashed the table.

'OK,' I said. 'I won't. You fancied Nico. You were pissed off at me for going out with him. It's all right, Barbara. It doesn't matter.'

'Obviously not,' she said. 'You look great.'

'Thanks.' So at least the make-up worked. I'd looked awful that morning – still pale as a ghost and still with huge black circles under my eyes. I didn't know why I looked so dreadful because I felt all right. I still had the occasional dregs of my headache, but paracetamol kept that at bay.

'So when are you getting married?' asked Barbara.

'January, I think.'

'Back in Ireland?'

'Obviously.'

She sat back in her chair. 'I'm still amazed.'

'Don't be.' I grinned at her. 'Just think of me back in

dreary old Dublin, up to my neck in housework, while you're still having a great time here.'

'Have you got a job?' she asked.

'Not yet.' I made a face. 'I'll get one, but I'm not going to try until after Christmas. Doesn't seem any point.'

'It's funny but I can't imagine you as a married woman up to your neck in housework,' said Barbara. 'I can only see you as you were with us – on the party trail.'

'Yes, well.' I sipped my coffee. 'That was a period in my life that I'd just as soon forget.'

'You had a good time,' Barbara reminded me.

'Oh, sure I did. But it wasn't really me, you know.'

'You don't think so?'

'I was under pressure then,' I said. 'I'm different now.'

She smiled at me. 'I hope you'll be very happy.'

'Thanks.'

'Really I do.'

'Would you like another coffee?' I asked.

She nodded and I ordered two more *solos.* I was pleased to have made my peace with Barbara. Even if she'd never realised that I'd gone through a period of disliking her intensely.

'How's Bridget?' I asked.

'So-so.'

'So-so?'

'She's OK,' said Barbara. 'But she's feeling a little under pressure herself.'

'Oh?'

'Tomás is out a lot,' said Barbara. 'Bridget is left at home with Christopher. She's not very happy about it.'

'I hope it gets better,' I said. 'Tell her I said hello.'

'Sure.' Barbara laughed shortly. 'Once the three of us went out every night of the week. Now you and Bridget are boring, married women.'

'Not quite married yet,' I told her. 'And I've had a slip-up on my way to the altar before.'

'You don't think it'll happen again, do you?' She sounded so horrified that I burst out laughing.

'Of course not! I was only joking. He wouldn't have the nerve to dump me a second time.'

'I think you're great to give him a second chance!' said Barbara.

'I don't look on it as a second chance,' I said. 'I feel it was always meant to have been this way.'

'I'm glad it's worked out for you,' she told me. 'Honestly.'

'Thanks, Barbara.'

She tapped her fingers on the handle of her coffee-cup. 'Can I ask you something?'

'Of course.'

'Would it bother you if I contacted Nico?'

'Contacted Nico?'

'Yes.' Barbara blushed slightly. 'Asked him out to dinner.'

I stared at her. 'You want to ask Nico out?'

'Yes,' she said. 'That's right.'

'Well, there's no reason for it to bother me,' I said, squashing the sudden spurt of – jealousy – that had rushed through me. Not jealousy, I couldn't be jealous of anyone going out with Nico. But it felt odd to think about it all the same.

'I know,' she said blithely. 'It's just that I'd feel awkward calling him without telling you first.'

'You go ahead and call,' I said. 'I'm sure he'd be delighted to hear from you.'

'You're a good friend, Isobel,' said Barbara. 'And I wish you the best of luck with Tim.'

'Will you come to the wedding?' I asked the question on impulse and wished I hadn't.

'I'd love to.' She beamed at me. 'Get you safely up the aisle this time.'

'Great,' I said. 'It'll be fun.'

I thought about them that evening as I arranged my six pairs of shoes at the bottom of my wardrobe. Barbara and Nico. They were probably more suited than Nico and I ever were. Barbara had no desire to move back to England. She'd look after Nico in a way that I hadn't.

I wondered if he'd accept her invitation to dinner.

Chapter 31

The Circus (Joan Miró, 1937)

'These are the follow-up files.' I double-clicked on the bright yellow folder at the top of the computer screen. 'The follow-ups are all labelled yellow. Green for the active folders and red for the completed ones.'

Nina nodded.

'All the standard letters are in the stationery folder.'

'I know, Isobel,' she said gently. 'I access them on the network.'

'Of course you do.' I pushed my hair back from my face. I was growing it longer for the wedding and it was driving me crazy. 'I'm sorry, Nina. I know I'm repeating myself.'

'It's OK.' She grinned at me. 'I'm making allowances because of the stress you're under.'

'I'm not under any stress,' I told her.

'Of course you are.' She smiled. 'You're packing to go home. You're trying to organise everything here. You want to be with your fiancé—'

'Oh, God!' I looked at my watch. 'I have to pick him up at the airport.'

'You've plenty of time,' said Nina. 'Don't panic.'

But I couldn't help panicking. The last four weeks had

been absolute chaos as I tried to streamline everything for my successor. I wanted to be sure that there was no chance of things going wrong because of anything I'd done, or failed to do. I had Nina driven demented.

Luis was taking over my job. I was glad it was Luis, that it wasn't a stranger. Which was silly, but it was how I felt. I hadn't talked much to Luis about it because I didn't want him to think I was trying to tell him how to do things. It was up to him to find his own way.

We'd gone for beer and tapas the previous night and that was the closest we'd got to a business meeting. We sat on the high barstools and shared *patatas a la romana* while the windows of the tapas bar dripped with steam.

'I'll miss this place,' I sighed. 'It was the first tapas bar I ever came to, and it's the best.'

'I'll miss you,' said Luis.

'Oh, Luis.' There was a lump in my throat. 'I'll miss you too.'

He took me by the hand. 'You're a good person, Isobel.'

'Don't be silly.' But I left my hand in his.

'You've been good for the company. You've been good to me.'

'And you to me,' I said.

'It might have worked between us.' His brown eyes twinkled.

'It would never have worked between us,' I said.

'But that night was wonderful,' said Luis.

'I get the impression,' I said, as I removed my hand from his, 'that you specialise in wonderful nights.'

He laughed. 'I enjoy making love, Isobel.'

'And you're good at it!'

'*Gracias.*' He grinned wickedly.

'But we would have been hopeless together.'

'*Por qué?*'

'I don't know why,' I said. 'We just would.'

'And now you are going to marry the man who made you too unhappy to go out with me,' he said.

'It wasn't because of Tim I wouldn't go out with you.' I made a face at him. 'It was because I couldn't sit in a restaurant with someone who thought it was OK to wear a red shirt and a yellow tie.'

'That's not fair!' He looked down at his chest. 'The tie was a present from Anna.'

'Why do they all buy you ties?' I asked. 'Maria was always buying them for you.'

'It's a female thing,' said Luis. 'You think of it as a leash!'

'We do not,' I said firmly.

'Well, I knew it was time to split with Maria when she'd bought me a dozen of them,' he said seriously. 'Talk about a noose around my neck.'

I giggled. 'That's outrageous, Luis.'

'Have you ever bought a man a tie, Isobel?'

'I bought Tim one for his birthday,' I admitted. 'But I also bought him a zip drive.'

'It's an ownership thing,' said Luis. 'Trust me.'

'Do you want another beer?' I asked.

'Why not?' He kissed me on the cheek.

~

I hadn't been drunk in a long, long time. Not like this, anyway. Not so drunk that I couldn't focus properly.

Luis helped me out of the taxi.

'I'm fine now,' I told him. 'Really I am.'

'I'll see you up to your apartment,' he said. 'I don't want to be responsible for you falling down the stairs or getting stuck in the lift.'

'I wouldn't.' But I stumbled up the steps.

'Oh, Isobel, I'm sorry.' He caught me under the arm. 'I shouldn't have made you drink the sambuccas.'

'I shouldn't have drunk them,' I said. 'I'm going to be so ill tomorrow.'

'I'll get you inside the apartment and make coffee,' said Luis.

I fell over the threshold and flopped onto the sofa. 'It wasn't even that much alcohol,' I moaned. 'Just a few beers and the sambuccas. That's all.'

'I like the posters,' said Luis, as he looked around.

I'd hung Miró posters on the walls, since he'd last been in the apartment.

'They look like I feel,' I said. 'Shaky.'

Luis laughed. 'You rest, I'll make coffee.'

It was nice to lie on the sofa and let someone else do all the work. And the good thing was that I felt safe and secure with Luis. Despite everything, he was the one man I knew who was like an ordinary friend to me. It was as though our night of mad passion had happened in another life.

'Here you are,' he said, just as I was dozing off. 'A good blast of caffeine should help.'

'Oh, thank you.' I sat up and sipped the coffee. 'I'll miss you, Luis.'

'And I'll miss you,' he said. 'Even if I never really got to understand you.'

'You don't need to understand me,' I told him.

'I'll miss our conversations,' said Luis.

'Me too.'

'And arguing with you about courses.'

I sipped the coffee, more cautiously this time because the first mouthful had burned my tongue.

'I'll miss lots of things about Spain,' I admitted.

'But you'll have a new, more exciting life back home.'

'Will I?'

'Isobel!' He looked at me in astonishment. 'Are you having second thoughts?'

'Oh, don't be silly.' I put the cup on the floor. 'It's just that I wonder what it'll be like, that's all.'

'What do you think it'll be like?' he asked.

'I don't know.' I shrugged. 'I'm scared I won't get a job, Luis. That I'll be dependent on Tim.'

'Does that matter?'

I tucked my legs beneath me and rested my head on his shoulder. 'It wouldn't have,' I said. 'A few years ago I wouldn't have cared. But I do now. I've worked so hard to be independent.'

'You'll get a job,' said Luis confidently. 'But you might decide to chuck it in and have babies, Isobel.'

'Gabriela has two children and she still works.'

'Yes.' He raised his eyebrows. 'But she also has a nanny and a housekeeper!'

I laughed. 'And I suppose I'll be the nanny and the housekeeper.'

'Not if you get another executive position like with Advanta,' said Luis. 'Then you can hire them yourself.'

'We'll see.' I yawned. 'Oh, God, Luis – I'm sorry, I'm just so tired.'

'I'll let you go to bed,' he said. 'All alone, Isobel.'

'I wouldn't be much use to you anyway,' I said. 'I'm far too tired to do anything.'

He laughed. 'Goodnight, Isobel. Sleep well.'

'Goodnight, Luis.'

I thought about getting up to go to bed but I didn't. I lay on the sofa with my eyes closed, and the next thing I knew it was the following morning and I had a hangover.

~

I looked at my watch again. There was nothing left to

do. The files were organised. Next week's schedule was printed. My presentation for AutosReal was ready for Luis to use. I had finished work. I'd plenty of time before I had to be at the airport.

Gabriela tapped at my half-open door. 'Can I come in?'

'Of course.'

She smiled as she looked at my empty desk. 'Finished?'

I nodded.

'So.' She sat on my visitor's chair. 'It is complete for you. Your time in Spain.'

'Mm.'

'You have enjoyed living here?'

'It's been wonderful,' I told her. 'I've loved it. This company is the best I've ever worked for – and you're the best boss I know.'

'Thank you.' She leaned back in the chair. 'I'm sorry you're leaving us.'

'I'm sorry to go.' I pushed my irritating hair out of my eyes. 'But I know I'm doing the right thing, Gabriela.'

'I never said you weren't.'

'No,' I agreed with her. 'But some people are afraid I'm making a mistake. I'm not making a mistake, Gabriela. I love Tim. I've always loved him.'

'And your friend Nico?'

I sighed. 'I cared about him a lot,' I told her. 'Maybe I loved him too, Gabriela. I don't know. Maybe he loved me. Although I don't think so. Not really. I think it was because I was a foreigner. He found me different. He was getting over a long-term relationship when he started to go out with me and I think I was what he needed at the time. But it was – oh, I don't know.' I stared into space as I thought about Nico. 'It was like one of those movies where they show a couple through a misty lens as they stroll hand-in-hand along the beach, or run through flower-filled meadows. It wasn't real, Gabriela.' I was silent. 'It was always a holiday romance. And when we argued we never had a proper argument. Maybe it was because we didn't know the words!' My voice was shaky. 'OK – I cared about him. But it wouldn't have worked.'

'Why not?' She fiddled with her beautiful emerald earrings.

'Because we're from different backgrounds. And I know that one day I'd want to go home.' I made a face. 'In a year at least, Gabriela. It came to me when I was in Barcelona. I didn't want work to be the most important thing all my life. I wanted to go home to a husband and a family. And that's what I'll have in Ireland.'

She said nothing.

'I'll be happy,' I told her.

'Of course you will.' She stood up. 'What time are you meeting Tim?'

'His flight's due in at eight.'

'Plenty of time. Can you come into my office for a few minutes?'

'Of course.'

Today was my last official day at work. A Thursday. Gabriela had brought forward the annual Christmas party and turned it into a combined Christmas, going-away and getting-married night. Tim would be there too. I was looking forward to the party and to introducing my fiancé to my friends.

Gabriela pushed the door of her office open. They were all gathered there – Magdalena, Sofia, Nina, Luis, José—

'We wanted to say goodbye to you,' said Magdalena. 'And good luck.'

'Thanks.' I couldn't think of anything to say. There was a lump in my throat.

'We will have the party tomorrow,' Gabriela said. 'But everyone wanted to wish you well today.'

'And to say that we hope you'll be very happy.'

'And that we'll miss you.'

'And we wanted to give you this, for yourself, to remember us.' Nina stepped forward and handed me a small, gift-wrapped box.

'Oh.' I took the box. I was going to cry. I knew I was. I fumbled at the red and gold paper, trying not to tear it but failing miserably. I'd assumed (cheekily, I suppose) that they'd get me a wedding-present. But I hadn't expected anything like the beautiful gold bracelet that nestled on the cotton wool in the box. 'It's beautiful,' I whispered, blinking the tears from my eyes. 'Really lovely. Thank you all.' I looked up. They were watching me, pleased expressions on their faces.

'This is for you, Isobel, and not for your house,' explained Magdalena. 'We wanted something so that you could think about us anytime, not just when you were in the kitchen!'

'I'll never forget you,' I told them fervently. 'Never. You're the nicest people I know.' Then I burst into proper tears, sobbing convulsively and laughing at myself while I did so. They gathered around me, hugged me, told me that they'd always remember me. It was far more emotional than my departure from DeltaPrint had been.

'So.' Gabriela finally broke up the gathering. 'We will see you tomorrow night, Isobel. At my house.'

'It's very good of you,' I said. 'Really good of you, Gabriela.'

'I enjoy it.' She beamed at me. 'I like having people to my house. And we'll have a great time tomorrow. Besides, we all want to meet the wonderful Tim.'

I looked at her suspiciously. Was she, even gently,

teasing me about him? But her expression was guileless, her eyes wide and clear.

'You'll have your chance tomorrow,' I said. 'And he's looking forward to meeting you all too.' I fastened the bracelet around my wrist. The gold glinted warmly in the office lights. I wanted to cry again. I was hopeless at these sorts of scenes. I brushed at my damp cheeks.

They lined up to kiss me, each taking it in turn to plant multiple kisses on my face. Then we hugged each other. The hugging and kissing went on for at least ten minutes before I finally managed to tear myself free and make my way out of the office building into the night.

The cold was rasping, the pavements dusted with a light covering of rarely-seen snow. I shivered, pulled my suede jacket tightly around me and shoved my hands deep into the pockets. I'd miss them all, I thought, as I clattered down the steps to the metro. They'd become so much a part of my life. And, because I had no family in Madrid, they'd become like family to me. I squeezed myself into the train that had just arrived. No more metro. Back to the grind of driving through Dublin's chaotic city traffic. Or not, of course. Maybe I'd get a job near Donnybrook so that I could get the bus to work. Or walk. I walked to work in Madrid sometimes. I leaned my head against the window. Maybe I wouldn't be able to get a job. Were there too many people equally, if not better qualified than me, already looking for jobs? I sighed. Of course I might get pregnant. Working might not be an option. I scratched my nose. My bracelet slid along my arm.

Señora Carrasco was at the letterboxes in the hallway. '*Buenas tardes.*' She nodded at me.

'*Buenas tardes,*' I replied.

'How is your packing going?' she asked as she took four white envelopes out of her letterbox.

'Not bad.' I unlocked my own box. It was empty.

'You will have to send me a photograph of your wedding.'

I grinned and pushed the button for the lift. 'Of course.'

'We all want to see you on your wedding day.'

'I'm sure I'll have plenty of photos.'

The lift doors opened and we got inside. As we glided gently up to the fifth floor I was suddenly overcome with terror that it would get stuck between floors, that we'd be there for a couple of hours while Tim waited – patiently, impatiently? – at the airport for me to arrive. Impatiently. He wasn't a patient person.

But the doors sighed open and we stepped out onto the fifth floor. I said goodnight to Señora Carrasco as I unlocked the door to my apartment.

It was quiet. That was the thing I both liked and disliked most about living alone. The peace when I wanted peace; but the terror of silence when I needed company. It would be different living with somebody. I wondered whether I'd be a pain in the neck to live with, so used to dropping my clothes wherever I liked or leaving half-read books and magazines lying around the place. And then there was my washing-up obsession – no plate, no cup, no pot allowed to wait around in the sink. It had to be washed immediately.

Of course Tim had lived on his own much longer than me. Untidy, easygoing Tim would probably be driven demented by my insistence on having jars and cans stacked neatly in cupboards with their labels facing outwards.

I shook my head. I'd never had these kinds of thoughts the first time we got engaged. The strain was definitely getting to me.

I changed into soft black trousers and a red chenille

jumper. I pulled on my shiny black boots and my padded black jacket. The festive look, I thought as I checked my appearance in front of the mirror. I was too pale, I decided – the black made me look like a ghost. I wrapped my red woollen scarf around my neck and instantly looked better. It was important to look right. To look perfect for Tim.

The flight had already touched down when I arrived at the airport. I looked around anxiously in case he might have already made his way to the arrivals area, but there was no sign of him. I stamped my feet on the tiled floor to warm them up.

Then he emerged through the glass doors and looked around.

'Over here!' I called as I waved at him. 'Tim! Over here!'

He saw me and his eyes lit up. I was glad that I had that effect on him.

'Isobel!' He dropped his suitcase and hugged me. 'Good to see you again.'

'Good to see me?' I teased. 'You're supposed to say that you've thought about me night and day.'

'I have,' he said. 'Didn't you get my messages?'

The e-mails had arrived every day. 'Sure did.'

'You probably didn't realise that I had the soul of a poet.'

'Yes, well—' I grinned. 'The last message wasn't very poetic: *Have lots of food in stock, I'm famished.*'

He smiled. 'I'm a growing man.'

'Come on.' I caught his hand. 'I made goulash last night. We only have to heat it up.'

'That's my girl,' he murmured as I led him outside to a taxi.

We sat in the back seat and he put his arm around me. 'It's bloody cold.'

'I know. Colder than usual for the beginning of December.'

'It isn't this cold at home.'

'Don't you remember your geography?' I said. 'A continental climate – hot, dry summers, cold, dry winters. That's what we get here.'

He pulled me closer to him. 'Good job I know lots of ways to keep warm.'

I snuggled into him. 'Good job I like them.'

~

He looked around the apartment with interest. 'I thought it would be smaller, more cramped.'

'It's small enough.' I stepped over a box full of books.

'I thought it would be like a studio.'

'Oh, no. I like having a separate bedroom. I couldn't have lived in a studio.'

'It's in here, I presume.' He pushed open the bedroom door.

'The bed squeaks,' I told him.

He sat on the edge and bounced up and down a couple of times. 'So it does. But I won't let that bother me if you don't.'

'You get used to it.'

'And did it get much use at squeaking?'

I felt myself blush. 'No.'

'Sure?' He got up and put his arms around me.

'Absolutely.'

'Nobody else got used to the squeaks?'

I gulped. 'I don't think so.'

'You don't think so!' He held me away from him and looked into my eyes. 'How many men have you gone out with since you came here? I thought there was only the one.' His tone was light but the question was serious.

'Hardly even one.' I smiled at him and returned his look.

'Oh, all right.' He pulled me to him again. 'I won't ask. It's not fair. But I hope none of them was better than me.'

Isabella querida. It was as though Nico was in the room.

I shivered, then I hugged Tim tightly and kissed him.

'Isobel.' His voice was husky.

'Tim.' I unbuckled the belt of his trousers.

'Isobel.' He slid my jumper over my head.

'Tim.' I unbuttoned his shirt.

'Oh, Isobel.'

It was frantic and quick. The bed squeaked loudly and I had to stop myself giggling each time it did. Tim held me tight, and was so fierce that it almost hurt. I wrapped my arms around his neck and clutched him.

'God, I've missed you,' he panted. 'I kept thinking and thinking about this moment and it's been driving me crazy.'

'I hope it was worth it.'

'It's always worth it.'

'Good.' I smiled up at him.

He closed his eyes and lay across me. He was heavy, squashing the breath out of me.

'Tim?'

'Mm?'

'Sorry. I need my inhaler.'

'Oh. OK.' He rolled off me. 'Are you all right?'

'Yes, more or less.' I took a puff. 'All this frantic activity.'

He laughed. 'Come back to me, Isobel. I'll show you frantic activity.'

'I thought you wanted something to eat.'

'Yes.' He looked darkly at me. 'You, Isobel.'

So we made love again and this time it was slower, less urgent, more pleasurable. And this time I closed my ears to the squeaking springs.

~

We went shopping the next day. I brought him to a furniture store near the Plaza de Colon and he looked at the heavy, darkwood table and chairs and asked me exactly how I thought we were going to get them back to Dublin.

'I wasn't thinking of these,' I told him. 'I just brought you to show you what they were like.'

'They're nice, I'll admit that.' He ran his fingers over the highly-polished surfaces. 'But they wouldn't go in my house, Isobel. That table's far too big.'

'I know,' I said. 'But we mightn't live there for ever. I want to put new ideas into your head.'

'New ideas about what?'

'I don't know.' I shrugged. 'Decor, furniture, all that sort of thing.'

'Please don't tell me you want to redecorate everything,' he begged. 'I've only just had the bathroom redone.'

'Have you?'

'Yes. And it's very nice, all green and gold, you'll like it.'

'I'm sure I will.'

'But you can mess around with the living room if you like,' he said.

'Thanks!'

'It needs to be redecorated,' he admitted. 'The wallpaper's peeling off the walls.'

'Why? The house isn't damp, is it?'

'No.' He shook his head. 'But I think the paper was

put up before the walls dried out properly or something. It's the original paper, I've never had it replaced.'

'Don't worry,' I told him. 'I'll do it for you. I want to make things – well, a bit different.'

'Why?'

'So's it's not just your house,' I said. 'I want to feel like it's partly mine.'

'It will be.' He looked puzzled. 'Once we're married it's automatically half-yours.'

'I know,' I said. 'But I want to *feel* that it is. By changing things.'

He smiled but I knew he didn't understand. 'Whatever you like, Isobel. Whatever makes you happy.'

He'd changed so much, I thought, as we strolled hand-in-hand down the Calle de Serrano and peered in the windows of the clothes shops. A couple of years ago he wouldn't have said 'Whatever makes you happy'. A couple of years ago it was whatever made *him* happy. It was great to know that he cared so much about me. That he loved me. I squeezed his hand and he looked at me. 'What?'

'Nothing. I love you.'

'Good,' he said and put his arm around me.

~

We took a taxi to Gabriela's house that evening. We'd almost come to blows earlier as we got ready – Tim spent hours showering and shaving and then he'd left the mirrors steamed up so that I couldn't see properly to do my make-up.

'You don't need make-up,' he said. 'You're fine the way you are.'

'Don't be stupid.' I rubbed the mirror with the damp towel and peered at my face in the smeared circle while Tim stood in the doorway and blocked the light.

'Honestly, Isobel. You've been working with them for over a year. They must know what you look like by now!'

'Of course they do.' I rubbed foundation cream onto my face. 'But we're going out, Tim. I always wear make-up when I'm going out. And I usually wear it into the office too.'

'You never used to.'

'That was because I didn't think I needed to.'

'Why do you need to now?'

'I meet more people. I like to look good.'

'That's rubbish!' He tucked his shirt into his trousers. 'You always look good.'

'Thanks,' I said impatiently. 'But I need to do my face. Now if you're finished in here would you mind giving me a bit of room?'

'Oh, have it your way!' He stalked out of the doorway.

'Oh, sod off,' I muttered sotto voce.

'I heard that.'

'And?'

'Not very nice, Isobel. To the man who's travelled two thousand miles to be with you.'

I was suddenly contrite. It wasn't Tim's fault that I was used to spending as long as I liked in the bathroom. It wasn't his fault that the mirror had misted up. I was just tetchy.

'Sorry,' I said.

'Oh, it's OK.' He put his head around the bathroom door. 'I guess I forgive you.'

It didn't seem like almost a year since I'd last been at Gabriela's house. We crunched our way up the gravel path and stood outside the door.

'Nice place,' commented Tim.

'Wait until you go inside,' I said. 'It's fabulous.'

'Come in, come in!' Gabriela held the door wide. 'It's wonderful to meet you, Tim.'

'We have met already.' He turned all the charm of his smile on her. 'When I called into the office to meet Isobel. Do you remember?'

'Of course I remember.' She smiled back at him. 'How could I forget?' She led us through to the living area. 'And how are you finding Madrid?'

'Colder than the last time I was here.' Tim rubbed his hands together. 'And Isobel dragged me around shops all afternoon so I was practically frozen.'

'Isobel!' She grinned at me. 'Tim does not look to me like a man who will spend much time in the shops.'

'Depends on the sort of shop,' I told her. 'Computer shops – can't get him out. Clothes shops – can't get him in!'

We laughed.

Most of the others had already arrived and were sitting in front of the log fire drinking red wine.

'For you?' Gabriela looked at us enquiringly.

'Wine is perfect,' I said.

'Beer?' asked Tim hopefully.

'Of course.'

Gabriela went to get the drinks while I introduced Tim to my ex-colleagues.

'He is most handsome,' muttered Sofia to me in Spanish. 'Very masculine. Very attractive.'

'Thank you.'

'Not as attractive as me, of course,' said Luis and I started to giggle.

'What?' asked Tim. 'What are you laughing at?'

'Nothing,' I assured him. 'They were just telling me what a good catch you are.'

Tim couldn't speak a word of Spanish but nearly everyone had passable English and they did their best to speak English all the time.

'Tell us about the wedding, Isobel,' begged Nina. 'What date is it? What will you wear?'

'We haven't set the date exactly yet.' I turned to Tim for confirmation. 'In January sometime, but I'll organise that when I go home. And I haven't decided on the dress either yet.'

'Will you make it yourself?' asked Magdalena.

'I don't know,' I replied.

'Oh, you should!' she cried. 'You made such a beautiful dress for me.'

I'd made her a dress for a black-tie function she'd gone to during the summer. It had been one of the nicest dresses I'd ever made – I'd found some white silk with almost invisible silver threads running through it and made a calf-length dress with shoestring straps. On Magdalena, with her almost black eyes and creamy complexion, it had looked absolutely stunning.

But I wasn't sure about making myself a wedding dress. I thought it might be unlucky. I'd done it once, after all, and I really wasn't sure I should do it a second time.

'Of course she'll make her own dress,' said Tim. 'She makes them for everyone else so the least she can do is make her own.'

'Will you make it long?' asked Nina. 'With a huge train and a veil?'

I couldn't see myself in a dress like that. Even my first one hadn't a huge train. 'I don't think so.'

'Oh, Isobel! You should.'

'It's not quite me,' I explained.

'What's you?' asked Luis.

'Not long trains and veils,' I told him.

'You have to have a veil!' Tim looked horrified. 'I like the bit where the bride comes to the church with the veil over her face and then lifts it back.'

'You've been watching too many movies.' I laughed. 'That doesn't happen much these days.'

'All the same, Isobel.' His voice was pleading. 'It'd be nice, don't you think?'

'Maybe.' I wasn't convinced.

'More wine?' asked Alfredo.

He refilled all our glasses, then Gabriela put on a party CD and we got up and danced. Then Tim and José (whose English was almost as good as Gabriela's) got into a conversation about computers. Luis and Anna were engrossed in conversation. I sat down in one of Gabriela's huge rose-pink armchairs and stretched my legs out in front of me.

'I probably shouldn't have spent so much time shopping,' I told Magdalena. 'My feet are killing me. And these shoes don't help.' They were lovely shoes in soft black leather, but they were a pair of the new ones I'd bought recently and I was getting a blister on my heel.

'Tim is a very nice man,' she said. 'I thought he would be more – no – not so very nice.'

'Of course he's nice,' I retorted. 'Why d'you think I'm marrying him?'

She shrugged. 'I do not know. I was surprised at the news, that is all.'

I smiled at her. 'I know that everyone thinks I'm crazy, but I've known Tim a long time and I love him.'

'I thought you did not love him any more. I thought you were in love with Nicolas.'

'Oh, Nico.' I dismissed him with a wave of my hand. 'A passing fancy, Magdalena! Someone to while away the time.' But I felt disloyal as I uttered the words and I wished I hadn't said it.

'He also was a very nice man,' she said dreamily. 'And also very good-looking. How do you manage that, Isobel? It is very unfair for you to grab all the good-looking men.'

'Must be my fatal charm.' I laughed. 'My good looks, my wonderful cooking!'

'Probably the wonderful cooking,' agreed Magdalena. 'My mother always says that cooking is a good way to get a man.'

I grinned. 'I think mine does too. And what about you, Magdalena? Any men on the horizon for you?'

She blushed. 'I am seeing Alejandro.'

'Alejandro!' I looked at her in amazement. 'I didn't realise that you were going out with Alejandro. I thought you said it was just a once-off thing.'

'It was,' she admitted. 'And then he phoned me, Isobel. Asked me to dinner. So I went.'

'How long has this been going on?'

'Four weeks and four days,' she told me.

'Does Gabriela know?'

'Not yet.' Magdalena bit the corner of her lip. 'I do not want to tell her yet, Isobel. She wasn't very happy when Alejandro left and—'

'I can guess.' I ran my fingers through my hair. 'So maybe you'll be inviting me to your wedding one day, Magdalena.'

She laughed. 'Maybe. But not yet, Isobel. We are taking it easy. No rushing into things.'

I smiled at her. 'Sensible Magdalena! But I wish you all the best.'

'Thank you,' she said. 'And for you I wish everything good too.'

Gabriela brought around some tiny vol-au-vents and slices of tortilla. Alfredo filled our glasses again. I danced with José and with Luis. Tim (despite his dislike of jigging around as he called it) danced with Gabriela and Nina. Then we danced with each other.

'I like your friends,' he told me.

'They like you too.'

'I can see why you enjoy working with them.'

'They're nice people.'

He kissed me on the cheek. 'But you'll be happier at home with me.'

I closed my eyes. 'I know.'

~

Later on we played Trivial Pursuit and the team of women easily beat the team of men.

'It's not fair,' said Luis. 'You girls got all the easy questions.'

'Rubbish!' Gabriela threw a cushion at him. 'We're just more intelligent.'

'It's called *Trivial* Pursuit,' said Tim. '*Trivial.* Not more intelligent.'

'Just because you lost,' I said lazily. 'And we had plenty to spare. You hadn't even got the pink wedge.'

'Huh.' Tim looked huffily at me and I laughed.

Alfredo filled our glasses again. Gabriela went outside and then reappeared with a huge gift-wrapped present. Another present, I thought. These people were far too good to me. She stood at the window and clapped her hands to get our full attention.

'I only want to say a few words. Isobel came to us nearly two years ago. Since then she has been a hardworking and responsible member of our company. She has been a good friend to all of us. We are very sorry to see her go.' She smiled at me and I blushed. 'But we are glad that she is going to marry Tim and be even happier than she was with us. And we wish her every success in her future. And we want to give you this, Isobel, as a memento of working with us here in Spain. We hope that you will come and visit us often.'

They clapped. I swallowed a couple of times, got up and stood beside Gabriela.

'Thank you all very much.' I looked at them all sitting in front of me, smiling at me. Suddenly I couldn't say anything else. My throat constricted and my eyes filled with tears. 'I'm sorry to leave you,' I croaked finally. 'I've loved being here.' I wiped the tears away as Gabriela hugged me and everyone else clapped.

'Sorry,' I said.

'Open your present.' Gabriela smiled at me.

I tore off the gift-wrapping. It was a magnificent reproduction of the Dalí painting that hung in my office. The girl looking out of the window. 'It's wonderful,' I said. 'Thank you all very much.'

'Luis wanted the Miró,' she told me. 'The lady walking the dog. But I thought this would be nicer.'

'You couldn't pick one I'd like better,' I said sincerely. 'Thank you, Gabriela. Thank you for everything.'

~

I was still strung out by the time Tim and I got back to the apartment in the early hours of the morning. I climbed into bed and put my arms around him, but I didn't want to make love.

'Why not?' he whispered as he ran his fingers along my thighs.

'Not tonight,' I said. 'I can't tonight.'

'Just as well I'm bringing you home,' he said. 'You're getting far too emotional over here.'

But he kissed me on the lips to show that he was teasing.

Chapter 32

Cat Catching a Bird (Pablo Picasso, 1939)

We slept late the following morning. I woke up at noon and didn't know where I was. I stared at the ceiling and struggled out of my sleep-filled haze. Then I turned in the bed and saw Tim lying on his back, eyes closed and snoring almost imperceptibly. I put my arm around him and he grunted but didn't wake up. I lay against his shoulder and closed my eyes again. Thank God it's Saturday, I thought, and then I suddenly remembered that it didn't matter to me what day it was. I'd left my job.

When I woke up on Monday I could roll over and fall asleep again if I wanted. No need for me to drag myself, mentally kicking and screaming, out of bed. There was no job for me to go to. I was dependent on Tim. The thought overwhelmed me. I'd never been dependent on anyone since the day I left school. I shivered and burrowed down beneath the duvet.

Tim didn't wake up, even when I got out of bed and made breakfast. He slept on, untroubled, dead to the world. I had a shower, washed my hair and was drying it before he stumbled out of the bedroom, rubbing his eyes and yawning.

'You woke me up,' he said.

'What?' I switched off my brand-new hairdryer.

'The noise. Woke me up.'

'I'm so sorry.' I made a face at him. 'Just as well something did, though, you'd have slept until tomorrow.'

'I know.' He yawned again. 'I was exhausted.'

'Poor thing. Here.' I threw a towel at him. 'The people in the building opposite can see into the apartment. We wouldn't want them to be driven into a frenzy by your magnificent masculinity.'

'Isobel!' But he wrapped the towel around his naked body all the same. He poured himself some coffee and bit into one of the croissants I'd left out on the table. 'I liked your friends.'

'Thanks.' I unplugged the hairdryer and left it on the sofa. 'They're nice people. Gabriela especially. She's been really good to me.'

'Classy lady,' he agreed. 'And she likes you.'

'We seemed to click.'

'Sorry to be leaving them?'

'Of course not.' I sat on his lap. 'Why should I be?'

'No reason. Isobel!' He almost choked as I undid the towel. 'Isobel, that's lovely but what about the people in the apartment opposite?'

'Let them watch.' I grinned at him. 'They might learn something.'

I'd booked a table in Quixote for that evening. When Tim had originally organised to come to Madrid we'd expected he'd be able to spend a week or two in the city, but he was very busy in work and we were going back to Ireland on Monday evening. So I thought it would be nice to go somewhere exclusive and romantic together before we went home. Besides, I wanted to impress him.

We took a metro into town and strolled to the restaurant. The city was crowded with people.

'This way.' I dragged him across the road and almost under the wheels of a Seat Ibiza being driven at high speed.

'Jesus, Isobel! Why did you do that?'

'We'd be waiting ages otherwise,' I explained. 'And you weren't in any danger.'

'Oh, really.' He tut-tutted at me. 'Just remember, you're not in the will yet.'

I laughed and turned down the sidestreet. The heavy wooden door of the restaurant was closed.

'Have we got the right day?' Tim looked at me doubtfully.

'Of course. I booked it.' I rang the bell.

The *maitre d'* answered the door and ushered us inside. We followed him down the steep flight of stairs into the basement of the building.

We were led across the highly polished marble floor to sit beneath a picture of the train station at Atocha. Fleetingly, I thought of Nico.

'A bomb went off there a few years ago,' I told Tim who looked at the painting with interest.

'While you were here?'

'No, well before that.'

'Good,' he said. 'I don't like to think you were in danger.'

'My hero.'

The waiter handed us menus.

'This is costing a fortune,' said Tim as he looked through it.

'It's my treat,' I told him. 'And it's worth every cent.'

We ordered *gambas mimosas* and *pollo cataluna.*

Tim smiled at me and yawned.

'Tired?'

He shook his head. 'Not really. Relaxed if anything. It's nice to get away for a couple of days.'

'It'll be hectic when we get back,' I said. 'Christmas, then the wedding.' I looked anxiously at him. 'You don't think it's all a bit much, do you? Maybe we should have the wedding later. March, or April.'

'Oh, Isobel, better off having it early. Anyway if we had it late people would say I was dithering again.'

'And are you?'

'What do you think?'

I smiled.

'You know I love you,' he said.

I nodded.

'I was a fool a couple of years ago. An absolute fool.'

'That's what I was thinking about,' I admitted. 'Rushing around for Christmas and then straight into the wedding – I thought, maybe—'

He smiled at me. 'Don't be an ass, Isobel.'

'OK.'

Tim ordered a Penendes white wine and we toasted each other before drinking it. 'To us,' he said.

'To us,' I echoed.

The restaurant was about three quarters full. I loved it here, the way the waiters seemed to glide rather than walk, the subdued hum of conversation, the clink of crystal glass and, in the background, the soft strumming of a guitar.

I'd jumped when the guitarist began to play but he wasn't Nico Alvarez, just a man in his twenties whom I'd never seen before. 'You OK?' asked Tim. 'You're in a trance.'

'No, sorry, I'm fine.' I looked up just as the waiter arrived with our prawns.

The food was wonderful. We didn't speak while we ate.

'It was good?' asked the waiter, and we nodded.

'You'll have to do a cookery course,' said Tim. 'Learn to produce things like that.'

'You should be so lucky.'

'I'll expect my dinner on the table every evening by seven.'

'You probably won't be home by seven.'

'Of course I will. Home and starving.'

'I thought your favourite food was a Big Mac and chips.'

'Almost,' he admitted. 'But if you started throwing *gambas mimosas* at me I might change my mind.'

'And what else do you want?' I teased. 'Your socks washed, your shirts ironed, your furniture polished?'

He laughed. 'There'll be a divison of labour, of course. But until you get a job—'

'Hopefully I'll get one right away,' I told him. 'I can't see myself sitting at home somehow.'

'I can't either,' he said. 'Although I could have. When we were engaged before.'

'Maybe,' I said. 'But I'm a different person now.'

'You still want a family.' It was a statement not a question.

'Of course. And you?'

'I'm sure we'll have the most beautiful children,' he said. 'Your eyes and my cheekbones.'

'What's wrong with my cheekbones?' I demanded.

'Nothing,' he said. 'But you always told me that you envied mine.'

The *pollo cataluna* arrived and the waiter refilled our wine glasses. Tim ordered another bottle.

'I'll be drunk. Again,' I said.

'Don't worry, you'll lead a life of total abstinence as Mrs Malone.'

Mrs Malone. I tried not to let myself think of being Mrs Malone. Whenever the name hovered at the edge of my consciousness I pushed it away, as though by thinking of it, letting it come into my head, it would somehow make everything go wrong. Mrs Malone. Isobel Malone. I couldn't believe that it was actually going to happen.

'This is fantastic.' Tim waved a forkful of chicken in front of me.

I cut a piece of my own and nodded. 'Delicious.' But I couldn't taste it. I wondered if I was getting a cold. My sense of taste always disappeared just before I started to sneeze.

'We'll go out at least once a week when we're married,' Tim told me. 'It's important that we should go out together and have fun, not just sit in night after night watching TV. Even after we have kids we'll have to make sure that we get time to be with each other.'

It was like talking to a different person these days. He never would have said things like that before.

'How long do you want to wait?' I asked.

'For what?'

'Before we have children?'

'That's up to you, Isobel. You're the one that'll have them.'

'But they'll be yours too.'

'I know. But whatever makes you happy.'

A completely different person, I thought. I drank some wine and it went down the wrong way.

'Are you all right?' asked Tim and I coughed and spluttered and my eyes watered.

'Fine,' I gasped. 'Just catching my breath.'

He watched me anxiously. 'Sure?'

I nodded. 'In a second.'

I took a puff of my inhaler. I hated doing that in public.

'OK now?'

'Yes,' I replied. 'I'll just go to the loo and repair my face.'

'It looks OK from here,' said Tim, but I wanted to be sure that I hadn't streaked mascara all down my cheeks in my fit of coughing. It was the sort of thing that Tim wouldn't actually notice.

The arched ceilings were in the ladies too, along with more murals of Spanish buildings and art deco mirrors surrounded by coloured mosaic. I redid my eyes and my lipstick and checked my dress. Not one I'd made myself, this evening. It was a pink wool I'd bought recently and it clung to every contour of my body.

I shivered. I didn't know why. It wasn't cold. I checked my tights for ladders, tucked my hair behind my ears and walked back to the dining room.

Nico and Barbara were sitting at the table directly in front of me. He was laughing at something she said, his eyes bright, his smile genuine. She leaned forward and touched his hand.

I stood rooted to the spot. Nico and Barbara. Here. Together. I didn't know why I was so shocked. She'd said that she was going to ask him out and she obviously had. So it shouldn't have surprised me. But I was surprised to see them here.

He saw me. The smile left his face, his eyes darkened and our eyes met. I couldn't see anything in them. Not hurt, nor accusation, nor even dislike. There was nothing. I swallowed and took a step towards them.

'Hi Nico, Barbara,' I said as I reached their table.

'Isobel!' The look Barbara shot me was triumphant. 'How are you?'

'I'm great.' The words came out but as though someone else was speaking them.

'What are you doing here?' she asked.

'Having dinner.'

I thought Nico smiled ever so slightly.

'It's Nico's birthday,' she told me. 'We're here to celebrate.'

'*Feliz cumpleaños*,' I said.

'Thank you.' He didn't look at me.

'So who are you with?' asked Barbara.

'Tim,' I said uncomfortably. 'I'm going home with him on Monday and I thought it would be nice to come here.'

'Monday?' This time Nico's glance flickered in my direction.

'Yes.'

'I thought you were staying until the middle of December,' said Barbara. 'That's what you told me, wasn't it?'

'I know,' I said. 'But Tim has to get back to work and there didn't seem much point in staying.'

'So have you set a date for the wedding yet?' She looked beautiful tonight, I thought. Beautiful and elegant and sophisticated in a way that I'd never seen her look before. Her eyes sparkled as she looked at me.

'January sometime,' I said. 'I'll be sending you your invitation, of course.'

'I can't wait,' she said. 'How about you, Nico?'

I looked at him, aghast. He couldn't possibly even consider coming to my wedding. Could he? Would he seriously think about showing up with Barbara?

'I would love to come,' he said, sending my heart plummeting to my shoes, 'but I do not think I can attend. I'm sorry, Is—'

'It's OK,' I interrupted. 'No problem. It's fine.'

Barbara looked at me in amusement. 'And where's lover-boy?'

'We're over there.' I indicated our table where Tim was reading the dessert menu with the look of someone who hasn't yet had anything to eat.

'God, Isobel, he's very good-looking.' Her sophisticated air slipped a little. 'I didn't realise—' She looked at me, then back to Tim, then at Nico. 'You certainly pick them.'

'Thanks.' I flushed with embarrassment.

'Will you introduce me?' she asked.

'If you like.'

'Isobel! I'm your friend! Of course I want to meet him.'

'OK.' I looked helplessly at Nico but he was studying the mural of the marina at Marbella.

'It's OK,' he said without looking at either of us. 'I will wait here for you, Barbara.'

She grabbed me by the elbow. 'I hope you don't mind about Nico,' she hissed. 'But you said you wouldn't care if I asked him out.'

'Of course I don't mind. Why should I mind?'

'Well, you know . . .'

'It doesn't matter. I was surprised though. I didn't realise you and he—'

'It's only our third date,' said Barbara. 'And the other two were at the Lux evening show so they don't really count. I thought it would be nice to bring him here as a treat.'

'It's lovely, isn't it?'

'And romantic.' She giggled. 'I'm hoping – well, you know.'

I wished she'd shut up.

'Hi, Tim. Look. This is another of my friends, Barbara Lane. She's one of the girls from the language college I told you about.'

'Barbara.' Tim's greeting made it seem as if he'd waited his whole life to meet her. 'Lovely to meet you. I've heard a lot about you.'

'All good, I hope.'

'None good.' He laughed and winked at her.

'So you're the man that broke Isobel's heart.'

He didn't bat an eyelid. 'And mended it again.'

'You think?' She grinned wickedly at him.

'You mean I didn't?'

'Well—' She smiled. 'Let's just say that there was a queue of people wanting to have a go.'

'Lucky that I managed to get her back then,' said Tim.

'Lucky indeed.' She smiled again. 'Lucky for me too.'

He didn't understand and I didn't enlighten him.

'I've invited Barbara to the wedding,' I told him. 'And Bridget too, of course.'

'I hope I can come,' said Barbara. 'I haven't been to a wedding in ages. I always cry.'

'So do I,' I said drily.

'I'd better get back,' she said. 'I don't like to leave him too long in case someone pinches him.'

'I know what you mean,' I said evenly.

'Where are you sitting?' asked Tim. 'Would you like to join us for a drink?'

I felt myself begin to wheeze again.

Barbara smiled. 'We've only just started dinner,' she said. 'But thanks, anyway.'

'We'll be here a little longer if you change your mind,' said Tim.

Barbara kissed me on the cheek. 'Don't worry, I won't,' she whispered and walked back to her table. Tim watched her go. From where he sat he could only see the back of Nico's head.

'Nice girl,' he said.

'Good friend.' I sat down and breathed more easily again.

'Going out with a local?'

I nodded.

'Will she marry him, d'you think?'

'I don't know.' She couldn't. Not Barbara. Not Nico. It wouldn't last.

And how the hell would I know? Maybe Barbara was exactly the sort of girl he needed. I pushed my escaping hair back from my face again. Maybe I'd get it cut. It was all very well to want elegant tresses for my wedding but it was driving me insane.

'Isobel?' Tim looked at me curiously.

'Yes?'

'You were miles away.'

'Was I?'

'Yes,' he said. 'I asked what the *Suprise Quixote* was likely to be.'

The apartment was bare. Not of furniture, of course, it had come furnished. But it was empty all the same. There were no flowers in the big pottery vases on the sideboard, there was no fruit in the multicoloured bowl on the table. The wardrobe was cleared, the bathroom shelves emptied. It was awful. I felt – bereft. I stood at the front door, reluctant to close it for the last time while Tim struggled with two of my cases and a box of Lladro ceramics that I was bringing home to Mum.

Señora Carrasco opened her door. She'd called over the night before and we'd shared half a bottle of port while she told me that I was one of the best neighbours she'd ever had and informed Tim that he was a lucky, lucky man and that he'd been fortunate to prise me from the arms of other (perhaps less scrupulous) men. And she looked knowingly at me and nodded sagely.

'Everyone keeps telling me I'm lucky,' muttered Tim as we climbed into bed that night. 'Come on, Isobel –

time to prove it.' He pulled me to him and I snuggled into the warmth of his body. We were both lucky, I told myself, as he gently stroked my thigh. Lucky Tim. Lucky Isobel. Lucky at last.

Chapter 33

Seated Woman (Joan Miró, 1938)

I was never very good at Christmas shopping. I'm not sure that many people are – crowds, jostling, and blank space where the ideas for presents should be. I suppose some enjoy the cut and thrust of it all, and some relish the last-minute panic of rushing out on Christmas week with a list full of people to buy for, but it's not me. Besides, I wheeze in a crowd. I was wheezing now, in the middle of Brown Thomas, surrounded by a mist from sample sprays for expensive perfumes that men were recklessly buying for their wives or girlfriends or mistresses. I tried not to breathe as I struggled through the throng. I was buying Tim a briefcase for Christmas. He'd told me about it in such a way that I knew it was the present he wanted, even though it seemed hopelessly unromantic and far too practical a gift.

'Maroon,' he said. 'Very dark. Not shiny.'

And I could see it now, in the centre of the display, understated in its elegance but (surely) overstated in its price. I peered at the label to make certain that the decimal point was in the right place. Oh well, I thought, next year it'll be woolly socks and thermals for him. We'll have settled into our domestic rut by then. In a year's time a briefcase will probably seem like a dangerously exciting present.

I knew that I was being cynical but I couldn't help it. I'd been in town since early morning. It was nearly one o'clock now and I hadn't even bought anything yet. I'd looked everywhere, of course, I'm a great looker, but I'd suddenly become hopelessly indecisive. I'd dithered between a blue angora jumper or a green silk blouse for Mum and bought neither. I'd made a mental note to buy a chunky jewelled costume bracelet I'd seen earlier for Alison, but hadn't bought it yet just in case there was something else I thought she'd prefer. I hadn't a clue what to get Dad. Or Ian. Or Jemima, Honey's replacement. Honey, it seemed, had got tired of Ian not asking her to marry him.

'But he's too young to get married,' I told Alison when she imparted this news.

'I know that and you know that,' she'd replied. 'But Honey loves him.'

When I asked Ian about it he simply said that she'd become too clingy. 'Wants to know where I am all the time. She doesn't bloody own me.' The words sounded very familiar. So did the sentiment. I hoped that Honey had found someone else.

I brought the briefcase to the sales desk. An assistant wrapped it lovingly in tissue paper before sliding it into the striped carrier bag. 'It's very nice,' he told me. 'Very popular this year.'

'Thanks.' I slung the rope handles of the bag over my shoulder and nearly took the eye out of a tired-looking woman waiting to pay for a soft leather wallet.

'Sorry,' I said. 'Really.'

'It's OK,' she said. 'If this is the closest I get to danger I'll be doing well this year. Last year I was mugged waiting for a DART. Nearly lost a tooth. I hate Christmas.'

'Oh.' I felt as though I was in the middle of *A Christmas Carol*. I left her to it and pushed my way into the main body of the store again.

I felt better now that I'd bought something. As though I belonged in the crowd. The bag marked me out as a shopper at last. I took the escalator upwards, walked around in a daze. I was really hungry now and feeling almost lightheaded. I'd put on weight since I'd come home. Lounging around with nothing much to do had seen me raid the fridge more often than I ever had before. In Spain I rarely snacked and if I did it was always fresh fruit. Except, of course, when Nico had brought me to the Chocolateria. I'd have to diet like mad after Christmas so that I'd look thin and beautiful when I married Tim. As always, when I thought of marrying Tim, my heart lurched and I felt the tingle of anticipation run through me. Isobel Malone. Finally.

Maybe it was thinking about my wedding that directed my footsteps, but quite suddenly I was standing at the bridal department, gazing at the truly incredible dress that was on display. It was a dream dress, the sort you imagined as a child when you pretended to be a fairy princess. Pure, dazzling white, with a skirt that took up incalculable yards of shimmering satin. An intricate pattern of white velvet rosebuds twined around the bodice and drifted onto the skirt. I'd made some dramatic dresses in my time, but this one simply took my breath away.

'Would you like to try it on?' The sales assistant was watching me.

I shook my head. 'It's beautiful, but it's too much. I couldn't possibly wear anything like that.'

'It'd look great on you,' she said. 'With your colouring. Absolutely stunning!'

I smiled at her. 'Maybe. But I couldn't wear it. Honestly I couldn't. Besides,' I made a face, 'I'm sure it's much too expensive.'

'It's the most important day of your life,' said the sales assistant. 'And you want to look perfect.'

I supposed she was right.

'Try it on, why not?' She grinned at me. 'It's quiet here today. People are buying Christmas presents not wedding dresses. And it would look great on you.'

I hesitated.

'Go on,' she said again.

'Oh, all right.' I followed her into the changing area and put Tim's briefcase on the floor beside a spindly chair.

'It's one of our most popular dresses.' She disappeared into another room and returned with my size. 'Everyone says that they feel like a princess when they put it on. Most of them end up buying it.'

'I promise you I won't end up buying it,' I told her as I slipped out of my jeans and jumper, thankful that I was wearing a really pretty set of underwear that I'd bought in a shop on the Calle de Serrano – cream and pink in soft cotton.

'Here you are.'

I stepped into the dress. She eased the zip upwards, pulled at the sleeves and rearranged the skirt. Then she stood back, looked at me and smiled. 'I told you,' she said. 'Like a princess.'

I wanted to say that looking like a princess wasn't any guarantee of a happy marriage but I couldn't speak. The dress was more than the sum of its parts, it had looked beautiful if over the top on the display, but wearing it – wearing it was a different story completely. I stared at the reflection of the lightly tanned, long-haired girl in the mirror and I hardly recognised myself. If I bought this dress, or if I made one like it, Tim would keel over at the altar.

'It suits you,' she said. And it did. I didn't think it would. I thought that acres of satin would look stupid on a woman of thirty. But I didn't look thirty. I looked young and eager.

'The dress is so important for every bride.' The sales assistant's voice seemed to come from miles away. 'It's a statement, of course. And that dress makes a very powerful statement.'

Isobel Malone. That was the statement I'd be making. Isobel Kavanagh loves Tim Malone and wants to be with him for ever. There was a lump in my throat.

'It gets some people that way.'

The sales assistant was looking at me understandingly. 'To be honest, it gets to me too.' She sniffed. 'You all look so wonderful.'

I smiled. 'Do we?'

'Oh, yes.'

'I suppose we should.'

'Why not? You'll only do it once.' She grimaced. 'Hopefully.'

'Hopefully,' I repeated. I blinked at my reflection again. 'I look – incredible.'

'Yes.' She looked at me critically. 'You do.'

'But I can't buy it. Not today anyway.'

'That's OK. I like seeing different people in it. And when you're ready to buy, even if it's not this dress, please visit us again. I'm sure we'll have something that you'll like.'

'I like this.' I turned around again. 'I really do. But it wasn't what I had in mind, you see. I wanted something simple.'

'Oh, simple,' she said scornfully. 'Why have simple when you can have utterly extravagant.'

I laughed. 'I'll come back.'

She unzipped the dress. 'I look forward to seeing you.'

It was a bit of a come-down getting back into jeans. I thanked her and retrieved Tim's briefcase. There was still the rest of the Christmas shopping to do.

But I was revitalised. I bought a couple of Mars Bars to sustain me, then stalked up Grafton Street ignoring the crowds and bought the green silk blouse for Mum, the bracelet for Alison, a jumper for Ian, and a hip flask for Dad. I bought a book on dogs for Peter Gaffney and perfume for Jemima. Then I bought myself a pair of black leather boots and a leather jacket.

Mum would go mad, I knew. She'd look at the boots and jacket and tell me that I should wait for the sales. But I wouldn't have time to shop in the sales – I'd be busy with wedding details. I stood at St Stephen's Green and waited for a taxi. I hoped that it would be warmer than this by then.

There were hordes of people waiting for taxis. I stamped my feet to keep them warm and wished that I'd worn a hat and gloves. I'd managed to lose my grey fake-fur hat in the move back to Dublin and I'm the sort of person who can't hold on to a pair of gloves for more than a couple of days. I cupped my hands and blew into them to warm them while my shopping formed a barrier around me.

Eventually a taxi arrived. I gave the driver the address and leaned back in the seat. Tim had wanted me to move in with him when I got home. He'd been surprised and, I thought, hurt when I said that I wanted to live with my parents.

'But we're getting married, Isobel,' he'd protested. 'And you practically lived with me before.'

'But I didn't,' I reminded him. 'I wanted to marry you. I still want to marry you.'

'And I want to marry you,' he said. 'I just think that we might as well be sharing the same house.'

'It's only eight weeks. You can wait for eight weeks, can't you?'

'It's not a question of waiting,' he said. 'It's a question of wanting you close to me all the time. Now that I have you,' he added, 'I don't want to let you go.'

'You say the nicest things.' I cuddled close to him. 'That's why I love you.'

But I hadn't moved in with him and I was glad I'd been firm about it.

The taxi drew up outside the house. I stood at the gate and looked at the necklace of yellow lights snaking their way around Dublin Bay, reflecting on the blackness of the sea. The sight was one of the advantages of living on the coast. I'd missed it while I was away.

'Tim rang,' said Mum as I walked in the door. 'He says that he'll meet you directly at the Chilli Club. He'll be going there straight from work.'

'Oh, bugger,' I said.

'Isobel!' Mum looked angrily at me. 'You know I hate that expression.'

I smothered a grin. 'Sorry.'

'As well you should be.'

I followed her into the kitchen. 'Did he say what time?'

'No.' She filled the kettle. 'What time are you supposed to be meeting him?'

'Eight.' I opened the fridge door and unwrapped a lump of cheddar cheese. 'Early.'

'It's late,' said Mum. 'Late to be eating a full meal. I don't know how you don't lie awake with indigestion every night.'

'I don't know either.' I nibbled on the cheese. 'But we didn't eat until much later in Madrid.'

'Foreigners are different.' She sniffed and arranged pork chops on the grill. 'Do you want one?'

I shook my head. 'Better not. This is Tim's pre-Christmas present to me – a romantic night out. Wouldn't do if I couldn't eat any of it. I'll make a sandwich. I didn't eat anything in town. I'm ravenous.'

'Your eating pattern is all out of sync,' said Mum. 'That's what going abroad does for you.'

'Don't be daft.' I kissed her lightly on the cheek.

'When you've finished that sandwich will you set the table for me?' she asked.

'Sure. Are you expecting everyone home for tea?'

'Yes,' she said. 'A rare occurrence in this household.'

'In every household,' I told her. 'Don't you read anything, Mum? It's all snacking and grazing now, not family meals.'

'There'll always be family meals in this house,' she said grimly as she sliced tomatoes.

'I'll keep that in mind when I'm in Donnybrook,' I said. 'Whenever I can't cope I'll come running home.'

'But you will cope, won't you?' She put the knife down on the worktop and turned to me. 'You'll be all right with Tim, Isobel?'

Her eyes were worried, her brow furrowed.

'Of course I will.' I smiled at her. 'We'll be fine, Mum. Honestly.'

'I don't like to interfere,' she said. 'It's all very well having my own ideas but I don't want to run your life. I've never tried to do that, Isobel.'

I raised an eyebrow. 'What about Barry Dillon?' I asked. Barry had been my second boyfriend. Mum hadn't liked him and he hadn't lasted very long. She'd made sure of that.

'Who?' She looked surprised.

'Never mind.' I smiled at her. 'It doesn't matter.'

'I don't remember any Barry Dillon.' Mum wiped her hands on her blue and white striped apron. 'But then you had so many boyfriends, Isobel. I never knew who you'd turn up with next.'

'That was me. Miss Popularity.'

'You were popular. You were – are – a good-looking girl. That's enough to make you popular when you're sixteen.'

'It's not a bad thing when you're older either.' I grinned.

'I know. And you're lucky, Isobel. You're still pretty.'

'Thanks,' I said.

'And it's hard for me to think of any of you as other than babies.'

'I suppose not.'

I thought, suddenly, of the baby she'd lost. Of the way it had all gone wrong for her.

'So I want what's best for you. I want you to be happy. I want you to have everything you want from life.'

'I am happy,' I assured her. 'I'm getting exactly what I want.'

She picked up the knife and began chopping mushrooms. 'It's not that I don't believe you—'

'But . . .' I supplied.

'There's no "but".'

'It sounded like a "but" coming on.'

'No. Really. It's just—' She turned around again. 'Are you absolutely sure this time?' Her voice was shaky. 'Are you certain that he's the one, Isobel?'

I put my arms around her and held her tight. 'I'm certain. Absolutely certain.'

~

Ian gave me a lift into town. He'd borrowed Dad's car to drive to Jemima's house which was in Rathgar.

'A southsider,' I teased as I fastened the seat belt. 'Honestly, Ian, I'm surprised at you.'

'She's nice,' he said defensively. 'She likes me and I like her.'

'Sounds intense.' I turned on the heater.

'It's – restful.'

'Restful?' I glanced at him as he pulled out into the main road, his eyes narrowed against the glare of the oncoming headlights. 'What on earth would you want with a restful relationship?'

'God, Isobel, we're not all voracious party animals, you know.' He accelerated along the coast road. 'I like to sit with a girl and just – rest.'

'That's fine,' I told him. 'No problem. I wish I'd had a boyfriend like you. None of them ever wanted to sit and rest. Sit and struggle more like.'

'I told you, we're not all animals. Maybe you just go out with the wrong sort of man.'

I glanced at him again. 'And who have you in mind?'

'Nobody.'

'Sounds to me like you do.'

'Don't be stupid.' He braked at the lights and swore under his breath.

'So Jemima likes to be restful, does she?' I switched the topic back to his love life.

'Yes, she does. Honey always wanted to do things. She couldn't sit still for more than five minutes. She exhausted me. "Ian, we must do this. Ian, we should go here. Ian, we have to meet these people. Ian, stop lounging around in front of the TV".' The lights turned green and he eased the car forward. 'Then, when she phoned, it was "Where are you going, what are you doing, who are you seeing?" It drove me nuts.'

'When I came home for Gran's funeral you said you couldn't live without her,' I reminded him.

'I was used to her,' he said. 'It's not exactly the same thing.'

'And are you in love with Jemima?'

He laughed. 'No, Isobel, I'm not. But I like her a lot and we have fun together and it's very, very unpressurised. Honey wanted to get married, you know.'

'Alison told me.'

'I'm too young to get married. It would have been a disaster. It's different for girls.'

'Is it?' I asked.

'Yes,' he said definitely. 'There's something about girls and being married.'

'Married women have a higher depression rate than married men,' I told him. 'In fact, I think married men are the most contented people there are. So there's something wrong about your theory.'

'Rubbish,' he said. 'I haven't yet met a girl who secretly didn't want to waltz down the aisle with some unfortunate sod.'

I smiled. 'I'm sure there are loads.'

'Name one,' he said.

'You see?' said Ian when I'd been silent for a couple of minutes. 'I rest my case.'

'We must all be mad then,' I said wryly. 'It's not the be-all and end-all of everything.'

We stopped at another set of lights. In the car beside us a girl, wrapped up in a black leather coat with a fur collar, snuggled against the man who was driving.

'And what do you think?' asked Ian. 'Really and truly?'

'Really and truly I don't know.' I leaned my head against the headrest. 'I want the companionship and the love and the stability, I suppose.'

'And for that you're going to marry that shithead.'

'Ian, you don't have to call him that. And there's more to it. I just don't have the words.'

'Or maybe you don't have the feelings.'

I shot a dark look at him but he was concentrating on the road ahead. 'I love Tim,' I said. 'And I don't see that I should have to keep justifying myself to everyone.'

'I didn't ask you to.'

'You didn't need to.'

He let me out at Trinity Street. Town was still crowded with people hurrying around with shopping or dressed up for Christmas parties. Much as I'd hated it earlier when I was shopping, I was now drawn into the festive mood of the city. People were in better humour now. The shoppers had finished searching for the perfect present and had decided to reward themselves with a drink in O'Neills or the Old Stand or anywhere else they could get in. Most of the pubs were jammed full, as though the beer was free. I cut through Exchequer Street, and across Grafton Street, where this time I noticed the animated display in the Brown Thomas windows and took time to look at it with a childish delight.

I remembered being brought to see Santa as a child, queueing for ages outside some city store (although I couldn't remember which). Then, when I finally came face to face with him and he'd put his arm around me, I screamed for my mother. I couldn't have been more than three or four. I didn't remember Alison being with us, even as a baby.

Nostalgic idiot, I told myself, as I rang the bell on the door of the restaurant.

'Malone for two?' The waitress smiled at me. 'In the corner. Your companion hasn't arrived yet.'

That was nothing new. Although he had tried, very hard, to be more punctual. 'I know how much you hate me being late,' he'd told me the second night I was home. 'So I'll do my best to be on time for everything from now on. Although,' and he'd smiled, 'if you just come and live with me now, you wouldn't have to worry about it.'

But I hadn't changed my mind.

'Can I get you something to drink?'

'Mineral water, please.'

She returned with a glass of sparkling water and a couple of menus. I sipped the water and read the menu, prounouncing the Malaysian words to myself and wondering exactly how they should be said. I always ordered the easy things, like *rendang beef* or *green curry*, simply because I was too embarrassed to get the names wrong.

I glanced at my watch. Only ten minutes late. That wasn't bad really, anything could have made him ten minutes late. I looked up at the sound of the doorbell and arranged my face into a smile, but it wasn't Tim.

It was a group of men and women, laughing and chattering as they made their way to a table in the corner. An office party by the sounds of things – they were ripping the reputation of someone called Vivi in accounts to shreds. Something to do with Jim in investments and Paul in finance. I hoped that Vivi could last the pace. I eavesdropped unashamedly, enjoying the office gossip. I missed office gossip. I missed my job. And where the hell was Tim?

I closed the menu with a snap and knocked over the glass of water.

The waitress flurried around while I apologised over and over again and she told me that it didn't matter and that there was no harm done and that it was only water, it wouldn't stain. Then she went off to get another tablecloth while I sat in my chair and tried to ignore the furtive glances of the other diners and pretend that this wasn't happening to me.

A new tablecloth was brought, the table was reset and I was given another mineral water. I said thank you and buried my head in the menu again. I wished Tim would hurry up. People were still looking at me, they'd realised now that I'd been sitting here on my own for twenty-five minutes. They'd be muttering to each other that my date had stood me up. I stretched out my left hand on the table so that the engagement ring sparkled in the light. Let them know that I had a man, a man who'd made a commitment to me. If he was a little late, it didn't matter. But I wished fervently he'd hurry up and arrive.

It was five minutes before he did, bringing with him a waft of raw night air mingled with stale smoke and beer. He sat down beside me and took my warm hand in his freezing one.

'I'm really sorry,' he said. 'Honestly, Isobel. I tried and tried to get here on time. I've come from work.'

'Work via the pub?' I hazarded.

'I had to,' he said. 'Everyone was going and I couldn't just walk out. I only had one.'

I said nothing.

'Well, two,' he amended. 'But I swear to God that's all, Isobel. I didn't even enjoy them, I left a full pint behind.'

I believed him. There was a sense of injured innocence about him that it was hard to doubt. Besides, Tim's eyes always went a delicate shade of pink after three pints, and they were still clear, if slightly hazy.

'I was having the most terrible time with Greg,' he continued as he released my hand so that he could open the menu. 'He wants me to finish another phase of this project we're working on before the end of the week. I asked him was he out of his mind – there's another three weeks of work there. But you know Greg, deadlines, commitments, all that sort of stuff.'

I nodded.

'So I told him that it'd be finished when it was finished and I was working flat out as it was.'

'And that was OK?'

'He huffed and he puffed but he gave in eventually.'

'That's good.'

'As long as it's finished before the wedding that'll do,' said Tim. 'Greg is like that. He sets an impossible deadline so that you end up promising something only barely achievable.'

I smiled. 'I hope you won't be tapping away at that computer on our wedding night.'

'Don't worry.' Tim grinned at me. 'I intend tapping away at something far more interesting.'

'Tim!'

'Sorry.' He squeezed my hand. 'I love you, Isobel.'

'Why?'

'What sort of question is that?'

'Why do you love me?'

'For millions of reasons. But mostly—' he leaned forward, 'because you're the sexiest thing on two legs in the whole universe.'

I smiled. We ordered food. I sat back in the chair and gazed around the room while Tim revisited his conversation with Greg about the project they were working on. I wasn't really listening to him, just the drone of his voice. All the stories about work were the same – Greg wanted too much, Tim delivered. Eventually. After a huge argument.

'So I'll have to go in on St Stephen's Day,' he said.

I looked at him. 'That's a bummer.'

'Oh, better get it finished. It wouldn't do to have him ringing me up on the morning of the wedding screeching for me to come in.'

I smiled. 'No.'

'How've you been getting on with things?' he asked. 'Everything under control?'

'Yes.' Because I wasn't working, I had time to organise everything. Much more time than on the previous occasion, although the closeness of the date made things awkward.

'Hotel booked, band booked, church booked—'

'Tim, everything is booked,' I said firmly.

'I just want things to go perfectly,' he said.

'Thanks.'

'So that when we're old and grey you can't complain about it.'

'I won't.'

'The honeymoon is more of a problem than I thought,' he said lightly.

'Oh?'

'I can only get a week off work.'

'Oh, Tim!'

'Well, what did you expect?' he asked. 'I took time off to come to Spain—'

'A few days!' I interrupted.

'I had some time off earlier in the year.'

'What for?'

He ignored me. 'And since our leave goes from April to April, I don't have much leave left.'

'So what are you saying?'

'That we'll go somewhere for a week.'

'Better than nothing, I suppose.' I made a face. 'And I guess I'll be aching to get back to work.'

'You don't have to,' said Tim.

'I do,' I told him. 'Like I said before, if we have children it'll be different. But I couldn't stay at home unless we had a family. What would I do all day?'

He shrugged. 'Paint? Knit? Sew?' He nodded. 'You could do that, Isobel. You could do dressmaking full-time.'

'I couldn't,' I said.

'Why not?' He smiled at the waitress who placed *satay chicken* in front of him. 'You like making clothes.'

'I know,' I said. 'But not full-time.'

'But you once thought of it.'

'Not seriously,' I told him. 'I wouldn't do it all the time. I wouldn't enjoy it.'

'Are you enjoying your time off?' he asked as he gently slid the delicate chicken from the wooden skewers. 'It must be nice not to have to get up in the morning.'

'Nice but strange,' I said. 'I keep thinking I should have something to do.'

'You have got something to do,' objected Tim. 'You're the chief wedding organiser.'

'That's me.'

'Have you started on your dress yet?' he asked.

I shook my head.

'You'll look gorgeous,' he told me. 'Everyone says so.'

'Do they?' I could feel myself blush. Not a deep, scorching blush, but a creeping pale-pink one.

'Of course,' said Tim. 'Dave thinks you're the sexiest girl he knows.'

'Tim!'

'It's true. He said that you were easily the most beddable thing at the Christmas party.'

Softsys's party had been the previous weekend. I'd worn the maroon dress I'd made for the dinner where Gabriela had been voted businessperson of the year.

'He said he could hardly keep his hands off you,' continued Tim.

I was blushing again.

'He said that if you weren't engaged to me, he'd have a go at you himself.'

'He did not!' I looked at Tim in horror. I hated the idea of them talking about me like this.

'He'd had a couple of pints at the time,' Tim reassured me.

'All the same.' I pushed my plate away. 'I don't like being discussed as though I was some sort of commodity.'

'You're not a commodity,' said Tim, 'and we didn't talk about you as if you were.'

'Even so. The idea of Dave having a go at me, as you so delicately put it!'

'He didn't mean any harm.' Tim's tone was defensive. 'And I'm proud that he feels like that about you.'

'Why?'

'Because it means that I made the right choice, doesn't it?'

'Does it?' I stared at him.

'Of course,' he continued blithely. 'It's great to know that the girl you're about to marry is the object of desire of so many people! I like knowing that you're mine and that there's nothing anyone can do about it. It makes me feel good.'

'Well it makes me feel like a piece of meat.'

'Oh, Isobel, don't be stupid.'

'I'm not.'

'You are. You're taking me up all wrong.'

'Tim, I'm not something you own, you know.'

He grabbed my hand again. 'Of course not. But I'm glad you're mine.'

I didn't reply. It was too complicated. But I hoped that Dave wouldn't be at our wedding. It would be too embarrassing to meet him and know he'd said the kind of things he'd said to Tim. Was I overreacting? Probably. I knew men talked like that to each other. I'd heard them in Delta. 'She's a looker, that one.' 'Hot for it.' 'Wouldn't mind a piece of that!' And they didn't mean anything by it. Not really. It was just the way men were.

I wondered if the men in Spain had talked that way. I'd never overheard them, but I supposed they must have. And Bridget had once said that Tomás treated her like a possession. Maybe it was just men. Maybe they never grew out of thinking of women like that. I didn't want to be a possession.

'What are you thinking about?' asked Tim.

'Nothing important,' I answered as I stirred my coffee. 'Nothing at all.'

Chapter 34

Basket of Bread (Salvador Dalí, 1926)

I didn't make my wedding dress. I bought it.

I'd gone into town to look at material. I'd decided to make myself something simple because I thought that I was too old for airy-fairy concoctions that bore no relation to the kind of person you were. So, nothing cute and puffy like the first dress I'd made. A plain dress, I thought, with a short jacket to go over it. And, despite Tim's wishes, I'd forget the veil and just wear flowers in my hair.

But somehow, without meaning to, I found myself in BT's and staring at their wedding dresses again. I told myself it was to rob ideas, but it wasn't. I just wanted a last look at the impossible dress I'd tried on before Christmas.

The same assistant was there. She smiled at me. 'You were here before.'

'Yes,' I admitted. 'I thought I'd take a look again. But I'll probably end up making my own dress.'

'You're a dressmaker?'

'Sometimes,' I said. 'I've made wedding dresses for other people and they've never complained!'

'Do you want to try one on?' she asked.

'Oh, I don't think so. I just want to get the feel of things.'

She smiled again. 'That's OK.'

'Did you sell the other dress? The one I tried on before?' I asked as I looked around.

She shook her head. 'Not yet.' Then she laughed. 'We have four of them in stock. Would you like to try it on again?'

I bit my lip. 'I told you I probably won't buy it.'

'I don't mind,' she said. 'Were you a twelve or a ten?'

'I don't know what size the one I tried was,' I said. 'Most of me is a ten, but I get occasional twelve days.'

She laughed. 'Come on, let's see what we can do.'

I hadn't put on as much weight as I thought. The ten fitted perfectly.

I stood in front of the forest of mirrors and looked at myself from every angle. It was still a fabulous dress.

But I didn't need a fabulous dress to marry Tim. I'd made a fabulous dress! I could still remember sewing all those bloody pearls on it. Stupid to have cut it up in a fit of temper.

I sighed.

'I thought you might like to try this with it.' The assistant handed me a veil and headdress. 'It goes really well, I think.'

'Does it?'

'Absolutely.'

I looked fantastic. I knew I did. It didn't look silly, or flouncy or over-the-top. It looked just right.

'You look wonderful,' said the sales assistant. 'Really wonderful.'

If I made a dress would I look this wonderful? I could copy it, I knew. But it wouldn't be quite the same thing.

'When's the wedding?' she asked.

'The end of January,' I said idly as I gazed at my reflection.

'The end of January and you still haven't bought a dress!' She looked at me in horror. 'Are you crazy?'

'Why?'

'Don't you think it's important to get the exact right one?'

'I think,' I said as I took off the veil, 'that it's more important to get the right man.'

I got dressed again and turned from Isobel Kavanagh, thing of beauty, into Isobel Kavanagh, girl with unmanageable hair.

'How much is it?' I asked the assistant.

'The dress or the veil?'

'The whole lot.'

She told me and I tried to look nonchalant. The price of the dress was almost as much as our week-long honeymoon.

'But worth every cent,' she said. 'For a day to remember.'

I could afford the dress. It just seemed like an incredible waste of money.

'Of course, it is reduced by ten per cent,' added the sales assistant.

'That makes a big difference.' I grinned at her.

Did I want to be Isobel Kavanagh, fairy princess? When everyone came to the wedding, what kind of Isobel did they expect to see? Someone revelling in the whole razzmatazz of getting married – like Julie, or someone in a sensible white dress and jacket? And if I was sensible, would they think that I was only being sensible because of what had happened the last time? Did I care what anyone thought?

The sales assistant watched me silently.

'It's such a lovely dress,' I said eventually.

'And it looked perfect on you.'

I smiled. 'You'd have to say that, wouldn't you?'

'Not at all. If you looked like the back of a bus I'd suggest something else.'

'I should make my own,' I told her.

'In less than a month?'

'It's not that difficult.'

'But you've other things to do, I'm sure.'

I didn't, really. I'd lots of time to slope off and do exactly what I liked. Even making my wedding dress and Alison's bridesmaid's dress, which would be time-consuming all the same.

'Could I try it on again?' I asked. 'I mean, would you mind?'

She shook her head. 'Try it on as many times as you like.'

The dress, when packed, took up the entire back of the car. It was a mountain of froth.

Alison was lounging in front of the TV, her legs dangling over the end of the sofa.

'Going out tonight?' I asked.

She shook her head. 'Peter's playing football with the guys from the office. They go for a few pints afterwards and I wouldn't dream of meeting with him then.'

'Good,' I said. 'I need to measure you for the bridesmaid's dress. And I want your opinion on mine.'

'My opinion?' Alison looked at me curiously. 'Have you made it already?'

'And how could I have done that?'

'Isobel!' She followed me up the stairs. 'Don't tell me you bought it!'

'OK, I won't.'

'Oh, my God!' She stared at the dress which I had hung over my dressmaker's dummy. 'It's the most gorgeous thing I've ever seen.'

'Thank you.'

'It's – wonderful.'

'I know.'

'You'll look absolutely stunning in it.'

I laughed.

'Where did you get it?'

'BT's.'

'How much did it cost?' She fingered the material.

'Lots.'

'Well, it was worth it.'

I laughed again. 'I hope Tim thinks so.'

'He'd have to be blind not to think so,' said Alison. 'And, whatever else he is, he isn't blind.'

'Give it a rest, will you.' I sat on the bed. 'If I've got over the last time, why can't you?'

'I've got over it,' said Alison as she sat down beside me. 'I didn't have much getting over to do, after all. But he was so bloody rotten to you, Isobel. And I just feel that he could be again. I'm sorry. I know you're not supposed to say things like this about people's boyfriends or girlfriends. Whatever. I know that I'm supposed to like him for your sake. But I can't forgive him.'

'Oh, Alison.' I put my arm around her shoulder. 'You're not the worst sister in the world.'

'I'm the best,' she said. 'Believe it!'

~

The phone rang at eight o'clock. Ian jumped out of the armchair and rushed into the hall to answer it. He came back a moment later looking rueful. 'It's for you,' he told me. 'It's someone from Spain.'

'Spain?' I looked up from *Irish Bride*. My heart had begun to beat faster. 'Who from Spain?'

Ian shrugged. 'Dunno. Didn't ask.'

'You're useless.' I put the magazine on the coffee table and walked slowly to the phone. 'Hello,' I said. 'It's Isobel.'

'Hi, Isobel.' I was surprised and somehow disappointed to hear Barbara.

'Barbara! How are you?'

'Not bad,' she replied. 'And you? How are the great wedding preparations going?'

'Oh, all right.' I laughed. 'That sounds terrible. They're going fine, Barbara, I'm just worn out, thats all. I'm fed up with lists of people and menus and all that shit.'

'Poor you,' she sympathised. 'I feel *so-o-o* sorry for you.'

'Shut up,' I said, amused. 'What have you been doing with your life since I left?'

'This and that,' she said. 'I've been very busy in work. We've got extra classes and I'm working two nights a week.'

'You mustn't get out much,' I said.

'Enough.'

'Is it cold there right now?' I asked.

'Yes,' said Barbara. 'But not as bad as last year. The frost melts very early. What about Ireland?'

'Not too bad,' I said. 'Misty.'

'Wish you were here?' she asked.

'Nope. My fiancé is here.'

'Ah, sweet love,' she teased.

'Speaking of sweet love,' my tone was light, 'how's Nico?'

'He's fine.'

'Keeping well?'

'Absolutely.'

'Still playing music?'

She paused. 'Not as much.'

'Why?'

'He's got a new job.'

'New job,' I echoed. 'He never said anything about looking for a new job.'

'He only got it recently,' she told me. 'He was headhunted.'

'Headhunted! Nico?'

'Why not?'

'It doesn't sound like Nico.'

'He's become very career-oriented lately,' said Barbara.

'Really?'

'Yes.' I could almost see her nod. 'He's taking life more seriously.'

'You must be having an effect.' My laughter was forced.

'I hope so,' she said.

'Are you seeing much of him?'

'When I can. He's so busy.'

'It definitely doesn't sound like him,' I said.

'He's changed,' she said. 'I think he's sort of matured.'

'Matured?' The echo was back.

'I've matured him.' Barbara laughed.

'Congratulations,' I said.

'Maybe not,' she conceded.

'I'm glad you're getting on together.'

'Oh, yes. Absolutely. He's a wonderful person, isn't he?'

'I – yes.'

'Attractive. That helps, of course. But he's a decent person too.'

'Yes,' I repeated.

'So warm, so sexy.'

'Barbara!'

'Well, he is, isn't he?'

'I – yes.' I didn't seem to be able to say much else.

'It's working well,' she continued.

'You don't mind?' I asked.

'Mind what?'

'That I went out with him first.'

'Isobel, Isobel! Bitchy.'

'Sorry.'

'I don't mind.' She giggled. 'It's me he's with now.'

'Yes,' I said. 'It's you.'

'Anyway,' her voice was serious again, 'I rang to say that I can't come to your wedding after all, Isobel.'

'Oh, Barbara. Why not?'

'Because of Nico, really. We're going to Seville. Unexpectedly.'

Seville. He'd told me he'd take me to Seville. Not that it mattered.

'That's a pity,' I said. 'I'll miss you not being there.'

'I'll be sorry to miss it myself,' she told me. 'Wanted to see you safely married off, Isobel.'

'Will Bridget still be coming?' I asked.

'Yes,' said Barbara. 'And Tomás! Didn't she send you a card?'

'Yes, she did. I just thought that maybe it didn't suit her.'

'We don't see that much of each other these days,' said Barbara.

'I suppose things change.' I clutched the receiver in my right hand.

'Of course,' said Barbara. 'Look, Isobel, I really am sorry I can't come.'

'At least Bridget can,' I said. 'And I'm glad one of you will make it. You were both very good friends to me.'

'Oh, Isobel.' Suddenly she sounded uncomfortable. 'Thank you. We had some good fun, didn't we?'

'Yes,' I said. 'We did.'

'Anyway,' she said brightly, 'I hope you have a wonderful day.'

'Thanks.'

'And a wonderful life.'

'Thanks again. You too, Barbara. And have a good time in Seville.'

'Absolutely.'

'Bye then. Keep in touch.'

'Sure,' she said.

But I knew she wouldn't.

~

The next day was 6 January. *Cabalgata* in Spain. I thought of Gabriela's children checking their shoes to see if they'd been filled with sweets and I felt a sudden wave of homesickness for somewhere that had never truly been home. But they'd been so good to me. All of them. And I missed them. I thought of Barbara and Nico going to Seville together.

But I was going to Venice, with Tim.

~

Mum asked me to do some shopping for her. When I agreed, she handed me a list a mile long. The supermarket was crowded and I grew more and more irritable as I pushed a trolley with a mind of its own up and down the aisles.

I was back at the car when I realised that I'd forgotten the washing powder. Mum had called after me as I got into the car. She hadn't put it on the list but she needed it anyway. Non-biological. The other sort brought Ian out in a rash.

I unloaded the plastic bags into the boot and went back into the supermarket. It seemed such a waste for one packet of washing powder. I stood in the express queue.

I had a sudden horrible vision of spending my life in supermarkets. Doing domestic things. Washing and cleaning and looking after Tim. I shivered involuntarily. But it wouldn't just be that. I was being silly. There would be the things I craved. The love and the companionship. The understanding. And, eventually, the children.

The woman in front of me had twelve items in her basket. The express queue was for ten or less. I wanted to say something but thought the better of it. Life was too short. There were more important things to worry about.

It was drizzling as I got back to the car. I wondered what the weather would be like in Venice. Hardly all that warm at this time of the year. Venice had been Tim's idea and I'd fallen in with it, but I wondered if I should have insisted on somewhere further away, like Barbados. I'd always wanted to go to Barbados. In fact, I thought, as I opened the car door and slid into the driving seat, I should have asked Tim if he'd like to get married there. That would have appealed to his new, romantic nature.

Too late now, Isobel, I told myself. You should have thought about it before. Besides, if I'd opted for a Caribbean wedding we wouldn't have been able to invite all our friends and I wanted my friends to be there.

Even if one of my friends would be too busy having days and nights of unadulterated passion with Nico Alvarez in Seville.

Three weeks to go, I told myself, as I started the car. I wondered where the nearest shopping centre to Donnybrook was. I'd never thought about that before.

Chapter 35

Dream (Salvador Dalí, 1931)

I was wearing the dress I'd made. The four hundred and twenty pearls glistened in the morning light and the skirt billowed around me, tugged by the breeze. The sky was stained pink from the morning sun which was peeping above the horizon.

Tim stood beneath the apple-tree. His suit was silver-grey and he carried a top hat. He smiled at me as I approached.

Father O'Brien had an old missal in his hand. It was a heavy prayer-book, bound with mother-of-pearl. He looked solemnly at us.

'Tim, do you take this woman to be your lawful wedded wife? To love and to cherish from this day forward, for richer for poorer, in sickness and in health as long as you both shall live?'

'I would,' said Tim. 'I intended to, Father, but look at her.'

Father O'Brien looked at me.

'How can you seriously expect me to marry her when she's dressed like that?'

I gasped in horror at his words then looked down at my beautiful dress and cried aloud. The pearls were falling off, one at a time, dropping around my feet and nestling in the lush green grass. And the dress itself was changing, dissolving before my eyes until suddenly I was wearing the net curtains – curtains that I knew Mum had thrown out years ago.

'She couldn't be bothered to make the effort,' said Tim. 'Why should I marry her if she can't even wear a decent dress?'

'You have a point,' said Father O'Brien.

I wanted to say that it was a mistake, that I had the perfect dress to wear, but my vocal cords were paralysed and I could say nothing.

Barbara Lane stood beside Father O'Brien. She was wearing the Brown Thomas dress and she looked wonderful in it. 'It's OK,' she said. 'I'll marry him. Don't worry, Tim. Everything is going to be all right.' And she kissed him on the lips while I was powerless to stop her.

'In that case,' said Father O'Brien, closing the mother-of-pearl missal, 'what God has joined together, let no man put asunder.'

My voice returned. 'No!' I screamed. 'No!'

I sat up in the bed, my heart thumping against my ribs. I was shaking. The dream had been so real, so vivid. I smiled feebly. But it was only a dream. I wrapped my arms around myself. I really shouldn't be suffering from nerves, but I must be to dream that kind of dream again. I hugged myself for a couple of minutes. 'It wasn't nerves,' I said out loud as I threw back the duvet and got out of bed. It was eating sweet and sour chicken at eleven o'clock the night before.

All the same I wished that the damn wedding was over and done with and that I was safely married to Tim Malone with nothing to worry about any more.

Alison pushed open the bedroom door. 'You awake?'

I faked a casual yawn. 'Just about.'

'Hurry up. Dad says he'll give us a lift into town if we're ready by nine.'

'OK.'

We were going shopping again. There was so much shopping to do I could hardly believe it. Each time I thought there was nothing left, I suddenly thought of something else. But today's shopping was important. We had to buy shoes for Alison and a going away outfit for me.

I'd finished her bridesmaid's dress the night before – that was what had me eating Chinese late at night – I hadn't wanted to stop earlier. I'd made the right decision, I knew, because her dress looked wonderful. It was red velvet, with long sleeves and a scooped neck. She'd tried it on when I'd finished and I'd slipped into my wedding dress and both of us had cried.

'It'll be you in a few months' time,' I said as I stepped out of my dress.

'I know.' She smiled at me. 'I'm really looking forward to it.'

'Well, it's a lot of hassle,' I said. 'I should've insisted we got married in Madrid.'

'Do you miss it?' she asked.

'Sometimes.' I hung the dress carefully on its padded hanger. 'I miss the job and the people at the office . . .' my voice trailed off as I thought about them and what they might be doing at that moment.

Gabriela and Alfredo sitting on the sofa in front of their widescreen TV while their children slept upstairs.

Magdalena and Alejandro having dinner.

Luis and Anna. Or Maria. Or Carlotta. Or Conchita. Or – well, Luis and anyone, I supposed.

Bridget and Tomás trying to make their marriage work.

Barbara and Nico planning for Seville.

'Do you regret coming back?' Alison's words broke into the picture of Barbara and Nico strolling hand in hand through the streets of Seville.

'No,' I said firmly, shutting out the images. 'But I wish that everything didn't seem to be so rushed.'

'Where do you want me to leave you?' asked Dad as we turned onto the quays.

'Anywhere will do, Dad. Which way are you going?'

'Doesn't matter. Through Dame Street.'

'Leave us opposite the Central Bank. We can cut through to Grafton Street that way.' Alison took a small mirror out of her bag and examined her face. 'I think I'm getting a cold sore.'

I looked at her critically. 'I don't see anything.'

'No. But my lip is starting to tingle.'

'We'll nip into a chemist. Get something to put on it.'

'Bloody hell,' she said crossly. 'It'd be just my luck to have a whopping great sore on my lip. I'll look horrible in the photos.'

I grinned at her. 'Don't worry, dearest sister. People won't be looking at you. They'll be looking at the radiant bride instead.'

Dad dropped us off, we bought some cream in the chemist and Alison smeared it over her lip. 'Hope this works.'

'It will,' I told her confidently. 'The pharmacist was very sure.'

'Peter hates cold sores,' she said.

'I'm sure he loves you warts and all,' I said sympathetically.

'Thank God I haven't got warts.' She stopped outside a plate-glass window and examined her reflection again.

'Come on, Ali,' I said impatiently. 'We'll never get anywhere if you don't speed things up a bit.'

I didn't think it would be difficult finding shoes for Alison because, unlike me with my stupid size threes, she's a nice, average five. But I reckoned without her quest for perfection.

We'd brought some of the fabric from her calf-length bridesmaid's dress with us and Alison insisted on getting a perfect match.

'It'll never be perfect,' I said, after she'd rejected another half-dozen pairs of shoes and we were entering yet another shop. 'I don't care if they don't match the dress. You can wear black shoes, Alison.'

'Don't be utterly ridiculous.' She marched up to a sales assistant and waved the red velvet fabric under her nose. 'It's not that difficult a shade.'

I was getting a headache. Probably because of eye strain. When I'd waltzed home with the shop-bought dress, Mum had decided that I had time to make her outfit too. So I'd been cutting and sewing non-stop for the past week.

'What about these?' Alison slipped on a pair of bright red shoes and posed in them.

'They're fine,' I said.

'Isobel! You're not even looking at them.'

'I am. Honestly. They're fine.'

'I'm not sure.' She stood in front of the mirror. 'They're brighter than the fabric.'

'It doesn't matter, Alison. Nobody will notice.'

'Of course they'll notice. People notice everything at weddings! And I know you think that they'll all be entranced by you in that divine dress, but they'll notice if my shoes are pillar-box while the dress is more cherry.'

She was right, of course. They weren't perfect. They were far from perfect. I couldn't understand why I didn't care more.

'Are you all right, Isobel?' She looked at me anxiously. 'You're terribly pale.'

'I'm OK,' I said. 'I just have a bit of a headache. That's all.'

Alison looked at her watch. 'Why don't we grab a coffee or something. It's nearly one. You're probably just suffering from caffeine deprivation.'

'Good idea,' I said. 'I could do with sitting down. My feet are killing me.'

I was wearing a pair of navy court shoes that I'd bought in Madrid. They were work shoes, utterly unsuitable for walking around town and I had no idea why I'd worn them. It wasn't as though I was going to be trying on shoes today. But I hadn't been thinking clearly this morning.

'Fancy a burger?' asked Alison. 'I don't know about you, but I'm starving.'

I made a face. 'I'm not hungry. And I'm on a diet.'

'A diet!' She looked at me scornfully. 'You weigh about seven stone. What are you dieting for?'

'I weigh eight stone,' I said. 'And I'm trying to purify my system.'

'No wonder you've a bloody headache.' My sister looked disgusted. 'Purify your system. That's a load of rubbish.'

'I need it,' I told her. 'I've been eating nothing but junk since I've come home. I used to eat healthy stuff in Madrid. Fruit and vegetables and pasta. Now I'm eating Mum's efforts at home cooking and Chinese takeaways at Tim's.'

'Well, I'm getting something to eat,' she said firmly. 'And if you just want to sip hot water, that's fine by me.'

There was a queue for burgers. I stood beside Alison and rummaged in my bag to see if I'd brought some paracetamol with me. Maybe Alison was right, maybe it was the detox diet that was doing it to me. Maybe I should eat something, even though I wasn't hungry.

'Hamburger and coffee, please,' I said.

The sales assistant, whose name badge said 'Betseigh', looked at me. 'Would you like cheese on the burger?'

I stared at her. 'No.'

'Would you like fries with that order?'

'No?'

'Anything else?'

I felt like Michael Douglas in *Falling Down*. If I had a gun I would have blasted it over the stupid girl's head.

'Burger and coffee,' I repeated. 'Hamburger. No fries. No cheese. No anything else. Just burger and coffee. That's my order, *Betseigh*.' I said the name in disbelief. Why did people find the need to spell their names in ridiculous ways? What was wrong with plain Betsy?

'OK, OK.' Betseigh made a face at me. 'I'm only doing my job.'

'You could add my order on to that.' Alison nudged me. 'Since you've obviously decided to eat, have you forgotten about me?'

I rubbed my temples. 'I'm sorry. I'm sorry.'

Betseigh stared at me, her finger poised over the register. 'There's more?'

'A double cheeseburger de luxe, large fries and a Coke,' said Alison.

The girl smiled. 'Would you like to upgrade that?'

'Nope.' Alison grinned at her. 'That should sort me out for a while.'

Betseigh went to fill the order and Alison turned to me. 'Are you all right, Isobel? Because I think you're starting to crack up or something. You were so rude to her and it's not like you.'

'I'm perfectly all right,' I said. 'Honestly. It's just so crowded.'

There was concern in Alison's face. 'If it bothers you we could skip this and go somewhere else.'

I nodded. 'No, it's fine. It's just stuffy in here. I'll be OK after the coffee. You're probably right. I need the caffeine.'

'Enjoy your meal,' said Betseigh as she put our order in front of us.

'Sure,' said Alison. 'Thanks.'

We sat down at a table. Alison pushed the chips at me.

'No thanks,' I said automatically.

'Isobel! Eat some.'

'I'm not hungry.' I unwrapped the burger. 'At least, I don't want chips. If I'd wanted chips I'd have ordered them from Betseigh!'

Alison grinned. 'Poor girl. You terrorised her.'

'I know it's not her fault,' I said contritely. 'But it drives me mad. If you ask for a burger, they want to know if you want chips. If you ask for a burger and chips, they try to sell you Coke. If you ask for all three, they want you to "upgrade" your meal – whatever that means. Why can't they just let you order what you want and leave you alone?'

'Sales techniques?' Alison hazarded.

'I suppose so.' I took one of her chips absentmindedly and ate it before I realised what I was doing.

'Have another,' she offered. 'It'll do you good.'

~

We stood outside the final shop and I took a squirt of my inhaler.

'Asthma at you?' asked Alison.

'Stress-related.' I grinned at her although my headache was pounding behind my eye and it wasn't being helped by my wheezing.

But we hit pay-dirt on the shoes. They were red suede, a shade darker than the dress. I held the fabric against the shoe and nodded. 'It's great. Are they comfortable?'

Alison slipped the shoes on again and walked up and down the shop. 'OK,' she said. 'A bit high.'

'That doesn't matter,' I told her. 'You won't fall off them, will you?'

'No. But I'll tower over you.'

'No, you won't,' I said. 'The shoes I brought from Madrid have a high heel. It'll only be your natural height that'll make me look like a midget.'

She laughed and hugged me. 'I'm looking forward to your wedding, Isobel.'

'So am I,' I told her. 'And it's a trial run for you.'

'At least I'll know which relatives to leave out.' She grinned. 'If Dad's cousin Cáit makes a total show of us, I'll feel quite justified in leaving her off the guest list.'

We only saw Cáit at weddings and funerals. She was a huge woman, big in every direction, whose personality matched her body shape. She wasn't even a blood relation, just some kind of connection by marriage. But she turned up at everything. She'd been at Granny Behan's funeral, sobbing as though her heart would break. She'd be the life and soul of my wedding, though.

Alison took off the red suede shoes and slipped back into her own. 'Come on, Issy. Will I take these?'

I nodded. 'Absolutely.'

'Thank God,' I told Alison as we walked towards Tara

Street to catch a DART. 'I was beginning to think you'd be wearing a pair of flip-flops.'

'They're nice.' She peered into the bag. 'Very elegant.'

'They're lovely.' I peered in too. 'I'm glad that's over with.'

We got on the train and I sat down with relief.

'Am I wrong, or are you getting fed up with the whole thing?' asked Alison.

I grinned at her. 'Just a little.'

She frowned. 'Why? Surely you should be enjoying it.'

'I am, in a way.' I made a face. 'It's just doing Mum's outfit and everything. It took more time than I thought. And I hate fussing about all the details.'

'I always thought you liked fussing, Isobel.'

'To a point,' I said. 'Right now, I wish it was all over.'

She was silent. The train sped through Fairview and Clontarf. I leaned my head against the window and closed my eyes.

I didn't realise I'd fallen asleep until Alison shook me on the shoulder to tell me that it was our stop.

Tim had organised a night out for both sets of parents. I hadn't wanted him to. It was too close to the wedding and, after the words that had been spoken between Mum and Denise Malone a couple of years earlier, I couldn't believe that they would sit down together and have a meal. But Tim thought it would be a good idea.

'Are we supposed to be there too?' I asked.

'Of course.' He looked at me in surprise. 'Why not?'

'I just wondered. Thought maybe it was just for them.'

'It's for all of us,' he said. 'We're all one family.'

'Tim, I've never heard such crap from you before.' I pulled gently at his hair. 'All one family! When you know your mother doesn't like me and my mother doesn't like yours and God knows what our fathers think!'

He smiled. 'Don't take it all personally, Isobel. They'll get on fine.'

'Will they?'

'Of course.'

I ached to have a night in front of the TV, but I sat in the restaurant while Mum and Mrs Malone tried to outdo each other with stories of their youth and Dad and Mr Malone chatted easily about the possibility of Manchester United doing the double again.

'It's an all-round team,' said Mr Malone as he poked at a sliver of beef. 'They've got the right balance between defence and attack.'

'Couldn't agree with you more.' Dad eyed his beef suspiciously. 'You know, I asked for this well done. It's still got pink in it.'

'Dad, please.' I put my hand on his arm. 'It's a French restaurant. They do everything rare here.'

'Huh.' Dad stabbed the beef. 'I don't care how the French do it, I asked for it well done.'

'Dad—'

'Would you like me to send it back?' asked Tim.

Dad turned it over as though it might get up from the plate and walk.

I sighed.

Tim called over the waiter and asked if the men's beef could be cooked a little more.

'No problem,' said the waiter.

'Thanks, Tim,' said Mr Malone.

'That's what I like in a man.' Dad grinned and thumped Tim gently on the back. 'Decisiveness.'

Decisiveness, I thought bleakly. Dad got over things quickly.

'Are you OK?' whispered Tim.

'Of course.' I swirled my risotto around on the plate.

'I can't help feeling that you're—' He sighed suddenly. 'Do you *want* to get married, Isobel?'

My heart thudded in my chest. Not again, I thought, despairingly. Don't tell me he's doing it to me again. The wall opposite me came in and out of focus and I felt my breathing stop.

'Isobel,' hissed Tim. 'Are you all right?'

I blinked a couple of times. The wall stopped shimmering. I took my inhaler out of my bag.

'Are you OK, love?' Mum looked anxiously at me.

'Yes,' I said. 'I'm fine.'

'You sure?' asked Mr Malone.

I smiled faintly at him. 'Yes.' I took a sip of water.

'What was all that about?' whispered Tim.

'I don't know. I – you asked me if I wanted to get married. I thought perhaps you'd changed your mind.'

'I asked *you* if *you* wanted to get married,' said Tim. 'There's nothing in there about *me* changing *my* mind.'

'I'm sorry,' I said. 'It's nerves.'

Tim smiled at me. 'I know. I get nervous myself sometimes.'

'Tim?'

'Yes?'

'Why are you marrying me?'

He sighed. 'Because I love you.'

'Why do you love me?'

'God alone knows.' He kissed me on the side of the cheek and turned to talk to my father.

I wanted to talk to him but this was the wrong place. I

couldn't understand why I was so nervous, why I couldn't relax. But I couldn't. I couldn't understand why I was becoming such a basket case. Everything was organised. All the replies had come back to the invitations. The tickets to Venice had arrived that morning. My dress was hanging up in the wardrobe at home. I'd booked an appointment for a manicure for the day before the wedding. I needed one false nail to replace the natural one I'd bitten in a moment of tension the previous week. I was going to get them painted blood red, to match Alison's outfit. There was nothing left to panic about, yet I still felt on the verge of hysteria all the time. I hadn't been like this last time. I knew I hadn't.

Maybe it was because I was still afraid that Tim would call it off again. Even though, deep down, I knew he wouldn't. It was the trust thing. I trusted him, I knew I did, and yet there was one little part of me that felt he could still do something completely unexpected and ruin my life.

He leaned over to me and nodded towards our mothers. 'They seem to be getting on quite well now.' They were exchanging recipes.

'It's definitely superficial,' I muttered and he laughed.

The waiter cleared the table and put desserts in front of us. Everyone was having a good time. I just wished that I didn't feel as though I was floating above them all, looking down on everything.

'It's going to be a lovely wedding,' said Denise Malone suddenly. 'And I'm delighted that these two young people have finally got their act together.'

'So am I,' said Dad. 'Although, Denise, I have to tell you that if your son leaves my daughter in the lurch a second time, I'll thrash him to within an inch of his life.'

'Dad,' I muttered.

'Fair enough,' said Brendan Malone. 'And if your daughter leaves my son in the lurch, I'll do the same to her!'

Everybody laughed. Tim put his arm around me. 'You can rest assured that there's no chance of this wedding not happening,' he said. 'I love Isobel and I know that she loves me. And we might have had a turbulent past, but that only makes our future together even stronger. When Isobel went to Madrid, I realised that I'd nearly lost the person who means the most in the world to me. When she agreed to marry me – for the second time – she truly made me the happiest person in the world.'

Mum wiped a tear from her eye.

'So here and now I want to thank Isobel for putting up with me and for understanding me, and I look forward to a long and happy life with her.' Tim smiled broadly at me.

'You've used up your speech for the wedding,' I said.

'Nope.' He grinned. 'I have another one for that.'

'Good grief.' I grinned back even though smiling actually hurt my head at the moment. 'Will you be producing a book? You know, Tim Malone's guide to a wedding speech for every occasion?'

They all laughed. Dad ordered some more wine. Tim kissed me.

I'd never felt more loved and wanted in all my life.

Or so terrified.

Chapter 36

Daybreak I (Joan Miró, 1946)

I hardly recognised Julie when she called around to the house. She'd always been pretty, but now she looked sensational. Her hair was lighter, her skin was clear and her eyes sparkled. She looked like someone who was very happy with life. I was conscious of my own lank hair (I hadn't washed it that morning) and the spots that had appeared on my face due to the fact that I was back on the detox diet. The spots would be gone before the wedding, I knew, but I was acutely aware of the one just under my right eye because I could see it out of my peripheral vision. Julie had no spots. I don't think she'd ever had a spot.

'How are you?' She hugged me tightly. 'I've missed you, Isobel.'

'Me too.' I grinned at her. 'It seems a lifetime since last summer.'

'Not to me,' said Julie. 'To me it's all gone in the blink of an eye.'

We went into the front room where three toasters were neatly stacked against the wall. I shivered and turned on the radiator.

'Mum's on one of her economy drives again,' I explained.

'It's lights off, radiators off once you step out of a room these days.'

Julie laughed. 'It seems weird to have radiators again. I'm used to air-conditioning now.'

'Lucky thing.' I opened the sideboard. 'D'you want a Southern Comfort or have you turned to some other American drink?'

She shook her head. 'Something non-alcoholic please, Isobel. Tonic or Ballygowan would be fine.'

'Are you sure?' I asked. 'I'm not trying to force drink on you, but as a celebration?'

'I want to celebrate with you.' She smiled. 'But I'm just not drinking alcohol at the moment.'

It took a second for the penny to drop. 'Julie! Are you pregnant?'

She beamed at me. 'It's early days, Isobel. Very early. So I haven't told anyone yet. But yes, I am.'

That explained the sensational look, I supposed, although I wasn't sure how sensational she'd feel in the sweltering heat of Florida.

'Congratulations.' I smiled at her. 'When's it due?'

'Not until July,' she told me. 'It was only confirmed a couple of weeks ago. I sort of thought I might be, but I was afraid to check. I couldn't have stood it if the doctor had just told me I had a stomach bug.'

I poured her a glass of mineral water and filled a glass with Southern Comfort for myself. 'Cheers.'

'Cheers.' She sat down on the sofa. 'You look tired, Isobel.'

'I am.' I nodded. 'It's been a bit of a rush and there always seems to be some last-minute thing going wrong. I'm deciding that they're lucky omens though. Nothing went wrong the last time!'

'And you're happy?' She sipped the mineral water.

'Oh, yes. I know I'm doing the right thing.'

'I couldn't believe it when you phoned,' said Julie. 'It was the biggest shock I'd ever had.'

'Sorry.' I smiled at her. 'It's all your fault anyway. I wouldn't have met him if it hadn't been for you and Andy getting hitched.'

'I know.' She frowned. 'I feel responsible.'

'Don't look so depressed about it! You should be pleased.'

Was Julie going to give me a lecture? I wondered. I couldn't bear the idea of someone else asking me if I was doing the right thing, if I'd thought it through properly, if I was sure – absolutely sure – that Tim Malone was the one for me. God knows, I'd thought about it often enough myself. It wasn't as though I'd simply seen him and decided that I still loved him and that was that. I'd agonised over it. Even, one day, written down a list of whys and why nots. Nobody could be more sure about their wedding plans than I was.

'I *am* pleased,' said Julie, after a pause. 'I'm delighted for you, Isobel. You deserve to be happy.'

'I will be.'

'So are you completely organised yet?'

I grimaced. 'Almost. I was prancing around in the shoes I'm supposed to wear – which I brought back specially from Spain – when the bloody heel broke! I couldn't believe it.'

'Oh no!' Julie laughed. 'Did you get them repaired?'

'Of course. But it was just something I could've done without.'

'It's not a real wedding until you've had a couple of near disasters.' Julie grinned at me. 'As long as *you* don't get hassled, that's the main thing.'

It was good to be with Julie. Of all the people I knew, she was the one who understood me the most. And she was helping me to relax by not taking the shoe thing seriously. I'd been absolutely furious when it happened – almost mute with rage. I'd thrown the shoe across the bedroom where the nail jutting out from the heel had torn the wallpaper that Dad had put up only two months earlier. I'd stuck it back and it didn't look too bad, but I felt terrible about it. Then Stella, the soloist we'd booked for the church, had phoned to say that she had a throat infection and that she wasn't sure about singing at the wedding.

'Tell me you're joking,' I begged, but she croaked that no, she wasn't, but she was on antibiotics and hopefully it'd clear up soon.

'And what if it doesn't?' I asked.

'There's a girl I know,' she whispered. 'Her name's Bernadette. She'll do it for you.'

But I didn't know Bernadette and I didn't want a complete stranger singing at my wedding. I didn't know Stella either, she was a friend of a friend of Tim's, but we'd heard her singing and she was good. This Bernadette could be utter crap for all I knew and the first I'd hear of it would be when she butchered the *Panis Angelicus.* No, I didn't want Bernadette.

But I might not have an option. I told Stella to keep in touch on the throat front.

'I'll say a little prayer,' said Mum when I told her. I didn't think prayers were what we needed. Stronger antibiotics might do the trick.

'What are you thinking about?' asked Julie.

I told her about Stella and Bernadette. 'So, as of now, I have absolutely no idea who'll be singing at the wedding.'

'It doesn't matter,' said Julie. 'They're all the same, these wedding singers.'

'No they're not,' I told her. 'When I went to my Cousin Linda's wedding about five years ago, the soloist was absolutely awful. She was Harry's sister-in-law and apparently had offered to sing and Linda didn't have the nerve to say no. But she said that every false note was like a dagger through her heart! The congregation were in fits of giggles every time she opened her mouth.'

'Oh, well, nothing like that will happen to you.'

'I hope not,' I said fervently. 'I keep telling Alison I don't want everything to be perfect, but trauma-free would be nice.'

'My trauma was that the underskirt of my dress caught on a nail or something at the top of the stairs,' said Julie. 'I heard a ripping noise and I nearly freaked out altogether. It wasn't that bad, just a small tear, but I thought I was going to faint all the same. And then Dad kept patting my hand in the car, telling me it was the proudest moment of his life.'

'I wonder why that is?' I mused. 'Surely they should be more proud of you when you leave school or graduate. After all, that's something that you've done all by yourself. Getting married is more luck really.'

'God, Isobel, you're a great advertisement for romance.'

'I am,' I protested. 'It's just – oh, never mind.'

I refilled the glasses. 'Anyway, let's talk about something else for a while. I'm sick to my back teeth of weddings. Tell me about Florida.'

'It's great,' said Julie. She settled back more comfortably in the sofa. 'I was lonely at first, and everything was very different. You know, even the English is very different – all that stuff about faucets and diapers and skillets. You don't realise how many words are different until you're there. And people are different too. So – enthusiastic about everything.'

I grinned. 'What about your house?'

'I brought photos.' Julie opened her bag and took them out. 'I know it's a boring thing to look at other people's photos, but I brought them anyway.'

'It's not boring at all!' I pored over a picture of the Jordans' home. It was a whitewashed, red-roofed villa, built three sides around a small courtyard. There was a fountain in the courtyard which was crammed with pots of brightly coloured flowers.

'Oh Julie, that's lovely,' I said.

'I know.' She flicked through the photos. 'This is the back.'

'Julie! I know you told me you had a pool, but this is huge!'

'It's not really. It's just the angle. It's quite close to the house.'

'It's fabulous.'

'Thanks. I keep wondering about what to do when the baby is born. You can't cover it up – you couldn't live there without having a pool. But I'm terrified of the idea of the kid wandering into it. You know the way they do.'

'Not really,' I said. 'But I'll take your word for it. Julie – this kitchen is incredible!!'

It was the last word in hi-tec – stainless steel and marble surfaces, softened by huge vases of different coloured flowers. Except for the flowers, it reminded me a little of Nico's kitchen. Except for the flowers and, of course, the photo of Carmen.

God, I thought. How could I have let Nico creep into my head like that? Nico and bloody Carmen. And it wasn't Carmen any more either. It was Barbara. Nico and Barbara in Seville.

'This is the bathroom,' Julie giggled. 'I know it's naff to bring photos of your bathroom, but I thought I'd show it to you anyway.'

'Is that a jacuzzi?!'

She nodded. 'It's Andy's favourite place.'

'You lucky, lucky thing, Julie Jordan.'

She smiled at me. 'I love it when people call me that.'

'Julie Jordan,' I repeated.

'I know it's stupid. I know I should be more mature about it. But whenever I hear it I kind of hug myself and thank God that I met Andy. Because I'm cracked about him.'

'I'm really pleased, Julie. You deserve him.'

'Thanks,' she said and showed me a photograph of their dining-room table.

~

I went to the doctor's the next day. I was still suffering from headaches which I suspected were brought on by stress, but no matter how relaxed I tried to make myself be nothing seemed to work.

Dr Byrne made me lie on the couch while she did a complete check-up on me.

'You're OK,' she said, 'but a little run down, Isobel. Are you eating properly?'

'I've been dieting,' I admitted.

'Well stop,' said Dr Byrne. 'You certainly don't need to lose weight.'

'It was more a detox thing,' I told her. 'To purify my system.'

Dr Byrne sighed. 'You're perfectly healthy. You don't need to do anything like this, Isobel. Eat sensibly and you'll be fine. Fresh fruit and vegetables would be good.' She pulled a pad towards her and started to write. 'These will shift the headache. And for goodness sake try to relax. I know getting married is a stressful time, but you don't need to get into a complete knot over it.'

'I know,' I said meekly.

She looked up from the pad. 'Is everything else OK?'

'What do you mean?'

She shrugged. 'Just that. There's nothing else bothering you, is there?'

I grinned at her. 'Only how to keep my mother and Tim's mother on civil terms until after the ceremony.'

She laughed and handed me the prescription. 'Have a few early nights,' she advised. 'And enjoy yourself on the day.'

~

The phone was ringing as I got home and I grabbed the receiver.

'Hello?'

'Hello, can I speak to Isobel Kavanagh, please?' It was a female voice, one I didn't recognise.

'Speaking.'

'Isobel, this is Marianne Leahy. I'm the personnel director of the Eastmann College. You applied for the position of administrator with us.'

'That's right.'

'I know this is somewhat short notice, but I was wondering if you could come in for interview tomorrow morning. Say ten o'clock.'

'Absolutely. Of course I can.' An interview! I'd applied for half-a-dozen jobs since I'd come back and this was the first interview. All of the others had sent back standard letters telling me that there were hundreds of suitable applicants and that they'd be in touch. Actually, I vaguely remembered that the Eastmann College had sent back something very similar.

'Do you know where we are?' asked Marianne.

I frowned. 'Merrion Square?'

'That's right,' said Marianne. 'I look forward to seeing you, Isobel.'

'I'm looking forward to it too,' I said.

I was surprised at how pleased the prospect of an interview made me feel. Even though my days were full of wedding preparations I'd felt as though something was missing. The idea that I might soon have a job again was more exciting than I'd imagined.

I went upstairs. My room was a mess. I was bringing some clothes over to Tim's that afternoon so that I'd have a basic wardrobe there for when we came back from Venice. Tim liked the idea of me leaving my clothes there. I planned to stay for the evening and cook him dinner. He liked that idea even more.

I stuffed several pairs of jeans, a few skirts, half-a-dozen tops and a selection of shoes into a suitcase and squeezed it closed. Dad had left me the car so I heaved the suitcase into the boot and drove across town to Donnybrook. Although Tim had given me the keys to his house the day I'd come back to Dublin I hadn't been in it on my own since my return. In fact, the last time I'd been in Tim's house on my own had been the day I'd wiped his computer files and thrown the earrings down the toilet. I'd have to confess that to him sometime, although I wasn't sure how I'd pluck up the courage to do it. It would be easier to explain the computer files than the earrings. I wondered whose they were. I hadn't thought about them in ages.

I let myself in the door and switched off the alarm. Still the same entry code, which was just as well because I hadn't thought to ask Tim if he'd changed it. I lugged the suitcase upstairs to the main bedroom. The bed was made, the dark blue and yellow duvet stretched carefully over the bed and the pillows, with their matching blue and yellow pillowcases, neatly plumped up. Tim had become terribly domesticated.

I opened the suitcase and laid my clothes out on the bed. It seemed creepy somehow, to be leaving things in his house. I wished I could get the feeling that it belonged to both of us, but I couldn't. The decor was all Tim. Sharp, definite colours. No pastel shades – even the yellow in the bedroom was a very vivid yellow. And it was clearly a man's bedroom. His dressing-gown, black and white stripes, hung on the back of the bedroom door. The shelves in the en-suite bathroom were laden with Gillette shaving foam, Paco Rabanne aftershave, and Imperial Leather soap. In Spain, my bathroom had had jars of pot-pourri on the shelves, along with pots of Clarins creams, Lancôme make-up and a selection of half-full perfume bottles. It had been tiled in pink and grey – feminine, even if that had nothing to do with me. Tim's bathroom was green, with a border of gold tiles.

I opened the chrome bathroom cabinet. Razor blades, Alka-Seltzer, Panadol, dental floss, athlete's foot powder (ugh!) and a half-full bottle of *Belles di Ricci* perfume.

I picked up the gaudy bottle and sprayed the perfume onto my wrist. Whose was it? I wondered bleakly. And why was it in Tim's bathroom cabinet?

I went back into the bedroom and sat on the bed. Was it going to be like this all the time? Was I always going to suspect the worst of him? And why, in heaven's name, should I be suspecting anything right now, when I knew that he'd come running back to me and that, more than ever, he was the one who wanted to get married? He wasn't sleeping with someone else. I knew that.

And if he'd had relationships while I was in Madrid – well, who was I to get upset about that? My God, if Tim only knew about the things I'd done in Madrid . . .

But the niggling feeling of distrust stayed with me so that I bit my lip as I hung up my clothes in the space he'd emptied for me the previous night. I wished that I didn't feel the way I did. I wished that I could trust Tim completely and utterly as I once had.

I made myself a cup of tea. Mechanically, opening the right cupboard door, taking out the tea caddy, taking out the mug with the picture of the Plaza Mayor that I'd brought back from Spain. I didn't have to think where any of those things were – I knew. And surely, I thought, desperately, surely that meant something. There were messages on his answering machine. I stared at the blinking light – four messages, popular bloke. I knew that I shouldn't listen to them but I couldn't help myself.

And none of them was a heart-stopping message from some secret lover. They were all simple work-related things. Which, I thought, just went to prove that I was hopelessly paranoid and that the sooner I actually married Tim the better.

~

'Honey, I'm home!!' Tim peered around the kitchen door and I jumped with fright. I hadn't heard the hall door open, I was immersed in a Robin Cook medical thriller which I'd found on Tim's bookshelf.

'You scared the living daylights out of me,' I told him.

'Sorry.' He kissed me. 'How was your day?'

'Is this practice for when we're married?' I asked.

'Sort of,' said Tim, 'but I won't always have these for you.' He produced a box of Belgian chocolates from a bag.

'Oh, Tim. Thanks.' I kissed him this time. 'They're great.'

'I thought you could forget about the diet for a couple of days,' he said as he dumped a pile of books onto the kitchen table. 'They have to be eaten within a week.'

I thought about the strict detox diet and Dr Byrne's advice. So I ate the biggest, creamiest chocolate of them all.

'Your dinner is ready,' I said with my mouth full. 'Are you hungry?'

'Even if I'd eaten a horse at lunchtime I'd tell you I was hungry,' said Tim. 'That smells delicious.'

'You didn't have a big lunch, did you?' I asked.

He laughed. 'No. How could I when I knew you were slaving away over a hot cooker for me?'

'Just as well,' I said. 'Go on, sit down.'

I put the plate of steak, vegetables and scalloped potatoes (another find in the freezer) in front of him. 'Eat up.'

'What are you having?' He eyed my plate of vegetables with distrust.

'Corn, peas, aubergine and red pepper,' I said. 'It's a mix you had in the freezer with a best-before date of next week.'

'Really?' He looked horrified. 'I tend to throw things in there and forget about them. Why aren't you having any steak? Or potatoes?'

'Not that hungry,' I said, and had a fit of the giggles when Tim put the box of chocolates onto the side of my plate.

We watched TV together afterwards. It was cosy and natural and I felt suddenly peaceful.

'Happy?' he asked, as I leaned my head on his shoulder.

'Mmm.'

'This time next week it'll all be over.'

'Don't say that.'

'Why? Don't you want us to be married?'

'Of course.' I looked up at him. 'It was the way you said it – it'll all be over – as though once we were married, everything would be different.'

'Everything will be better,' he said confidently. 'And I'm wrong anyhow. This time next week we'll be walking over the Rialto in Venice.'

I smiled. 'It sounds great.'

'I'm sorry it's only for a week,' said Tim. 'Truly I am. I'll make it up to you, though. We'll go somewhere really special for the summer.'

'Where?' I asked lazily.

'Mexico, Jamaica, Pattaya Beach, Langkawai, The Seychelles—'

'Keep talking,' I said, 'they all sound great.'

'We'll go anywhere you want,' Tim told me. 'I just want you to be happy.'

I snuggled closer to him. 'Tim?'

'Yes?'

'Can I ask you something?'

'Of course. What sort of something?'

'It's stupid.'

'So?'

'I don't want you to think I'm paranoid.'

'I know that already.' He ruffled my hair. 'What's wrong?'

'Nothing. It's just—' I took a deep breath. 'I was in your bathroom today and I opened the cabinet. There was perfume in it.'

'And?'

'And I wondered why.'

There was a brittle silence. He sat up straight and looked at me. 'What d'you mean – you wondered why?'

'Why there was a woman's perfume in your bathroom cabinet.'

I stared at the floor, my face red, feeling guilty.

'Isobel, you are an awful fool,' said Tim. 'That's been there for ages.'

I glanced up at him.

'It's Laura's perfume,' he said and I felt my heart thud in my chest.

'She stayed here one night.'

I swallowed.

'We were working late and she stayed here. She did that a couple of times.'

I said nothing.

'It was perfectly platonic,' said Tim. 'She looks too much like you, Isobel. I couldn't possibly have taken her to bed, even if I wanted to.'

'Why?'

'I don't know,' he said irritably. 'There's probably some perfectly decent psychological reason, but I couldn't. And I didn't. Which, I think, I've told you before. More than once.'

I bit my lip.

'For God's sake, Isobel.' Tim looked angry. 'I can't believe you're actually upset about this.'

I looked down at the floor to hide the tears that were about to fall. 'I don't know,' I whispered. The tears fell. They slid down my cheeks and dripped onto the green carpet, leaving dark spots where they landed.

'Do you think I'm having some sort of relationship with her?' he asked. 'Do you?'

'No,' I muttered.

'Well, then. Why the tears?'

'I don't know.'

He pulled me to him. 'You're being silly, Isobel. Really silly.'

'I know.'

He sighed. 'I don't know what it is about Laura. I knew you were upset about her before. But honestly, I never slept with her. I never even kissed her.'

'I'm sorry.' I wiped away the tears. 'I don't know what's the matter with me, Tim.'

'Come here.' He pulled me into his arms. 'I love you, Isobel.'

It was good to hear him say it. He stroked my hair. I closed my eyes. Then I remembered something.

'I want to ask you a question.' I opened my eyes and looked at him.

'Another one?'

'Please. It's not an easy question.'

He stared at me. 'What?'

'Did Laura – well, did she – did—'

'Isobel!' He looked exasperated. 'What?'

'Did she ever leave earrings here?'

'Earrings?' He looked at me as though I was completely insane. 'Earrings? Why would she—' He broke off and stared at me suddenly. 'Gold ones. With rubies?'

I nodded.

'One afternoon, when we were working, she was using headphones and the earrings were digging into her. She took them off and then went home without them – or so she thought. She asked me about them. I thought I'd put them away somewhere, but I could never find them. Isobel – what about her earrings?'

It had been a secret that had weighed on me for a long time. 'I flushed them down the toilet,' I told him miserably.

'You flushed them down the toilet.' He stared at me. I wanted to curl up and die. 'You flushed them down the toilet.' Then suddenly he started to laugh. 'Oh, Isobel. You're quite mad! I think that's why I love you.'

'Are you sure?'

'I've never been more sure of anything.' And he folded me into his arms again.

I stayed the night in Tim's house. We made love twice.

Chapter 37

Daybreak II (Joan Miró, 1964)

I woke up at eight o'clock, just before Tim's alarm went off. I had to get home, Dad needed the car. And I'd forgotten, until I was almost asleep, about my job interview. I needed to get home, have a shower and dress in something more suitable than baggy jeans and a sweatshirt. I slid out of the bed.

'Where're you going?' mumbled Tim sleepily.

'I've got to go home,' I said. 'I promised Dad I'd have the car back. He needs it today.'

'Come back to bed.' Tim stretched his arm out over the duvet.

'I can't, Tim. I'm in a hurry.'

'Your dad doesn't need the car at eight in the morning.' Tim was awake now.

'No, but I want to get home and have a shower. I've an interview today.'

'A what?' He sat up in the bed. His hair stood spikily on the top of his head.

'Interview.' I pulled my sweatshirt over my head. 'At ten o'clock.'

'What sort of interview?'

'Job interview,' I said. 'What other sort is there?'

He didn't say anything. I brushed my hair and fastened my watch around my wrist.

'Why didn't you tell me about it last night?'

'I forgot.' I leaned forward and kissed him on the head. 'I was carried away by you and it completely slipped my mind.'

'Tell me about it,' he demanded.

'There isn't a lot to tell.' I sat on the edge of the bed. 'The ad said administrator. It's for a place called the Eastmann College. They're in Merrion Square.'

'Never heard of them,' said Tim.

'Neither did I before I read the ad.' I yawned. 'I sent off my CV before Christmas. I didn't really expect to hear from them.'

'It seems a bit crazy going for an interview today.' Tim was grumpy.

'Why?'

'Isn't it obvious?' He stared at me. 'We're getting married next week!'

'They'll hardly expect me to start next week,' I told him. 'They're probably interviewing lots of people. I'd say it'll be at least a fortnight before I know. Plenty of time.'

'All the same.' He sounded aggrieved. 'You should have told me.'

'I would have told you,' I said. 'But I already said. I forgot.'

He sighed and threw back the duvet. 'I suppose now that you've woken me I might as well get up.'

'You'll be on time for once.' I grinned at him. 'I'd better go, Tim. You know Dad. He'll be hopping up and down wondering if I've forgotten. And he won't ring to check. All that'll happen is that his blood pressure will soar.'

'I'd hate to be responsible for landing your dad in hospital,' said Tim. 'I'll give you a buzz later.'

'OK.' I kissed him again, only this time it was a proper kiss.

'Take care of yourself.'

'You too,' I said and ran downstairs.

As I suspected, Dad was pacing up and down the hallway when I arrived home.

'Plenty of time,' I told him as he looked at his watch. 'Don't fuss, Dad.'

'You should have been here last night,' he said.

'Oh, Dad.' I hugged him. 'Don't be such a fuddy duddy daddy.'

He didn't smile. I made a face at his back as he let himself out.

Mum was in the kitchen, reading the *Irish Times* and sipping tea. Alison was doing her make-up at the kitchen mirror.

'Morning,' I said brightly.

'Uh.' Alison outlined her lips.

'Good morning,' said Mum. 'You took your time in getting home.'

'You knew I was staying with Tim last night,' I said as I buttered a slice of toast.

'I don't like it,' said Mum. 'It isn't right.'

'Oh, God.' I sighed. 'Don't give me a hard time now, Mum. I'm in a hurry.'

'What sort of a hurry?'

'The sort where you don't linger around the place,' I said through a mouthful of toast. 'I've got an interview this morning.'

'A what? I wish you wouldn't speak with your mouth full.'

I swallowed. 'An interview.'

'Interview? Who with? What for?'

'With some woman for the job of administrator in Eastmann College,' I told her.

'A job interview?'

Sometimes my mother could be very dense.

'Yes.'

'Isobel, you can't go to a job interview when you're getting married next week.'

'Do you know that you sound just like Tim?' I demanded. 'Of course I can. And I have to get a move on. It's at ten o'clock and I need to shower.'

'Good idea,' muttered Alison from the other end of the room.

'Oh, shut up,' I said.

Ian had obviously been the last person in the bathroom. The towels were scattered on the floor, across the sink and across the toilet cistern. His razor was still in the sink and he'd left a scum of bristle around it.

It took ages to dry my hair and even then I wasn't happy about it. I used handfuls of mousse to try and keep some sort of shape on it but the final result was still too curly.

I took my Louise Kennedy suit from the wardrobe. It was three years old, I hadn't brought it to Spain, but it still fitted me and it still looked smart. It was olive green with bronze buttons on the jacket. For one horrible moment I thought I'd taken my plain black court shoes over to Tim's last night, but I found them at the bottom of the wardrobe, under a black refuse-sack full of socks and well-worn jeans.

I wiped them with some tissue, then decided that I'd better polish them properly, then got polish on the cuff of my cream-coloured blouse so that I had to change it for a white one, which I didn't think went with the suit half as well. Maybe Tim and Mum were right. Maybe I was off my rocker going for an interview today.

It was drizzling by the time I was ready. I took Dad's golf umbrella from under the stairs and walked to the bus stop. I really, really missed the metro.

The bus was late and the traffic was appalling. By the time I reached the Eastmann College building it was exactly ten o'clock.

It was a Georgian building with a fanlight window over a shiny black painted door. A gold plaque on the wall said *Eastmann College – founded 1977.* I pushed the door open and walked inside.

The entrance hall was impressive. A chandelier hung from the high ceiling. The walls were painted primrose yellow and were hung with portraits – Oscar Wilde, George Bernard Shaw, Seamus Heaney, Edna O'Brien and Mary Robinson. A girl whom I guessed to be in her early twenties sat behind an almost antique desk. She looked enquiringly at me.

'I'm here to see Marianne Leahy,' I told her. 'My name is Isobel Kavanagh.'

She looked in a red appointments book. 'Yes. Can you wait a moment, please.'

I nodded and sat down on one of the velvet upholstered chairs. I knew nothing about Eastmann College but they didn't stint on the furniture. The students must be pretty mature, I thought. The chairs wouldn't have lasted a minute in the Madrid college where I'd done my Spanish classes. Of course, it had been a very different place. The building had been old, as this was, but completely modernised inside. I rather liked this. It was very beautiful.

'Can you go up to the first floor?' asked the receptionist. 'Marianne is the first door on the left.'

I nodded and went upstairs.

I tapped on the door marked *Administrator* and walked inside.

For some reason I'd expected Marianne Leahy to be a clone of Gabriela. But she wasn't. Marianne looked to be in her late forties or even early fifties – although I might have got that impression from her iron-grey hair which was cut very short. She wore very little make-up, and no jewellery. Her suit was navy blue. I hadn't felt nervous until now, but suddenly I realised that my mouth was dry and my palms sweating.

'Isobel.' She smiled and I felt better. It was a genuine smile, reaching her eyes and softening her stern features.

'Hello,' I said.

'Take a seat.' She opened a folder and took out my CV. 'I'm glad to meet you.'

'Thanks for taking the time,' I said.

'You've an excellent CV.'

I nearly said, no, not really, but then I realised that I could blow the job instantly if I was stupid. So I said 'thank you' again.

'Tell me about your career.' Marianne sat back in her leather chair while I talked about DeltaPrint, Advanta and the work I'd done.

She listened carefully, asked occasional questions and made notes. She raised her eyebrows when I told her that I was getting married the following week. Then she told me a little about Eastmann College and the sort of work I'd be doing if I got the job. She only came in to the college a couple of times a month so the entire responsibility for running things would be mine. It sounded exciting.

'It was very nice meeting you,' she said. 'Obviously, I've other candidates to talk to. So I won't be able to give you an answer this week.' She smiled. 'In fact, not before you're married! But I will give you a call as soon as I can.'

'Thank you.' I stood up and shook hands with her.

'I hope you have a lovely wedding,' she said as I left the room.

It had been OK, I thought, as I walked to Pearse station. I'd answered her questions readily, and nothing she'd talked about seemed out of my capabilities. I was hopeful.

I wanted that job. The more I thought about it, the more interesting it became. I wished I didn't have to wait for two weeks to find out whether or not I'd been successful. I wished she'd given me some hint straight away.

The train slid into the station and I hopped on. Merrion Square would be handy enough for Donnybrook. I could walk it in the summer. I enjoyed walking to work, it gave you time to plan your day. I hoped I'd have lots of planning for Eastmann College.

Mum was hoovering the hall when I opened the front door.

'Why on earth are you doing that now?' I asked.

'I opened the door and that little runt of a dog from next door ran in,' she said furiously. 'He'd been digging in the flowerbed, the dirty little beggar. He got muck all over my hall.'

'Oh dear.' I smothered a smile.

'It's nothing to smile about.' She switched off the hoover. 'As you'll no doubt find out yourself.'

'They don't have a dog next door to Tim,' I said. 'And if they had it'd be too scared to run in. He doesn't like dogs and he'd give it a boot up the bum before it knew where it was.'

'I wish you wouldn't use language like that,' complained Mum.

'I've used a lot worse.' I made a face at her.

'Not at your interview, I hope.'

'What d'you think I am?' I took off my coat and hung it over the banister.

'How did it go?'

'Not bad, actually.' I followed her into the kitchen where she filled the kettle. 'It sounded like an interesting job.'

'But what about Tim?' asked Mum.

'What about him?'

She looked uncomfortable. 'It's just that I thought you were getting married to have children.'

'Mum!' I looked at her in despair. 'I want to. Sometime. Not this year, though. And I need a job in the meantime.'

'I just thought it'd be good if you got yourself something nice and easy,' she said. 'Answering the telephone or something.'

'Helen Kavanagh! Answering the phone can be very stressful. Do you realise that it's being at the bottom of the pile that can stress you? Not having any control over what you do or when you do it? Worrying about being five minutes late for work? *That's* stress.'

She sighed. 'Well, you know what you want.'

'Yes, I do.' I spooned instant coffee into two cups. 'And by this time next week I'll have it.'

Although we'd wanted to get married on a Saturday, we had to settle for Monday. It had been absolutely impossible to book a hotel for a Saturday wedding with the amount of notice that we'd been able to give them. Because it was a Monday I'd been doubtful whether any of the people from Spain would be able to come. I'd imagined that they might all discover reasons why they couldn't – like Barbara. But Luis, Gabriela and Magdalena arrived on Saturday afternoon as promised and I'd booked the El Paso in Howth for ten o'clock that night. Peter and

Alison and Julie came along too. Despite all my longings to have more nights in, this was a night out I'd looked forward to for ages.

The restaurant was full and buzzing with conversation when the four of us arrived.

We ordered a pitcher of beer and Julie asked for mineral water.

I hadn't told either Alison or Peter about her pregnancy but Alison looked at her in the knowing way that women look at each other and Julie blushed. Alison grinned and said 'congratulations' and Peter looked at us as if we'd gone crazy.

Gabriela, Luis and Magdalena arrived at the same time as the beer.

'Gabriela!' I called. '*Aquí*!'

'Isobel!' She swept towards me. 'Isobel! *Cómo estás*?'

'*Muy bien.*' I hugged her and kissed her. 'And you?'

'I'm very well also.'

'*Hola, Isobel.*' Luis got in on the hugging act.

'It's lovely to see you,' said Magdalena.

'And all of you,' I said. 'I've missed you so much.'

And I had. It was only seeing them all again that made me realise quite how much. I introduced Peter, Alison and Julie.

'We have heard a lot about you,' said Gabriela as she sat down. 'Isobel told us lots of stories about her life in Ireland.'

'She probably lied,' said Alison. 'Made herself out to be an angel.'

Gabriela laughed. 'Only sometimes.'

'Did you have a good flight?' I turned to Luis who was looking very well tonight in jeans and a denim shirt. For once nothing clashed.

'It was OK,' he said. 'We were delayed a little at Barajas but we made up the time.'

'And your hotel?'

'It is near the sea. On the other side of the river. I have a wonderful view of Dublin Bay from my bedroom window.'

'Yes,' Magdalena chimed in. 'Me also. The sea is fantastic. I have never seen it that colour before. And the white tops of the waves!'

I could understand her amazement. I'd felt equally amazed the first time I'd seen the azure calmness of the Mediterranean.

'Have you got everything ready, Isobel?' asked Gabriela.

I nodded. 'Nothing left to do but turn up.'

'And you can always change your mind about that!' Magdalena blushed the moment the words left her lips. There was a frozen silence and everyone looked at me.

'No fear of that,' I said as I filled my glass with beer.

Everyone started to talk at the same time then, chattering about the first thing that came into their heads. I looked at the menu and tried to ignore the desperation in their voices.

We ordered chicken wings and tortillas, and an assortment of main courses. The atmosphere lightened a little when the food arrived and everyone got their fingers messy with the chicken wings.

'How is business?' I asked Gabriela.

'Very good,' she replied. 'We have signed a contract with Amicar Insurances for two years and I am making a presentation on Thursday morning to one of the banks. It's been a good start to the year.'

'How about you, Isobel?' asked Luis. 'Have you been enjoying your time of leisure?'

'Actually, I was at an interview today,' I said.

'An interview!' Julie looked at me in amazement. 'I didn't know you were going for an interview.'

'It was sudden,' I told her.

'Where?' she asked.

So I told them about Eastmann College and Marianne Leahy and how I hoped I'd made a good impression. 'I gave your name as a reference, Gabriela,' I added.

'You know I will give you a good reference,' she said. 'In fact, if you ever want to come back to Madrid there will always be a job waiting for you.'

I swallowed the lump that had suddenly appeared in my throat. Gabriela had been so good to me and she was still being good to me. 'Thanks,' I said.

'It's not quite the same without you.' Luis laughed. 'There is no one going around the office singing.'

'Very funny.' I joined in their laughter. Anytime I even hummed a bar of a song in the office people ran for cover.

'Tell us about America.' Luis turned his charm on Julie. 'What is life like there?'

She talked for a while about Florida and about Andy and his work and their house. I noticed that she spent a lot of time talking about the house. I wondered if I'd become like that when Tim and I were married. Would my priorities change completely? Would having a chrome bathroom cabinet instead of a gold one be one of those life or death questions?

'I like gold myself,' said Gabriela. 'But only in a big room. It takes over a small one.'

'That's what I think,' Julie agreed. 'And the en-suite bathroom is very small.'

I caught Peter Gaffney's eye and we both started to giggle. Alison wanted to know what was so funny but I shook my head. 'Nothing, nothing.'

We stuffed ourselves with *enchilladas* and *fajitas* and then we ordered margharita cocktails.

'I shouldn't drink this,' said Julie, who'd asked for one made very, very weak.

'Oh, don't worry about it,' Alison advised. 'It's probably good for you.'

'The trouble about being pregnant,' murmured Julie, 'is that you think of absolutely everything relative to the baby. You completely forget that you're a person yourself.'

'Don't drink it if you don't want to,' I said. 'But if you do, please don't go into paroxysms of guilt.'

She grinned. 'I'll drink a little.'

Julie sipped at her weak margharita while we ordered another round. And another. I was feeling happier than I'd done in ages.

'What are you going to do tomorrow?' I asked as I put another empty glass on the table.

'We will go into the city,' said Magdalena. 'I have a guide book.'

'Some of the shops will be open,' Alison told her. 'You can do a little shopping if you like.'

'Really?'

Alison nodded. 'From about one o'clock. It's a nice time to look around. Not too crowded.'

'Not shops,' groaned Gabriela. 'I have had a bad month with my credit card.'

'Did you buy that with it?' I asked. She was wearing an amber-coloured suit which looked wonderful on her.

'Yes,' she said. 'And I bought jeans and trousers and shoes and jumpers. Alfredo said that if I bring any more clothes into the house he will divorce me.'

'You keep that in mind.' Peter hugged Alison. 'If you ever go on a spending spree like that – it's curtains for our marriage.'

'Dream on, honey.' She grinned at him.

Luis ordered more cocktails.

'Oh, no, Luis. Please don't,' I begged. 'If I drink

any more I'll have a hangover tomorrow and I have things to do.'

'I thought you said everything is done,' he protested.

'I have to bring some presents to Tim's house. And I want to polish my nails. It's hopeless trying to do that on Monday morning. All that'd happen is that I'd smudge them or get nail polish all over my dress.'

'How about an Irish coffee?' he said.

I sighed. 'All right. But that's absolutely it.'

We had the Irish coffees – except for Julie who just had ordinary coffee. The alcohol had made me mellow; I sat back in my seat feeling very relaxed and very at peace with the world. These were my best friends. It was good to be with them.

'We'd better go,' said Alison as she checked her watch. 'It's nearly one o'clock.'

'I'm tired,' admitted Julie.

'Me too.' Gabriela yawned and set us all off.

I paid the bill, waving away Luis's protests and his attempts to pay instead. Then we walked outside into the cold night air. The moon shone frostily down onto the black sea and a wind whistled across the bay. Julie shivered.

The steel wires of the boats clanged in the wind. Just as they had done the first night I met Tim. Almost here, in fact. When he'd put his arm around me and we'd walked along the pier and afterwards he'd kissed me and I'd said 'wow'. I stared unseeingly across the bay and felt as though I had fallen back in time. It was as though it were that night again, as though the last few years hadn't happened, had been merely a vivid dream.

'Are you OK, Isobel?' Alison nudged me.

'Of course.' I returned to the present with a jolt.

The Spanish contingent climbed into a taxi and waved goodnight.

'See you on Monday!' cried Gabriela as their car disappeared down the road.

Alison, Peter, Julie and myself got into a second taxi. I leaned back in the seat, suddenly tired. I was asleep before we reached the house.

~

I wasn't too bad the next morning. I had a slight headache but it was an ordinary hangover headache, not the pounding ones of a few days ago. It disappeared almost immediately when I took a couple of Dr Byrne's tablets.

In the afternoon I bundled up the remaining bits and pieces that I wanted to leave at Tim's house. Although, I told myself as I turned into his road, I'd really have to start thinking of it as my house too. Perhaps once I'd moved in permanently, I'd be able to feel differently about it.

Tim was drinking coffee when I walked in.

'Afternoon,' he said. 'Have you got all the stuff?'

I nodded. 'I'll put it in the spare room and we can rummage through it later.'

'OK.' He drained his cup. 'Help yourself to coffee or tea if you like. I've got to go out for a while.'

'Oh, Tim. Where to?'

He looked embarrassed. 'I'm meeting Greg and the lads for a few drinks.'

'Tim!' I looked at him in horror. 'I thought you were going out last night!'

'I was,' he said. 'But my folks had invited some old fogey relatives over to dinner and they wanted me to make an appearance. So I told the guys I'd meet them tonight instead.'

'Tim Malone, whatever you do, don't get blitzed tonight.'

'Of course I won't.' He put his arms around me. 'I'll

probably have one or two too many, but don't panic. I'll be there tomorrow. On time. Waiting for you.'

'I'll be on time too,' I said. 'You know me. Always punctual.'

He kissed me gently on the lips. 'I know. Honestly, Isobel, I'll behave myself. It's not like we're a bunch of kids, you know. We can be sensible.'

I looked at him in disbelief. I couldn't imagine, in a million years, a group of men in a pub being sensible.

'Honestly,' he repeated as he nibbled at my left ear. 'And I won't let them do anything awful to me.'

'They wouldn't, would they?' The thought was dreadful. I could see Tim stark naked, chained to a railing. Or Tim, his drink spiked, being bundled into a taxi and sent to Kerry. Or Tim, passed out, having his head shaved.

'Isobel!' He laughed. 'I told you. We're mature adults.'

But I had an awful sense of foreboding as I drove back to Sutton. I wished that he hadn't told me he was meeting his friends tonight.

~

There was a taxi parked outside our house.

Mum was in the hallway and, much to my surprise, so was Bridget Evans-Medina.

'I was just going,' she explained when I said that I hadn't expected to see her before tomorrow. 'I wanted to leave a gift for you, that's all.'

'Oh, Bridget, thanks. Wouldn't you like to stay for a cup of tea or anything?' I peered at the taxi. 'Is Tomás with you?'

She shook her head. 'He couldn't come. He's at home with Christopher. But I'm staying with some friends in Monkstown so I don't mind.'

'How are things with you and Tomás?'

She smiled. 'A bit better now, I think. It was hard at first, Isobel. It wasn't what I expected. But we've both changed.'

'What did you expect?' I asked curiously. 'How was it different?'

'I don't know.' She made a face. 'I think I expected him to be as romantic when we were married as he was beforehand. And, of course, it can't be like that. Not when you're with someone every minute of the day. And I got pregnant too quickly. I thought he just wanted me chained to the house, you know.'

I smiled sympathetically at her.

'And he does have a bias towards me being at home and looking after things.' She sighed. 'We compromised.'

'I'm glad,' I said. 'I'm glad it's working.'

'So am I.' She smiled at me. 'Do you know, at first I just wanted to walk out. But then I realised that I loved him. That he was important to me.'

'I know how you feel,' I said. 'Well, it's nice to know we're all getting sorted out. You and Tomás, me and Tim, Barbara and Nico.'

'Barbara and Nico?' She looked at me in amazement.

'They've been going out,' I told her. 'Didn't you know?'

'I know that she asked him to dinner one night,' said Bridget. 'And that she went with some friends to hear them playing in the Lux. But they're not going out together.'

I stared at her. 'They're going to Seville this weekend.'

'No, they're not.' She shook her head. 'Barbara is in Liverpool. She's been there for the last week.'

'Are you sure?'

'Of course I'm sure. I rang her last night. I wondered

if she was coming over for the wedding. I know she told you she couldn't because she was doing a course, but I thought she might just make it.'

'She never told me anything about a course,' I said slowly. 'She told me she was going to Seville. And I thought it was with Nico.'

Bridget grinned. 'Maybe she just wanted to be sure you were over Nico. You know Barbara. Maybe she was afraid that if you thought he was footloose and fancy-free you'd have second thoughts about your wedding!'

'That's ridiculous,' I said.

'Of course it is.' Bridget smiled. 'But Barbara was never very rational about Nico, I'm afraid. She really thought she'd get something going with him. And she was pissed off at you, Isobel, both for going out with him and then for dumping him!'

'Silly,' I said dismissively.

'Oh, well.' Bridget shrugged. 'It doesn't matter. Anyway, as far as I know, Nico's fine. Tomás told me that he doesn't play in the Lux any more.'

'He doesn't?'

'No. Apparently he got some promotion in work. So he's incredibly busy. Working evenings, Saturdays – you name it. I don't think he's been in the Lux for weeks.'

'He probably still plays in the Retiro Park,' I said.

'In December?' Bridget laughed. 'He might be mad, but not that mad, Isobel.' She looked at her watch. 'I'd better go. I'm supposed to meet the girls soon.'

'OK, Bridget,' I said. 'Thanks for calling.'

'You're welcome.' She smiled. 'It was great seeing you. And I can't wait for tomorrow!'

'Neither can I.' I hugged her. 'By this time tomorrow night, we'll both be married women.'

'Absolutely.' She kissed me on both cheeks. '*Buenas noches*, Isobel.'

'*Buenas noches*,' I said as she walked down the garden path.

Chapter 38

Hair Dishevelled by the Fleeing Constellation
(Joan Miró, 1940)

I left the milk bottles outside the front door before I went to bed and shivered in the raw night air. The white smudge of the Milky Way cut through the dark night sky and made me feel small and insignificant. All those stars, perhaps with planets of their own. And maybe people like me living on them, worrying about the fact that their fiancé was off with a bunch of blokes the night before his wedding. I prayed that nothing awful would happen to him. It would be a complete nightmare if we discovered in the morning that they had played some trick that had gone horribly wrong and that he was stranded in the depths of the countryside, totally unable to get back to Dublin.

I imagined what Mum would say. And Dad. I almost smiled at the thought of it. 'We told you,' they'd mutter grimly. 'He was never right for you, Isobel.'

I shivered in the cool night breeze that came in from the sea and closed the front door. I put on the latch and drew across the safety catch.

Everybody was home. Ian was listening to CDs in his room. Alison was lying on the sofa. She'd plastered a skin-purifying, high-moisturising, turn-you-into-a-sex-goddess face mask over herself.

'Any luck?' I asked.

'Huh?'

'Has it turned you into a cross between Sandra Bullock and Sharon Stone yet?'

'Sod off,' she said. 'You'll want me to look the part tomorrow.'

'I have every confidence in you,' I told her. 'But I'm working on the basis of beauty sleep. I'm going to bed.'

'That's a good idea.' Mum was filing her nails. 'You should get some rest, Isobel.'

'Absolutely.' Dad looked up from Ian's copy of *Four-Four-Two*. 'Get your rest now.'

'OK,' I said. 'Goodnight, everyone.'

'Goodnight,' they echoed.

I went up to my bedroom and closed the door behind me. I wasn't sleepy but I needed time to be alone. All evening the family had talked about the wedding, about getting our hair done, about the church, about the soloist (Stella's antibiotics hadn't worked, it was the untested Bernadette tomorrow!), about the champagne reception, about the band, about the hotel – they went on and on until I was sick of it. And when I didn't answer Mum's ridiculous question about whether or not I should have had a smoked salmon starter, she asked me if I was feeling all right, if I had a headache, a temperature, anything at all?

'I have a temperature,' I'd snapped. 'But it's normal.' Then Mum looked hurt and I felt terrible.

'Nerves,' Ian had muttered and taken himself off to his room.

I could hear the rhythmic thud of guitar through the bedroom wall but it was comforting not annoying. I sat in front of the mirror and went through the cleanse, tone and moisturise ritual that I'd started the day I got my first spot. This time tomorrow, I said, as I wiped away the cleanser, this time tomorrow I will be Isobel Malone. I will be married. I will be Tim's wife. Isobel Malone, I mouthed at my reflection. Is-o-bel Ma-lone.

Isabella querida. Isabella.

Would this have happened anyway? I asked myself savagely. If Bridget hadn't shown up and told me that Barbara and Nico weren't an item and that Nico had turned into a workaholic? Would I have thought of Nico tonight?

It wasn't as though he'd left me for Barbara. I'd left him. For Tim. And I knew I was doing the right thing. I was certain. But I couldn't help thinking about him. *Isabella querida.*

I'd have probably thought about other boyfriends if Tim and I had married when we were supposed to. It would have been Alan Davenport or any of them. Whispering, oh Isobel!

I closed my eyes tightly and summoned up a picture of Tim. Tim looking handsome and wonderful in his black tux, a carnation in his buttonhole. Tim smiling at me as I walked up the aisle to him. Tim's face as he saw me in my ridiculously extravagant dress.

I opened my eyes again. The dress wasn't ridiculously extravagant. It was perfect. My heartbeat slowed down and the raggedness in my breathing abated. Everything would be all right. It was normal to have nerves. I would be OK.

The bed was cold. I hadn't got used to sleeping in a single bed since I'd come home. I hated the way I couldn't pull the duvet right around me, under my chin, turning it into a cocoon. The bed in my apartment in Madrid had been a double bed. Just as well, really, given the amount of time Nico had spent in it.

Not Nico again, I screamed silently. Not Nico, not now. Nico was over and I'd kind of loved him and he'd kind of loved me but it wasn't the getting married sort of love and what Tim and I had was.

Isabella querida. I didn't even *want* to think about him. *Hadn't* thought about him. Not for ages. So why now? Why tonight? When I needed to be calm and relaxed. When it was Tim I was worried about, Tim who could (even now) be handcuffed to a lamppost in Donnybrook!

I loved Tim and he loved me. He'd told me at least a thousand times since I'd come home: I love you, Isobel. I need you, Isobel. You're the only one for me, Isobel. This time Tim loved me with the same need as I'd loved him. This time it was Tim that wanted all the trappings of a big wedding, it was Tim that talked about redecorating the house, it was Tim that couldn't wait until our wedding day.

So I didn't have to worry that he wouldn't show up and I didn't have to imagine how I'd react if he rang me to say he was sorry, but he'd changed his mind. It wasn't going to happen. Everything was fine. Everything was sorted out. All I had to do was get a good night's sleep and look my radiant best in the morning.

I heard the rest of the family come to bed. Mum called in to Ian to turn off the CD. He lowered it down but I could still hear the bass. Alison poked her head around my door and whispered goodnight. I grunted back at her. She was really looking forward to tomorrow. The dress I'd made looked fabulous on her and she loved it. Mum's suit looked great too. We'd all look great tomorrow. It would be fine.

It was around two when I fell asleep. And I dreamed the dream again, the one about Father O'Brien and wearing net curtains instead of a dress. I woke up at three, sweating. I fumbled for my inhaler, knocked it off the bedside locker and under my bed. I hated it when that happened. I hated feeling around for it under the bed. When I was small I'd believed that there were spooky creatures underneath. I knew there weren't any spooky creatures there, but I still didn't like waving my hand under it. Childish. Immature. Silly Isobel. I took two puffs and felt better. I hoped I wouldn't be wheezy tomorrow. My bouquet was of fresh flowers and if I didn't deliberately sniff them I'd be all right. It was very traditional: red and white carnations surrounded by gypsophilia. My other bouquet, the one for the first wedding, had been roses.

I lay down and closed my eyes but I was wide awake and couldn't go back to sleep so I turned on the light. I could read, I thought, but I knew I couldn't concentrate long enough to read anything properly. Three o'clock is a horrible time of the night to be awake.

Eventually I went downstairs and made myself a cup of tea. I was as quiet as possible, but Alison walked into the kitchen just as I was pouring milk into the cup.

'I thought I heard something,' she said.

'You shouldn't have come downstairs.' I took a second cup from the rack and filled it for her. 'What if I'd been a burglar? I could've smashed your head in.'

She laughed. 'Risk I had to take. Besides, I heard the fridge door opening. I don't think burglars would be bothered about the contents of our fridge.'

'Probably not.' I sat down at the table and sipped my tea.

'Can't you sleep?' asked Alison.

'D'you think I'd be sitting here drinking tea if I could?'

'I suppose not. I wonder will I be the same?'

'I don't know,' I replied. 'Maybe it's par for the course.

You lie awake and you wonder if you're doing the right thing, and you think back over your life and you hope that the future's going to be OK.'

Alison nodded. 'I understand.'

'It's not that I don't want to marry him,' I said. 'It's just that you hope that everything turns out the way you want, that's all. And you realise how final it is.'

'Not really.' She grinned. 'You can always get a divorce.'

'But nobody thinks like that going into it,' I protested. 'You don't stand in the church and think that it doesn't matter because you can get a divorce. You want it to work.'

'So – are you having second thoughts?' She added some more milk to her tea.

'No,' I said. 'Just thoughts.'

We sat in silence. The hands on the kitchen clock suddenly whirred around the face in a frenzy. It was a radio-controlled clock – the manic spinning of its hands meant it needed a new battery.

'You don't have to marry him,' said Alison blandly. 'If you don't want to.'

'Oh, don't be bloody silly.' I got up and rinsed my cup under the tap. 'He went out with the blokes from his office tonight. I'm worried in case he's too hungover to turn up tomorrow!'

'Isobel! Not really?'

'No.' I sighed. 'Not really. He'll probably be hungover though.'

She grinned. 'And his eyes will be pink.'

'Do you notice that too?' I asked. 'That his eyes go pink?'

'Most people's do.'

'But he doesn't have to drink very much.'

She laughed. 'And when they send back the photos

they'll have a little comment about how to avoid pink eyes! By standing further back when you use the flash!'

I laughed too. 'And avoiding all alcoholic drink the night before.'

Alison yawned. 'I'm tired. I think I'll go back to bed.'

I was feeling tired myself now. 'Me too,' I said and followed her upstairs.

~

It was an absolutely beautiful morning. The sun shone from a cloudless blue sky and the breeze – miraculously – was from the south so that it was almost warm.

The house was in a state of chaos. Mum had commandeered the bathroom; Ian, trying to be helpful by ironing for the first time in his life, had singed a hole in his shirt; Alison derided him for not knowing that the three dots on the iron meant hot and Dad wandered around the house looking for the notes for his after-dinner speech.

I remembered Julie's idea of going to the Berkley Court for a pre-wedding breakfast and I wished I'd followed her example. I hadn't fallen asleep until nearly five o'clock, there were black bags under my eyes and, despite everything, a spot had chosen today of all days to reappear on my forehead. I dabbed Clearasil on it in the hopes that it might dry out before I got around to doing my make-up.

Alison and I went to the hairdresser's at eleven. We were both wearing our hair the same way, although hers was now long enough for the style and mine only just made it.

'As soon as I get back from Venice I'm going to get it chopped off again,' I told Tanya, the hairstylist.

'It suits you like this, Isobel.' She stood back and

admired her work. 'You should be patient, let it grow a little longer.'

'Patience was never one of my stronger points.'

'We'd better put some spray in,' she said.

I nodded and took a deep breath. Hairspray made me sneeze and wheeze. I held my breath until a few seconds after she stopped spraying and the tiny molecules had stopped floating around the air in front of me. But I sneezed anyway.

'Are you OK?' asked Alison.

'I will be.' I sneezed eight times in a row and tears ran down my cheeks.

Tanya giggled and I made a face at her. When I finally stopped I paid her and we left the salon. Usually I walked to the hairdresser's but today we'd driven, on the basis that the breeze might whip up into a wind and ruin Tanya's good work before we got home again. But it was still mild and warm as we got into the car and drove home.

'It's exciting, isn't it?' Alison smiled at me. 'It's the one day when everyone does exactly what you want.'

'It's the one day when nobody wants to upset you,' I amended. 'And that's not a bad thing.'

Peace had been restored at home. Dad had found his notes, Mum was doing her make-up and Ian had managed to iron another shirt, this time without ruining it.

'Your hair is lovely,' said Mum. 'Really pretty. You look very young like that.'

'Thanks.'

'I've just made some soup and sandwiches,' she said. 'Don't forget it'll be late before you get anything to eat.'

'I'm not hungry,' I said.

'I'm starving,' said Alison. 'Lead me to it.'

'You have to eat something,' Mum told me. 'Even

if you don't think you're hungry now. You'll be hungry later.'

I didn't think so. My stomach was in a knot and every so often a wave of adrenalin shot through me, sending acid into my tummy and making me wince with pain.

But she almost force-fed me with chicken soup and ham sandwiches and I supposed she had a point.

'By the way, Tim rang when you were in the hair-dresser's.'

'Did he?' I looked anxiously at her.

'He said that he was tucked up safely in bed by midnight and that he'll be waiting for you at two o'clock.' She beamed at me. 'I must say, Isobel, I had grave doubts about you marrying him. I really had. But I think it's all worked out for the best. He wasn't mature enough before. He's changed and that's a good thing.'

'I've changed too,' I said.

'But you were always mature,' she said confidently. 'Girls are.'

~

The only thing left was the veil. Alison helped me to secure it onto my head, then we both stepped back from the mirror.

'Oh, Isobel.' Her lip quivered. 'You look beautiful.'

'Thanks.'

'And the veil is wonderful.'

I made a face. 'I didn't really want a long veil. It was Tim that wanted that.'

'Why?'

'I think he has some male fantasy about virginal brides or something.'

She chortled. 'Well he's barking up the wrong tree there.'

'Alison Kavanagh!' I shoved her gently. 'That's a terrible thing to say to me.'

'Truth hurts,' she said blithely.

I adjusted the veil.

'You *do* look wonderful,' she said. 'And the dress is perfect.'

Mum knocked on the door. 'Are you ready yet?'

'Yes,' I said.

She came in and started to cry. I hugged her and told her that I loved her but she kept her face buried in my shoulder and I was afraid that her make-up would rub off on my dress.

'It's OK,' she sniffed. 'And I haven't ruined your dress.' She dabbed at the sleeve with a tissue.

'Don't worry,' I said. 'Everything's fine.'

'Your dad wants to take a photograph in the garden,' said Mum.

'The garden!' Alison threw her eyes to heaven. 'What's he thinking of? It's bleak in the garden.'

'He wants to,' said Mum defiantly.

'I don't mind,' I said.

We trooped downstairs. Dad took a photo as we walked into the kitchen.

'Oh, really, Dad!' Alison made a face at him.

'Come on,' he said. 'A nice family photograph.'

He set the camera on timer and we stood under the bare branches of the apple-tree, Mum and Dad, Ian, Alison and me. The camera whirred into action and took the photo.

'That'll be lovely,' said Dad. 'Just the five of us.'

We went inside again and Mum peered out of the front window.

'The cars are here.'

'OK,' I said.

'I'll be going, then.'

'See you there.'

'You'll be OK?'

'Of course.'

Dad went with them to the door. I stood in the kitchen and gazed out at the back garden. It was nice to have thirty seconds to myself.

~

Dad held my hand all the way in the car. He didn't talk and I was grateful to him for that. But Dad wasn't a chatterer. And he understood me more than Mum.

The photographer bustled around with his camera. He made me get out of the car twice because he said I'd bent my head at the wrong moment the first time.

'Look up!' he cried. 'Come on, Isobel.'

I looked up, he got his photograph and then we walked into the church.

It was the strangest sensation. I stood at the end of the aisle and it had never seemed longer. The red carpet stretched into infinity in front of me and the guests in the pews seemed to be insignificant dots miles away in the distance. But I could see Tim at the top of the church. He was there, as he'd promised. Relief flooded over me, so strong that I felt myself shake. Dad squeezed my hand again and I felt better. I wished that I'd taken a squirt of my inhaler before I'd come into the church, but I'd forgotten. I knew it was only nerves that was making my breath come in short gasps.

The organ wheezed into life. Dad and I walked slowly up the aisle. I was lightheaded, but I didn't know whether that was from hyperventilating or whether it was the sense of occasion getting to me.

The little posies of red and white flowers, tied with white satin ribbons, looked very elegant at the end of each pew. The red and white flowers on the altar were magnificent.

I recognised people as I walked by. Christine and Siobhán. Greg Roberts. Mum's sister, Rachel. Dennis, holding Sorcha by the hand. Luis. Magdalena. Gabriela, dabbing at her eyes with a tiny handkerchief. Julie. Her sister, Danielle. Other relatives. Mum. Denise Malone. And, finally, Tim. He smiled at me. His eyes were pink.

The congregation sat down. People cleared their throats. Someone coughed. I wanted to sneeze. I wriggled my nose to stop it.

It seemed very solemn all of a sudden. Very solemn and very religious and very final. I kept my breathing slow and easy.

Father O'Brien smiled at us and I looked down at my dress to make sure it hadn't turned into net curtains. Tim squeezed my hand, already sore from all the squeezing Dad had done in the car.

The priest started to talk about love. And marriage. He reminded everyone that Tim and I had had our ups and downs. But that we'd grown through that adversity and become stronger people as a result. People who were now committed to living a Christian marriage and a Christian life.

Because we were older, he said, we had past experiences to help us. I thought of some of my past experiences and bit my lip. Ignacio. Stefan. John. Luis. I almost smiled when I thought of Luis. At least I'd been able to look him in the face again. Eventually. And I thought of Nico.

Father O'Brien smiled at us again and then, unexpectedly, because I hadn't even been listening to what was going on, he was saying to Tim: 'Do you, Tim, take Isobel as your lawful wedded wife?' It had happened before I realised it was going to happen and the suddenness of it all made me hold my breath.

Tim was saying the words: 'For richer for poorer, in sickness and in health, as long as we both shall live.'

I gasped.

Father O'Brien smiled at me. 'Do you, Isobel, take Tim as your lawful wedded husband?'

The words echoed around the church, bounced around in my head. 'Sickness, health, richer, poorer, as long—'

I stared at him. He smiled encouragingly at me. This was it, then. This was my dream come true.

I cleared my throat. 'I, Isobel—'

I stopped.

There was a ripple of laughter from the church and Tim grinned at me. Father O'Brien smiled again too.

I cleared my throat again. 'I, Isobel—' And there was thunder in my ears and a mist in front of my eyes and a feeling that time was standing still. I could sense everyone as though in a movie still, watching me, listening to me, waiting for me to say the words. But the words were stuck in my throat and they wouldn't come. I wanted to say them. They were there, somewhere inside me. But I couldn't get them past my lips which remained stubbornly closed.

Tim was looking anxiously at me. Father O'Brien watched benevolently. The crowd waited expectantly.

And suddenly the bubble burst, time moved forward again and I looked at Tim and at Father O'Brien and gasped, 'I'm sorry. I can't.'

Then I dropped my bouquet on the steps of the altar, picked up the skirt of my dress, and ran as fast as my spindly heels would allow out of the church.

The chauffeur was leaning against the car door smoking a cigarette. He looked at me in complete amazement as I came flying down the steps.

'Start the car,' I commanded as I jumped into the back seat, yanking the dress in with me. 'And drive.'

'What?'

'Don't argue, just do it,' I snapped.

He did what I said. I suppose he was too terrified by my manic look to refuse. As we drove down the road I looked back through the rear window and saw the crowd of people appear in the church door and I was both appalled and relieved at what I had done.

'Where to?' asked the driver.

I wondered whether this had happened to him before. He was remarkably relaxed.

'The Summit,' I said clearly. 'Howth Summit.'

He said nothing but drove at a steady forty miles an hour. It only took a few minutes to reach the summit.

'What now?' He stopped the car and looked around at me.

'Wait here,' I said.

I got out of the car and walked to the edge of the hill.

Suddenly the driver was beside me. 'Don't do anything stupid,' he said, his eyes full of concern. 'For God's sake, girl. Nothing is that bad.'

I turned to him and laughed and it was a real laugh, full of joy. 'I'm not doing anything stupid,' I said. 'I've just saved myself from doing something stupid. Honestly. It's OK. Wait for me.'

He stayed where he was while I picked my way uncertainly through the rough, damp grass. The end of the dress would be stained green. I didn't care.

The breeze was much stronger here. It pushed me and pulled at me so that I struggled to keep my balance on my high-heeled oyster-white shoes.

I stood and looked out to the horizon where the blue of the sky and the green of the sea met. My breathing was better now, helped by the freshness of the air.

I closed my eyes. I had done a terrible, terrible thing.

People would say that I'd done it to get my revenge on Tim and, I supposed, lots of them would believe that. But I hadn't. Up until the moment that Father O'Brien had asked me the question, I'd intended to marry Tim. I'd gone through a night of doubts and fears and I'd woken up certain that I was doing the right thing. Even walking up the aisle, though I'd been nervous, I was still certain that I was doing the right thing.

And thinking of Ignacio and Stefan and John and Luis I was sure I was doing the right thing.

And thinking of Nico . . . When I thought of Nico, I wasn't sure of anything any more.

Yet I still would have gone through with it. But when Father O'Brien said the words out loud, when he asked me whether I wanted Tim as my husband – then it was like a bolt of lightning, like an electric shock. *I didn't.* And at first I didn't believe it myself. My body tried to say the words but my mind wouldn't let it. And I couldn't believe it.

But I knew that I'd made the right decision. Even if I'd left it very late in the day. I felt as though a huge weight had been lifted from my shoulders and, for the first time in weeks, I didn't have a headache and I didn't need to puff my inhaler.

The wind tugged at my veil and whipped it around my face. I reached up and untied it. I held it out in front of me and it stretched out, long and white, like a banner in the air.

They'd never forgive me. Never.

Then I let go of the veil and the wind took it, spinning it around and around before carrying it high off the hill and out to the blue-green sea.

Anyone But Him

Sheila O'Flanagan

Andie Corcoran and her sister Jin have never seen eye to eye. Andie doesn't envy Jin her wealthy husband and luxury lifestyle, while Jin can't believe Andie's happy with her quiet and man-free existence (if only she knew!).

But when their widowed mother Cora comes back from a Caribbean cruise with more than just a suntan, Andie and Jin are united in horror. Who is this gorgeous young man who's swept their mother off her feet? And what exactly does he want? On top of this, both sisters are about to face crises of their own.

What they really need is a friend to set the world to rights with – but can they ever be friends with each other?

Praise for Sheila O'Flanagan's bestsellers:

'Highly readable' *Daily Express*

'The Sheila O'Flanagan guarantee is a pretty powerful one' *Irish Independent*

'Another fantastic book' *Irish News*

'Witty and touching' *Family Circle*

0 7553 0758 5

headline

SHEILA O'FLANAGAN

Dreaming of a Stranger

Jane O'Sullivan is a dreamer. She dreams of white sands, blue skies, and one true love, the man who will turn all her dreams into reality. She's famous for losing her heart too easily. And when Rory McLoughlin turns his blue eyes, framed with ridiculously long lashes, on her, it won't be long until her dream of walking up the aisle comes true.

But weddings just mark a new beginning, not a happy ending. And dreams aren't always what they seem. Jane has to take control of her own destiny. And only time will tell if real life can be as satisfying as a dream . . .

Praise for Sheila O'Flanagan's bestsellers

'Chick lit at its very best' *Irish Examiner*

'A must-read' *Woman's Own*

'Engaging characters and flowing dialogue . . . an eventful, compelling and ultimately satisfying journey' *Irish Independent*

0 7472 6564 X (A format)
0 7553 3000 5 (B format)

headline
review